Praise for

Nancy Adams

The Soul Within is an intriguing story that grabbed me from the start and never let go. The storyline was a mish-mash of many different paranormal elements that worked perfectly together to draw me into the sexy and suspenseful world of two souls brought together through a higher power to keep the innocent safe...It's a satisfying story with unique paranormal aspects and I'll definitely be on the lookout for more by this author. ~ *Words of Wisdom*

THE SOUL WITHIN

NANCY ADAMS

The Soul Within
ISBN # 978-1-78184-552-6
©Copyright Nancy Adams 2012
Cover Art by Lyn Taylor ©Copyright June 2012
Interior text design by Claire Siemaszkiewicz
Total-E-Bound Publishing

Published in 2012 by Total-E-Bound Publishing, Think Tank, Ruston Way, Lincoln, LN6 7FL, United Kingdom.

THE SOUL WITHIN

Chapter One

The soul is not where it lives, but where it loves...~Proverb

The right honourable Brad Rhodes jumped at the knock on his office door. Quickly closing the files on his laptop, he called out. "Yes, who is it?"

"Security, Mr Rhodes."

"Shit." He muttered under his breath. "One sec." He glanced nervously over at the door to his private bathroom.

His hands shook as he ejected the flash drive from his laptop, and slid the data on the new Defence contracts into his pocket. He stopped before the door, took a deep centring breath as he buttoned his suit jacket and smiled, his nervousness now hidden behind a mask of absolute confidence. Opening the door, he had only time to gasp before he went flying back into the room.

The sheer force of the kick to his chest had him gasping for air. With his chest burning and head spinning Brad was quickly pinned to the floor by two men. Stunned, he stared up at a masked face leaning in close. The vivid blue of the eyes that stared back were beautiful, divine and yet deeply disturbing. Those eyes saw more than just the government employee, husband and father, those eyes saw the dark secrets sitting on his soul.

"Who are you?" There was no answer as he was quickly patted down. A hand stopped on the pocket that held the Flash drive. Pulling it from his pocket the man with the blue eyes held it up and tossed it to his partner. He then stood, settling his celestial eyes on him, before stepping over him and proceeding behind his desk.

"Now, Bradley," The second attacker began. This man was different from the other—his eyes were black, empty chasms. "You know very well who we are."

The quiet words sent a shiver through him. "Oh, God!" These men were part of the Guardian Project and they were here. That meant the other members knew what he had been up to. That meant these men were here to kill him. "But you can't...I'm a member on the committee that sanctions you."

"Yes, you are." The man reached into a pocket hidden on his sleeve and withdrew a syringe.

"That's the reason why we didn't shoot you. We don't want any unwanted attention, so you will die of natural causes." The man squatted down next to him. "Your wife will be taken care of for the remainder of her life and your child will only know of a father that worked incessantly to improve our country." The masked man paused and shrugged casually. "If you ask me, that's pretty good considering the amount of shit you stirred up." The man turned to his partner who was behind the desk. "Ace?"

"Just cleaning his hard drive." There was a brief silence before he announced, "Done."

The man, Ace, walked around the desk and stopped by his feet, giving his partner a quick nod.

"Wait." Brad began to panic. "Please. You can't do this. The people that want this…"

"Are dead." It was 'Ace' who finished. "Just like the soldiers you sold out."

"I didn't know they would kill so many. Please…" Brad held up his trembling hands, his face now coated with a light sheen of sweat. "I have a…my family."

"Those soldiers had families." Ace gritted out between clenched teeth.

"Your family will be better off without you." The killer next to him said. "Now, are we going to have to hold you down or will you take your punishment like a man?"

Brad's heart began to race, blood pounded in his ears. He was going die. He didn't want to die.

The basic need for survival had Brad fighting the men the best he could, but they were too strong, too fast. He felt the pinch at the base of his hairline, before the killers released him. Their mission now complete.

Two sets of eyes stared down waiting for him to die. Both so dramatically different, yet both the same. "You're monsters." He mumbled.

Miles nodded. "We have to be, in order to protect the world from people like you."

In the last seconds of his life, Right Honourable Brad Rhodes watched as the man who killed him took off his mask and he realised that the head of his own security team had killed him.

"Well that's six months of my life I won't get back." Miles sighed. Standing, he snapped the cover on the end of the syringe and slid it back inside his sleeve. "This guy was a real dick. Next time we're tasked with a job like this, you're on point."

Alex 'Ace' Hunter raised his eyebrows. "Stop whining like a bitch. We could still be in the desert roasting our asses off."

"Yeah!" Miles snorted. "That was by far the easiest part of this job. I didn't have to do anything." Miles narrowed his eyes. "You still miss all that shit don't you?"

Alex shrugged. "Not always. I have missed using my rifle though. It was nice to blow holes in things again."

Miles laughed out loud. "Let's set up the scene and get the hell out of here. I'd like to say goodnight to my kids tonight..." Both men turned at the sound that came from the opposite side of the room. Alex kept watch on the wood panelled wall while he drew his pistol from behind his back. Stepping quietly forward, he crossed the short distance and reached out, pushing gently on the dark wood panelling. Nothing. Then again, further along the wall, but still nothing. He moved two steps to the right and pushed again, the wall clicked and a hidden door opened. Alex moved to one side of the door as Miles moved to the other. Only black was visible through the small crack. Alex held up his hand giving the sign to stop when he saw Miles tense. Closing his eyes, he listened. He had heard someone, he was positive. He held his breath, slowed his breathing so he could pin point... There it was again, coming from inside the black room, a muffled cry.

With his eyes glued to the dark room, Alex watched for any type of unfriendly movement. When none was detected he angled his already raised hand in the direction of the sound, then gave the go. He pushed the door open with his foot as Miles entered the room. Alex followed, hitting the light as he entered. Guns raised, both men descended on the figure as it cowered in the corner of Rhodes' private bathroom.

Alex fixed his eyes on the target as he moved closer. Then stopped, stunned by what he saw. A woman. A pregnant woman. He grabbed Miles' shoulder. "Wait."

"What for?" Miles asked quickly.

The woman turned her face, showing her tear-stained brown eyes. Those beautiful eyes grew wide when she saw Miles. "Rick?" The woman called Miles by his cover name. "What's going on? Why did you...?" She couldn't finish, tears slipped over onto her cheeks as her lips began to tremble.

Alex studied the woman. "Who is she?" *And what is she doing here with Rhodes?*

"Jillian Reid, Rhodes' secretary." Miles pulled his lips into a tight line and lowered his gun. "What are you doing here, Jillian?"

Alex watched Miles silently. Body tense, eyes flat, although, his voice did carry a slight emotional attachment. Something was off.

The woman sniffed and peeked at him between her fingers. "We were late coming out of a meeting and I had to catch up on a few things. I ended up missing my bus. Mr Rhodes said he would give me a ride home." She sniffed again. "He said I could use his bathroom before we left, so I didn't have to walk upstairs." Her face crumbled a second time. "Why...why did you kill him, Rick?"

Miles raised his gun. The woman whimpered.

"Hey," Alex warned. "You *are* seeing what I'm seeing, right?"

"We have the *go* to eliminate witnesses. She's a witness."

Alex's stomach twisted. He knew Miles could be vicious, they both could, but this woman went far beyond the normal witness. "We're not doing this."

"She can identify me." Miles glared at the woman on the floor. "I have more to lose than you."

Like Alex, Miles was a trained killer and he was good at his job. But Miles had the one thing that could be used against him, a family. A wife, children, a house with a white picket fence. Christ, he even had a dog. All Alex had, was his job. He had had a family once, when he was still in his teens. But he had lost them, so he understood where Miles was coming from. Though that didn't make killing this woman and her unborn child right, even he knew that.

"What is she going to do? Look at her." Alex slid his pistol back behind his back as he straightened next to Miles. "Let's take her back to the shop and give her to the CO. Let him deal with her."

Miles turned, his face blank. "This is still my op and I'm still on point. She dies."

Alex's decision was made before Miles could squeeze the trigger. Alex slammed him into the wall, his fist smashing into Miles' face. The blow knocked him down, but he was far from out.

Alex reached for the woman. "Get up." He bent down barking, "Now!"

Grabbing her by the upper arms, he yanked her to her feet and dragged her through the office and out into the main corridor. They had made their way down the dark hall, to a set of stairs before the first shot was fired. The bullet caught Alex in the meaty part of his shoulder and he hissed when he felt it slice his skin open.

As they descended the steps to the parking garage Alex pinned her close to the wall with his body and out of Miles' line of sight. They moved between the parked cars, Alex's senses in overdrive as he kept watch on the access door to the garage. He opened his back zippered pocket and took out a single key. "Take this." He ordered, thrusting the key in her hand. "There is a grey, four-door BMW on the next level with Alberta plates."

Alex jerked her down when he saw the door swing open. The woman inhaled sharply when the door to the parking garage slammed shut.

"Oh God, that's him isn't it?"

"Shut up and listen." He hissed. "Take the car. It has secured plates so local and federal police can't trace it."

She placed a hand on her swollen belly and exhaled slowly. Alex studied her, "How far along are you?"

"Six months." She exhaled slowly once again. It was obvious she was breathing to help control pain.

"Is it the baby?" What a stupid question. What else would it be! With all of his training in first aid and as a combat medic, he still had no idea how to help a pregnant woman.

"Yah! She's kicking up a storm."

"Can you make it to the next level?"

"Do I have a choice?" she asked sarcastically, pulling her long blonde hair over her shoulder.

"No you don't."

She acknowledged the truth. "I know. I can ma—" Alex covered her mouth when he heard Miles walking closer. He grabbed her hand and keeping low, he led her between the cars, moving closer to the ramp that led to the next level.

He pulled her up against a concrete pillar and listened as Miles systematically checked each and every car. If Miles was anything, he was a patient bastard.

"Not much time. Listen very carefully to me. You will drive out of the city and head north on highway 18. Keep heading north until you reach the town limits of Montcalm. Drive straight through the town and take the fourth dirt road on the right. It's overgrown so watch that you don't miss it. Follow it to the end. It will bring you to a small lake. Follow the road around the lake to the other side." He paused and looked over the cars to see how close Miles was to their present location. "Shit!" He was starting on their row. Alex spoke faster.

"You'll find a house, it's the only one there and very isolated. Park the car in the shed. The key is hidden under a rock in the front garden. There's lots of food and water and a generator. But don't waste the gas. It has to last until I can come and get you. If someone comes, hide. On the off chance you need them there are guns and ammo hidden in the sidewall of the bathroom closet."

"Can I go home first?"

"No you can't." Alex paused. "Is someone waiting for you? The baby's father?"

"I thought..." She looked down, her cheeks pink. "No. I just wanted to get some clothes."

"The BMW's front seats flip forward. There is enough cash to get gas and whatever else you need. Don't use your credit cards and don't stop in one place for too long."

"I won't." The woman squinted at him. "Can I at least see your face, so I know who is coming for me?"

Jillian stared as the man pulled the black mask over his head and stared back at her. So this was her saviour. She scanned his face. She saw the scar running through his left brow first. Then saw how his eyes were the same colour as the sky and that they were in direct contrast to the black-brown hue of his hair. If she had just passed him on the street and didn't know he was a killer, she would have thought he was handsome. But all she could see was a man that was trying to save her and her baby. She would never allow herself to forget this man's face.

"My name is Jillian Reid."

"Alex."

"Thank you, Alex."

He gave her a curt nod. "Time to go. I'm going to draw his fire. I'll cross to that row of cars and then to the other aisle. When you see me running back towards the access door I want you to run down the ramp to the car. It's not far, parking spot two-E. Exit out the east side, don't come back this way." Alex moved to the edge of the thick grey pillar.

"Wait." Jillian grabbed him.

Alex looked down at her hand gripping his arm. "What?" He glared at her over his shoulder.

"What if…you don't come?" Her voice wavered. She couldn't help it, she was terrified. Her baby was due in three short months. What if something happened? This baby was everything to her.

Her fear must have been very evident. "If I can't get to you, I'll send someone to you, you can trust."

"Who?"

"Time to go."

Jillian watched in horrified amazement as bullets started flying the moment Alex ran across to the opposite row of cars. He weaved by a minivan and a

SUV and out into the next aisle, all the while firing back at his partner. The echo of the bullets hitting the cars was almost deafening and Jillian covered her ears as she ran as fast as her body would allow, down the ramp to the waiting car.

Looking back over her shoulder, the last thing Jillian saw was Alex running towards his partner firing his gun.

Chapter Two

Standing at the end of the hospital bed, Alex watched as the nurse switched the empty IV bag for a full one.

"What the fuck is a median?"

"From what I understand," The little blonde leaned her hip into the rail at the end of the bed, while Alex went to stand next to the nurse and watched as she punched commands into the intravenous pump. "It's a soul that has become separated from its living body."

"Say again." He ordered. He kept watch on the nurse, waited for the smallest of signs that the woman knew she wasn't alone in the room.

"That's your body." He could see the petite blonde point to his body lying on the bed out the corner of his eye. "And you," —she waved her hand up and down the length of him—"are the soul. Together you are whole. But because you are in a coma, your soul has separated from your body."

He pulled his eyes from the nurse and focused on the blonde who had appeared at his side an hour before. "I'm separate from my body!" He blinked...once. "Do you know how crazy that sounds?"

"It's very crazy. But it's also true, because here you are," — she pointed to his body in the bed — "and there you lay."

"How long have I been like this?"

"I don't know." She shrugged her slender shoulders. "Read your chart."

Annoyed by her casual tone Alex glared at her, then stared over the nurse's shoulder. As he searched the page for his admission date he noticed the nurse shiver and goose bumps appear on her arms. She finished with her notes, then signed and dated the sheet before she left the room.

"Well?" The blonde huffed.

"I was admitted on the eighteenth." And the nurse had dated her rounds as the twenty-sixth. He had been here for eight days.

"Does this happen to everyone who's in a coma?" Alex thought out loud. He couldn't be the only one.

"There are others here in this hospital, that are also in a coma." A sad undertone clung to her as she spoke. Alex looked, across his body, at her.

"But are they like us?" He watched her stiffen and his gut told him something wasn't right. "You're not like me, are you?"

She broke eye contact with him. "No. I'm dead."

Alex didn't move. He simply stared at her. This pretty little blonde with her hauntingly beautiful brown eyes was dead? She didn't look dead. She looked like him. Then again, he wasn't sure what he was and was undecided if he believed any of this median crap.

"How long have you been dead?"

"Two days," she said casually. "Give or take a few hours."

Crossing his arms, he looked down his nose at her. "For someone that hasn't been dead for very long, you sure know a lot."

"I know." She caught and held his stare. "It's a little scary."

As Alex observed her body language, he realised she was telling him the truth. She was unnerved by her unexpected knowledge.

"When do I go back into my body?"

"I don't know." She shrugged again. "It's different for everyone. For some medians, it only takes hours or days for them to re-enter their bodies. Some take months or years, others never."

Alex straightened. A sudden urgency rose and lodged in his chest. He couldn't wait days or weeks, or years. He had to get out of here to… What? What did he have to do that was so important?

"Are you all right Alex?" The blonde suddenly appeared at his side. He could see her small hand grip at his arm, but he couldn't feel her touch.

The sight jogged a memory of another small hand touching his arm. He looked into the woman's brown eyes. Big brown eyes.

"Jillian Reid?" He blurted out.

The woman nodded knowingly. "Yes."

"She's in danger."

The blonde waited patiently, as the reason for him being in his present state came flooding back to him.

Congressman Brad Rhodes had been selling military Intel to factions in India that had ties to the Taliban. The result, was the deaths of many soldiers. Miles was planted as Rhodes' new head of security, to gain more information as to Rhodes' contacts. The Congressman was either not very bright or too cocky for his own good because it took less than six months to confirm and eliminate all levels of contacts. It was just bad timing that Jillian had stayed late to help her boss. Bad timing that she had used his private bathroom and bad timing she had seen them kill Rhodes.

Without a doubt, Miles would have killed Jillian if Alex hadn't stopped him. Even now when Alex wasn't sure if he was dead or alive, that feeling of disgust turned his stomach. He didn't understand how Miles, a husband and a father, could want to kill a pregnant woman. The roles should have been reversed. Between the two of them, Alex was by far the more ruthless. It should have been him that had wanted to kill Jillian — not Miles.

After years of having Miles as a partner, he should have been able to read Miles like a book. He squeezed his jaw. This was fucked. Miles was more than just a friend, he was the closest thing he had to a family. He looked down at the holes in his shirt, a permanent reminder of how not to get too comfortable. It would also serve to remind him of a friend's betrayal. Why was protecting a life far more dangerous than taking it? Being the good guy sucked some serious ass. Yet Alex knew without question, he would do it again.

"I need to get back into my body. Jillian is still in danger. Miles has already had a week's worth of time searching for her."

The blonde nodded again before turning towards the door. "I have heard others talk about a woman who has helped medians re-enter their bodies, you should find her."

"How in the hell, am I supposed to do that? I can't just ask who she is. No one can see me, or hear me. Christ, it took me over an hour to figure that out."

And, he couldn't afford to waste time by listening in on conversations. Miles would find Jillian eventually and when he did, Jillian and her baby would die.

"Don't get your panties in a bunch, I know her name." The blonde smirked.

He waited...impatiently. "Well? What is it?"

"I think you need to ask nicely."

He lowered his head and levelled his eyes on her. "That was me asking nicely."

She laughed. "You're not very patient."

"I don't respond well to being teased. Now give me the name."

"Well since you asked so nicely..." She smiled sweetly. "Evening Sinclair."

Surprised, Alex ordered, "Say again."

"Evening Sinclair."

"Her name is Evening?"

"Yes. But she goes by Eve."

"I'm not surprised." Alex said dryly. "What does she do?"

"She heals soldiers."

"She's a doctor?"

"No. She heals the body and the soul." The blonde's eyes became unfocused as her voice dropped, sounding distinctly male. "When one is brought to her broken, not only does she heal the body but the soul as well. The act brings her joy, which makes her a true healer. Evening is part of a dying lineage, and one that must be cherished." Her eyes cleared as she looked up at him. "What was I saying?"

Alex stared at the blonde. What the hell was that? He was not the most religious man on the planet, but if he didn't know better he could have sworn something divine had just happened. "You said she works with soldiers, where?"

"I'm not sure. But I do know this entire floor is dedicated to soldiers and that the other wing on this floor has more patients. You could start there."

Alex watched as the blonde turned back towards the door, her golden hair swung back, brushing the top of her shoulders. Making no attempt to stop her, he simply asked, "Where are you going?"

She lowered her head before answering him. "I'm going to say goodbye to my family."

"You can just do that?"

She turned back once again to face him. Her fleeting smile accentuated the tears in her big brown eyes. Alex froze, a sudden feeling that he had seen her tear stained eyes before. "Well, I'm allowed to say goodbye to my husband. But my sister is different. She already knows I'm dead. She knew the second I died. But, I'm still not supposed to go to her."

"But you're going to."

The blonde shrugged. "Of course. She's my sister." Alex nodded. He couldn't help but admire her loyalty. "I am a little nervous though, she is in a delicate situation right now and I don't want to make it worse." She took a deep breath and sighed. "I'll figure it out."

Alex held the blonde's stare. "What's your name?"

"Justine."

Alex nodded. "Thanks for the Intel, Justine."

"You're welcome." She smiled. "Good luck, Alex Hunter." And with that said, she turned and left the room.

* * * *

From the moment Justine had appeared at his side, Cade had known something wasn't right. Her smile had been genuine and full of love but there had been sadness too. Then she had broken the bad news. He was in a coma, and his soul had become separated from his body. This explained why he had been staring down at his own body for the last day and a half. It had sounded completely ridiculous, except Justine didn't lie. She believed lying only complicated life. God, he loved that about her.

When he had first woken up, he'd thought he was stuck in a dream. And that Justine was surprising him at work for lunch. The truck losing control and pinning them against a wall, was all part of the dream. Then he had woken up here in the hospital, where every single person ignored him even after he had called them every rude and insulting name he could come up with. It had soon dawned on him that they couldn't see him and no amount of yelling would get their attention. He had felt like he was going crazy. He still felt that way.

"There's something else I need to tell you." Sorrow clouded her lovely face.

Cade instinctively moved to her and tried for a third time to pull her into his arms. He couldn't, his arms simply floated through her…again. He sighed, irritated. "What is it?"

"I was killed when the truck hit us."

He felt the blood drain from his face. "What?" His voice cracked.

Justine traced her small hand down his cheek to his chin as she had done hundreds of times before, except this time he couldn't feel her touch. "I died Cade." The tender stroke always calmed him. But this time he felt nothing but anger and confusion.

"Please don't look at me that way." His heart squeezed at her plea. "You know I can't stand it when you're angry and I can't soothe you the way you need right now."

Raising her deep brown eyes, Justine looked up at him with such love that his heart ached. This was his fault. They should have driven to the restaurant, but it had been a warm day and he'd suggested they walk. If they had driven, the truck would have just hit the building. Justine would still be alive and he wouldn't be in a coma. Life would have continued.

"Christ, Justine what do you expect?" He wanted to grab her arms and shake some sense into her. "You just told me you're dead. And you're so calm about it."

"I'm not going to lie." Her shoulders slumped. "This really sucks. There was so much I wanted for us. A big house, kids, and at some point…being part of the mile high club." She winked at him, then sighed loudly when he didn't smile. "I thought it was funny." She shrugged. "I was told it was my time." She rolled her eyes. "I know, not very original, but that's what he said."

"Who said?"

"You'll see soon enough."

Cade grabbed the back of his neck. "I don't understand."

"Honey, look at your body. It's a mess. And you're not strong enough to repair the damage done to it."

"What are you talking about?" He stared at his body, his chest and head wrapped in bandages. His right arm in a cast, tubes in his mouth and arms. "It will take some time but it will heal."

"Cade!" Justine's sudden sharp voice caught him off guard. "This part of you," —she waved her hand up and down—"is the soul. Your soul is not strong enough to heal your body. If you re-enter your body, your soul will be trapped there until your body finally dies. I have no idea how long that will be or if you will suffer any pain." She was now very agitated. "Please. Please trust me."

"Okay," he soothed. "So what happens? I just sit here and wait for my body to die or what, I go with you?"

"You can't come with me, yet."

He was confused. He wasn't dead and he couldn't go into his body or he'd be trapped until it died and now Justine was telling him he couldn't die and go with her. "So I can't die now either?"

"No, you have to wait for him." There was a sudden blank look on her face that was disturbing — and her voice — it had dropped unusually low.

"Wait for who?"

"The hunter, he'll need your help."

Cade scanned his wife, something bizarre was happening. She was her normal beautiful self, she wore the same clothes as the ones she'd died in, but her posture was suddenly stiff and awkward. "Honey." He paid close attention to her face. "What hunter?"

Justine's stare became haunted. It was as though she was staring through him. "The hunter is the one who will save Jillian."

"Jillian?" Cade asked.

She acknowledged him with a nod. "The instinct to protect comes naturally to him and he is strong. Stronger than you. He will fix what you cannot. But you must give what is yours to him freely, before you can join us."

Cade stared down at his wife and got a creepy feeling that it wasn't his wife staring back.

"He'll need what you do not."

And as suddenly as it happened, Justine's voice and posture were normal once again. "I think I'm starting to get used to that." She shook her head and grinned.

He narrowed his eyes. "Justine you're not making any sense. What am I supposed to give freely?"

Her smile was tender. "You'll know when the time comes."

Cade instantly matched Justine's steps as she backed away from him. "I have to go."

"Where?"

She shrugged, as her eyes searched the room for an answer. "I'm not sure." She focused on his chest. "But as strange as it sounds, I know it's going to be okay." She raised her face to his and, once again, stroked the side of his face.

This time a light feathery touch tickled his cheek. He closed his eyes savouring her touch. When he opened his eyes she was gone.

Chapter Three

The first time Eve had seen him — the man in grey — he had been standing across the street from her house. With his legs braced apart and his arms crossed, he had stood as still as a statue, just staring at her. Though her stomach had flipped, which was usually the first warning sign, she had ignored it and hoped he was waiting for a friend or maybe a ride.

The next time she had seen him was later the same day when she had gone to meet Noelle at the bus. She had felt him before she had seen him. As she'd stepped out of the house and closed the door, she had noticed him leaning casually against the far corner of the porch. There had been no intensity like the last time, only a show of interest. Their eyes had locked briefly and she had seen even from where she stood that his eyes were a bright blue. His stare had been so unnerving that she'd turned and walked away. This time not only did her stomach flip, but she suddenly felt nauseous. That was the second sign.

As the evening passed into night, Eve fought the urge to look out the window. He was still near — she could feel him. This was odd because she never felt the presence of a median until they were very close, usually within arm's reach. She peeked hesitantly over her shoulder. Nope. No creepy man dressed in grey standing in her office.

She sighed, resting her head in her hands. What was going on? Medians at her house—this was a first. She had never encountered one *outside* the hospital. She had always believed that the fear of the unknown had kept them close to their bodies.

However, the man in grey was at her house, close to her child. At that moment the third and final sign became apparent—she was scared.

Taking a deep breath, she tried calming her racing pulse. She was going to have to tell this median that she couldn't help him. She didn't merge anymore. Denying him what he wanted—what they all wanted—was the main reason behind her fear. Refusing a desperate soul usually ended up with them becoming violent. She hated that and this time she knew it would be worse. The man in grey must have incredible strength or she wouldn't be so receptive to him.

What would happen when she told him no? With the power he wielded he could cause a lot of damage. She stared at the computer screen as her stomach twisted into a knot. The last time she had encountered a desperate soul, she had been verbally assaulted and all she had done was look at the woman. The waitress had screamed in her ear during all three of her appointments at the hospital, calling her nasty, hurtful names. Of course, that was all the waitress had been able to do and the energy the waitress had given off hadn't been anywhere near as powerful as the man in grey. God, she didn't want to deal with this new, stronger median, but the alternative was not an option.

Eve went to bed still feeling the power of the man in grey. She woke when her alarm went off, feeling tried and cranky. She had woken throughout the night with the feeling that she wasn't alone. Yet, each time she had sat up and turned on the light, nothing had been there.

She showered, hopeful that it would help her mood, threw on blue dress pants and a cream turtleneck, and went downstairs to start Noelle's breakfast. As she entered the kitchen, she stopped short when she saw him leaning against the counter. He was at complete ease, standing in her kitchen like he had been there before. All he needed was a cup of coffee and she would think he was an old friend stopping in to say 'hi'.

As she stood in the doorway, Eve stared him in the eye. "You're not welcome in my home. You have to leave."

He raised his eyebrows, amused by her demand.

"I can't help you." Eve glared at him. "You need to go."

He pushed away from the counter, moved closer, displaying his greater height.

She tried not to notice the small holes in his grey shirt, or how each one of them had a dark inky stain circling them. Was he... No! She couldn't see the dead. She had never seen the dead. That talent belonged to her mother and grandmother. Although, Gran had told her, that could change at any time.

Crossing her arms, she let him know without words that he didn't intimidate her — which was a total lie — and for several minutes they stood staring at each other. Eve wanted to turn away from his intense blue stare but she didn't.

Finally he spoke. "I need your help Evening."

Eve felt her mouth drop open. She turned from him and began preparing Noelle's breakfast. He knew her name, her real name. Her heart pounded in her chest as her hands shook. She had no idea who this man was or had been, she had never told a median any personal information and she had never told anyone, needy soul or otherwise, her real name.

She focused on breakfast with the hope he would give up, but when she turned to the fridge to get the milk, he was still there watching her. She jumped when she heard a door close. Noelle was up and moving around.

Panicking, Eve broke the silence and whispered. "You have to leave."

"I need your help, Evening."

Her eyes grew wide. "You can't stay here. Please go."

"I need you to put me back in my body."

"No. I can't." She glanced towards the door, praying Noelle was slow in coming down this morning.

"I was told otherwise."

"Whoever said that is wrong," she cried. "I can't help you."

One minute he looked mildly annoyed and the next his face was a mask of rage. He stalked towards her, his blue eyes glowing as if beams of light were behind them.

Startled, Eve staggered back but the damn counter blocked her. He stopped just before her and lowered his face so they were nose to nose. "If you can do it for six year old Jimmy Chen and for Debbie Wilcox and for Emily Spencer, you can do it for me."

How did he know all of this? With her eyes wide, she moved her way along the counter, desperate to get away. "They…" Condensation floated between her parted lips as she spoke, thanks to the sudden drop in temperature. "They were…different." The surrounding cool air caused goose bumps to prickle her skin.

He closed the small gap and loomed over her. "Stop moving."

Closing her eyes, Eve prepared herself, tensing her muscles, waiting for whatever might happen next.

There was an unnatural silence until she heard him curse, then breathe out in a long frustrated sigh. "Open your eyes." Eve did as he asked and stared at him. "Different how?" He demanded quietly.

"You've been shot." She didn't see her breath this time when she spoke.

"Yes." Alex agreed. It wasn't like he could hide it. "How is that different from the others?"

Alex studied her as he waited for her to answer. Evening was clearly more than just scared, she was terrified. He decided to use that fear to his advantage but, when he saw her close her eyes and her body tense, he stopped. She had been preparing herself for a hit. It was sobering to realise she had been expecting *him* to hit her. He took a breath.

"Evening." He pressed for the answer.

She closed her eyes. "Please, stop calling me that."

"But that's your name."

Her eyes flew open. "I know what my name is." She snapped. "Just Eve. Okay. Eve."

"Okay, Eve. How is being shot different from the others?"

She shook her head. "It just is. But that doesn't matter. I still can't help you."

He kept direct eye contact with her as he crossed his arms over his chest. A loud thump came from upstairs and Eve's head shot up. He saw the pulse beat wildly in her neck. He needed to exploit her one weakness. "I was shot by a man that wants to kill an innocent woman." He paused. Another thump came from upstairs. *Her daughter again*. He fixed his sight on her. "An innocent, pregnant woman."

Her eyes locked with his. "What?"

Happy with her shocked expression, he continued. "She witnessed the murder of a guilty man. The men responsible had no idea she was hiding there, or they would never have performed the task. She can identify one of the men. That man cannot afford to be identified. If he's caught, the authorities could track him back to his house. His career, family and life depend upon him being invisible. So he panicked and tried to kill the woman."

"But you stopped him?" Eyes narrowed, she shifted slightly, her body turning towards the exit.

"There were other ways to silence her rather than killing her. He didn't care and we fought…"

"That's when he shot you?"

"Yes."

She glimpsed nervously towards the door of the kitchen and then back to him. "What happened to the woman?" The suspicion was still there in her eyes, but her question about Jillian gave him the result he was hoping for…he had her hooked.

"She was able to get away. But she's still in danger." Alex decided he should be blunt. Eve needed to know the kind of person Miles was trained to be. "The man is a trained killer — he will hunt her down and dispose of her and her baby in a manner that is untraceable."

The truth caused her to flinch and she stared up at him with horror in her hazel eyes. "He could do that so…easily?"

Alex paused. Strange, he never hesitated in his job, he couldn't afford to, but for the first time since his parents had died, he'd second-guessed his methods. He wanted Eve's help and being honest was the right thing to do, but it wasn't his intention to give her nightmares either. In spite of his good intentions and of how odd it seemed, he knew deep down that it would be hard to lie to her. "Yes, he can. That's why I need your…" A loud thump at the bottom of the stairs caught his attention and Alex turned just in time to see Eve's daughter walk into the kitchen, tucking a necklace inside her blouse.

"Good morning, Mummy."

Turning to face her daughter, Eve ignored him and smiled. "Hey." She cooed and opened her arms. Eve hugged her daughter and kissed the top of her head. "Have a good sleep?"

Alex focused on Eve. Her voice…it sounded different. He stepped back and listened, his muscles relaxing, his breathing slowing.

"Yup! What's for breakfast?" The girl pulled away and moved to the fridge.

"I was thinking scrambled eggs and toast, so grab the eggs while you're in there."

As he watched mother and daughter, Alex noticed it again. Eve's voice had changed, there was a calming, almost musical lilt to it now and he realised that he felt calm and not so restless about getting back into his body.

"Okay."

The girl's response snapped him out of his stupor. Wait! He blinked hard and shook his head. What the hell was going on? How did she do that? He went from being wound as tight as a spring to feeling…tranquil. He *never* felt tranquil.

Alex took a step towards Eve, staring intently at her face. As she met his stare, the smile faded away.

"What just happened to me?" he demanded. "I felt… Did you do that?"

She didn't answer him, only shook her head, pleading with her eyes.

Alex looked to the girl and then back to Eve. "You don't want her to know I'm here."

Eve shook her head again and quickly turned away when the girl closed the fridge.

Alex stared at the back of her auburn head. She had somehow taken control of him and that was something he would not allow to happen again.

Despite the fact her daughter was in the room, Alex strode up behind Eve and leaned over her shoulder. "Don't ever do that again or you'll be sorry you did."

He didn't miss her shiver and satisfied, he turned, stepping back, unintentionally blocking the kid. Out of habit he instantly moved to the side as to avoid hitting her, the same instant she moved to avoid him.

Chapter Four

Miles slowly sipped his coffee as he studied the police reports.

Detective Cade Taylor remains in I.C.U at Memorial. Resident Doctor reports that, although Cade is in stable condition, there has been no sign of improvement. The severity of his injuries will in all likelihood result in a permanent state of vegetation. Detective Taylor's wife, Mrs Justine Taylor, 30, was killed instantly. An autopsy was performed, cause of death resulting from impact of a moving vehicle. Her remains are currently located at Memorial, until such time as a family member steps forward to claim her body.

Unlike the first report filed three days before, this new report included the details of the autopsy. No mention of a pregnancy. Miles sighed. He had killed the wrong woman. And a cop. *Shit.* This complicated things. The locals would be raining down a shit storm until they locked someone away for trying to kill one of their own. He would have to walk a little softer until the investigation was over.

Gripping his hands behind his head, Miles remembered how the driver had fought to keep the truck on the road. He was the only one who knew the old-timer had been fighting a losing battle. As he had watched from a distance, Miles'd had full view of the accident, which was what it appeared to be — nothing more than an accident. Just like he had planned it.

* * * *

As Eve walked Noelle to the bus, the grey guy decided to tag along. Waving goodbye to Noelle, Eve felt him standing behind her. Of course she felt the stares of the other mothers too. At least that was normal. Standing next to a man that could possibly be...dead was not normal. *Is he dead?* Her stomach dropped, terrified at the thought. No, he can't be dead. She didn't see the dead.

"Why are those women staring at you?" he asked.

Ignoring him, Eve folded her arms over her stomach and marched back to the house. With a man, who could very well be dead, following her? Nope, definitely not normal. She wanted to run, get as far from him as possible and fast.

Eve ran up the steps, reached the door first, and opened it just enough for her to slip through, and then quickly shut it behind her. Holding it closed, she could see him standing on her porch watching her through the window in the door.

"You can't stay here. Go back to your body."

He cocked his head, studying her briefly, then slowly shook his head.

Eve rested her forehead against the door. "Please," she moaned. "I can't help you. Why won't you listen?"

"Because you haven't given me an acceptable answer."

The answer came from behind her.

Startled, Eve whirled to face him and snapped. "What are you doing?" She was shaking from fear, anger and suddenly frustration. "Go. Go. Go. Go."

She almost yelled the last 'go' and, embarrassed, stepped back from him.

Locking eyes with him, she waited for him to do something, but he just stared at her. No anger, no frustration, no amusement. It was getting kinda weird…and kinda scary. "What?" She threw her hands up. "Are you just going to stand there staring at me?"

This time he smiled. The pull of his lips was slow and she couldn't help but stare back. The look, described in one word…sexy. *No wait, I mean evil. No! Not sexy. What the hell. Not sexy. Just evil. Plain old evil.*

"Yes," he clarified. "I am, until you answer my question."

Her shoulders slumped as she sighed. "I told you, I can't help you."

"That's not the question I want an answer to. Why were those women staring at you? Do they know what you do?"

"Oh!" She hadn't been expecting that and wasn't quite sure if she should answer him, it was none of his business. But…if she did answer him, maybe he would disappear. She placed her hands on her hips. "Do they know if I'm a Physical Therapist? I have no idea and don't care. And I have no idea why they stare, they just do. Now please go," she asked politely. Maybe nice manners would help her cause. "I don't have time for this. Go find someone else to help save that secretary."

His eyes drifted over her face. "There is no one else, only you."

Actually there was at least one other she knew about with the same ability, and she knew, that person would not appreciate any name-dropping, especially when *this guy* was the median.

"Please try to understand I..." She stopped when she heard a car pull into the driveway.

"Who's that?"

Eve blinked and found him standing only an inch away from her, his gaze directed at the car parked outside of her house. His strength and power vibrated through her body, it caused her muscles to tingle and her stomach to clench. The intensity was so strong she had to take a step away from him. She wanted to take another when he looked down at her. She sucked in a breath. His eyes were glowing again. Like miniature blue lights.

"Evening." His voice was low, just above a whisper. "Who is that?"

Opening her mouth didn't make the words come out, she just gawked up at him. She couldn't believe this was happening. Since when did medians have glowing eyes and when had she become such a coward?

Anger over her own cowardice rose quickly when the question popped into her head. She was not a coward. This was her home, not his, she would not allow this...this...soul with beautiful, glowing eyes to scare her.

"That is my first patient of the day." She reclaimed her original spot.

Raising dark eyebrows, he looked down his nose at her. It was the look of someone used to getting their own way.

"Who is he?"

"That's none of your business." She moved to the door.

"Make it my business."

"Why? It's not like he can see you. What difference does it make?"

How could Alex explain his need for control to this woman? She had no concept of the man he was. The years spent training with the military had sharpened his mind and strengthened his body. Yet, it was the years he'd spent with the Guardian Project that had developed his natural desire for control. Controlling all aspects of the world around him was a simple fact of living and dying. That control had also saved many lives. But she wouldn't know that, no one would.

Alex inhaled slowly, struggling to find patience he wasn't sure he had.

Eve brushed past him as she moved to the door. He knew he wouldn't feel her touch, yet he felt...something when she passed.

She turned as she reached the door. "Go. Please," she implored again. The look on her face caused him to frown. Not because she had recited those words, yet again, to him but because he was actually considering giving her what she wanted and leaving her alone. He wished he could give her that, but he wouldn't.

Besides, he didn't like it when people lied to him and she was lying. She was capable of putting him back into his body—he read it on her face, in the movement of her hands and body.

The Guardian Project had spent long hours and millions of dollars teaching their soldiers how to read and interrupt body language. After all, if the people he hunted were on his kill list, they'd been good enough to avoid traditional police and military forces and he had to be better in order to stop them. So it was easy for him to recognise Eve's fear and anxiety, just as it was easy for him to recognise when she was lying.

Though he didn't like the lying he could handle it, now the fear...that was unusual for him to deal with. Never in his life had a woman been so afraid of him. That fear puzzled him. Deep in his gut he knew there was more—she wasn't telling him the whole truth. Shit she wasn't really telling him anything. It didn't matter—he would not walk away just because Eve was scared. He would not let Miles kill Jillian. She and her baby would live.

He shook his head. "No."

She closed her eyes and drew a deep breath. "I won't help you."

"Yes you will." He took a step closer to her. "And I'm going to haunt you until you give me what I want."

"Haunt me." Her eyes grew wide as a shiver shook her from head to toe.

"Mmm." He winked. "I'm not leaving your side until you put me back in my body."

Heavy footsteps echoed on the front porch.

"No," she whispered, her eyebrows pressed together. "I won't help you."

"Yes. You. Will." Then, nodding towards the door. "Want me to get that?"

Chapter Five

Plastering a smile on her face, Eve threw the door open and greeted Sergeant Dave Mills. Dave had been coming to see her for weeks, the time he had spent with her had done wonders for him and not just for his injured leg. Dave's overall wellbeing had improved since his first appointment with her — although she could see that today wasn't a good day for him.

Eve stopped next to the door to her studio and waited for Dave to enter. The man in grey suddenly stood directly behind Dave, watching her. She did her best to ignore him and focused on Dave. "Are you coming in?" When he didn't answer she spanned the small distance between them and, using the gift God had given her, Eve began Dave's treatment in her front hall.

"Would you like me to take your coat?" Eve asked, using her voice to soothe Dave.

The man studied her with a deep frown, then shook his head.

"Okay," Eve began, keeping her words in the same light tone. "Why don't we sit here and you can tell me what's going on." She paused briefly, but knew she would have to keep talking, if she wanted him relaxed enough so he would tell her what was going on. "Or we can go into my office where the chairs are more comfy, or into the studio and I can give that leg a look-see and a nice massage?"

The long-winded sentence worked, he expelled a long breath. "You talk a lot."

Eve hid her relief in a smile and rolled her eyes. "Like I haven't heard that one before."

Dave was feeling better but he needed more, so she kept her voice at the same level.

"You do talk a lot." The median commented. "And your voice is different again." There was an underlying warning to his words. "Why?"

Ignoring the comment, Eve urged Dave into the studio. "Come on."

He followed her in and she shut the door quickly before the median could enter. She wasn't about to be courteous to him—if he wanted into this room he could bloody well float through the damn wall.

Turning to Dave, she heard a deep chuckle from behind her. "Closing the door isn't going to stop me." The words were spoken next to her ear in a low amused tone. The median's enjoyment at the situation pissed her off, but not as much as the fact that she couldn't answer him back.

Eve looked at Dave and did the only thing she could do with an annoying median, she ignored him. "Okay, soldier drop'em and have a seat."

Dave did as she asked, then looked seriously at her. "I hope you weren't offended by what I said in the hallway?"

Eve focused on massaging what was left of his calf muscle. "Of course not." The wound had healed but the scars still looked red and sensitive.

"I like how you talk, I find it very comforting. Whenever I have a shitty day, I come here and listen to you talking about Noelle or whatever else and it has a way of calming me down and I feel better." He wrinkled up his nose. "I always dread talking to women about emotional stuff, but not you."

"That's because I'm a fantastic therapist and a wonderful human being," she teased, then saw him grimace when she ran her thumb over a tender area. "Still sore here eh?"

He gave her one nod, then flared his nostrils.

They were quiet for some time as Eve worked on his calf and once she had moved down to his foot, she levelled her voice and asked. "What's going on Dave?"

Sighing Dave laid back, covered his face with a big muscled arm. "I saw his wife last night."

"That must have been uncomfortable." Eve watched him from the end of the table. She needed to keep him calm while he talked about his friend's widow. "How did she handle it?"

"She cried when she saw me…"

"And?"

"She hugged me, and said she was happy I was back home."

"So…it went better than you thought it would?"

"Yah. It still fucked me up though. I keep thinking about him and how he died."

"Dave," Eve began. The faint musical pitch was barely audible and had taken her years to perfect, but it would help heal the pain Dave felt. Not the pain from his injury but the pain that was lodged deep in his soul. When *that* pain was healed, he would feel better or at the very least, it would help him come to terms with the loss of his friend. "It's okay to remember your friend and you are going to think about the day he died. It's only natural. I used to think about my mom's death all the time. Then I had Noelle and, as time passed, the memory faded and my life went on. A screaming baby has a way of snapping you back to the land of the living."

Dave pushed up on his elbows and looked at her. "So you're saying I need a screaming baby?"

She chuckled. "No, smart ass. I'm saying you need someone to help you through this."

Dave's gaze dropped away from hers, his brows wrinkling together. "Deb wants me over for dinner. She'll want to talk about Jeff."

"Of course she will," Eve agreed. "But isn't sharing it with her better than keeping it to yourself? You both have a chance to lean on each other for support. Who better to understand what you are feeling than her?"

Alex stood behind Eve, listening to the conversation. It didn't take a genius to realise that this soldier had lost his friend in the same incident in which he had been wounded. He seemed to be still coming to terms with it, which, no doubt, would take some time but Eve was helping, Alex could see that. The sergeant had been in bad shape when he'd first arrived, the anger clear on his face when he had turned towards the house. It was that look that'd had Alex demanding that Eve tell him who this man was. His apprehension was unwarranted, however. Eve and her short one-sided conversation had soothed away the anger. In seconds, Dave had been feeling better and had admitted as much.

Alex wasn't a fool, it wasn't her advice that was helping this man it was her voice. It was hard to catch because it was so subtle, but he had heard it. The lilt was almost feathery, a musical brush to the skin. The different range and tone for each word had a calming effect not just on the sergeant, but him too. It was the same sensation he felt in her kitchen earlier when her daughter was there.

A sudden realisation had Alex turning to Eve. She hadn't been trying to calm him this morning. She had been using that musical lilt on her daughter. Was she trying to keep the kid calm while he was in the room? He remembered the love on Eve's face when her daughter walked into the room. No, it wasn't a one-time thing—it was a natural response and probably a habit. He focused on her, studied her. No fake smiles, no nervous movements, no avoiding eye contact, Eve was what she appeared to be...a person that cared.

She heals the body and the soul. Alex remembered the words. *When one is brought to her broken, not only does she heal the body but the soul as well.* Alex watched as she joked with the soldier and worked on his torn up leg. She was a healer. The blonde was right.

He shouldn't torment her when she was helping this man. And he was tormenting her. She was doing her best to ignore him but he saw her eyes swing over his way occasionally. He should respect this soldier and leave the room, letting Eve to do her job in peace, but he wouldn't.

Alex spent the remainder of the day watching Eve with her three other patients. He stood on the opposite side of the room so she could see him and he had a clear view of her face. Every so often, he would comment on something she said, and would grin to himself when she gritted her teeth and carried on with her task.

Her last patient of the day was a young infantry private. He had damage to both knees and one ankle, leading Alex to believe that the private belonged to a jump unit and had injured himself in a practice jump. As Eve worked on the soldier, she spoke in the same calming voice she had used with her other patients, except this time the patient looked at her as more than just a therapist, he was looking at her as a woman. Before he could stop himself Alex inched closer and taunted her. "Stop teasing him already and put a smile on his face." Her nostrils flared. Alex fought to contain his laugh as he continued. "Come on Eve, do your part for our young warriors." He stood up, satisfied when she closed her eyes and sighed loud enough for the kid to hear.

"Is everything okay Eve?" the private asked.

Eve opened her eyes and smiled sweetly at him. "Yup. I just have an annoying buzzing in my ear and it will stop once it realises I will not help it."

The kid blinked, confused over her bizarre statement. Alex laughed.

By the end of the appointment she was pissed off and showed it the moment the young private drove away.

"Really?" She slammed the heavy front door. "Do you have to be so tacky?"

Alex raised an eyebrow.

"Don't look at me like you don't know what I'm talking about." She huffed and turned, stomping into her office. Smiling, Alex had to follow her. Apparently, he had got on her nerves more than he thought. A few more days like this and he'd be back in his body.

He followed into her office and walked around as she noisily shuffled folders on her desk. Like her bedroom, which he had spent a few hours in last night, this room was feminine. But not so much that a man would cringe when he walked in. One wall was covered from floor to ceiling in books, another had a large window. Her black, antique desk was a good size and stood out against the cream walls, and the over-stuffed chair in the opposite corner had a bold black and cream print that went well with the rest of the room.

There were pictures of her daughter on her desk and more pictures of what he guessed to be family members on the walls around the room. He walked around, looking at the pictures and stopped when he saw a picture of a little girl, maybe five or six with dark hair, standing with a woman who resembled Eve. It was an older picture and the surrounding edge was a bright red tartan with stripes of white, black and blue running through it.

"Well?" The demanding tone had him smiling before he could stop himself. He turned.

"Well what?"

"Argh," she huffed. "I wish I could throw something at you."

Alex knew what had her worked up, but he shrugged anyway. "Every man wants a 'happy ending' at the end of his massage. I was just looking out for my fellow soldier." He winked at her.

She narrowed her eyes and gave him a very fake smile. "Well, that service isn't offered in my practice."

The opening was there. He had to take it. "What about in your bedroom?"

"If I did, you certainly wouldn't be able to afford it," she replied straight-faced.

Eve watched the sexy smile drop from his face as he approached her. He slowly lowered himself so they were face to face, his eyes flat and emotionless. "I have enough money to pay for that service for a life time. Would you like a down payment?"

Eve felt her eyes grow wide. "No, I wouldn't." *What am I doing? Arguing with this median over sexual services! Geez!* He didn't flinch when she snapped, "Go away!"

His smirked pulled his mouth up to one side. "No."

"Then leave me be while I'm working. Those men can't afford me to be distracted."

"This problem can be solved, if you just put me back in my body."

"Merge. Merge you back into your body, not 'put'," she corrected. "If you're going to nag me about this, at least get the terminology right." She turned and sat at her desk. "And no, I already told you I don't do that anymore."

"Anymore?"

She cringed when she heard his question. *Damn it.* "That's right." She pulled out her first chart and began writing her notes. Except she couldn't concentrate on her notes, he wouldn't let her.

"Let's say I was a ten year old boy, who wanted nothing more than to go home with his parents and the only way that would happen was for you to merge me back into my body." He moved to the side of her desk, resting back against the wall. "Would you help me?"

Eve answered him honestly. "A ten year old boy would not be standing in my house talking to me. He would be with his body in the hospital and we would never meet."

He scowled down at her. "So you wouldn't help him?"

Eve lowered her head. "I don't go to the hospital, so I wouldn't even know about him."

"What if he comes here and he tells you his story, how about then?"

Eve raised her head and looked at him, *really* looked at him. He had no idea that medians never left their bodies. He was the only one she had ever seen let alone heard of leaving their body. She was about to fill him in on that simple fact when she froze, not knowing what to call him.

"What's your name?" She asked lightly.

He scowled again but answered her. "Alex Hunter."

"Alex," she began, "I've never had a median come to my house. You're the first. Every median that I've had contact with, which for the record is not that many, remained close to their bodies in the hospital."

The dark grey, long sleeved shirt Alex was wearing pulled tight against his arms when he crossed them. "What do you mean? They can't leave their bodies?"

Leaning back in her chair Eve thought out loud. "They were always in the hospital." She met Alex's watchful gaze. "I saw all of them while I was doing my rounds." She opened her mouth but Alex interrupted, "You're a nurse?"

"Was." She tapped her pen against her lips. "I did see Emily Spencer at the nurses' station, but her body was just down the hall. I remember that 'cause it scared the shit out of me to see her standing there, staring at me. But the others, I saw them all in their rooms. I always believed medians couldn't leave their bodies, that there was some kind of weird psychic link between soul and body. But now that you're here, it blows my theory out of the water. Maybe a median doesn't leave their body because they're scared too."

"So you're not a nurse?" he asked.

"No. Did you hear what I said?"

He raised an eyebrow as he repeated it back to her word for word. Eve's eyes grew wide and she threw up her hands. "Okay, just checking to see if you were paying attention."

His brows lowered into black-brown slashes. "I always pay attention."

Eve rolled her eyes. "Lucky me."

Crossing her legs, she examined him from her leather chair. He'd wait for her to finish before he asked why she was doing so.

She finally sighed.

"Well?" he asked.

She leaned against the arm rest. "How come you were able to leave your body?"

"I'm trying to save a woman and her baby, I wasn't thinking about anything else." He shrugged. "If it means leaving my body to get what I need to help them, then so be it. I'll do what I have to."

Eve straightened in her chair and swung her legs back under her desk. It was obvious she didn't like being reminded why he was here. She adjusted her papers and began to write her notes.

Alex left her alone until she had to go to the bus stop to pick up Noelle. As he did in the morning, he followed and waited behind her as the bus approached. Once again the women stared at Eve. He looked from the women to Eve and then back. Eve was standing alone as the other parents gathered in groups and chatted away. He found it curious that Eve stood by herself when her entire day had consisted of socialising with her patients. She wasn't a loner but she didn't seem to fit in either, just like him.

He had to be both. Although not everyone agreed with him, the type of life he led was not suited for family or friends outside of the project, but he needed to be social enough to get his kill and then disappear. Eve was very similar to him, except he wasn't sure if she was being alienated or alienating herself. He also found it curious that their stares irritated him.

Back at the house, Alex followed Eve around and realised quickly that she was as regimented as any soldier he had met. First up was Noelle's homework, then Eve made them supper, then the pair of them cleaned up the kitchen. Up next was 'free time' which meant Noelle was free to do whatever she liked, and the evening ended with Eve and Noelle on the couch watching T.V. He observed mother and daughter when they laughed at something on the screen. A long time had passed since he had been with his own family. He'd forgotten how comforting it could be just to sit and be with family. Except this wasn't his family.

After Eve said goodnight to Noelle, she went into her room and began pulling off her turtle neck. She stopped and turned, facing him.

"You almost forgot I was here."

With a slight blush, she gave him a fake smile. "No."

He rubbed his chin and said, "Guess I need to be stepping up my game, if you're forgetting about me that easily."

"No. You don't need to step up anything. You need to go, I want to change."

"So change." He waved his hand out before him as he leaned into the door frame.

"You're funny," she grumbled, snatching up her clothes and stomping into the attached bathroom. He moved into the room before she closed the door and waited for her to turn. Her startled look and gasp was priceless when she saw him and he couldn't help but laugh out loud.

"Would you get out?" She pulled the door open and pointed. "Get out."

Alex shook his head.

She narrowed her eyes, then the look dropped away as she spoke to him. "Alex." The muscles in his chest and shoulders responded to her voice instantly and he felt the tension ease from his body. "I would like to change and I am honest enough to tell you I'm not comfortable with you here in the same room with me while I do that." Her voice was incredibly smooth and it flowed over his skin like the caress of a lover's hand.

He edged closer, pulled to her by the call of her words, and focused on her face. She was using her voice trick, like she had with the others. Except this time, she was using her gift as a means of defence. He should be pissed. He wasn't. He was in enough control of himself to do what needed to be done, but he wasn't heartless either.

"Please," she asked, cheeks pink.

Stepping closer still, he looked down at her, into her hazel eyes, noticing the flecks of green flickering in them. He hadn't missed the fact that Eve was an attractive woman, but right then, at that moment, when she spoke to him and pleaded with her soulful eyes he wanted to give her anything she needed, including leaving her.

"I'll be waiting in your bed—" he paused when her eyes grew wide, " —room." He finished.

Chapter Six

"Don't you sleep?" Alex asked, sitting on the side of her desk.

Eve continued getting the next day's charts out, then stood and looked him in the eye. "Usually."

She turned, scuffing her slippers as she walked into her studio. She had got into the habit of preparing for the first patient the night before, anything to get that extra ten minutes of sleep in the morning.

"It's late, why aren't you sleeping now?" Alex asked from behind her.

"Well…" She pulled a fresh pillow case out from under the treatment table and began changing the dirty pillow case. "I had charts to finish, which is hard when someone is staring over your shoulder, plus I like to prepare for the next day. As for sleeping, I'm not sure, because you're here. And if tonight is the same as last night, I doubt I'll be sleeping at all."

"Are you avoiding going to bed because of me?"

"Ah yah!" She moved to the corner and pulled a resistance band from a shelving unit. "How would you feel if you knew a strange man was wandering in and out of your bedroom at night?"

"How did you know that?" The intensity of his words made her stop in her tracks.

Eve turned back to face him. "You don't know..." She began. He didn't know that she could feel his presence. She wasn't sure she should share this information with him—it might give him an advantage when he already had so many. Playing on his ignorance could only help get rid of him. Right?

"Know what?"

Eve tilted her head back as he closed the gap between them. She felt the need to look away but stayed where she was. "Nothing. Are you leaving anytime soon?" She pulled a loose piece of hair behind her ear.

"No," he answered, then asked, "Why are you lying to me?"

This time Eve did look away, it happened before she could stop it. How did he know she wasn't telling him the truth? She shook her head. "I'm not—"

"Yes you are." Then very quietly he warned. "You do not want to play this game with me Eve."

She bit her lip waiting for him to continue or leave her alone. He didn't move.

"Look at me."

When she followed his order she expected to see anger gleaming in his eyes but there was nothing but staunch curiosity. "Know what, Eve?" he repeated.

Huffing, she told him the truth. "I can feel you. I don't need to see you to know you're there."

He raised his dark brows studying her intently. "How many times did you feel me last night?"

"You don't believe me."

"I didn't say that."

"Yah right!" Why did his doubt annoy her? Who cared if he believed her or not? "I felt you seven times. But I couldn't see you, even when I turned the light on."

He raised his eyebrows. "What did you feel?"

She shrugged, trying to convince herself that she wasn't relieved that he seemed to believe her. "You know that feeling you get when you know there is another person in the room with you because you can see them?"

He nodded.

"It's like that but much, much stronger. Plus I get nauseous."

"You get sick?" He seemed disconcerted by the idea.

Eve couldn't help but laugh. "I don't throw up or anything, just an upset stomach."

"Do you feel that way now?" Concern was attached to his words this time.

"A little."

He surprised her by taking a step back. "Are you done?"

Now what was he doing? She searched his face, trying to figure out what his game was. She shouldn't trust him, didn't trust him. Yet, there was something about him, she couldn't quite figure out.

They stood facing each other. During that very brief moment, Eve came to three conclusions. One, he was a median, and though most were scared and confused, medians were not trustworthy. Two, he could very well be dead. She swallowed hard. God above, she *really* did not want to see the dead. But if that was the case, she knew from Gran that the dead would do anything to get back into a body and that made them not trustworthy. Three, he was very nice to look at. Eve struggled to hide a smile over her last conclusion, her sudden fear so easily overshadowed. Good looking men were definitely not trustworthy. At the same time she found herself wondering if his eyes would be that vivid when he was back in his body and if his mouth would be that sexy.

Alex broke the silence first. "Eve?" She looked up from his mouth and met his amused stare. "Are you done?"

Nodding like an idiot, she left the studio for bed.

* * * *

Alex sat on the floor, resting his back against Eve's bedside table. The room was dark and except for Eve's slow breathing, the room was quiet. "Go to sleep."

"I can't, you're here," she sighed, turning onto her back.

"Well in that case let's discuss why you won't merge me." Alex suggested.

The duvet was pulled up to her chest. She rested her arm above her head, and toyed with an auburn curl. The casual act appealed to him. The light stroke of her fingers had him wishing he was that strand of hair. It caused a thirst for something he had no business craving for in the first place.

He shoved his new thirst aside and focused on the woman. Eve was interesting. A single mother, with her own practice and the ability to merge a soul back into its body, as well as the added talent of controlling emotions by using her voice. A number of questions ran though his head, most importantly, why was Eve alone? He studied her profile. Small nose, thin eyebrows the same brownish-red hue as her hair and supple pink lips, and though she was on the shorter side, her hour-glass curves were full and lush. Why was this sexy little brat single?

Then he remembered how stubborn she was. He also remembered the fear. He hadn't liked seeing that fear on her lovely face, not when she was backing away from him in her kitchen and he didn't want to see it now. He wasn't a fool, he knew forcing Eve might become a possibility but he did not want fear to control her actions when the time came.

Pestering her would get him what he wanted, irritating to the point she would give him what she wanted just to be rid of him. He had to be as stubborn as she was.

"I already told you," she murmured. "I don't do that anymore."

"Why is that?"

"Because."

The simple answer irritated him. He was used to getting what he wanted, not having to wait for it. He held his temper in check, knowing it wouldn't help his cause.

"You're a soldier," she stated.

"Yes."

"But you're different from the other soldiers I've met."

"Not really." He leant back.

"But you are, I can feel it." She rolled on her side to face him.

He locked his eyes on her. "Can you?"

"Yes."

"What do you feel?"

A thoughtful look creased her brow. "Anger. But I don't think that's because of me. Frustration—" she huffed, "—which is because of me."

He had to fight to hide his smile. "Anything else?"

She nodded. "You're twitchy."

What the hell! "I'm not twitchy."

"Yes you are." She chuckled. "You're used to getting what you want, in this case me merging you back and I'm not giving it to you. Which in turn, makes you twitchy."

"I'm not twitchy." He growled the words.

"Fine!" she sighed dramatically. "How's restless?"

"Better."

She laughed, quietly this time. "But you are different aren't you?"

Even though it had been drilled into him from the first day he'd entered the Guardian Project to keep his mouth shut, Alex answered honestly. "Yes."

"You're trained in special operations?"

He sighed, bent his knees and rested his arms on top of them. "And then some."

"Have you been on many tours?"

"When I was with my old infantry unit."

"But not now?" She stared at him, her eyes questioning. Alex stared back wondering if he would be able to see the green slivers.

"I belong to a different type of unit now. We specialise in Urban Combat Terrorism." She gave him a confused look.

"We track and eliminate persons that have become a danger to society."

"You mean terrorists?"

"Sometimes. If the local police force or military can't track them down or if they can't get close enough to make the kill, we'll lend a hand. But most of the people that make the kill list are a danger to the society in which they live." He watched her face as he explained. "Like a drug lord who kills an entire village to send a statement of power or a politician who sells a list of tactical operations dates and locations to a terrorist group." He stopped.

The Rhodes op was still fresh in his mind. He had been pissed when he had found out why members of his old unit had been killed and he had demanded to be put on point. *He'd* wanted to kill Rhodes. As it was, Miles had been granted that gift. And, though it took him three months of hunting in that stinking hot desert, he had got to clip each and every one who participated in the ambush.

"That sounds like Secret Service or CIA stuff." She yawned covering her mouth.

Alex didn't respond until she looked at him again. "We don't have the government ties, the agencies in the States have, because we are not a government agency. We are a military unit." She stared back at him and he could read on her face that she didn't know whether to believe him or not. Not that it mattered, but he was telling her the truth.

"My turn. Can I ask a few questions now?"

"No." She rolled onto her back once again and began toying with another curl.

Alex couldn't help but chuckle. "Too bad."

Eve smiled into the darkness at the sound of Alex's laugh. It was a deep laugh. A sexy laugh.

"When was the first time you saw a median?"

Eve concentrated on the ceiling. "The first median I saw was on the same floor in the hospital as my granddad. He was a young man mid-twenties, nice looking. Of course, at the time I had no idea he was actually a median. He was standing in my granddad's room when we went for a visit. At the time I remember thinking granddad had a lot of visitors but then my mum spoke to the man and when I was older I learned she had gone back and merged him."

"Your mom could merge as well?"

"Yup, she was an amazing person." Her mother's face flashed before her eyes, and like every other time, she wanted to reach out and touch it.

"How'd she die?" His voice was low.

Eve closed her eyes. She remembered coming home from work just as the ambulance had been pulling away. When Gran had told her what'd happened, Eve had refused to believe it and had rushed into the house to see for herself if her mum had gone. The house had been quiet. Her house had never been quiet, her mum had always had on music or been singing, and that day it had been dead quiet. Then the guilt and the 'what if's' had crept into her mind like they always had. What if her mum hadn't given her the medallion? Would she still have tripped and fallen down the stairs? The 'what if's' gave her chills.

"Are you still here?"

She shook her head. "It's really none of your business."

"I know. But you're still going to tell me."

Why was he right? "It was crazy how she died, a total accident." She took a deep breath. "She fell down the stairs vacuuming. She did it for me because I was pregnant at the time and she was worried about me falling down the stairs and getting hurt."

He was silent for a few minutes and Eve had no idea what he was thinking, and she certainly didn't have enough courage to ask.

"I wouldn't call that crazy. Accident yes. Crazy no."

"Why isn't it crazy?" She asked surprised by his response.

"A man broke into my house when I was eighteen and shot both my parents. When I hunted him down I asked him why did he did it, his answer was because someone bet him twenty bucks that he couldn't. My parents were killed over a stranger's bet. *That's* crazy."

Sadness poked at her heart. How terrible to have both parents taken away in such a manner. Her need to heal was always present, and the only difference was that Alex was sitting on her bedroom floor instead of down in her studio.

Eve gripped the blanket and very carefully spoke. "I'm sorry."

She didn't know if she would get a response so she kept talking using a delicate pitch. "You hunted down the man who killed your parents when you were eighteen? How did you do that?"

He sighed. "Don't use your voice on me," was all he said before he continued, "I have no idea. It seems to come naturally to me."

Eve didn't know if the goose bumps on her arms were because of his answer or because he'd caught her using her gift to help him.

"You're a natural at hunting down and..." She stopped hoping he would fill in the blank with arresting or catching.

"Killing," he finished.

Eve stared up at the ceiling exhaling a long breath. "And you wonder why I can't sleep?"

His deep chuckle made her relax a little, a very little. "You have nothing to worry about unless you plan on becoming a danger to society."

"Sorry, my schedule is full for the next ten years." She chuckled. Geez this was nuts. Joking with a man who had just confessed he was a trained killer—like her life wasn't full enough already.

"Too bad, I think I would enjoy hunting you down." His voice had become deep, with a sexy twist.

Air caught in her throat. "You would?"

"Oh yes. I can think of a few sweaty ways to deliver your punishment."

Eve felt her eyes grow wide the same moment her stomach fluttered. It had been a long time since a man had made *that* kind of suggestion to her.

In the dark part of her mind, she wondered how many people she would have to bump off before Alex came knocking on her door to deliver his…punishment.

"You're wondering what you would have to do in order for me to deliver my punishment, aren't you?" The sexy humour in his voice had her smiling into the darkness.

"No." Her face heated up.

"I'll tell you anyways. Jaywalking."

"What?" Eve rolled back onto her side to face him.

"All you have to do is jaywalk." She could see him turn his head in the dark to face her. "And I'll come knock on your door."

Eve froze, she didn't even blink. He had to be joking, except…he didn't sound like he was joking. "Would you like to hear what your punishment would be?"

Absolutely she would. But for some reason she couldn't tell him that, couldn't even move.

"Undecided eh?" Sitting up, he turned. "How about I tell you anyway?"

She stopped breathing then and waited.

"I would come to you in the middle of the night. Slip into your bed while you were sleeping and begin to remove that see-through T-shirt of yours."

In the dark as she listened to his sensual summary of her punishment, she saw two small flickers of light.

"Your panties would be next. I'm going to love sliding those down your legs—feel how wet you are for me."

She blinked, focusing on the flickering that grew brighter and brighter, until she was looking into small beams of blue light.

"Here's where I'm having a little difficulty—you see I'm torn between bending you over the bed and getting my fill of you from behind or just pulling you down to the floor and riding you hard." His eyes were beautiful and freaky, but the way they flickered like miniature flames was almost hypnotic.

His voice dropped low. "It's a little rougher on the floor but it's deep." He ran his hand along the top of her carpet and she wished that he was running it over her instead. A hot ache pulled between her legs as he continued. "There will be a lot of panting and sweating and by the end you'll be begging me to let you come."

Her throat was dry and she swallowed a hard lump of desire. Was he serious? That wasn't a punishment. It was a single mother's dream come true. Her heart jumped.

It was strange though. Should he even be having these thoughts? Did medians feel desire and passion and need? Did the dead? Besides that, how could he feel that way about her...he didn't even know her...

"Wait a sec," she blurted out. "Oh my God!" She covered her warm face. "Nice try." She bit out. "But doing this whole 'oh babe you turn me on, now merge me and we'll screw all night' isn't going to work. So just piss off, go away, leave, get out." Did he think she was a fool? She had been burnt by enough guys to know when they were spouting bullshit, even really hot sexy bullshit.

Eve turned, facing the opposite side of the room and closed her eyes. She was still aching, turned on by his detailed description and also pissed off. Not just at him, but at herself as well. She had actually begun to feel… It was probably because she hadn't had sex in a while, but damn it she knew better. Trusting a man was bad enough, but trusting a median was worse and the dead…she didn't even want to go there.

"You will merge me." She flinched when the words were spoken next to her ear. "And I meant what I said. All you have to do is jaywalk to have me knocking on your door." He paused before whispering, "Maybe, even less."

Chapter Seven

Alex watched Eve sleep for the better part of an hour until he finally got up. He was done tormenting himself. He stared down and watched as she stretched, extending her arm over her head. The movement was innocent but it turned sultry when it caused her breasts to lift and push against her T-shirt.

Shit! There it was again, that need to touch her. He took one step back, keeping his eyes on her face. There was something about Eve that turned him on. The feeling had come out of nowhere, catching him off guard and he silently wished he was in his body, so he could feel if her skin was as soft as it looked.

He took another step back. This was not him. He didn't allow himself to become attracted to a woman he didn't know. He didn't feel much for the women he did know. And Eve was not the type of woman he slept with. She wasn't what he wanted in a woman. He liked them tall and leggy, with straight hair. Eve wasn't short but she wasn't what he would call tall and those auburn curls. Curls always reminded him of a mess and he liked things orderly. She was also a mother. She had an attachment in her life, a family, families were a distraction, they could be used against him, and that was something he would not allow.

No attachments. No feelings. It was a self-imposed rule and one he had kept. He only slept with woman that wanted what he wanted, sex. No more, no less. None of the women he spent the night with had a family or kids, and none of them would pose a threat to him. He made sure of it by researching each one of their backgrounds before he took them to his bed.

No, Eve was not his type and the sooner his body realised it the better off he would be. He turned from Eve's still form and moved to the door. Why was he feeling anything? Emotions, sure, but his body was turned on. He had felt his cock swell at the thought of Eve's naked body wrapped around his...except he didn't have a body for her to wrap around.

Stopping at Eve's bedroom door, he sighed. There didn't seem to be any clear cut guidelines for a median. He felt emotions, which he guessed were generated from the soul, and could feel the physical stir of his body yet he wasn't a solid mass. He could walk through doors when Eve shut them on him, or in the case of her trying to lock him out this morning, all he did was think about being in her house and he was. Yet, he could sit on the floor or lean against walls and not fall through them, like he imagined a ghost would.

Slowly extending his arm, he reached for the door handle and watched as his hand floated right through it. He pulled back and tried again, with the same result — nothing. Annoyed, he stood back and studied the handle. There must be more to it. He thought about the day. Every time Eve had closed a door on him, he had been irritated enough that he had walked through to her. Everything he had done today had occurred when he'd had an emotional response to Eve's comments or actions.

He turned back to Eve and remembered the shaky way she had exhaled after he had said he would come back and pay her a visit, once he was whole again. He meant it too, even though it went against his normally strict practices. And it pissed him off that he knew he wouldn't be able to fight the urge. He would come back here all right and spend a very long, very sweaty night getting to know her body. If she knew what was good for her, she would hurry up and merge him and get away from him a-sap. But she was so damn stubborn.

He shook his head. Why couldn't the only person that could merge him be willing to help him instead of fight him? And why did she have to be so damn sexy? With agitation, flowing through his veins he reached for the door and turned the handle. It swung open and he stalked down the hall.

* * * *

"So doc, what's on the agenda for today?"

Eve groaned loudly when she heard Alex behind her. "I'm not a doc. And I thought I told you to go away."

"And I thought I made it pretty clear last night when I said I wasn't going anywhere."

Eve sighed. "Really, I must have tuned you out." She turned to face him and found him leaning against the counter next to the fridge.

He crossed his arms, displaying the well-developed muscles of his biceps and shoulders and gave her a smile that only curled up one side of his mouth.

Eve almost allowed her mouth to drop open. He looked so casual and sexy and before she could stop it, her body reacted. Her skin heated, her arms and legs felt tingly and her insides twisted into a hot eager knot. Oh man, this couldn't be good. Getting turned on by a median or…dead soul…maybe dead, maybe not. This might be easier if she knew what clues to look for in the dead but she didn't because there weren't any. *Oh Lord.* She groaned, hoping he wasn't dead, because, if that was the case and he was, not only would she be out of her mind but what kind of fulfilment would she get? Nothing. And it certainly wouldn't be like her dream. A vivid image popped into her head of Alex making love to her on the floor. Of his hot, sweat covered body pinning her against the rough carpet, his hand slipping between their bodies, fingers teasing her moist lips and clit, his mouth nipping and licking, covering every achy, wet inch of her.

The sound of running water from above snapped Eve back to where breakfast was waiting to be made, and the hottest median she had ever come into contact with, smirked knowingly at her. Heat spread though her face again when she realised she still needed to get the milk for Noelle's cereal. Alex gave her a wink when she sighed again. He had the ability to irritate her and make her blush at the same time. *Fantastic.*

She walked over to the fridge, despite the close proximity, and withdrew the milk. Straightening, she faced him and gazed into deep pools of blue. Alex had the most vivid blue eyes she had ever seen — they were beautiful — considering he might actually be dead. He gave her a playful wink, hinting that he knew exactly what he did to her insides. Her stupid stomach fluttered in joy and annoyed she quickly turned, placing the milk on the table. Remembering the door to the fridge was open, she turned to shut it but was too late, it was already closing.

Eve froze, watching the door to the fridge being pushed closed. She shifted her eyes to Alex, who was staring back. "Guess what I can do?"

Oh shit! He had done that, he had shut...the...door. She exhaled a slow breath, an eerie chill causing the hair on the back of her neck to stand on end. Medians couldn't touch...stuff. The dead, well they were different. Her Gran had told her about the different things she had seen the dead do. Some weren't able do anything, others could move objects or open and close doors. The rare few had the ability to appear to the living. And a very select few were able to talk and move as if they were still living. Gran had explained to her when she was young, that the abilities the dead had were directly related to the age of their soul. Young souls were the weakest, with little or no experience at living, only dwelling in one or two bodies, they could do very little. The older, more experienced souls were stronger, having lived many lives in many different bodies and therefore had the ability to do more once they passed.

She should probably talk to Gran. Make sure she wasn't wrong. Make sure Alex was what she believed him to be, an old soul. A dead, old soul.

Noelle arrived shortly after Alex displayed his new trick. So he never got the chance to ask Eve why it scared the hell out of her. Instead, he stood back and watched mother and daughter. He listened as they talked about the day ahead.

"We have gym today with Mr Larson." Noelle said, before scooping more cereal into her already full mouth.

"Chew first please," Eve commented, and then asked, "Who's Mr Larson?"

"He's our new gym teacher."

"I thought Miss Penny taught you gym?"

"She does. But she broke her foot playing for her soccer team. So she can't." The girl shrugged.

"Oh that sucks! Tell Miss Penny I hope she feels better soon." Eve took a sip of her coffee and licked her lips.

Alex felt a tug in his groin and he clamped his teeth together, annoyed that the simple gesture could do that to him.

"I will." Noelle blinked up at Eve with wide hazel eyes. "Hey! You should help her mum. You can fix anybody."

"Honey. You know I can't."

"But you help all those sick soldiers. You make them better. Why can't you help Miss Penny?"

"For one, I'm sure she already has a very good physiotherapist, and two I have a contract with the Military saying I will only treat soldiers."

"What's a contract?"

Eve sighed. "Well, it's a—" She paused, struggling to find the words.

Alex didn't want to interrupt, and though he knew Noelle saw him, he never spoke when in her presence because he didn't want to frighten her, but Eve looked as though she needed the help. "It's like a promise," he suggested.

Eve shifted her eyes slightly in his direction but then focused back on Noelle's questioning stare. "It's kind of like a promise. I promised the Military that I would only help soldiers."

"That's because they're really special, right?" Noelle asked shovelling in another scoop of food.

"Yup. Some of them are," Eve confirmed, taking another sip of her coffee. "So what's this Mr Larson going to be teaching you?"

"Football."

"Gran's version of football or American football?"

"No, not soccer. Real football." The girl put down her spoon and looked serious. "I don't know how to play football. Do you Mum?"

"No, I'm sorry honey I don't." Eve reached forward when Noelle's frown didn't disappear. "It's okay." Alex could hear the calming lilt to her words. "We'll sit down together tonight and look online. We'll read up on it, okay?"

"Okay," the girl sighed, and stood, taking her dirty dishes to the sink. "I wish I had an uncle."

Eve turned to face her daughter. "You do?"

"Sometimes." The girl stared thoughtfully at her mum. "Then I would have someone to show me how to play sports like Kylie's uncle. He plays soccer with her in the park when he comes to visit."

Eve stood and wrapped her arms around the girl. "You never told me you wanted to do that. I'll play soccer in the park whenever you want."

Noelle pulled away and shrugged. "It's not the same. Is my lunch ready?"

Eve nodded. "Yup, it's in the fridge." She checked her watch. "Get your shoes on, time to go."

Noelle grabbed her lunch and went to get dressed.

Eve began cleaning the kitchen.

From where he stood Alex could see the hurt on her face. "Kids are fickle." He began not knowing where he was going with his statement. "They always want what the other has. If Noelle had a father or an uncle or even a brother, she probably wouldn't even spend time with them."

"Says the man, who's a self-confessed killer. Had a lot of experience with kids have you?"

Straightening, Alex gave her a hard look. "I'm saying the grass is always greener on the other side. Even us self-confessed killers know how kids think, even if their mothers don't."

Clearly insulted, Eve turned and left the kitchen.

Eve ignored him for the next two days. Not even when they were alone did she answer his questions or respond to his comments.

Only at the end of the second day when Noelle was asleep did he finally get a reaction from her. He was pissed off enough to do the only thing that would guarantee a response. He stood, walked over to her bedroom door and slammed it shut.

Eve shot up onto her knees and hissed. "Are you crazy?"

"Little bit," he conceded. "I'm glad I finally have your attention." He stopped when he heard Noelle call out to Eve in fear.

"Mummy? What was that?"

Eve glanced at him questioningly.

"Answer her, she's scared."

Eve narrowed her eyes at him and called out, "It's okay honey, I slipped. Go back to sleep."

"Okay, night Mummy."

"Night, honey."

Still scowling, she hissed at him again, "What is the matter with you?"

Alex calmly walked back to her bedside and stood looking down at her. "I don't like being ignored."

"That's bullshit." She stared up at him defiantly. "I'm not giving you what you want and that bugs the hell out of you."

He shrugged but agreed. "True. But you haven't answered one of my questions and like I said, I don't like being ignored."

"I don't really care what you like or don't like. You came into my house, unwelcome by the way, and you expect me to be courteous to you. Buddy you are living in a dream world if you think this is going to change."

Alex felt his teeth clench together, the muscles pulled in his jaw. He wasn't used to being told what he could and couldn't do and he wasn't used to being called buddy. Buddy? He honestly didn't know which was worse. The one thing he did know was that Eve's attitude was about to go through a serious overhaul. He wanted the woman he had spoken to two nights ago, not a brat having a hissy fit.

He purposely leant down, closing the gap between them. "Is that right?" He spoke coolly.

"Yes that's right," she answered, her voice wavering slightly.

"In that case I think we should invite Noelle into my dream world, see what she thinks about it?"

Straightening to his full height, he turned and walked towards the door. It flew open before he reached it and passed through. Eve jumped out of bed.

"No," she whispered. "Please don't."

He kept walking. Eve needed to know that he wasn't a man to be challenged and he never made idle threats. Reaching Noelle's door, he entered the room.

"Please Alex. Please. Don't scare her." Her words were whispered once again but her voice was calmer this time.

Alex instantly recognised what she was doing. He could hear the flowing musical undertone to her words. He stopped and turned back to her once he was standing at the foot of Noelle's bed. "I can handle any insult you throw at me, but I will not stand by and let you chastise me when all I was doing was trying to comfort you. Do not talk to me like that again."

Eve stood in the doorway, hands clenched together, anguish on her pretty face. Then he saw them — the tears. They pooled quickly in her huge eyes and slipped over her lashes when she blinked at him.

"Have I made my point?"

She gave him a tearful nod.

"Not good enough," he said a little louder. He knew Noelle could see him, but he never pushed the issue because he recognised she was ignoring him for her mother's sake. And he didn't want to wake her now but if he had to in order to make his point, then he would.

"Yes." New tears slid down her cheeks. "I'll answer your questions. Please don't hurt her."

Hurt her? Alex turned to the girl and saw the same mixture of colours that formed her mothers' eyes. Those eyes were wide in fear and he guessed the kid had heard what her mother had said. He responded to Eve's plea, "I would never hurt a child and I'm insulted that you would think so." Yet in all fairness, he had told Eve about his occupation, it would be only natural for her to assume he would 'hurt' to get what he wanted.

He studied Noelle's face, taking note of every feature that was similar to Eve's. She blinked up at him, eyes still wide. He should probably apologise for scaring her, but he wouldn't.

"Okay. I'm sorry," Eve whispered. "Please come out of there. I'll answer anything you want."

Alex almost sighed when he heard the delicate undertone to her words. "What would you like to talk about?"

Giving Noelle a smile and a wink, he turned from her and moved back towards the door. He passed Eve, knowing full well she would want to check on Noelle before coming back to her bedroom. Alex stopped, blocking her path and said loud enough for Noelle to hear. "Don't worry she didn't hear a thing, she's a sound sleeper." Let's hope the kid got the message and closed her eyes before Eve went in. Now was not the time for Eve to find out her daughter shared her talent for seeing medians.

* * * *

Eve closed the door to her bedroom and climbed on top of the bed. Alex was already sitting in his normal spot next to her bed, on the floor. Sliding under the covers, she reached over and flicked off the light. Strips of orange light filtered through her blinds from the street lamp across the street.

"What are you doing?"

"I don't need the light on to answer your questions." Eve exhaled slowly as she rested back against her pillow. Her fear wasn't gone, but there certainly was less of it. Alex was a ruthless man or rather ghost or dead person. The fear she felt when Alex walked into Noelle's room was so intense she had been reduced to tears and begging. She would have done anything, given him everything, just to get him away from

Noelle. And then he had to flip things around and become insulted when she begged him not to hurt Noelle. The look on his face and his words actually sounded genuine. But it didn't matter now, he was away from Noelle and she had promised to answer his questions. "Okay, what do you want to know?"

He chuckled. "Guess I found your weakness."

Eve clucked her tongue. "That's the stupidest observation I've ever heard. Of course Noelle is my weakness. She is my child. I would give my life for her."

"You're pretty ballsy saying that to me."

"And you're an idiot for pointing out the obvious." She sighed and did her best to sound apologetic. "Okay look. I said I would answer your questions and I will. So ask away."

Alex chuckled again. "Your apologies are almost as bad as mine."

"That's because I'm not used to having to apologise." Eve smiled to herself, she couldn't help it.

"Me neither. Okay, first question. Why were you scared when I closed the fridge door?"

"You shouldn't be able to close doors. That's what scared me."

"Why shouldn't I be able to do that?"

She could picture a frown on his face as she stared up at the ceiling. "I don't know." She shrugged. "That's what I was told."

"Couldn't any of the other medians you ran across do that and you just didn't see it?"

Eve seriously thought about it, then finally guessed, "I don't think so."

"But you don't know for sure."

"No, I don't. But they felt different from you."

"How so?"

Eve wasn't sure she should tell him her theory about him being an old soul, not only would it give him a boost to his ego but it may give him more leverage over her. As for telling him, she thought he might actually be dead! Well, that wouldn't be any fun either and his reaction to that might become violent. If that happened, she had a feeling she would see what Alex was capable of.

"I'm not sure. How were you able to find me when other medians can't leave their bodies?"

"I did what needed to be done. I didn't think about anything else."

"Then maybe that is why you can move things too." *Or maybe it's because you're dead!*

"Who told you about medians, your mother?" he asked.

"Yes." She cringed when she dragged the answer a little long. He would know she wasn't telling him the whole truth.

"And who else?"

"My gran," she answered him honestly.

"She can see medians too?"

"Yes."

"And merge them?"

"Not anymore. She's too old." Eve shook her head.

"How old?" Now why would he ask that question? Did he know more than he was letting on?

"Old."

He paused and she could feel him looking at her but she refused to meet his stare. "So you, your mother and your grandmother can all see and merge medians?"

"That's us. Welcome to the Sinclair family curse."

Chapter Eight

What was she not telling him? Then the words from the little blonde in the hospital began circling around his head. *Evening is part of a dying lineage, and one that must be cherished.*

Dying lineage. Eve's family was that lineage? How far did her family go back? He wanted these new questions answered, but decided to address her last comment first.

"How is it a curse?"

"Really?" she asked surprised. "You can't see how my merging souls, is a curse? Look what's happening with you. You barge into my home, threaten me, and threaten my daughter. Yes this is a curse."

Alex levelled his stare. "But you already said I'm not like most medians, so I'm predicting this is a one-time thing. Regardless of my presence, it's obvious that you are a good therapist, you heal people. Isn't merging a soul back with its body like a type of therapy?"

She turned away shrugging. The gesture was meant to be casual, except it was anything but. Her hands clenching into fists gave a different meaning.

"It's hard for you to say no to me isn't it?" he guessed out loud. "It goes against your natural instinct."

"Is there anything else you want to ask me?" Her change of topic wouldn't deter him. In fact it made him all the more curious.

"Answer me Eve." He demanded quietly, though he was sure he already knew the answer.

Remaining silent Eve rolled onto her side facing away from him.

He stood and walked around to the other side of the bed and squatted down, his forearms resting on his bent knees. She opened her eyes and focused on him. There was a hint of sadness in those hazel beauties.

An unusual urge to reach out and comfort her made the muscles in his arms flex. "Make it easier on yourself," he encouraged gently. "Merge me back and all of this will be over."

Her eyes began to shimmer as she shook her head. "I can't," she whispered. "It's better this way, trust me."

He wanted to know why it was better he remained a median. And why should he trust her? He had put his trust in Miles and what had it got him? Three holes in the chest and a coma. Trusting wasn't his strong suit right now. He looked into her eyes full of unshed tears and sighed loudly, "Go to sleep, Eve."

* * * *

Standing next to the bed, Miles listened to the rhythmic pace of the heart monitor. Medical proof that Ace was still alive. He should have known Ace wouldn't be easy to kill. He was a tough bastard and too fucking stubborn to die.

Miles was still surprised that Ace had gone against him. They had always thought alike and covered each other's backs. He still wasn't sure what had come over Ace, siding with Jillian had put both of them in a difficult position. As Ace had pointed out, bringing her to the shop and having her relocated would have been the right thing to do, but there were other factors involved, besides her witnessing Rhodes' premature death. She would be able to identify him. She could lead the cops to him and his family. He would never allow that to happen. Nicole and the girls meant everything to him and he would protect them at all cost. And as distasteful as it was, if he had to kill Jillian and his best friend to keep his family safe, then so be it.

But it wouldn't happen tonight. This floor was under surveillance with a mandatory sign-in at the only entrance. They knew he was in here and it would draw unwanted attention, not only from the hospital security, which he knew were military, but unwanted attention from his unit. He had led the bosses to believe a perpetrator had caught Ace off guard and shot him. He had to play the role of concerned partner, which wasn't really a lie. He was concerned...he was concerned that Ace would wake up.

Miles inhaled, the air in the room was suddenly cool. Actually, the entire room was cold. Exhaling, he saw his breath. "What the hell?" He looked around. Why hadn't he noticed it before? Had one of the nurses left a window open? He crossed over to the row of windows and pulled back the blinds. The windows, solid pieces of glass, were sealed from top to bottom. Frowning, he walked back to stand next to the bed and wondered if he should mention to the nurses how cold it was in here. He reached out and touched Alex's arm. It was cool too.

Miles murmured, "Maybe I should let you freeze to death, and then I wouldn't have to kill you."

Miles turned and went to the door, the cold air filtered through the door with him and followed him down the hall.

* * * *

The next couple of days were much calmer, now that there was a quiet understanding between Alex and Eve. Although he didn't leave her when she was working, he did keep his comments to himself while her patients were around and Eve spoke to him whenever they were alone. He had also realised, during the past couple of days, why he had reacted so harshly when she'd ignored him. He needed her company. She was his only link to the world and when she shut him out, he had nothing and, when she ignored him, he felt very much alone.

The day grew dark and, after the usual night routine of watching some TV and having a snack, Eve put Noelle into bed. Alex stood behind Eve this time. He wanted to see what Noelle's reaction would be to him standing in her room after the episode a few nights past. He was pleasantly surprised when the kid looked up at him without any fear. He winked at her then and left Eve to say good night.

Eve wasn't long coming into her room. He leaned against the far wall and watched as she gathered her clothes and went into her adjacent bathroom. She looked at him with her hazel eyes and he could have sworn he saw a flash of green before she closed the door. Wishful thinking…maybe.

Alex stared at the door a long time, imagining Eve removing her clothes. First her snug fitting T-shirt that she layered on top of another T-shirt with long sleeves. Both hugged her waist and breasts. Next, her grey pants that clung to her thighs but didn't hide the nice flare to her hips. Her bra would be next, then panties. He imagined they would be a matching set, something that went with her shoulder length hair, like an earthy-green tone, in silk. He could see her, in his head, taking off the ensemble. Her eyes heavy and focused solely on him. Her hands running over her tight pink nipples, down the sides of her waist to her hips, as she hooked her thumbs inside the silk panties and slowly pulled them down her legs.

Before he could stop himself, the door opened and he was standing in her bathroom. The steam rose from the shower but he could see Eve's figure clearly. Her auburn hair was wet and hung down her back as soapy bubbles slowly made their way over the pink nipples of her full breasts. She raised her arms and scrubbed at her head which made her breasts swing, then arching her back, she rinsed the shampoo from her hair.

He moved slowly towards her. Images of Eve's naked body stretched out before him. Of his hands kneading her breasts, pinching her nipples. Of him sliding his hand between her thighs, sliding a finger deep, searching for her wet need of him. Then he was in her, the slick heat gripping him like a fist. He could see himself driving into her over and over, but not on the floor, it was in a bed and he wouldn't tease or torment her, he wouldn't have the patience. He would fuck her fast and hard, but she would enjoy it, he would make sure of that.

He watched mesmerised as she scrubbed her body a light, flowery scent filling the room. Lifting her arms she ran the soapy body-puff down their length in turn and back up, then bent to do the same with her legs. He took another step closer when he caught sight of her smooth behind. It was pink from the warm water and nicely rounded. Another step. *Shit!* She wasn't saying a damn thing to him and yet he was still drawn to her. What the fuck? He never allowed himself to crave for anything, least of all women he had no business craving in the first place.

As she began to cleanse her breasts she stopped in mid-motion and looked in his direction. She knew he was here, she had said she could feel him.

"Alex?" she called nervously covering her chest.

He knew she could see him, what was the point of hiding. "Yes."

"Why are you in here?"

He smiled when he heard the shyness of her words. "There's a sexy, naked woman in here. Where else would I be?" he said lightly, even though his throbbing body wasn't taking anything he said lightly.

"Alex," she breathed.

"Relax," he soothed. "I'm leaving." He turned for the door but stopped, looking back over his shoulder and mumbled, "Damn sexy." Then left the room.

* * * *

To keep his mind off Eve, her lush body and his now hard cock, he walked around the house, checking the perimeter. It was an old habit and he had done it every night since he arrived, and continued to do it despite the fact that Eve had a top of the line security system, which she set faithfully every night.

When he reached the second floor, he checked the spare rooms, then quietly entered Noelle's room. He expected to find her asleep but was amused to see the bright beam of a flashlight under her covers and the rustle of pages.

"Good book?" he whispered so as not to startle her.

The light turned off and Noelle popped out from under her flowered sheets. Her eyes widened when she saw him.

"I didn't mean to scare you," he whispered again.

She blinked up at him and opened her mouth but nothing came out.

Alex thought that she had got over the other night, maybe he was wrong. "Do I scare you?"

She shrugged. "A little at first, when you were in the kitchen and when you came into my room a couple nights ago, but not so much now."

"Good." He gave her a sideways glance. "Am I the first median you have seen?"

She pressed her lips together. He studied her, tilting his head. He guessed, "Are you worried I'll tell Eve?"

She nodded silently.

"Well you don't have to worry about that. I'm good at keeping secrets."

"You're the first one I've seen." She looked thoughtfully at him. "At least I think you are. Gran said it will be hard to tell at first."

"Your Gran, she knows you can see medians?"

"Yah." She nodded eagerly. "But mum doesn't want me to. Gran says it scares her."

"It scares her that you might be able to see medians?"

She nodded her answer again, then added, "But also because Gran says that medians have hurt mum before, because she said no to them. I think she's scared of them."

Alex kept his reaction to himself. That was a huge piece to the puzzle and he was one step closer to understanding why Eve was fighting him. He would, of course, keep at her until she merged him. He just had a better understanding now as to her behaviour towards him.

The topic was a bit heavy for a kid so he changed it. "So, what are you reading?" She turned the book so he could see the front cover. "Not Another Flying Turtle." He couldn't help but smile at the title.

"It's about a little girl who has magical powers and how she gets into trouble every time she uses them. It's really funny."

"Sounds like a page turner." He stood smiling and turned to leave.

"Are you going to tell mum I was reading?"

"No. Are you going to tell Eve that I was in here asking you questions?"

She shook her head. "No. Then I would get into trouble too."

"All right then. We keep this to ourselves, deal?"

"Deal." She gave him a wide smile, showing him that she was missing a bottom tooth.

He smiled back. Damn this kid was cute. "Pull up your other blanket. It will help hide the light while you read," he said, before leaving the room.

Chapter Nine

Lying in her bed, Eve stared up at the ceiling. She was still thinking about what Alex had said. *Damn sexy. He thinks I'm sexy?*

Her first thought was that he was trying to use compliments to win her over like before. But he had mumbled the words subtly to himself, as though she wasn't meant to hear them. Could she be wrong about before, when he had told her he wanted to come back when he had a body, and spend the night with her? He had been so detailed in his description and then said she was *damn sexy.* She smiled despite herself. She was flattered. Who doesn't want to hear that? But it was kind of creepy too because she couldn't forget the fact that there was a good possibility that he might be dead.

Better yet, why was a 'possibly dead man' having sexual feelings anyway? The dead that refused to leave were either lost or confused, or they wanted to be alive again. Gran had never mentioned anything about dead souls hitting on her. As for medians, her experience was limited to the few souls she had merged and none of them had displayed any sexual characteristics. Then again, none of them had Alex's unusual strength either.

Still, what if Alex wasn't a dead soul? What if he was just a very strong median, who could still feel the same emotions and needs as the soul in a living body? Was that possible?

She pressed her hand to her forehead. She wished she could ask Gran. It had been days since she had visited her. But Eve had been putting off seeing her because Alex might realise something was up and begin pestering Gran instead and she didn't want that. Gran had helped enough people in her very long life and it was time she got some rest. Even if she did complain about being bored half the time.

"Something bothering you?" Alex asked. He was sitting on the floor in the same spot next to her bed, resting his large frame against her bedside table.

Eve turned onto her side to face him. Thanks to the streetlight she was able to see him lean his head back and look up at the ceiling. She studied his profile. Sharp chin, straight nose, his eyebrows were black slashes over his intense eyes, and the scar he had running through his left brow just made him all that more appealing. The muscles in his arms and chest were well defined, she knew this, thanks to the dark grey shirt he wore, and she guessed his legs were just as athletic. Alex was a very attractive man, there was no denying that.

Impulsively, Eve reached out to touch him. She was actually expecting to touch the solid mass of muscle that was his shoulder, but she was disappointed when her hand floated through instead. Alex turned his piercing eyes on her.

"I'm sorry." She pulled her hand back. "I just wanted to see something."

"No you wanted to feel something."

"Yes." She focused on his shoulder.

"What were you expecting?"

She met his blue stare. "I'm not sure. Nothing I guess."

"Try again."

Eve pressed her lips together and slowly stretched out her arm, her hand coming to stop just under his chin. "Do it," he ordered gently.

She ran her fingers along the faint outline of his chin and up the side of his cheek grazing it with the back of her fingers. "It's warm." A slow smile curled her lips as she pulled her hand back.

Alex scowled at her.

"I'm sorry—"

"Don't be." He cut her off, shaking his head. "Do it again."

Eve sat up when she saw the scowl on his face. "What's wrong?"

"There was something—" he sounded confused, " — Do it again." He paused looking at her hand. "Please."

Seeing the look of confusion on a man who usually radiated confidence was a little troubling. "Okay."

Reaching out to him once again, he stopped her. "No. Come sit here in front of me."

Eve blinked. It was close and very intimate but she accepted and slipped out of bed, settling herself between his outstretched legs.

Leaning towards her, Alex rested his hands palms up on his thighs, ready for her. "Go ahead."

Taking a slow breath, Eve ran her fingers down the length of his forearm. She could feel his warmth as she touched him. It was the same as a living, breathing person. "My God," she breathed out.

"I can feel you touch me." Alex raised his head, a half smile on his face.

Her eyes met his. "You do?"

He nodded. "Again."

This time, she started at his shoulders and ran her hands down the entire length of his arms to his hands, where she made an attempt to clasp them in her own. The same sensation occurred, but now she could still feel his warmth seeping into her as she rested her hand in his. Smiling, he shook his head. "How are you doing this?"

"I don't know? How can you feel me?"

He chuckled. "I don't know?"

Staring down at their hands she asked. "What do you feel?"

"It's like when your foot falls asleep and you get that 'pins and needles' sensation, mixed with a warm tingling."

Eve met Alex's stare. "You're really not dead."

He studied her intently. "Is that why you won't help me, because you think I'm dead?"

Embarrassed, she turned away. "I thought you might be and that you were having trouble…moving on."

"Moving on?" he repeated. She heard him exhale in a huff but didn't want to face him yet. "Eve?" He used her name to get her attention but she didn't budge. "Evening." This time her name was said with more force.

Her cheeks were warm when she faced him. She expected him to be annoyed but he only showed concern. "Do you see the dead too?"

"No. Never, just medians. My mother did, I thought maybe it had started for me too. It was the only explanation I could come up with as to why you were still hanging around me." Her throat felt like it was beginning to close up with the thought of it, but she asked him anyway. "Have you seen...them...out there?"

Alex was going to ask if she wanted the truth, then saw the fear in her eyes and lied. "No, I haven't."

The truth was he had seen many dead people walking around the hospital, mixing in with crowds sitting on benches in the waiting rooms, following around nurses and patients. The difference he noticed between the dead and the living was purpose. The living had a purpose, work needed to be done, people needed to be taken care of, the living had things to do, places to go. The dead didn't do anything but follow the living. None of them had any direction, all of them were lost. All of them were unnoticed.

After a long silence, while she rested her hands in the ghostly shadow of his, she finally asked, "What hospital are you in?"

Surprised, he studied her carefully. "Memorial. Seventh floor, east wing."

"That floor is for military personnel."

"You know it?"

She nodded. "I have a few patients there. I'll switch appointments and go there instead."

As she began to move, Alex tried to keep her hand from slipping away but it was pointless. He came to his feet, as she slipped back under the covers.

Standing next to the bed, Alex gazed down. Eve's arm rested above her head again, an auburn curl wrapped around her finger. She appeared calm, but he knew she wasn't. The thought of merging him terrified her and he had no idea why. And that really worried him.

He shouldn't care why he was bothered by her fear. All that mattered was that Eve merged him. He could then get his hands on Miles and finish what he had started, then Jillian and her baby would be safe. He had wasted so much time here with Eve and Noelle. He was frowning before he finished the thought. No, they were not a waste of time and though he wished Eve had agreed sooner, he didn't regret coming to her.

"Alex," she exhaled. "There's one thing you must understand first."

"What's that?" He watched as she focused on him. Once again his body reacted to her, except this time it was strong enough to cause the muscles in his groin to harden without the added torment of erotic visions.

"If your body has too much damage to it, I won't merge you."

Crossing his arms he demanded quietly. "Why not?"

She looked directly at him. "If you don't have enough strength to fix your body, you'll be trapped."

"Trapped?" he asked carefully. "In my own body?"

She nodded.

"That doesn't make any sense. Getting back in is the main objective."

"The soul heals the body on re-entry," she began with a sigh. "But that can only happen if the soul has the strength to repair it, because once you're back in, you're back in. If you, the soul, don't have the strength needed, then you're trapped until your body heals itself, however long that might take, or your body dies, in which case you too will die."

He huffed, not bothering to hide his frustration. "You couldn't have told me this sooner?"

"I only just figured out you are really a median and not a dead soul." She pushed up onto her elbows, the dim light helping to shape her breasts as they pulled her T-shirt tight.

He squeezed his teeth together, focused hard on her face.

"You deserve to know all the risks, and what I won't do."

Arms still crossed, he braced his legs apart. "You've seen this happen. A soul trapped in a wounded body?"

"No." She shook her head, the movement causing a few unruly curls to frame her face. "I haven't experienced it but Mum has and so has Gran. They both drilled it into me not to trap a soul and, with my nurse's training I have been able to prevent it from happening. Then again, the ones I merged weren't new cases. Their bodies had had time to heal before I merged them."

He digested the new Intel and asked. "So it would be like being in a prison cell?"

Another curl fell when she nodded, this time resting on the side of her face. He squeezed his hand into a fist before he gave into the urge to brush it away.

"Probably worse, depending on your wounds. You might be able to hear and feel everything but not speak or move. I could never do that to you. So I will make my decision when I see your body." She tried to make the last sentence a command but her efforts were wasted on him. How could someone with a mess of auburn curls hanging in her face be considered authoritative? He smiled.

"I'm very serious Alex. It would hurt me to know I caused you pain. I won't allow it to happen." She revealed, straight-faced.

He lost the smile when he heard the admission. It was an odd feeling to have a person care for him after so long. She wasn't bullshitting him, it would really do her some damage. He saw the truth on her face, but there was something else behind her confession. "I know you're serious. But I can't help feeling that there is another reason why you're fighting this merge."

Her hazel eyes grew wide. "I don't know what you're talking about."

Resting back down on her pillow she closed her eyes, ending the discussion.

He put extra effort into his long drawn out sigh and chuckled when she huffed. "I'll find out what it is sooner or later, it would make things simpler if we dealt with it now."

Her response was to fling her arm above her head, her fingers tangling in her hair. He would let it go for tonight. He didn't want to argue over something that made her uncomfortable when she just agreed to go to Memorial. He would have to figure out the rest once they were there.

He watched her breasts rise and fall. Eve had just admitted that she didn't want to hurt him. That was pretty good considering she had told him to 'get out' less than a week ago. Hell, at this rate he might even get her to admit that she's attracted to him in another week. Not that it mattered. She would merge him and he would be out of her life very soon, he doubted he would be around in a week's time. The contented feeling he had vanished and was replaced with annoyance.

At that very moment, Eve sighed and pursed her lips. He closed the distance to the bed, silently swearing. It would be for the best if things turned out that way. She was not his type at all, and she had a kid. But, damn it, she tempted him like no other woman had and he had no idea why.

He bent down closer to her, trying to understand what he found attractive about her. The skin on her face was smooth, with small pin point freckles on her nose. Her thin brows were a darker shade than her hair and her lashes, though they didn't appear to be long on first inspection, were actually very long and deceptive, because the tips were lighter in colour. And then there were her lips. Light pink and smooth. He guessed they would taste even better than they looked.

She sighed then. The innocent sound had an embracing lilt that urged him closer to her lovely face.

She was lovely. And incredibly sexy. On the other hand she was also lippy and stubborn, yet her compassion and firm protective streak balanced her out nicely. Maybe that's what pulled him to her. Or maybe it was the fact she was finally going to merge him.

Whatever the reason, she deserved his appreciation.

"Thank you, Evening," he whispered. Then, as if instinct took over, Alex brushed his mouth against her tempting lips. The tingle on his lips lasted long enough for him to reclaim his spot next to her bed.

Chapter Ten

"Well if I didn't know better, I'd say Evening has come early today."

"What are yah on about Dawn? It's one in the afternoon." Mrs Winkle, a short woman with an odd yellow wig said, moving to the window. "Is your glaucoma bothering you again?"

"I don't have glaucoma, you daft old bird."

"Oh! That must be mine then."

Eve chuckled as she hugged her grandmother. "Hi Gran." She kissed the older woman's cheek. "You look wonderful."

"Hello my doll—" Was all Gran managed.

"Why thank you Eve, that's very nice of you to say." Mrs Winkle beamed while adjusting her wig.

Eve gave the older woman a smile. "You're welcome Mrs Winkle."

Gran's snort caught her attention and she did laugh when she saw the disgruntled look on her face. "Come on, let's go for a walk."

"Oh that sounds like a—" Mrs Winkle began.

"Not you, Fiona," Gran snapped, pointing her hand-carved Hornbeam cane at the other lady. "You sit here and wait for your grandson. It's Tuesday, he'll be by soon for a visit."

"Oh! It's Tuesday." Mrs Winkle jumped up from the chair Gran had ordered her to sit in. "I better go put on my good hair."

Eve pressed her lips together to stop herself from laughing and watched as the older lady shuffled out of the common room and down the hall.

Gran took her arm and they walked out through the French doors and into the back garden of the retirement home. It wasn't really a retirement home as much as it was a retirement community with assisted living and a nice one at that.

"Does she really have good hair?" Eve asked pointing to a bench by some late blooming flowers. It was a sunny fall day and sitting in the sun would do them both some good.

"Course not." Gran tisked. "She'll just put a bow in the one she has on." Gran shook her head. "Daft cow. If I hadn't known her for so long I probably would have whacked her with my cane by now."

"You can't do that Gran, that thing is really hard." She pointed to the old white cane. It had been her great-grandmother's and had come over with Gran from Scotland, apparently it was very old and been in their family for a very long time.

"Oh, stop your worrying. I'd never hit Fiona. She's one of my best girls. Can keep any secret I tell her." Gran sat down and patted the spot next to her. "Mind you, she has a bit of old-timers so that helps."

Eve chuckled.

Gran looked at her, her green eyes clear and as sharp as ever. "Well?" she asked expectantly.

Eve rolled her eyes, reached into the bag she had brought and pulled out a thermos and two plastic mugs.

"Hurry up, I've been waiting for this for days." The older woman rubbed her hands together. "That's the only thing I don't like about living here. No booze."

Shaking her head Eve commented. "You're like a junkie waiting for her next fix."

"I'm not," Gran gasped pretending to be shocked. "Now pass it here."

Laughing, Eve handed her the mug and watched a youthful grin appear on Gran's face. She inhaled the scent of fresh coffee and Irish cream and was about to take a sip when the smile fell from her face.

Eve stopped filling the second cup when Gran hissed, "Go away Philip. Can't you see my granddaughter is here?" There was a pause, followed by Gran glaring over the bench. "Not while Eve is here, we'll talk later. Now sod off." Gran had a satisfied grin when she turned back to Eve.

If Eve hadn't know what Gran's gifts were she would have thought she had fallen out of the crazy tree—and it probably looked that way to others—but Eve had grown up with Gran snapping at medians and dead souls as far back as she could remember.

Eve continued pouring her coffee. "Who's Philip?"

Gran waved her hand. "A long time ago, Philip was the farmer who owned this land."

"What does he want?" Eve was trying to act casual about it for Gran's sake but dead souls scared the shit out of her. She took a sip of her coffee hoping the Irish cream might help relax her.

"He wants to know if I can call to his wife. He seems to think that if I call to her she will come back to him."

"But she's dead!" Eve felt the need to point out the obvious, just to be on the safe side.

"Yup. Got scalped when Indians attacked their farm."

"Oh!" Eve gasped, almost choking on her coffee. "That was long ago! Have you told him he must go to her?"

"Yes, but I guess I'll have to tell him again." Gran took another sip then sighed, "So, where is my wee lass today?"

They talked for over an hour about Noelle and school, and Eve's patients. Eve dragged on about each subject intentionally stalling the inevitable. She was thoroughly disgusted with herself. Why couldn't she just ask Gran what she needed to know? Why was Alex able to move things? Why was he able to leave his body? Why did he turn her on? Well maybe she didn't need the answer to that question, but still she needed to talk to somebody about him. And she didn't have much time. She had got him to agree to stay away while she was visiting with Gran, yet she knew he wasn't far away because she could still feel the slightest vibration of his strength.

"Out with it doll, your babbling is driving me batty," Gran demanded.

Eve sighed, she should have known Gran would notice. "I have been... There is a..." Eve took a deep breath. "A median came to my house, and is now staying with me."

The older woman's eyebrows rose in surprise. "Staying with you?"

Eve raised her shoulders and with a guilty look, confessed, "Actually he's been haunting me. Well that's how he put it."

"Haunting you?"

Eve nodded. "Until I merge him. Which I'm not sure I'll be able to do." Eve turned so her side was leaning against the back of the bench. Resting her elbow on the top of the bench she pressed her hand to her forehead. "He's driving me crazy."

Gran turned and mimicked the way she sat. Looking at her, Gran appeared to be in her late sixties, the cane and her frequent conversations with imaginary people helped to complete the look. The truth was, Gran was anything but frail, in fact for the oldest living person on the continent she looked amazing thanks to the Sinclair blessing...or curse...or whatever this thing was.

"Why can't you merge him?" she asked, her green eyes sharp.

Eve rested her cheek into her hand. "He has three bullet holes in him — one is very close to his heart, one probably in his liver and the other in his shoulder."

Gran remained quiet taking in the information.

"He can move things too. Opens and closes doors." Her heart began to beat faster when she recalled Alex closing the fridge door. Even now goosebumps crawled their way up her arms.

"Doll." Gran leant forward and touched her bent knee. "I know the idea frightens you but are you sure he isn't dead?"

"Yes."

"But you just said that he came to you, that he could move objects and that he has three bullet wounds one close to his heart. It sounds as though he's dead." Gran shook her head. "I told you seeing dead souls might happen sooner or later."

"That's just it, for a while I was so sure he was dead, then I touched him and—"

Gran sat up straight. "You touched him?"

"Yes," Eve moaned covering her face. "I couldn't help it, there's just something about him."

"What, doll?" Gran asked gently.

"I'm not sure." She lied. She had wanted to feel, no that wasn't right. She had wanted to know that he was real, that this man, who thought she was damn sexy was more than just a soul and why it was, that when she felt his heat seep into her hands, it felt as though her own soul sighed in relief?

"What did you feel?"

"Heat. He was warm. That's when I knew he wasn't dead."

"Why did he come to you?"

Eve told Gran everything that Alex had said to her apart from a few conversations that were more sexual in nature. Gran did not need to know that she found Alex's threat about jay walking a turn on.

"Well," Gran began, casually peering over her shoulder. "Looks like you have a very, very old soul following you around."

"Have you ever had this happen?"

"I'm sorry doll, I haven't." Once again, Gran shifted her eyes looking into the distance.

"What do you think I should do?"

Gran's eyes were back on her. "I think you should merge him before he does something he might regret."

Eve straightened. "What does that mean?"

"He has a great deal of violence in him, yet he has it under control. Right now it's his frustration over your stubbornness that is controlling his actions."

"Why are you talking about frustration? He never looks the least bit frustrated. It's actually quite annoying."

A deep chuckle from behind had Eve exhaling a heavy sigh. "It's good to know that I at least annoy you."

Eve raised her arm and pointed her thumb over her shoulder. "This is Alex," she introduced. "This is my Gran." Eve glared back over her shoulder at him. "Mrs Sinclair."

Alex chuckled again. "It's nice to meet you, ma'am."

"Ma'am!" Gran said with a snort. "Dawn is just fine."

Eve watched as Alex gave Gran a wink.

"Oh for heaven sakes," Eve huffed and looked at her watch. "It's time to pick up Noelle." Standing, she began to pack up the plastic cups and thermos. "I'll see you in a few days."

"Leave that." Gran grabbed the thermos. "I think I'll sit here and finish it."

Grinning, Eve leant down and kissed her cheek. As she grabbed her bag and began to walk away, Eve turned back wagging her finger. "Be nice to Mrs Winkle."

Gran snorted in response, then called, "Give my wee girl a kiss."

* * * *

Alex went to follow Eve but stopped short when the white cane flew up in front of his legs. It didn't block his path but that was her intention, so he accommodated her.

Eve's grandmother turned back to him. Her green eyes were sharp and, after about a minute of her studying him, she finally said, "If Eve says you can't go into your body, you need to trust there is a good reason for it."

Alex felt the rush of power that accompanied the woman's words. She was asking him to do her bidding. He could feel the force of her silent command. The underlying hum was strong, much stronger than Eve's, but different. When Eve used her talent, her words were a subtle caress. They slid across his skin like delicate silk. They calmed him, yet made his body burn. The strength surrounding Dawn's words was bold and very much in evidence. He rebelled when she pushed him to follow her command.

"She's a good girl, wouldn't hurt a soul." The older woman winked at him.

"You're stronger than Eve." He stared down as she took a sip of her coffee.

"That's because I've been doing this longer."

"How long?" Alex lifted his chin.

She looked up at him with a sly smile. "A very long time."

Dawn was just as cryptic as her granddaughter. "Then will you tell me how long Eve has been able to do this?"

The woman went deep into thought, taking another sip of the steaming brew. "She began early. Earlier than her mother. Five or six, I think."

"Shit." Alex studied Eve as she walked away, the sway of her hips calling to him. She stopped briefly to talk to a tiny little woman with strange yellow hair, who seemed to be fussing over something. Eve patted her shoulder in an effort to calm her and took a small red object the woman handed her. A minute later the woman was smiling up at her, a red bow now firmly placed in her bizarre hair.

"Do you see?" Dawn turned back to face him. "She knows how to heal. You have noticed that haven't you?"

"I've noticed." He hated having something pointed out he had seen repeatedly over the last week. He had seen first-hand how she'd healed men drowning in battle scars and brought them back. He was amazed by it. He admired her for it, and was strangely proud of her.

"Then trust her to do what is right for you." The pitch to her words was so strong that he almost willingly agreed. Almost.

Alex narrowed his eyes and gave her a crooked smile. "You're strong."

She raised her eyebrows. "Honey, you have no idea." And gave him another wink.

He laughed out loud then said, "But I'm stronger." And winked back. "I've agreed to let her have a look at my body, but nothing more. She will merge me back. She doesn't have a choice."

Dawn's smile became serious. "Then you better be damn sure you can save this broad with the baby. I don't want my Eve getting hurt over your mess."

"All Eve has to do is merge me and then I'm gone from her life."

"You're leaving once she merges you? After the way you just looked at her?" She looked up at him in disbelief. "I doubt that."

Chapter Eleven

"You do know where Memorial is don't you?" Alex asked, sitting next to her.

She looked over at him once again. "How are you able to travel in the car?"

He gave her the same answer as when he had said he could feel her touch, "I don't know."

"Eve." He pressed. "Do you know how to get to Memorial?"

"Of course," she snapped back. "I used to work there."

"Then why are we taking the long way?" She could feel his blue gaze on her. "I...I don't like hospitals," she sighed.

"I thought you were a nurse?"

"Ex- nurse." She glanced quickly at him.

"Is there such a thing? Take the highway it's faster." He switched topics pointing to the on ramp, then swore when she ignored him and continued on her present course. "Isn't a nurse always a nurse?" he pointed out.

He was right of course, a nurse didn't just stop caring for the weak or injured, they simply shifted their focus. She lied to him anyway. "No...I don't think so. When it's time to move on, it's time."

"And you've moved on?" he asked slowly, "To merging souls and providing therapy to wounded soldiers?"

She gripped the steering wheel. Why did he have to point out the very thing she was trying to lie about? She ignored the second part of his statement but answered the first, "I was trying to move on until you had to share your story with me. Now I'm going back and not liking it in the least."

"You said you have patients at Memorial? Don't you visit them to see how they are doing?"

"No," she said too quickly. "They come to me. I told you, I don't like hospitals."

There was blissful silence for a minute or two. "What happened Eve?"

No! She couldn't tell him. That would mean talking about it, and talking about it would lead her to think about it and she did *not* want to do that. So she answered him by shaking her head. Right from the start Eve knew Alex wasn't used to being denied anything, and now wasn't any different. But it had to be this way.

"Did I give you the impression I give up easily? Turn left up here," he ordered again.

Ignoring his order for a second time Eve turned right at the intersection taking them further away from the hospital.

Trying to hold onto his patience was worse than getting shot. Why couldn't she just answer his question? And why did she try to hide the fact that going to the hospital terrified her? She was such a contradiction, always willing to help but never allowing anyone to help her. He shared his thoughts.

"That's not true." Was she hurt by his allegation?

"Who helps you?"

"Gran. Gran helps me, whenever I need it."

"But she's the only one. And I bet you don't ask her for much."

Her hands tightened on the steering wheel as a frown pulled at her delicate brows. Alex gazed over at her. He couldn't stop looking at her today. She looked good, stylish with her white button shirt and jeans. Maybe it was the low heels and beige fall jacket that caught his interest? Or maybe it was because her hair was pulled back into a loose ponytail which accented her hazel eyes and pretty face. Whatever the reason she looked damn good.

He took note of her stiff posture and sighed. "Eve, you can't go in there like this. Someone will pick up on it."

Focusing on the traffic in front of her, she simply nodded.

"Is it death that bothers you or the sight of blood?" he guessed. "Bad luck with a patient? Bad luck with a merge?"

Her eyes widened and her arms went stiff as she clutched the wheel. Alex narrowed in on her face, finally understanding.

He began slowly, "A merge gone wrong?"

"You could say that," she replied.

"What happened?" She remained silent, gripping the wheel until her hands turned white. "That bad huh." Still no response. "Jesus Eve. Do I need to start slamming things again?"

"Fine," she snapped, closing her eyes while stopped for a red light. "You are so stubborn."

"Eve," he demanded.

"All right! I was working in hospital a few years ago when a young teenage girl was brought into the ER with internal head and abdominal injuries. She had been in a car accident. After she was stabilised she was moved to surgery and then to ICU where, due to her head injuries, she was put into a medically induced coma."

She swallowed hard but continued, "I was covering a friend's shift when I first saw her. I was at the nurses' station filling out a chart, when I turned to leave she was standing there staring at me. It scared the hell out of me." Eve flipped on her signal and turned right.

"That was the girl Emily Spencer?"

"Yes!" she sounded surprised.

"You mentioned her before. Keep going," he encouraged.

"She asked me if I could see her. When I nodded she started to cry. I wasn't sure what to do and there were so many people around that day and I couldn't stand there like an idiot so I continued on with my rounds. She cried harder and chased me into another room."

They took another right. "Eve, we're going around in circles." If she heard him he couldn't tell.

"Come to think of it, she was a bit dramatic." They stopped at a red and she turned to him, a serious look on her face. "I hope Noelle doesn't grow up to be like that."

He realised then that her anxiety level was very high. Her nervous chatter and driving around aimlessly were clear signs. How could he have missed them? Because he had been concerned with himself, his needs and hadn't bothered with Eve's fear. Which, if he had been paying attention, had been present all along.

She stared at him waiting for an answer. He answered her with what he believed to be the truth. "I don't think you need to worry about that, Noelle isn't a dramatic kid."

"You don't think so?"

"I've been around her for over a week. That's plenty of time for her to show her true colours. I haven't seen anything dramatic." That was the truth. Once Noelle had got used to him, they'd talked more and more when Eve wasn't in the room. She was a bright kid, very observant with a great sense of humour and she loved her mother very much. He actually enjoyed her company.

"Light's green," he pointed out. "What happened next?"

"Once I got her calmed down, I told her to wait in her room. When I finally got around to checking her vitals and made note of them I could see she was a mess. She looked so lost and confused. I felt terrible for her, she was so young. I read over her chart and saw she was making a very good recovery and that she was scheduled to be taken off the meds that induce the coma she was in. I explained why I could see her and what I could do and that because she was doing so well I could merge her back into her body. She was so excited. But I had this gut feeling something wasn't right, I didn't feel...she didn't feel strong enough."

"What do you mean strong enough?"

"Every soul is different and each soul has its own energy. Some souls are young, some are old, and some are in-between. Young souls are new souls. Their energy level is low and therefore they are not very strong. Old souls are the opposite. Their energy level is high which indicates how strong they are. Emily looked so tired for someone so young. I could tell her soul wasn't strong enough to re-enter her body and help repair the damage."

He knew that Eve was able to feel his presence but he'd had no clue just how sensitive she really was, until now. "You can feel the strength of different souls?" he repeated, amazed.

"Yes." Her cheeks flushed.

He nodded his head. "Keep going."

"She must have noticed I was unsure and then begged me to help her. She was so young and so pretty. Lying in a hospital was no place for her to be, she didn't deserve that. So I agreed, and told her that once the meds were decreased I would merge her."

"Why wait for the meds to be cut?"

"Remember what I said. When you're back in your body then you're back in. If the docs planned on keeping her in a coma longer, then she would be trapped until her body either died or woke on its own. I wanted to give her the best chance and make it easier for her."

He shook his head sorting out the Intel. "And then things turned bad," he guessed.

"Yah! Real bad. When I began to merge her back with her body another soul attached onto hers."

He blinked, looking at her, and saw how pale she was. "Pull over, right now!"

She did as he asked and her hands shook as she threw the car into park. "Explain that last part to me."

"Because her soul wasn't strong enough. Another soul," — she paused taking a shaky breath — "a dead soul attached itself to her. And I merged both into one body."

Alex did not know what to say to that.

"The rule is…" Eve closed her eyes. "One soul to one body. No exceptions. The flesh and bones of a living body can't handle two souls, let alone one that is dead."

He didn't want to upset her more but something didn't make sense. "You said you can't see the dead. How do you know it was a dead soul?"

"I can't see them. I…I should have performed the calling faster, but Emily was scared. So I moved slower than I normally would have. I felt this sickening feeling right before I merged her, but I'm not sure if that had anything to do with it. I only knew it was a dead soul because I saw someone…on her face." She made a pulling gesture in front of her face with her hand. "It was a man's face. It was angry."

Alex didn't need her to continue to know the outcome was bad. But he asked anyway, "What happened?"

"Have you ever seen the part in The Exorcist when the demon jerks the kid's body around on the bed?"

"I remember."

"Well"—she tightened her hands on the steering wheel—"it was kind of like that but worse. Her body twisted and heaved, it looked like the two souls were fighting under her skin, inside her body. Her screams were horrible, like the dead soul was killing her." She swallowed hard. "By the time it was over, her body was distorted and bruised, her skin was torn. It finally stopped when her body died from the trauma. It was…" She blinked away the tears in her eyes. "I've never seen anything like that before," she whispered.

Alex placed his hand on top of hers as she held the steering wheel, giving her the only comfort he could give, his heat. Although it didn't seem to be enough, because she drew in a shaky breath. Fuck, he wished he was in his body, she needed more than his pathetic attempt at compassion. She needed a man to hold her and tell her that everything would be all right. He wasn't sure if he was that man, but he was willing to try. "You okay?"

"No." She sniffed, turning her flushed face to him. The tears that shimmered in her hazel eyes brought the green flecks to life. "I'm not. I did that Alex. I caused that. And you want me to do that to you." She shook her head, turning away.

"Hey, look at me." He placed his hand on her thigh and squeezed. She spun to face him, her hair flying into the side of her face, then looked down at her leg. "Look at *me*," he ordered.

When she complied he saw that her eyes where bright, her pupils large.

"You said you can feel the strength of a soul. How do I feel?"

"That's not the point."

"Answer me," he demanded. "Do I feel tired or weak?"

No he didn't. She couldn't feel any sort of weakness in him at all. The truth was, strength radiated off him. It was so powerful at times she was surprised he hadn't been able to get back into his body on his own.

"Your grandmother said I was a very, old soul. And you said the older the soul the stronger the soul." He squeezed her thigh a second time and for a second time a jolt of heat flew through her. "When you merge me, nothing will happen, I will not allow it."

"I told you, I have to see your body first before I…"

He cut her off. "You will merge me Eve. I can't afford for you not to."

She didn't comment, just pressed her lips together as she pulled back into traffic, once again slowly making her way to Memorial.

'*I can't afford for you not to*'. The words stirred something in her she hadn't experienced before. She wished she didn't cut her nails so short, because the urge to scratch something or rather someone's eyes out would feel pretty satisfying right about now. Not that it would happen. Alex wasn't hers, in fact she was under the impression that Alex didn't want to belong to anybody. Clearly, that assumption was wrong.

"Don't you mean the pregnant secretary can't afford for you not to?" *Geez*. Eve rolled her eyes. That couldn't have sounded any more jealous if she actually tried.

"I suppose." Eve checked her rear-view mirror and could see his puzzled look out the corner of her eye. "But I was thinking more of myself. I don't want the death of an innocent woman on my hands."

"You don't want her death on your hands, but you're willing to sacrifice yourself for her?" Wow! This broad had better know what she had in Alex, there weren't many men out there that were willing to sacrifice themselves for a woman.

"Yes."

"I'm so jealous..." Her face heated before she finished the thought. She had meant to mumble that in her own head not out loud.

"Of what?"

She answered him truthfully. It was too late to lie now, when she had put her foot in her mouth. "Of the secretary. I wish I had what she has."

Confused, he asked, "What does she have?"

"A man that loves her." Eve waved her hand and feeling like an idiot she began to babble. "All the guys

I've met are twelve-year-old boys stuck in thirty-year-old bodies. Besides my life focuses on Noelle and my practice, most guys hate the competition."

"She doesn't have me."

Now it was Eve's turn to be confused. "Sure looks that way. Look at all the stuff you have been doing and people you have been tormenting. She must mean something to you."

"I don't even know her. She was a woman that was in the wrong place at the wrong time and was witness to a murder. I don't love her," he clarified. "I just want to keep her and her child safe."

A self-sacrificing male. She had read of them in stories, heard about the odd one in the news, but to meet one in person was...strange. "You're doing this for a person that you don't know?"

As Alex shrugged it caused his shirt to move and Eve caught sight of the bullet hole as it slid up and down along with his movement. "Doing nothing would have been the same as shooting her myself. I've done a lot of bad things in my life, but not one of those acts was done on an innocent person." He pressed his transparent fingers into her leg for a third time. "I need you to help me keep it that way."

* * * *

For close to two weeks, Jillian had ambled around the old cottage. When she'd first arrived she had been terrified that Rick had followed her. That he would burst through the door and shoot her in cold blood. Then as the days passed, she had realised that Alex had kept her safe from Rick. Now all she had to do was wait for Alex to come and get her, but sadly, that might not be a possibility now. She had learnt from a reliable source that he had been shot and was in a coma. Now she was stuck in northern Quebec and had no idea what to do. She had asked her ghostly informant—who had been making appearances— what would happen, and what she should do? The only answer she received was to wait for Alex.

Wait for a guy who was in a coma? That made no sense, but what else could she do?

The days had crawled by slowly, she'd been used to being kept busy at work, it had been hard to suddenly slow to a snail's pace, but she soon found things to keep her occupied. She had spent time each day searching room by room for any information on the man that had sent her here. When she hadn't found anything useful she had gone out onto the porch, sat in the whitewashed rocking chair, and read a book she had found in a box she'd discovered in her room.

Today was no different. Once she had finished reading a long-winded detective novel, she had made herself dinner that consisted of canned ham, canned beans and canned potatoes. She was almost canned out.

"Hey!" The familiar voice made her smile.

Jillian looked over her shoulder and forced a dirty look. "Finally decided to come back have you?"

"Give me a break. It's harder than you think to get away from those guys. They're always watching me."

"Not really surprised by that." Rolling her eyes, Jillian turned back to washing her plate and glass in the sink. "But as usual you were able to charm them, because here you are."

"Didn't work. I had to break the rules and skip out."

Jillian turned and laughed. "Escapee already! That has to be some kind of record."

She received an impassive shrug. "I'm sure it won't be the first time. How's it going?"

Jillian reached for her glass and began drying it. "I heard a car drive up to the house this morning. It totally freaked me out. So I hid upstairs and peeked through the curtains. Other than that, everything's fine"

"Well…who was it?"

"Local police. They checked out the area and left shortly after."

"Don't scare me like that."

Jillian grinned, placing the glass in the cupboard and shrugged. "You asked."

"That's not funny, Jilly. So much stuff has happened, I wanted to know how you are, not have a heart attack."

Closing the cupboard Jillian turned back with a sad smile. "Well, you don't have to worry about that now, do you?"

"Sorry. You know what I mean."

"I know. I'm fine, don't worry," Jillian soothed.

"I'll worry until Alex gets you out of this."

"Oh yah!" She couldn't keep the sarcasm from her question—she didn't want to. "And how's that coming?"

"He's working on it."

"Oh…good." That was not the answer she was hoping for. Better than she expected, but not 'he's was on his way', or 'everything is fine', or even to hear that Rick had decided to not kill her. *Oh boy that would be nice.*

She had to be patient. She had to put her faith in Alex, a man she had just met and who was also a killer, but at least he was trying to help her. Most people wouldn't have bothered to help and just looked the other way.

She sighed inwardly. She could wait.

"Want to go sit out on the porch with me?"

"Yes." Justine grinned back at her. "I need some Jilly time before these jokers come looking for me."

Chapter Twelve

Eve parked her car on the opposite side of the street from the main entrance. Alex had disappeared from her side by the time she reached the revolving door. Once in the elevator, she pulled her binder with her patient charts from her bag and clipped her ID badge to the pocket on her shirt. She opened the binder and double-checked the times for each appointment and had been careful to book them around a spot for Alex. They had come up with the idea together and agreed it would look more believable this way.

Adjusting the heavy book still left in her bag, she marched onto the seventh floor and came face to face with Alex. Intensely focused, he locked his blue eyes on her.

"Wha…" She stopped abruptly when the cool mist of her breath floated around her mouth.

"Don't stop, keep moving," Alex ordered. "You don't want to draw suspicion."

She walked to the security booth and signed in. Her bag, coat and binder all went through a metal detector and she was scanned from head to toe before she was allowed to continue.

When she was out of earshot from the guards and others moving around the floor she whispered, "What's wrong?" She was beginning to get nervous. The area around her was still freezing. Something was definitely wrong.

"Don't talk to me. Go to your patients." His voice was hard and unbending, but then took the sharp edge off by saying, "I'll be right behind you."

Those last few words gave her great comfort as she began her day. The idea of having her own private guard protecting her from old ghosts was nice indeed. When she approached the nurses' station she was surprised to see two of her old work friends behind the counter. Both came around the desk and gave her a quick hug, caught her up on all the gossip and then walked her down the hall to the therapy room where her first patient was waiting and her day began.

In between appointments, she took the time to see her other patients still at Memorial. As they teased and joked with her, Eve found she relaxed as the morning progressed.

By the time lunch rolled around she was nervous again. Alex was next up on her list.

"Do what we talked about," Alex ordered gently.

She took a deep breath as she walked to the nurses' station and began flipping through her appointment schedule.

"Relax," Alex said next to her ear. "You're doing great." The area around her wasn't cold anymore but she still shivered.

"Hey, Gloria," she began casually. "My next patient," — she flipped her pages — "Alex Hunter, is either new or missing because I can't seem to find him."

"Alex Hunter?" Jan said. "He's east wing."

Both nurses looked at a woman who stood close by. She wore green combats under her white lab coat. "You have an appointment to see Alex Hunter?"

"Yes, I do."

"Under whose authority?"

Eve felt her heart race as she once again flipped through her notes. Did anyone notice her shaky hands?

"Calm down," Alex soothed. "She would ask the same question for any other patients in the east wing. I'm no different."

"I received the referral from Defence Health Services like I always do." She handed her a standard request form from the Director of Military Health. "It's a request for an initial assessment," she pointed out.

Straight faced, the nurse asked, "May I see your clearance please, Ms…"

Eve unclipped her ID badge and handed it to her. Apparently everything was in order because the woman handed back her badge and said, "This way please." Eve turned back to her friends and raised her eyebrows mouthing the words 'this way please'. Both women chuckled.

As they approached the east wing, heavy metal doors blocked them from entering. The nurse punched in a code and the doors opened. The east wing was smaller than the west wing with only eight rooms. There was a very large station with two nurses working behind it. When they approached the station her escort explained the reason for Eve's visit and left. The two nurses exchanged puzzled looks but in the end they directed her down to the last room on the left. As she walked away she heard one say, "There's a standing order to call this number should Hunter have any visitors."

Eve felt the area around her grow cold as she walked the short distance to Alex's room. There was something wrong again, but she couldn't ask him, not with people watching her.

When she reached his room she paused just inside the door. A large body was lying unmoving in the bed. Alex moved past her and went to the bed. "My chart is here." He indicated the end of the bed. She slowly moved further into the room, studying Alex's still form.

Once she stood next to the bed, she noticed that his black hair appeared soft, curling due to the longer length and the beard on his chin had recently been trimmed. His chest was bare except for the bandages and IV tubes. By the gleaming white dressings, all wounds had recently been changed so there was no need for her to disturb them, and there didn't appear to be any sign of red or swollen skin indicting an infection. She reached down and felt for a pulse on his wrist, mentally taking note of the strong steady beats. Next, she bent forwards over his muscled chest and looked at his closed eyes for any type of movement.

Nothing.

She was about to lift his eyelid when she noticed the scar that ran through his left brow. It was much deeper than it appeared on his soul.

"This must have been very painful," she said and ran her finger gently down the length.

"I don't remember. It happened a long time ago."

She continued on with her task and lifted his eyelid. The shade of blue that blankly stared back was so startling, so breathtakingly beautiful that she released his lid and staggered back.

"Eve?" Alex asked from the other side of the bed. "What's wrong?"

She looked over at him and blinked. "Nothing." Her heart pumped feverishly as she lied. "Your body is healing nicely." She looked down, avoiding his curious gaze and noticed the mark on his arm. "You have a tattoo," she babbled out, lightly touching his skin.

"It's my unit tattoo. We all have it."

She liked it, and she liked that Alex had one, it made him more of a living person than just a soul. She also happened to think tattoos looked sexy on a man's biceps, especially this man.

"Eve, my chart."

Eve looked at him again with a strange expression. What the hell was the matter with her? And why could he feel it when she touched his body? He hadn't paid much attention when she had first touched his wrist, but then she'd touched the scar over his eye. He was sensitive about that scar and didn't like anyone touching it, which was why he'd noticed when she did. He studied her as she moved around the bed, others must have touched him while he was stuck here, nurses, and doctors, why hadn't he felt them, why could he only feel Eve's touch?

She pulled out his chart and began reading the notes out loud giving him a narration at the same time. "You were brought in with multiple gunshot wounds. Right shoulder clean exit. Upper right abdominal with puncture wound to your liver and mid-chest with a puncture wound to your lung and it looks like it just nicked the pericardium."

"What's that?" He leaned over her to look at his chart.

"It's a sac that surrounds the heart for protection." She shook her head and flipped the page. "This doesn't make any sense." She flipped to the third page. "Everything looks good. Your pulse is good, blood pressure is good. CT scans on your head came back normal. You've responded well to the surgeries and antibiotics. You did lose a lot of blood, more than half your total amount but it's been replaced." She shook her head. "You shouldn't be in a coma."

"Then why am I?"

She looked at him worried. "I don't know."

"Could my injuries have caused it? Maybe the trauma of having two serious wounds was too much for me?" He wasn't a doc but knew any damage to the liver wasn't good and the heart and lungs was worse.

Eve sighed, pulling her lip between her teeth. "Maybe. Combined with the blood loss. I'm sorry Alex, I just don't know."

"What about when people are put in comas? Could they be doing that?"

She trailed her finger down the pages. "I don't see any meds on here that would induce a coma. Besides, there is no need, your body is very strong. Unless..." She paused.

"Unless wha—" Alex froze. He could hear people talking in the hall, they were getting close. A male voice spoke. His anger rose fast and he clenched his jaw trying to contain it.

Miles.

Eve turned and looked warily up at him. He breathed.

"Miles is here," he spoke quickly when she became stiff, keeping his voice calm. He was actually nervous.

He didn't want Eve anywhere near Miles. He saw the fear in her eyes. "Be calm. Miles will pick up on your fear right away. Just act like a physical therapist."

"I am a physical therapist."

"Yes, I can see that," a male voice said from the door. Eve jumped and turned. Miles sauntered into the room as if he owned it. Alex's partner held out his hand to her, his wide friendly smile seeming genuine.

As the room suddenly grew cold, she felt Alex put his hands on her hips. The heat from his hands seeped through her jeans, she guessed he was standing close behind her because her back was warming up too. He must be doing it for her benefit, helping to keep her calm, except it didn't feel like it was working.

"Good afternoon Mrs…?" Miles gripped her hand and looked directly into her eyes.

"Ms Sinclair." She forced her smile to reach her eyes as she looked back. He wasn't a bad looking guy. He was dressed casually and wore his brown hair a little longer than Alex did. He wasn't as tall as Alex was, but he did have more bulk across his chest.

She searched his eyes and fought against the impulse to shiver. If she didn't know he was a killer she would like to think she would have figured it out by his eyes. The dark brown appeared almost black. Hadn't Gran said time and again that the eyes mirrored the soul? Well the old proverb was certainly proved right by the looks of this guy.

"How can I help, Ms Sinclair?" He stood back, inspecting her.

"I was asked to come and perform an initial assessment on Mr Hunter here." She pointed the chart at Alex's body on the bed. Did he see that her hand was shaking? She lowered the chart.

"And who was it that asked you for the assessment?"

"He's just probing," Alex suddenly said. "Wants to see what you know. Calm down, I'm right here."

Calm down! Like that was going to happen. This man was a killer. Well, so was Alex but this guy was evil, she could almost feel it.

"Who are you?" Eve pretended to be confused. "You're not a doctor?"

He chuckled. "No, no. That's too much school for me. My name is Remy Castillo —"

"Cover name," Alex said next to her ear.

" —I work for the Department of Veterans Affairs. Did you know that this floor is for military personal only?"

"Yes of course. I have patients here." She blinked up at him, hoping to appear naïve.

"Who did you say referred you here?" he asked giving her a sweet smile.

"My referrals come from the Director of Military Health." she answered him honestly, there would be no point in lying to him when he could ask any nurse or doctor on the floor.

"Why did they send you to Mr Hunter?" He was studying her now, looking her over from head to toe. The action almost made her cringe.

"I'm a physical therapist." She shrugged, hoping she was pulling off the innocent look.

Miles' expression was blank.

Eve felt he was waiting for more of an answer, so she rambled on, "I get called...you know, usually after the patient has recovered from their wounds...to begin treatment." He continued to stare at her. Confused and a little freaked out by his behaviour,

Eve suddenly blurted out, "You do know what a physical therapist does, don't you?"

Alex tightened his hold on her hips. "Watch what you say to him, you do not want to piss this man off."

In defence, Eve threw up her hands and apologised. "I'm sorry. That was rude. I'm just confused." She held out Alex's chart. "This says that he is in a coma. And I'm not usually brought in until the patient is...at least awake." She gave him a worried look. "I can't help him...well I could I suppose." She purposely glanced sadly at Alex's body. "I just don't know what good it will do." She handed him Alex's chart.

"I apologise for the confusion. Perhaps when Mr Hunter wakes up you will be able to help then."

Alex's hands dropped from her hips as she moved for the door. "I'd like that," she replied truthfully, stepping through the door. She fought the overwhelming urge to look back at Alex's large body one more time.

Miles walked down the hall next to her. "This is all new to me. Do mix-ups like this happen often?"

Eve shrugged. "From time to time, although coma-boy is a first."

"Coma-boy?" Alex mumbled next to her.

Miles laughed. "You sound as though you've seen worse."

"Ooh yes! When I was training, there were two patients with the same name except spelt differently. One was in for a hysterectomy and the other for a tonsillectomy. But the docs picked up the mistake before anybody was cut open."

"How did they figure it out?"

"Because the eighteen year old boy in for the tonsillectomy was wheeled in front of a gynaecologist."

"Oh!" He laughed out loud. "Ouch!"

She couldn't help but laugh. "You're not kidding." They reached the heavy doors and Miles punched in the security code.

"You have more patients to see?" he asked casually. The area around them suddenly grew very cold.

"One more and then I'm gone." She tried not to look at Alex standing next to Miles. The look on his face should have killed Miles on the spot. She realised right then, when Alex was back in his body, Miles was in for some serious trouble. Who was she kidding? Miles was a walking dead man. Goose bumps tingled their way to the surface of her arm. Boy, she was sure glad she wasn't in Alex's bad books.

"Too bad. I was going to see if you wanted to grab a coffee."

"No!" Alex growled the word. "He only wants to get more background on you. He doesn't feel anything for you. Stop. Being. Nice." There was a snarl attached to each word.

"Oh, well." She didn't have to act indifferent to his suggestion, it came naturally. Of course she wouldn't go anywhere with him. She almost huffed aloud. She was totally insulted that Alex would ever assume she would. He had hurt Alex.

"Gotta go. Nice meeting you." Eve faked one more smile and turned, walking away. When she heard the doors close behind her, she exhaled a shaky breath.

Chapter Thirteen

Eve walked back down the hall checking the room numbers. She wasn't lying when she told Miles that she had one more patient, Master-Corporal Jean LeBlanc. The only problem was, she couldn't seem to find him. She scanned her schedule for a third time. He was supposed to be in room seventeen, but that room was being prepared for a new patient.

"Why are you walking up and down the hall?" Alex asked next to her. She had continued to ignore him ever since he had accused her of being 'nice' to Miles. What the hell had he wanted? She had acted curt with Miles, Alex had said don't, so she'd acted nice to Miles, Alex hadn't liked that either, when the whole time she had been freaking out. What did he want from her?

Giving up her search, Eve walked to the station and leaned on the counter. "Jan, you're not going to believe this, I've lost another one."

The short and very wide nurse chuckled. "Who this time?"

"Jean LeBlanc."

"The resident hotty. We gave him the boot when we found out he was married," Gloria called over her shoulder from the other side of the desk.

"Oh!" Eve laughed. "Where'd you kick him to?"

"Just down on six. Room eight I think." Gloria walked over. "He's doing real good under your care Eve. He's a different person than when he first arrived."

Eve blushed. She wasn't good at accepting praise. "It's not all me, he's worked his butt off."

"Has he ever," Gloria mumbled wiggling her eyebrows.

After collecting her jacket and bag, Eve said her goodbyes, promising not to stay away so long next time and walked down the hall towards the elevator. Waiting for the doors to open, Alex commented, "She's right, your patients do very well under your care."

The doors slid open and she stepped inside, Alex moved next to her as the doors closed.

She turned to him. "Was that your way of apologising for being snippy?"

There was a smirk on his face as he stared up at the glowing numbers. "I don't get snippy."

"Uh! Yes you do." She shook her head. "I'm here trying to help you, remember?"

"I remember." He crossed his arms, suddenly agitated. "Speaking of which, you didn't get a chance to finish your sentence when we were talking about induced comas."

"Yah. I've been thinking about that and I don't think it's a possibility."

"What?"

"I thought that maybe you were keeping your soul out of your body on purpose."

Alex hit the emergency stop button. He pulled his finger away and turned back to her grinning.

"I can't believe you just did that." Eve pointed at the buttons and then at him. "Why *did* you just do that?"

"What do you mean I'm keeping my soul from my body?"

"It's a stupid idea." She blinked, still stunned by his abilities. "I can't believe you just did that!"

"Evening!" he growled her full name.

"Fine! I thought because of the circumstance and the danger involved with your employment, that your soul had left to give your body time to heal so that when you re-entered you would be strong and fully healed and could fight back. Right now, you're safe because Miles thinks you might die, or at the very least not wake up. But if you were to wake up he would kill you, and right now you're too weak to fight back." Eve pointed to the elevator buttons again. "But that proves you are not weak."

He focused on her for a moment, then asked, "Would I be able to heal my body if I was to re-enter it?"

"I think so. Yes."

"But you can't get near it now to merge me," he sighed. She could hear the disappointment.

"Maybe we could try again in a few days, come at a different time," she offered.

"No." He dragged his hand through his dark hair. "You're on Mile's radar. He'll check into your story and research your life. It would be suicide if you came back here."

She hated hearing that defeated sound in his voice, she didn't want to quit, she wanted to help him. "Maybe I could try and get you moved to a different floor?"

"You don't have that kind of pull."

"Alex, I—" she began, but he cut her off.

"Don't worry. I'll figure it out." He jammed the stop button with his finger and the elevator began to move. "You just focus on getting your appointment done. I want you out of this hospital."

She didn't get a chance to respond as the doors slid open and he vanished from sight.

* * * *

Alex found the room first and waited in the doorway for Eve to arrive. She chatted with the nurses behind the counter, then finally made her way to him, her thin brows were knitted together as she approached him. He was the cause. He *had* been snippy with her, not that he would ever admit to it. He just didn't like the idea of Miles and Eve together. Even though he knew Miles had never been unfaithful to his wife Nicole, the idea made his insides twist with a rage he couldn't understand.

"Smile." He inclined his head towards the room. "His wife is in there with him." Eve glared up at him and turned into the room, coming to a dead stop. Stepping in behind her Alex was about to ask why she had stopped, when he saw the answer.

Eve's jaw dropped open. Another one? And both in the same room. *Ah great.* This must go against some law of physics. What were the odds of having two medians in the same room? She watched him as he sat on the window ledge looking back at her. His posture became stiffer when he realised she could see him.

"You can see me, can't you?"

She couldn't answer, where she stood by the door a curtain began and cut the normally large room in half giving each patient their own privacy. On one side, her patient, Jean, and his wife were staring at her, on the other side was a median demanding her attention.

"You can." He stood and moved towards her. "How can you?"

She walked to Jean smiling, trying to ignore him. "Don't walk away, talk to me."

"She can't answer you." Eve heard Alex say.

"What? Who are you?" She could hear shock from the new median.

"*Bonjour* Eve. How are you?" Jean's French accent was thick.

She shrugged answering back in French, *"D'accord."*

"How can you hear me?" The new median's question cut into her train of thought as he spoke to Alex.

"Because I'm like you."

Okay this was way too many conversations. Eve shook her head missing Jean's question. "Pardon?" she asked in French. It had taken years to learn the language even with her talent for manipulating words, but she was glad she had. After all, she did live in a country where French was one of two official languages.

Jean repeated his question and she answered, the words rolling smoothly off her tongue.

"You're a soul?" the median asked.

"Wait one—" Alex stopped the median. "You speak French?" When she didn't answer he commented, *"C'est un bel accent."* Then, in a flawless French accent, he proceeded to ask what else she could do with her tongue.

A smile tugged at her lips as her face burned. She couldn't believe he'd just asked her that and in front of people. Not that they heard...but that wasn't the point.

"Who are you people?" the median demanded.

"Quiet," Alex ordered. "Wait until she's done."

Eve was thankful that Alex had taken control of the other median and began chatting with Jean, purposely using a soothing pitch. Her words, even spoken in French, would lull him into a relaxed state so she could obtain an honest reaction from him.

He answered each of her questions sincerely, a sweet smile on his face the whole time. The truth was there, plain to see. Her job was done.

"Well," Eve returned to English. "I think you have done a great job Jean. So, I'm cutting you loose. I'm recommending you be released. I'll call your doc when I get home."

"Fantastic! *Merci*!" Jean's wife laughed.

"Try to get them to leave the room," Alex suggested next to her.

Right the other median. She couldn't very well have a conversation with two medians when her patient was listening to every word she said. "May I recommend a celebratory walk in the park? It is a beautiful day to sit and have a latte."

"*Oui*. Good idea." Jean swung his legs off the bed. "Want to come with us, Eve?"

Eve graciously declined, "I would love to but I can't. I have to finish up my notes and then pick up Noelle."

"Okay. Give *la petite fleur* a kiss from *moi*." Jean gave her a wink as he walked out of the room holding his wife's hand.

"I will," she called.

Alex joined her. "You're happy."

Eve grinned up at him. "Yes. Jean couldn't walk five months ago."

"Really?"

"His tank rolled over an IED. He was diagnosed with multiple compression fractures and now look at him."

Alex raised a dark brow. "Can't, he just walked out the door."

"I know. Great isn't it?"

Alex chuckled. She was beaming, there was no other way to describe it. It was true what that 'Being' inside Justine had said, Eve was a true healer.

"Come on." He nodded to the curtain. "There is a confused median over here."

"Yeah." The smile dropped from her face as he followed her.

Stepping around the curtain Alex suggested to Eve, "Maybe we should close the curtain?"

She nodded and pulled the material around them blocking the view from the hall.

"Okay, now you can talk." He squared his shoulders and studied the man closely. He was a good sized man, maybe an inch or two taller than Alex's six foot one, with sandy blond hair and dark brown eyes. With that hair and the tan he sported, the guy looked like your typical California beach boy, except he wore a hardened expression that had been practiced for years.

With his fists clenched at his side, the median focused on Eve. "How can you see me?"

Eve shrugged. "I've been able to see souls since I was young."

"But how can you, when no one else can? What makes you so special?" Alex had wondered that same questions many times. Why did Eve have this particular talent?

"I don't know. It's been in my family from the start. All Sinclairs can see and merge souls."

"Merge souls?" Alex tensed when the blond moved towards Eve.

"I have the ability not to only see souls but I can merge them back with their bodies if the situation allows it."

Another question answered without giving away too much information. Eve was almost as good at being vague as he was.

The blond remained still—deep in thought—until Eve made the introductions. "My name is Eve Sinclair and this is Alex—"

"He doesn't need to know my name." He cut her off, glaring at the median. It had been drilled into him to never give his real name, and even though he was nothing more than a *very old soul* he still followed protocol. He could see Eve look up at him, then roll her eyes.

"And just who is he going to tell?"

He shrugged. "When he wakes up, who knows?"

He noticed Eve look over at the body lying in the bed. This median was in a worse condition than he was in, tubes in both arms, IV bags hanging close by, the only difference was this median had bandages wrapped around his entire upper body and his face was a mess, plus his blond hair had been buzzed short on one side and a row of stitches were visible through new hair growth. She was probably thinking the same thing he was...this guy wasn't waking up.

Eve gave the median a smile that didn't quite reach her eyes, then gave him a wink, "Alex Hunter."

He sighed, irritated with Eve's deliberate show of defiance.

"Cade Taylor." He nodded in greeting. "I am...or rather was, a detective with vice." He crossed his arms and Alex caught sight of the curious way he looked at him, almost like he knew him. Cade raised his head and nodded. "What happened to you?"

"Got shot, and you?"

"Got hit by a truck. It pinned me against the wall and killed my wife." He looked down at Eve when she sucked in her breath.

"I'm so sorry."

"Don't be." He gave a warm smile. "I get to see her now. I've been waiting for you."

"For me?" Eve blurted out. She couldn't help it, the words burst out with her surprise.

The cop had a deep laugh. "Not you." He locked his eyes on Alex. "You."

Eve looked to Alex. His only reaction was to cross his arms and stare back at Cade.

The room was quiet for some time. Eve became irritated over the lack of communication. What was wrong with Alex, didn't he want to know why Cade had been waiting for him? Well she did, the suspense was killing her. "Why?"

Cade glued her to the spot with brown eyes. "Because he's the Hunter."

"Excuse me?"

Cade sighed and explained, "I was told I had to wait for the hunter and that I would give him something I don't have any need for. I've been racking my brain trying to figure out what I don't need and it just came to me." He looked over at Alex. "I don't need my body."

Alex's reaction was non-existent. He didn't even ask why Cade didn't need his body.

Eve wanted more than that. "Cade, what do you mean?"

"My wife is dead," he said flatly. "She isn't here anymore and let's face it..." He turned and walked to the end of the bed his body was lying in. "I'm not getting up. Look for yourself."

Eve walked to the bed and pulled his chart free, she flipped through the pages then saw it. She felt sick as a deep sense of sadness swept through her, nobody could help this man, not even her and he knew it.

"Eve?" Alex moved to her side, his heat slowly spread up her side when he touched her waist. She wasn't sure how he knew she was upset, she didn't want to know, she was just glad that he was there. He amazed her again by squeezing her side.

She took a shaky breath. "I'm okay."

"What's it say?" he asked quietly.

She shook her head. She couldn't say it, not with the guy standing less than a foot away. In the end she didn't have to.

"It says I'm a vegetable." He turned and looked at them. "I was told that in my present state, that if I was to re-enter my body" — he directed his brown eyes on her — "I guess that's where you come in — I wouldn't have enough strength to fix my injuries and that I would be trapped until my body dies." Cade slid his gaze to Alex. "But apparently you do have enough strength."

"How do you know that?" Alex asked.

"Because my wife told me," he said straight-faced. "And she doesn't lie."

"What makes you think I need your body?" Alex asked.

"Because I was told 'you will need what I do not' and I don't need my body, which means you do."

"Your wife again?" Alex asked, a hint of amusement in his voice. "Sounds like she knows a lot."

"Mmm, I think it freaked Justine out a little bit," Cade shared.

Alex's hand dropped away from Eve's side as he turned to face Cade. His intense look was shadowed as he gave Cade a sideways glare. "Your wife's name is Justine?"

Cade nodded.

"Petite, blonde hair above her shoulders, big brown eyes," Alex ventured.

This time Cade frowned. "You know Justine?"

Eve stepped around Alex in time to see him nod. "She showed up in my room a few days after I woke up in here." He turned informing Eve, "She was the one that suggested I look for you."

Eve's heart stopped as she looked back and forth between the two men. "She's dead?" she asked.

"Yes." Alex was the one to answer her.

She locked her eyes with his. "You said you didn't see the dead." He had lied to her. She shouldn't be surprised. He wanted to get back into his body and was willing to say anything to get what he wanted. "Why did you lie?"

He looked down at her, his gaze bright and clear. "Frankly, because I saw that the idea frightened you and I didn't think there was any point in scaring you further. Plus, I thought if you knew the truth it may have you changing your mind about coming to the hospital."

For a second her heart jumped. Alex was actually concerned about her and her fear, but then he had to ruin it and become all manly, only thinking about himself. What was the matter with her? Did she actually believe that Alex was concerned about her? He was like every other man she had met, self-centred, life was all about his wants and needs. 'Merge me back...I have to help a woman...blah, blah, blah.' The worst thing...she had allowed his arrival to jeopardise her simple existence. Allowed it, even after he told her about his occupation.

Awesome. She pressed a hand to her forehead. Who allows a man like Alex to enter into their life, let alone their home? Median or not, it was the stupidest thing she had ever done. She should have just got all this over with right from the start. She sighed. None of this would have happened if she had, it was her own fault.

She shook her head and tried not to let it show that his words had any importance. "Okay." She shrugged. "So now what?"

Alex scowled when she inched around him and addressed Cade. "So did your wife leave any other words of wisdom?"

"No." Cade looked from her to Alex and back. "She just said I would know what to do."

"Which is?" Alex asked from behind her.

Cade shrugged his wide shoulders. "I want you to have my body. I don't need it."

The sadness crept into her chest again. "But—" Eve began.

Cade cut her off—"The only thing I want is to be with my wife," he reassured. "I've been away from her for too long. God only knows what trouble she is causing."

"You must really love her."

"Yes, I do."

I want a man like that. The thought, caused a lump to squeeze her throat. Instead she had a bossy median who lied to her about seeing dead souls.

"Can you merge me into Cade's body?" Alex enquired.

Eve shrugged. *Jerk.*

Damn it. He knew she was pissed at him, although not sure why. One second they were fine and the next she was acting indifferent towards him. "Give me a better answer than that," he directed.

"I see you still need to work on your patience."

Alex turned to the window where the voice had come from and, though surprised, he grinned all the same. "She's worse than you."

"Who's worse than me?" Eve asked confused by the sudden change in topic.

Justine looked at Eve and snorted, "I doubt that." She turned to her husband as he moved towards her.

The two stopped short, an inch separated their souls.

"What have you been up to?" Cade gave his wife a suspicious grin.

"Same as you, making new friends." She gave him an innocent pout.

Alex almost laughed at the look that crossed Cade's face. "What kind of friends?"

Eve peered around the room nervously. "Who are you talking to?"

Alex, knowing it would cause her discomfort, happily informed her, "Cade's wife is here."

Eve visibly stiffened, her face becoming white. "W-what?" she stuttered. "She's h-here now?" Her eyes became huge as she nervously scanned the room.

Alex immediately regretted telling her when he saw her reaction. It wasn't his intention to scare her to death—just a little payback for being cold all of a sudden—especially when he thought things were going so well between them.

"Eve, calm down," he tried to soothe her.

"Tell me where she is." Eve shivered. When he was slow in answering, she begged, "Please, Alex."

"Tell her, Alex," Justine ordered. "She's terrified."

He crowded close and hoped the heat from his soul would warm her. "She's standing in front of Cade."

Eve looked at the spot in front of Cade, her lips trembling.

"Why is she so scared?" Justine asked.

Alex watched the pulse pound in Eve's neck. He wanted to pull her into his arms but he couldn't. So instead he ran his hand down her arms and tried to cup her hands in his, savouring the tingle she caused. "Eve had a very bad experience with a dead soul. It merged with a median, it ended up destroying the body and killed the soul in the process."

"Oh! Please tell her I'm not like that," Justine said, then added sincerely, "I would never hurt her. I've only come for Cade."

Alex turned his attention back to Eve. "Justine wants you to know that she isn't like that, and she has only come for Cade."

"And that I wouldn't hurt her. You forgot that."

He looked up and took a deep breath, gaining some patience, then back to Eve, "And that she wouldn't hurt you."

Eve only nodded.

Alex gave the couple a sideways glance. "So, Cade just leaves with you?" He studied the blonde. "No, get ready, get set, go?"

"No. But if it makes you feel better I can say that?" She grinned at him.

Alex shrugged at Cade. "You married that smart mouth?"

Laughing, Cade reached for his wife. "Sure did." His arms encircled her and he stopped surprised. "I can touch you."

Nodding Justine informed, "That means it's almost time."

"Almost time for what?" Cade asked dumbfounded.

"Time for you to come with me," she announced happily.

Cade leant down. "'Bout time." And hesitantly, like she would disappear, he kissed his wife.

"That was really weird," Eve whispered. Alex shrugged. It wasn't weird from where he stood. A husband had just kissed his wife. Even though they weren't among the living anymore it was clear the love and passion they shared was still strong and very much a part of their relationship. It was an encouraging sight.

"No more," Justine scolded when Cade went back for more. "I need to get my job done." She turned in Cade's arms and faced Alex. "There isn't much time. You'll have roughly seven to eight minutes for Eve to merge you. If you go beyond that Cade's body will be clinically dead and you're stuck. Got it?"

Alex gave her a curt nod.

Justine pulled from her husband's arms and stopped in front of Eve. She studied Eve briefly, her head moving in awkward jerks, and then gazed over at Alex with all-knowing eyes. "Jillian is not the only one you need to help," a deep male tone rumbled. Her voice had changed like this before, *something* was talking through her. "The other women in your life. They will need you just as much as Jillian, if not more." Dark eyes blinked. "They can give you what you have been missing."

Justine's eyes returned to their normal brown as she blinked. "Damn it." She hissed up at the ceiling, "I wish they would stop doing that."

Alex raised an eyebrow.

"What did they have me say this time? Wait," — she held up her hands — "I don't want to know." She swung around and motioned to Cade. "Come on, honey. Let's get the heck out of here. I want to figure out who keeps doing that to me." She walked over to him and gripped his hands. "Remember." She turned to face Alex. "You have no more than eight minutes, after that you're screwed."

Alex watched as the couple simply faded from sight and the clock started ticking.

Chapter Fourteen

"What the hell just happened? Where's Cade?" Eve blinked in shock. One second Cade looked like he had been making out with air and the next he had just disappeared. It was like watching an old creepy film, with bad special effects.

"Justine took him away." Alex focused on her face, his expression humourless. "It's time Eve."

"Time for what?"

"Time for you to merge me into Cade's body." She began shaking her head before he even finished. "Yes you will," he commanded quietly.

"No. I can't." She didn't know what to do. She couldn't merge him with that body, it had too much damage.

His hands suddenly reached out and gripped her shoulders. She slowly lowered her gaze to his hands and then back to his face.

"How are you doing that?" She could feel his heat and the weight of his hands on her.

He ignored her question. "You will merge me."

Her mouth opened but nothing came out. She shook her head. She was still waiting for her heart to start beating again. His strength amazed her and terrified her.

"Yes. You. Will." He pronounced each word clearly. He was deadly serious and that scared her more than the idea of merging him.

She began pulling away but he was so strong. He held her in place. Then, she noticed his eyes. The blue was so clear and bright that it sent shivers down her spine. She hadn't seen him this angry or worked up since the first time she had seen him standing in her kitchen.

"There is so much damage. What if you can't...I don't want to hurt..." She began shaking.

"You can't hurt me," he stressed, then ordered, "I need you to put me in that body, *now!*"

She jumped at his order and almost fell back when he released her. Then he shocked her with a prediction, "If you don't merge me, you might as well shoot Jillian yourself because she is as good as dead without my help. Think you can handle that resting on your shoulders for the rest of your life? Or think about what Jillian's baby could have grown up to be each time you look at your own child?"

Tears came to her eyes and slipped over the edge. He was so cruel, using her own fear and child against her. "That's not fair."

"But it is fair, because it's what you deserve for being so selfish."

"I'm not selfish," she called back. "I just can't bear the thought of something hurting you." Her heart thumped in her chest and she placed a hand over it. "Or of you being trapped in that body. It would kill me if I...lost you," she whispered the last part. She hated that she was crying and she hated it more that she had admitted feelings she had just realised herself.

If her admission shocked him, she didn't see it. She lowered her head, mortified by her confession.

His hands were suddenly back on her shoulders, his heat seeped through her clothes spreading over her skin as he gave her a squeeze. "Nothing is going to happen to me."

What about his leaving once she merged him? If this whole merging Alex's soul into Cade's body worked, once he woke and was on his feet, he was gone, he had said so himself. And then what? She went back to her normal life? The idea wasn't as satisfying as she had once thought.

"Please Eve. I'm strong enough, I can do it," he urged quietly.

She gave in, praying she wouldn't regret her decision. "I hope so."

She moved to the chair on the opposite side of the room from the door and dragged it half way down the bed until she sat staring at Cade's knees. Dropping her bag on the floor, she flipped open the top, pulled an old leather bound book from within and placed it on the bed.

Taking a deep breath she forced the fear out and the serenity in. She needed to be calm and in control, because if there was a dead soul nearby and they heard her fear while she was calling, it would be drawn to her. Gran said the dead fed on fear.

"Eve, we don't have much time. Cade's body has an expiry date."

She repeated the deep breathing exercise, pushed all thoughts of Alex rushing her and Cade's beaten body aside, and concentrated on merging soul with body.

Untying the leather straps, Eve opened the book and began turning the pages searching for the chant that would call to Alex. "Once I begin the calling—" She continued to turn the old paper as she spoke to Alex. "—every other soul, dead or otherwise will be drawn to it. There might be none or there could be many that answer it." She pointed to the spot across from her on the other side of Cade's body. "Stand there."

Alex did as she asked. "Are you going to look at me?"

She ignored him and continued searching the book. "It's always hard to find this poem. It was scribbled down in the outside margin. You'd think after years of studying this damn thing I'd know where it is," she babbled.

"Eve will you *please* look at me." He emphasised the 'please' with a tender push.

She raised her head as far as his stomach and he bent down the rest of the way. He locked his brilliant blues on her.

"You concentrate on merging me and I'll take care of any problems."

She jerked her head up and down.

"Eve"—His deep voice surrounded her name in warmth, and chased away her growing fear—"Everything is going to be okay."

She nodded, blinking away the burning she felt in her eyes and scanning a few more pages, she caught sight of the small print. "I found it. Are you ready?" She looked up.

It was a stupid question. His face was void of all emotion, the muscles in his arms and chest flexed, his hands were clenched into fists and he was deeply focused. Oh, he was ready. He gave her a curt nod.

In the delicate yet smooth pitch Eve used on her patients, she began reciting the poem.

"Hear me." The words were spoken in an endless flow of an awkward language. *"Hear me call to you, Alex. Listen to my words and put your faith in me. I call to you."*

He had no idea what language she was speaking but understood every word.

"I call to you Alex. Allow me to unite body with soul so that both are whole. You are the essence of life. Bring your light and join with the strength of this body. Without your warmth the fire that is within will never be."

Alex felt the feathery touch of Eve's voice flow over him. Her words were drawing him closer when he suddenly felt the most foul, stomach-turning sensation. He blinked and it was gone.

Once more, he concentrated on Eve, peace washed over him again and he almost sighed. Eve had a beautiful, sultry voice. The way it brushed over his skin caused a need so deep he wanted nothing more than to bury himself in her body and get lost in her for days. He felt his lips curl up at the thought, when that vile sensation flooded him for a second time. His stomach tightened and he fought against the overwhelming nausea. The feeling was so strong, so…there was only one word that came to mind…evil. Something pure evil was near. It was so heavy and all consuming, that he was sure it would crush him if he allowed it to.

Fighting against the seductive pull of Eve's voice, Alex peered over his shoulder in time to see a dark, muddy figure hovering in the door. There was no face or clear definition that resembled anything that used to be human, only black inky holes where eyes and a mouth might have been. It moved into the room and glided towards him.

Eve stopped her chant. "Oh no," she breathed. "I feel it. Like the last time."

The fear in her voice cut through his haze and he turned fully to face the soul.

He cocked his head to the side when it stopped. He shook his head. The soul screamed with rage. A deep accented, male voice pushed above the screams — "Ours, ours."

Alex shook his head again. "Mine," he growled. The word a clear cut warning.

This time, the screams of rage became stronger and the muddy figure, hovering inches off the floor, began to twist and coil in on itself. What looked like its attempt of an arm, separated from the rest of the figure and pointed at him. "Be ours. Be one." The voice that rose above the screams was distinctively female this time. It pointed to Eve. "Kill."

Eve shook, she couldn't help it. She felt it — the dead soul — and not because the room was suddenly freezing, although Alex could have been the cause of that. She felt the rage and the hate and the complete and utter evil filling the room. She focused on Alex. The ring of light that surrounded him was a light blue and increasing in strength. His fists were clenched at his side and his legs were braced apart. She suddenly heard him growl, "Mine."

She was right, it was a dead soul, it wanted the body and by his posture, it looked like Alex was blocking its way. Alex shook his head a second time and she almost jumped from the chair when the room began to vibrate. She grabbed Cade's legs to help secure his body to the bed when a low menacing rumble swirled around them. *This* was scary. The vibrating in the room intensified and so did the growl. She realised then that Alex was the one responsible for both. In the blink of an eye Alex lashed out. "Both mine!" he roared and shot forward.

Her heart was in her throat and her entire body was shaking. The anger radiating off Alex was heart-stopping, she had never heard anything like it before. She hoped she never heard it again.

As fast as the room filled with evil, it emptied, taking the cold air with it. Alex turned to face her, fists squeezed tight and body rigid. She met his intense gaze just in time to see the last flickers of blue fade away. It was almost the same colour as the blue that surrounded him.

She swallowed hard and sat back on the chair.

"Finish it," — his voice was low, rough, and not to be questioned — "time is running out."

The command snapped her out of her stupor. Her hands shook as she reached for the book.

"*I plead* — " Her voice cracked and she cleared her throat and took a slow deep breath. She began again — "*I plead to you Alex*," she spoke in Gaelic. The words rolled off her tongue in one long sentence. "*Use your heat to warm this cold shell. Give it heart so that it may love. Give it emotions so that it may laugh and cry. Give it spirit so that it may fight and endure.*" The light that surrounded Alex became even brighter as he bent over the body lying on the bed.

"*Give it a conscience so that it may know the difference between right and wrong.*" She took a_breath. "*I ask of you Alex. Allow this shell to shape a new identity. Guide it gently through the years with all the wisdom you have earned.*"

For the last part of the poem she had to drop her voice and give him a command. What if he didn't follow it? Alex is so stubborn. *"I command you, Alex."* She put as much strength behind the words as she could. *"Complete this union, fuse with flesh and bone and no longer will you dwell alone."*

The light that surrounded Alex lit up the room, so bright that she had to close her eyes from the glare. When it finally died down, she turned back expecting to see Alex standing there frowning down at her, but he was gone.

She slowly shifted her eyes to Cade's body.

She scanned his face for signs of movement and then his body. Nothing. She wouldn't know anything until Cade or rather Alex opened his eyes. That was *if* he could open his eyes.

The hand closest to her clenched the sheet and Eve shot to her feet, she scanned his face a second time and staggered back, her jaw dropping open. The scar that ran through Alex's left brow appeared on Cade's face. Next she saw Cade's lighter hair darken to Alex's black and then become light again. At the base of the bandages wrapped around Cade's chest, a small scar the exact size and shape of a bullet wound appeared on the right side of his abdomen. Eve slid her eyes to his right shoulder — she felt her mouth drop open as a bullet scar appeared there as well.

Alex was filling Cade's body, making it his own. She stumbled back when he opened his mouth and inhaled a deep breath. Cade's thick arms rose and he rubbed at his face with his hands displaying the bottom half of Alex's unit's tattoo.

Eve took another step back, tripping over her bag and landed hard in the chair. The scraping of the metal chair caused Cade...Alex to jump. Eve froze like a deer caught in headlights but was jerked out of her trance when she heard loud voices in the hall. Reaching for her bag, she quickly jammed her book inside and was standing by the end of the bed when the nurse came around the curtain.

"What was that light?" she asked crossing to Cade's body.

"I'm..." Eve's voice cracked again. "I'm not sure. I was next door here, finishing—"

The nurse cut her off. "Mr Taylor?" she called out forcing his arms down. "Detective Taylor can you hear me?"

Eve stood and stared in horrified amazement when Cade...Alex opened his eyes. They weren't Cade's brown as she was expecting, they were blue, they were Alex's blue. So it was easy for her to see them clear across the room, he lifted his head and pushed up on his elbows ignoring the nurse's protest. He was trying to look at her, she could see him moving his head but the nurse kept blocking his view and he finally pushed her out of the way.

He stared at her for a moment, then a slow easy smile claimed his face. It was a triumphant smile and she waited for him to say 'told yah'. He didn't, but he did seem happy to see her.

Her heart jumped and she felt a nervous laugh build up inside her. She didn't know what to do. She was shocked and thrilled that Alex had been able to merge with Cade's body. That he had been powerful enough to ward off the dead soul and still heal Cade's wounds. It was so nice to see him in a body even though it wasn't his, he was solid now. He could touch...her heart jumped again...and be touched. On that same note, she was terrified that Alex was able to pull it off and merge with Cade's body. The man had confessed to her that his job entailed eliminating people who were a danger to society. He had killed many, many people. And she had helped him merge into a body, setting him free.

She took another step back. The smile dropped from his mouth as he studied her. A startled voice came from behind her and she jumped, turning in time to see a second nurse enter the room and rush over to the bed, checking the pulse of the body Alex now claimed.

Eve automatically stepped back as more people entered the small room, and did so again even when the flow of people stopped.

This was insane. Not five minutes ago she was concerned he would vanish from her life and not look back. Now she was concerned that he knew who she was. Still, she wanted to go to him, tell him how relieved she was that he was okay. But she was afraid of who and what he was. The conflicting emotions were too much, she turned and glanced over at the door, she needed to get away.

As the nurses fussed over him, Alex watched her quietly, his head cocked slightly to the side.

She backed away again angling herself towards the door. This was too much. Fear was now the only driving force. She froze to the spot when his face went dark. He slowly shook his head, a warning in his eyes.

Oh my God, he knows. Eve swallowed the hard lump of fear in her throat and turned away. That fear drove her hard and she walked faster than ever before. Her heart pounded nervously in her ears when the elevator took a lifetime to stop on her floor. She rushed in almost knocking down an elderly lady and turned expecting to see Alex walking down the hall towards her.

Chapter Fifteen

Alex fought the nurses when they tried to hold him down. He wasn't a fool, he knew he wasn't up to chasing Eve down the hall, he just wanted out of bed, so he could see.

It took a bit of effort but he finally swung his legs over the side and stood. His legs felt a little shaky and the tubes in his arms pulled at the skin as he dragged the IV stand with him to the window. He hoped he was on the right side of the building. He also hoped he wasn't too late. Because he knew it would happen, and he needed to see it firsthand so when the time came he could give her a detailed description.

Bracing his hand against the window for support Alex breathed when he saw Eve's car still parked across the street from the hospital. Then he saw her, she began crossing the street, as traffic sped by. She was being reckless, which meant she was scared. She didn't care what the risks were, she just wanted to get away. He sucked in his breath when a white, two door hatchback nearly ran into her. She reached her car and flung open the door, getting a loud honk from a blue minivan that passed by. There was a brief pause and then her black sedan took off, cutting two cars off in the process.

Alex moved back to the bed, gaining approving nods from the nurses in the room. As he allowed the tubes in his arms to be adjusted he smiled to himself. Eve did the one thing that he told her not to do if she didn't want to see him again—Eve jaywalked. His smiled deepened. Scared or not, the reason didn't matter Eve would receive her punishment and he would enjoy every sweaty minute of it.

* * * *

From the main lobby of the hospital, Miles had watched as Eve Sinclair had darted across the busy street and opened her car door. He had waited in the lobby in the hope she would pass through. He wanted to talk to her again, see if he could get more background on her before he dug into her life—it would make his task that much faster if she could give him more places to look.

Unfortunately, he'd never got the opportunity. From the moment she had shot from the elevator, she'd pretty much flown through the lobby and out the main doors. There was no question she had been scared, but of what or who? It wasn't him. He had hid in plain sight blending in with the crowds of people walking around. Curious, he had waited a few minutes to see if she was being followed and frowned when no one had come looking for her. What the hell had had her so scared?

His cell vibrated and he checked the number before answering it.

"Mike?"

"Got a positive return on the BMW."

"Wait one," he ordered into the phone and quickly moved out of the building and onto the sidewalk. "Go." He walked down the street blending into the surrounding crowds.

"Caught on security cam eleven days ago."

"Location?"

"Milley's Eats. I sent the coordinates to your GPS."

Watching for cars as he crossed the road, he inquired, "You're sure it was ours?"

"Same colour, four-door, Wild Rose plates." Miles didn't expect Mike to rattle off the plate number, if this call was being scanned the people listening wouldn't get much info. "It's yours."

"See the occupant?" Reaching his car he unlocked the door and slide inside.

"Nope, only the tail end of the car." There was a pause. "How's Ace, any progress?"

"No." He tried to sound disheartened, but was getting tired of keeping up the appearance of a worried friend and partner. "Still the same."

"Fuck." Mike the unit Adviser, as he was called, sighed sadly. "I'll contact you with any new Intel."

"Roger." Miles hung up the phone and reached for his GPS. The co-ordinates were flashing on the screen. He tapped the display to activate the search.

As he waited he started the car and pulled out of the parking lot. "Destination found," the GPS announced. He grabbed the handheld unit and scowled. Guess he was taking a drive to Montcalm.

* * * *

Even though the drive to Memorial Hospital had taken over an hour — thanks to her delaying tactics —

Eve was able to make it back to the house in half that time. Once back home she had only enough time to throw her purse on the counter, before she had to meet Noelle at her bus. Noelle was the most important part of her life. She came before everything, medians, patients, and even Alex. However, that fear of Alex following her was still twisting her stomach, growing stronger when she thought about Noelle. Would Alex hurt Noelle, or use her like before for some reason? If something was to happen to Noelle, she'd be lost. Her sweet, beautiful child was her saving grace, which she proved again by keeping Eve busy with stories from school. If it was any other night, the endless chatter would have driven her crazy, but tonight she was thankful for the distraction, as short as it was.

Once Noelle was in bed, she raced downstairs and locked all the windows and doors and set the alarm. Grabbing a knife from the butcher block and a rolling pin from the drawer, she headed to her office to finish her notes on the patients at Memorial. She pulled up the first chart and began to write her notes, finishing off with personal comments on each patient.

When Alex's phony file came up she stopped in mid thought and just stared at his name. After everything that had happened today, how could she forget that she had faked his appointment on her schedule? The whole idea, was for her paperwork, patient files, and schedule she brought into the hospital to look valid. Of course everything was valid except the file on Alex. She blinked and focused on the screen. Alex had told her what to type into his file, and she knew it was all the truth because she couldn't go into east wing with false information.

She knew his real name, which was Alex Hunter. He had told her his real date of birth, his height, weight,hair and eye colour, even the city he had been born in.

Leaning forward, Eve rested her chin in her hands. What was she going to do? She knew so much about him, information that he said not many people knew. She blinked and stared at Alex's name on the screen. She knew personal information about a killer who had been trained by the government. And now he was in the body of a dead cop! If she went for help, the cops would believe one of their own, before they'd believe a crazy woman who claimed to merge souls. Oh yah! She couldn't forget about Miles, another killer, who was probably right now checking to see if she was legitimate. If he found out she wasn't legit, she almost certainly would have problems with him, and she hoped it would only be the cancellation of her contract with the government. "Oh my God," she groaned. "I'm so screwed."

Turning off her computer, she grabbed the knife and rolling pin and went to bed, cursing Alex the whole time. This was his fault, all his fault. It would never have happened if he had just stayed away. He had brought all this trouble with him, and now Noelle was in danger, her baby...baby.

Eve sat on the side of the bed. She had forgotten about the woman Alex was trying to save. Jillian. Alex had said she might as well shoot *Jillian* herself if she didn't help him. She was pregnant. And she was alone, right now with a killer searching for her.

Shame pressed down onto her shoulders, and though she was alone, Eve was embarrassed. She was acting so selfishly, worrying about herself when Jillian must be in a constant state of fear, which wasn't good, considering her condition. That poor girl was waiting for Alex to save her and she was waiting for Alex to…what?

What would he do? She placed the knife under her pillow, the rolling pin on the bedside table Alex used to sit against and slid under the covers. There was no way Alex would be jumping out of bed anytime soon. Though he was strong and was able to heal Cade's wounds it would still have taken a toll. He needed to rest. She still had time. But time for what? She flicked off the light and rested back on the pillow, she lifted her arm above her head, automatically.

What could she do, run away? Alex would find her. She believed that now. There would be no safe place for her and Noelle to hide if Alex wanted to find them.

* * * *

After the trip to the window and back, Alex hadn't been able to jump anywhere, let alone out of bed, until the next morning. He'd stared at the ceiling most of the night as the nurses and doctors had fussed over the new body he owned, checking vitals, taking blood samples, asking him a million questions. And just when he had thought it was over and he'd get some time to rest…in came the cops.

He was told about Justine's death by an older, hard looking man, who he guessed was his 'boss'. It was hard showing any type of grief towards his 'wife's' death. He'd only known Justine when she had been dead, and though she was quite the smart mouth, she had also been very likeable. He also knew she was now with Cade and that both were happy. So he opted to keep his head down when he was given the bad news.

He silently listened to the condolences and the promises. They would catch the perp responsible for blowing the tyre of the old guy's truck and he was ordered to take as much time as he needed to recover. Alex stiffened. "How did the tyre blow?"

Trevor, Cade's partner, who had black eyes, a bald head and a red goatee looked to his boss and received a nod. "The delivery truck that hit you and Justine had blown a tyre. Stan, a veteran trucker, kept saying that he didn't understand how that could have happened because he checks his truck daily and had been present when new tyres were installed just two weeks before. He kept on and on about something not being right with the tyres." Trevor sighed. "He was so damn persistent that I did some digging. As it turns out Stan's gut feeling was right. The lab checked the tyres and the air pressure had been lowered on the left side enough to cause the truck to become unstable but not enough for the driver to notice."

Alex shook his head. "That wouldn't be enough for a veteran driver to lose control."

Trevor nodded. "Stan loads his truck at night for his deliveries the next day. All tether straps holding his loads in the back were eaten away."

"Eaten away?"

Trevor nodded, his red eyebrows lowering over his black eyes. "That's what they looked like. It was bizarre the lab tests came back with traces of a bunch of different organic chemicals but mainly —"

Salt. Alex thought.

" — salt."

Trevor went into detail about the organic acid but it was a waste of time. Alex had used that classified compound to remove a few targets himself. He wasn't familiar with all the chemicals used to create the lethal mix, but he did know it included acids found in nature, a heavy dose of salt acid and a few other things. He also knew that the company that had accidently created the concoction had been forced to close down by the government and all trace of the new organic acid had disappeared from the public's eye. The blend wasn't particularly affective on hard surfaces, such as metal but natural materials—the heavy woven cotton straps used to hold down cargo— the acid would eat through in a matter of hours. Ingestion of the acid was faster—only taking a single drop in a glass of water or on food to kill its victim— and because the mix was created from biological ingredients it dissolved in the body with little or no trace.

Alex felt his nostrils flare as he took a deep breath. Why the fuck would Miles kill Cade and Justine? What was happening here? First Miles had wanted to kill Jillian and then he'd killed Justine and put Cade, who was a cop of all things, in a coma. What the hell was the connection? If he didn't know better he would say Miles was either panicking or enjoying the kill. Alex silently prayed that Miles was panicking, because if the Project found out he was enjoying the kill, Miles would be put on the list, with more than one team targeting him. And then he would never get his chance to hunt Miles himself.

Shit. And into the middle of all this, he had dragged Eve—he had put her in Mile's line of sight, and knowing Miles, he probably already knew most of her background and where she lived.

Rubbing his face he murmured out loud, "What a fucking mess."

Trevor gripped his shoulder, like a friend would and tried to comfort him. "We'll get him, you just take it easy."

His first instinct, when the cops had entered his room was to bin the job, he didn't need someone or something getting in his way when he went hunting for Miles. He'd decided against it when they had proved how capable they were by tracing the acid. It had also helped when Trevor handed him a gun and badge. He almost grinned when he saw the two-tone Sig Sauer pistol sitting in his hand. Alex looked up at the man and nodded. His unit was taught to avoid all police forces. They were bound by different laws, defective laws. Yet, with the state he was in, he didn't have much choice. He'd take all the help he could get. Especially, if they were giving out free guns.

* * * *

Sitting on the side of the bed, Alex rested before he forced his new body to take another circuit of the room. His thoughts constantly turning to Eve.

Eve.

He squeezed his jaw when he remembered the fear in her eyes. At first, he'd wondered if it might have been his actions when the other souls responded to her calling. He had only acted so viciously because they'd wanted him to kill her. Something in him had snapped at the idea of anyone or anything hurting her. That'd been when things had become a little hazy, his vision had clouded over and his chest had burned. The glowing eyes and growl had probably been a bit of overkill, but the message had been received. He would not let any of them hurt Eve or take Cade's empty body.

Flexing his muscles he stood once again and moved around the room, smelling antiseptic, and sickness. He swung his arms over his head and stretched. He felt good. Solid. Alive.

He moved to the bathroom again and looked at himself in the mirror. Cade's body was in mint shape, a little more muscle mass in the upper body than he was used to, but he'd have no problems adapting. He was taller too, by about two inches, and his hair was a sandy blond and longer than he liked but not bad either. He ran a hand along the side of Cade's head that still had hair. He needed to shave this off before he went anywhere.

Staring back at the face in the mirror he saw it again. He wasn't sure if his mind was playing tricks or just plain wishful thinking, but he could see himself. Features that were distinctly his were becoming very apparent. The most obvious were his eyes, the colour and his old scar. He touched the deep scar above his left eye and noticed the bottom half of a tattoo on his right arm. He raised the sleeve of his white T-shirt.

"Holy shit!" he breathed, touching his unit's insignia tattooed on his arm. He stared back into his own blue eyes, his mind processing the new Intel.

The scar he'd received from the man he had tracked down and killed for murdering his parents and the tattoo of his unit—both were unique to him. He rubbed the golden stubble on his face, paused then tugged up the hem of his white shirt and pulled it over his head. The cop's body was well defined and was lightly tanned, different from his own. He spent the majority of his time out at night, when others were at their most vulnerable. Yet the golden torso that was now his, also held tell-tale evidence. Three round scars marked the chest he now owned. A reminder of a friend's betrayal.

Chapter Sixteen

Three days had passed since Eve had merged Alex into Cade's body. Three days of her wondering if he was going to leave them alone like he'd said he would, or if he would come 'knocking on her door' as he'd put it, feeling she was a liability. The constant fear was driving her crazy—if he was going to come she wished he would get it over with. But she hoped that he would come for a different reason altogether. Her face heated slightly at the idea. There was more than that, she missed him, *actually* missed his company.

She shook her head and cursed him again as she climbed the stairs to bed. This was becoming a nightly ritual. Working a little, then getting distracted and thinking about Alex, before finally blaming everything on him and carrying her knife and rolling pin to bed.

She reached the top floor, quietly checked on Noelle, then closed her door and walked slowly to her own room. Who was she kidding? He wasn't coming back. Her stomach dropped like a rock. She came to a halt just inside her room. She needed to come to terms that she had feelings for a murderer and that she might not see him again. "How can I feel that for him it doesn't make any sense?" she asked out loud.

"Depends on what you're feeling and who you're feeling it for," the voice came from behind her in the hall. Without looking back she jumped into the room reaching for the door blindly behind her in an effort to swing it shut. She then cleared the height of the bed landing in the centre, then quickly turning she faced the door holding out both knife and rolling pin while she shifted back and forth, her feet almost getting tangled in her sheets thanks to her nervous tizzy.

The door opened and Cade…Alex walked into the room. She froze as she stared at him, her mouth dropping open. He was in her house and she hadn't heard him enter, he had walked behind her almost into her bedroom and probably up the stairs and she hadn't heard him. A part of her was terrified but there was a part that was happy and excited to see him.

"You're dropping your rolling pin." He nodded to her hand. She jerked it up still gawking at him. "Don't hold the knife like that," he suggested calmly. "Hold it so it faces up towards your attacker, the movement is harder to stop."

He slowly closed the door.

She adjusted the knife in her hand.

Alex casually approached the bed and stopped, crossing his arms. "Now," he began fixing his blue eyes on her. "What feelings are we talking about here? Warm and fuzzy or"—he gave her a wicked grin—"hot and wet?"

Eve felt her mouth drop open again. "I…I… What are you doing here?"

"Rolling pin," he pointed out.

She jerked it up and pointed it at him. "How did you get in here?" She noticed he had shaved the other side of his head so that his hair was all the same length, and though the stitches were removed she could see the scar running across his head, which looked to be healing nicely. Cade's body looked good, Alex had done a good job healing it.

"I saw you activate your alarm system at least a dozen times." He shrugged. "It wouldn't have mattered though, I would still have gotten in." Then, straight faced, he divulged, "It's what I do."

"Get out!"

"No." He edged closer to the bed, his gaze trailing over her face.

Eve took a step to the side, keeping a tight grip on the knife and rolling pin. "Please get out."

"No," Alex answered with a lop-sided smirk. He stared at her for a few minutes while she thought of a way to get him to leave. Finally, he sighed out loud, "I don't get you. You've bitched about me for three nights now. You want me here, don't want me here. I've caused all the problems and I'm not here to help you and now that I am here, you want me out."

Eve felt her mouth drop open again and her face burned. "I...I... No I didn't say that."

She watched as he took another step closer, she didn't move this time, just followed his movement.

"Yes you did." He grinned up at her. "I think you want me here. What I don't know is why you're fighting it."

She didn't answer his question. She just stood there like an idiot, feeling her heart pound in her chest and her face burn. Three nights. He'd been in her house listening to her...for three nights and she hadn't even noticed.

"I'm not going to lie. There is something that attracts me to you, it makes me want to throw you down and fuck your brains out. I wish I knew what it was, because you're really not my type. I like my women blonde and I like them tall so they can wrap their legs around me. Your hair is curly and you're a little on the short side."

Alex raised his brows when she put her hands on her hips.

"I'm not one of your women. So you don't have to worry about me wrapping anything around you." The bite in her voice suggested she was about two seconds from throwing the knife and rolling pin at him.

He kept on with his attack and pointed to her hair again. "And the auburn. It has a lot of red in it, I've heard redheads—"

She didn't let him finish—"Oh wait, let me finish this one. Redheads have bad tempers and are bitchy. Thanks but I'm not a redhead."

He studied her auburn hair. She wasn't a redhead in the conventional sense of the word but her hair was reddish and he actually liked it. "That wasn't what I was going to say. What I was going to say was that redheads are supposed to be fantastic in bed, so you do have that going for you."

He leaned to the side as the rolling pin flew past his head and thumped against the wall. They both paused waiting to hear if Noelle would call out. When the house remained silent, Eve hissed, "You are an asshole."

"Sometimes," he confessed. *One down, one to go.*

Alex planned on insulting her skills as therapist next. She didn't oblige and turned, huffing out loud as she jumped off the bed. The second her back was turned he moved, coming around the bed fast. He grabbed her arm holding the knife, locked her elbow straight and pulled the knife from her grip.

He loosened his hold and glared down at her. "Don't ever point a knife at me again." He then pulled her stiff frame up against his chest. He lowered his voice, "I never want a reason to hurt you."

Eve looked at his chest. She tried to hide her fear but he saw it the second she looked up at him. "But you are going to hurt me? That is why you came back isn't it?"

Sighing he tossed the knife on the bed and lightly took hold of her other arm. "Is that what you thought? That I would came back here and kill you and Noelle?"

She looked him in the eye. "Yes."

He gave her a hard look.

"What do you expect? You're a trained killer that belongs to a unit of trained killers that no one is supposed to know about. Yes, I thought you would come back and kill me and Noelle."

He squeezed her arms so she understood. "I am not going to kill you or Noelle. My unit doesn't just kill random people. I told you, we track and kill people that are a danger to you and Noelle and every other good person."

"You keep saying people, what people?" Her voice became a little high.

He pulled her to the bed and sat her down.

She looked up at him with big expectant eyes.

"You want an example?"

"Yes please." Her response was polite and curt at the same time.

He began pacing in front of her trying to think of an example that she would be familiar with, but wouldn't scare the crap out of her. It didn't matter which example he thought about, all of them were bound to scare her.

"Two years ago, hookers started going missing from all major cities in the Prairie Provinces. No one thought there might be a connection. It wasn't until the girls from smaller cities started disappearing that police seemed to take notice. The girls that went missing all had two things in common. One, they all had tongue studs. Two, they all had their own car." He stopped and looked down at Eve. She was sitting crossed legged on the bed listening to him intently.

He sat down facing her. "This was a public case and quite a few details never made the papers because of how violent these acts were."

"Okay."

"Eve, I don't want to scare you."

She blinked as her cheeks flushed. "I'm..." She nodded. "Okay."

Alex sighed at her reaction. For some reason she was embarrassed that she was attracted to him. He didn't even need the blush to know what she was feeling. Her pupils always grew large and took over the pretty hazel of her eyes whenever she looked at him.

"When the police from each city found no trace of the girls, we were called in. There was one detail that no one picked up on. Each of these girls had a car and in almost every case the car was also missing."

"Oh, I remember that case. The Used Car Murders. But the police caught that guy."

"They caught that guy. But not the others."

"Others?"

"Wait for it," he ordered. "We focused on the cars. Even though they had been unregistered, they'd been easier to trace, and not one car had been found. Miles and I had thought that odd, then had wondered if the cars were hiding in plain sight. We'd come up with a theory. What if the girls had been lured away by the promise of big bucks but had had to drive to meet their john at an isolated meeting point?" He clenched his jaw remembering the grisly details of the hunt.

"We dressed up in suits and ties and went…"

"Wait," Eve interrupted him. "That can't be right. How could the police miss an important fact like each of these girls had cars and they too were missing?"

He frowned at her question. "Some of the cars were never registered, a few were stolen and the others… Well let's just say that's still being looked in to."

She gasped lightly, "You mean a cop might have…"

"It's still being looked in too." He ended the discussion. "Do you want to listen to the rest?"

She snapped her mouth shut and nodded silently.

"Like I said Miles and I got dressed and went up to random girls and told them we couldn't do anything at the time but would like to call them later and meet up. Every girl gave us her cell number. When we'd called them later that day and suggested a place to meet, everyone with a car had shown up. That was when we met Amy. As it turned out the last john that had asked her to meet him at a later time, jumped in a waiting car and taken off when she'd shown. When I asked why, she'd thought it was because her pimp had driven her to the meeting point. That was when we'd realised we were right about the isolated meeting point and learnt there were now two targets to hunt. This made sense, because in every case no body or car was found."

"One to drive the first car and one to drive her car," Eve pointed out as she began toying with the handle of the knife.

Alex casually slid the knife away from her and stood, crossing to her dresser. "Yes." He put the knife down and walked back to the bed. "We focused on the cars again. We scanned the net for several makes and models of cars we knew were missing and got several hits from a couple of dealers. We ended up searching the entire list and most of the cars were at one of two dealerships. After that Miles and I each went to a dealership and had found the cars on their lots. All VIN numbers were different, but the make and models were identical."

He sat down on the bed again. "Are you convinced yet?"

"It's too soon to tell, keep going."

He scowled when he heard the interest in her voice.

"We called in a trace for both owners of the dealerships. As it turned out they were both from the same small town in Serbia and both had fought in Bosnia during the early nineties. And both of them placed a number of calls to a wrecking yard midway between their dealerships. We traced the owner of the wrecking yard and he was also Serbian and fought alongside his two partners. Everything fell into place after that."

Eve had a horrified look on her face. "They hunted down girls, killed them and then sold their cars. How does the wrecker fit in?"

"He chopped up the cars they couldn't sell, for parts and disposed of the bodies. Initially, we didn't find any remains, only the tongue studs and DVDs with each of the girls mur—"

Eve cut him off shaking her head. "I don't want to know anymore. I believe you." She stood and moved around him in a wide circle.

"I told you it wasn't nice," he said following her to the bathroom.

"I know," she answered quietly. "The other two? What happened to them?"

He didn't answer her, he didn't have to. "You killed them," she stated, her back still towards him.

Before she could enter the bathroom, Alex grabbed her by the waist and turned her to face him. "You okay?" he asked, slowly pulling her closer.

"I...I think so." Her thin brows puckered together. "I'm feeling a little confused."

"Why?" He shifted her back from the door. She didn't seem to notice.

"The thought of people out there like that scares the shit out of me. Now, I know about you and your unit, and how you protect us from evil people like that. I think that scares me more than the murderers, because you are better than they are, yet I'm glad you're out there protecting us." She looked at him as he continued to lead her away from the bathroom. "See...confused."

Stopping next to the bed Alex pointed out, "You're not scared of me now."

Eve glanced around. "Wait...how did you do that?"

He held tight when she tried to pull away. "You're not scared of me now, or you would still be on the bed."

"Yah and you would still be insulting me." She crossed her arms in a huff.

"I'm not sorry about that. I needed you to lose the baking weapons. I didn't come here to get beaten into a pie," he teased.

"Why did you come?" She threw her arms in the air.

He felt like laughing at her dramatic gesture but didn't. He slid his gaze over her face. Enjoyed the way her cheeks turned pink like her lips. He then focused on the green flecks in her eyes. "I told you I would come knocking on your door if you were to break the law and you did."

Her eyes grew wide when she remembered their conversation. "But I didn't…"

"Yes you did. When you left Memorial." He pulled her closer and slid his hand through her curls to the back of her head. "You should know better than to run out into traffic, that white hatchback almost turned you into road kill."

Eve gasped, "You saw that?" He smirked at her. "But I…that shouldn't count…"

"It counts." He looked at her lips and as though she knew he needed to see it, she ran her tongue along the seam.

"But you didn't knock." She pushed lightly against his chest, a pathetic last attempt to save herself. He lowered his mouth brushing his lips against hers feeling the tingle that only she caused. "This is me knocking."

Chapter Seventeen

Eve inhaled as Alex pressed his lips to hers. It was wonderful, this nervousness he caused. It had been so long since the last time a man had kissed her. Then again, the last time — she could even remember. Alex was a truly gifted kisser, he made her lips tingle the way he caressed them with his own. Her legs began to shake. He slid a hand down to her lower back and pulled her so close their bodies were touching. She felt her breasts press against his chest as he bent over her, the muscles of his shoulders hard under her fingers. His new body was taller and easily overshadowed her.

I like my women tall and blonde. She unexpectedly felt small and inferior. Well she wasn't tall or blonde and had no desire to be. She pushed against his shoulders until he pulled away. His eyes opened as he licked at his lips.

He frowned at her sharp intake of air. "There was no way I was that bad." He gave her a wicked smile.

"Your eyes..." She couldn't finish. Alex's features were taking over Cade's. How was that possible?

"What about them?" He straightened.

Eve blinked up at him still stunned by what she saw. She swallowed. "They're...blue."

"Yes, and...?"

"They're glowing." She realised, quite suddenly, that Alex wasn't angry or irritated in anyway. So why were they glowing?

"And that bothers you?"

She pulled away, separating herself from his warmth. "A man with glowing blue eyes really isn't that appealing to me." She couldn't help but give him the dig.

He raised a golden eyebrow. "Really. That's good to know. What *do* you find appealing?"

"Why do you care? I'm not your type, remember."

"I remember." He studied her briefly. First her body, then her face. It was odd, it seemed like he was reading her body. "Just because you aren't the normal type of woman I'm attracted to, doesn't mean I'm not attracted to you."

As he fixed his intense eyes on her, she began to feel small again. She snorted and stepped back. "I think the merge has scrambled your noodle." She skirted around him and into the bathroom. "I'm not blonde." She grabbed the door and began to swing it shut. "And even though I'm not as tall as you would like, I'm certain I would be able to wrap my legs around you. Not that it will happen now. I'm having a shower." She closed the door but not before catching the blue flicker in Alex's eyes.

Alex sat on the edge of the bed staring at the door to Eve's bathroom for five minutes. He had listened to the water run, had imagined Eve's naked body wet and soapy. He had stopped himself from following her for five goddamn minutes.

Fuck! He scrubbed at his face. What was he doing? He shouldn't be wasting his time here. He needed to find out where Miles was, he needed to get into his main apartment and pick up his rifle and a few other supplies, and he needed to make sure Jillian was okay. What he needed wasn't what he wanted. He wanted Eve. He wanted to join her in that shower, watch the soapy water slide over her body.

He sat forward, rested his elbows on his knees and tried to block the image. It didn't work. He stood and moved to the bathroom door. Would she be pissed if he joined her without asking? Probably. Would she kick him out? Maybe. The most important question was—would he leave if she asked him to?

No. He knew he wouldn't. He would stay and use his mouth and body to convince her otherwise.

Leaning into the door he braced his hands on the frame listening to the water. His decision was made when he heard her sigh. He swore as he pulled his shirt over his head and kicked off his boots.

The warm water was doing a good job of easing her stiff neck. She'd had no idea she was so tense until she was covered by the warm spray. She did know that Alex was the cause. It was either the kiss that caused it, the insults, or the fact his new body...Cade's body was just that little bit taller—she had to look up at him when he stood so close to her.

Their whole conversation had been confusing. He'd said he wanted her but she wasn't his type. It was like he didn't want to be attracted to her. Well, she didn't want to be attracted to him. He was a dangerous man—his life could easily destroy hers. Closing her eyes she let the water work its magic until the memory of Alex's kiss had her wondering if he was still in her room. She opened her eyes and jumped when she saw him standing in front of her. Standing *naked* in front of her. How had he got in…she hadn't even heard him enter…

"I was just wondering why you were frowning." He smoothed the skin between her eyes with the back of his finger.

Her entire body burned from embarrassment. She opened her mouth to tell him to get out but answered him instead, "It seems like you don't want to be attracted to me."

He studied her then shook his head. "I don't want to be attracted to you. You have Noelle. I don't date women with families. But this attraction to you is different. It's stronger than anything I've ever felt, and nothing seems to override it."

She lowered her eyes. "You should probably leave."

"Do you want me to leave?" He raised her chin so she was staring into his face. Alex's face. She could see his features—the scar running through his left brow, his bright blue eyes, even Cade's blond hair seemed to darken to Alex's black. She blinked up at him amazed, while he stared back waiting to hear her answer.

"No, I don't want you to leave." Her faced burnt with the admission, but not as hot as her body when he proceeded to push her back and take his time looking at her. She had never stood in front of a man like this, allowing him to look at her when she felt vulnerable. Of course, the other men she had been with weren't the same type of man as Alex. The others would ask, he would take. Her body tightened in anticipation of Alex taking.

When she couldn't stand another minute of his gaze she inched closer and caught his attention. "What I do want is for you to fuck my brains out. I think I would really like that."

He gave her a wicked grin as he traced her waist and hips then roughly pulled her forward covering her mouth with his.

Alex warmed her front as the water warmed her back. His heat seeped into every pore and surrounded every nerve and she thoroughly enjoyed it. His mouth was soft, yet demanding, wanting her to give as much as he was. He moved his hands, one to the back of her head, the other to her behind. He tugged her forward, sealing their bodies together. Her breasts flattened against his chest, the coarse hair tickling her already stiff nipples. Eve couldn't stop the moan that escaped when his hard cock rubbed against her belly. Shit, this felt so good, so natural. She couldn't remember why she was nervous of him to begin with.

As he held her pinned against his body, she licked at the seam of his lips. His response was to inhale and swear under his breath. She opened her eyes and met his glowing gaze.

Eve couldn't help but smile when his nostrils flared and he pulled at her hair tilting her head back. His mouth roughly covered hers and she opened her mouth, eager for his tongue to enter.

Never had he been so turned on by the slightest of touches. It took all his control not to swing Eve around, pin her against the wall, and slam into her wet body. That might still happen, if they didn't slow down.

He savoured the rich taste of her mouth, enjoyed how she slid her tongue seductively against his. He honestly hadn't expected Eve's response to him to be so...agreeable. Especially, since she thought he had come to kill her and Noelle. He wished he knew where she came up with that ridiculous idea.

Not wanting to break their kiss, he continued to hold the back of her head as he ran his other hand over wet skin, exploring her lush body. She moaned as he moulded her rounded behind. He ran his hand up her back. God, her skin was smooth. She felt as good as she looked, all soft and curvy. Her large breasts were tipped with rosy hard nipples and the flare to her hips and small waist gave her a seductive shape. He cupped a creamy mound, squeezing the fullness, taking pleasure in the size. She drew in a shaky breath when he circled her nipple with his thumb.

Separating himself from her mouth, Alex kissed his way to the tender skin under her ear and tasted. Goosebumps appeared on her skin from the slight touch. He moved to another spot on her neck and kissed her again. This time he felt her body quiver. He repeated the kiss and stroked her skin with his tongue. Eve turned her face to his. Her wet lips brushed over his, causing his mouth to open and she slipped her tongue inside tangling with his. The kiss was tender and enticing, yet intensely passionate, by the time he pulled away, Alex was out of breath and struggling to stand.

His heart pounded and his cock stiffened. Damn, she was hot, with her swollen mouth and heavy eyes. She was as turned on as he was. "We need a bed."

She smirked up at him, stroking his chest. "We do?"

Alex's laugh was deep and very sexy. He reached behind her and turned off the water. Pulling her from the shower, he handed her a large towel and grabbed one for himself. She barely had time to dry herself before he was dragging her out into the bedroom and towards the bed. She stood with her back to the bed as Alex began to crowd her. His eyes were dark and his face intense, he looked like a wild cat hunting his prey. It both excited and frightened her. She slipped onto the bed and scooted back. He grabbed her hips and pulled her forward. "Where are you going?" He moved between her legs.

Eve leant back onto her elbows. "On the bed."

He pinned her to the spot with his eyes. "You looked nervous all of a sudden."

"I did?" It was kind of a lie, but she was excited too.

He bent over her, forcing her to lay back on the bed, her body now open and stretched out before him. "But you're not now, are you?" It was a cross between an order and a plea. Of course, neither was necessary. She didn't want to stop anymore than he did.

She curled her hands around his neck and pulled him down. "No," she breathed against his lips just before she slid her tongue into his mouth and tasted the sweet heat. He stopped before too long and trailed his lips across her cheek to her neck again and she shivered when he ran his tongue along her pulse. As he moved his hand to her breast, his mouth followed, the wet trail, causing her to tremble. Lifting his head, he very gently caressed her breasts. The touch was so painfully tender, that it caused a heavenly pressure in her chest. "Beautiful." He lowered his head tormented the hard nipple with his breath. She inhaled sharply. "I'm glad you found something about me to like," she teased lightly.

Locking eyes with her, he cupped her now aching, breasts firmly in place. "I've found more than just these two beautiful creations." Then, watching her expression, he took an oversensitive nipple into his mouth and swirled his tongue around the hard tip. The muscles in her stomach clenched, as a high like no other flew through her damp body.

Closing her eyes she moaned, arching up against him. She ran her fingers through his short hair, trying to hold him in place. This was crazy, this feeling. She was swamped with such a ravenous need, just when he kissed her, God only knew what would happen when they finally made love? Her nipples tingled under his warm mouth. Her body burned hotter when he kissed and licked the rest of her breast, taking care not to miss a single spot before moving to lick and tease the other one.

Eve felt her insides coil tighter and tighter each time his mouth touched her skin. She wanted more, she ached for more. As Alex lavished attention on her nipple, she felt his fingers trail down her stomach and slide between her legs, stroking her swollen core. She moaned again and pulled at him lifting her hips searching for his touch. Alex must have noticed her need because he didn't spend time teasing her, he simply slipped a finger deep. Her back arched automatically. "Better?" Her groan was husky as he kissed the smooth skin between her breasts.

Pushing up onto his elbow Alex watched Eve. She arched her hips again as he palmed her slick lips, the same time as he slid his finger in and out of her tight opening. He scanned the length of her body, watching how she moved under his touch. My God, this woman was sexy, the way she moved, the way she kissed, the way she touched. He grew harder just watching her. "Alex," She pleaded, pulling him down again and brushing her mouth against his. She petted his chest, grazed his stomach with the back of her hand, before gripping his cock. "Stop teasing me." She ran her hand down the hard length. "I need you."

I need you.

He liked her saying that. He liked the way she touched him too. How she squeezed his cock, pumping slowly up and down, steadily increasing the pressure and speed.

Alex breathed into her mouth, "Soon," he promised, clenching his jaw as she tightened her grip. "You need this first." Covering her mouth with his own, he slid a second finger in to join the first. He drew her breath into his lungs, as he tasted the sweetness of her mouth, his tongue exploring every corner. God above, she tasted good. Her mouth was as soft and as satiny as the rest of her.

He kissed her deeply one last time, then nibbled on her chin, making his way to her neck. He made small circles with his hand, his palm rubbing and teasing her clit as his fingers continued to slide in and out of her wet folds. He sampled the skin under her ear, her flowery scent filling his head when he licked at the pulse pounding in her neck. The combination of all three sensations proved too much, her shallow breaths stopped and she sucked in a breath as the orgasm shook her body.

Alex used her dazed condition to move her further onto the bed. "Condoms?" He asked, moving over her.

"What?"

Grabbing her legs, he chuckled at her dreamy tone, the shaft of his cock parted her slick lips as he moved up and down between the folds. "Do you have condoms?"

She gazed up at him, her eyes heavy and inciting, a silent invitation.

"We're not done yet."

A sly smile tugged at her swollen mouth. "I hope not. Top drawer." She pointed to the bedside table.

Alex felt the muscles in his groin flex as he pulled away. He quickly found what he needed, throwing the remainder of the box on the bed.

Climbing back to join her, he moved over her as she framed his face pulling him down. Grinning, he kissed her lush pink lips. He thought he might have to spark up the heat again but it wasn't necessary, because there was no desire lost between them. God that made him hard, she made him hard.

Eve pulled on his neck wanting more, then raised her hips. Her body called to him the same way her voice did, smooth and seductive and full of promise.

He couldn't wait any longer. She was just too tempting. He bent his knees, spreading her legs apart and slowly entered her, closing his eyes as he sank into her luscious depths.

He kissed her, then sucked in her breath when she raised her hips. Her body clamped around him, silken muscles holding him in place. He pulled out and slowly entered her. Her moist heat welcomed him, gripped him like a wet, slick fist.

"Alex," Eve called out, her breathing coming in fast choppy bursts. He liked hearing that desperate edge to her voice. "Faster, Alex." And she proceeded to wrap her legs around his waist, locking her feet.

He lost a little control after that and drove into her harder, faster, deeper. He kissed her hard, sweeping his tongue in her mouth searching for that heavenly touch. Her breasts skimmed against his chest as she clawed at his shoulders, while she licked and nipped at his at his earlobe. Every time their bodies joined, everywhere she touched, his skin began to tingle and come to life.

"I need to...make me come." It was a whispered command, and one he could do nothing but follow.

Those simple words were his trigger point. He licked two fingers and moved them down between their joined bodies. Moving deeper inside her, he stroked her clit until he felt her dripping core clamp around his cock. She pressed her face into his shoulder crying out as her strong muscles gripped and pulsed around him. Grunting, he held her down and did precisely what he said he would...he fucked her brains out, rammed into her convulsing body over and over, until her cries were overshadowed by his own, until he felt his limbs shake and a savage pulse-pounding sensation had him coming hard and deep.

Chapter Eighteen

It was one thing to find out that the cop who had been hit by the truck had come out of his coma. Shit, who was he kidding? It was great. The cop was never his intended target. But things became entirely different when he saw the cop appear out of nowhere and enter Eve's house.

Crossing his arms, Miles relaxed against the side of the house across the street from Eve Sinclair's house. Until the cop had shown up he was going to leave her be. She was what she appeared to be, a single mom with an eight year old daughter and a physiotherapist that worked with members of the military. A quick tour of her house had proven it to be true.

He had also found out, while researching her background, that she had no prior offences or convictions, she'd been born in England and had moved to Canada when she was young. Although he was unsure how accurate that data was because it stated 1968 as the year of entry into the country. It was probably a typo and should have been entered as 1986 based on her age. It was odd however. He had never run across any problems when dealing with Immigration. This one flag had made him question every other aspect of her life, which was why he was standing across the street in the dark watching her house.

He had also found it curious how she had ran out of the hospital a few days before. When he'd learnt that the cop had awakened from his coma, he'd been surprised to hear that Eve was the only person in the room when he'd woken up. He'd spoken with her patient, Master-Corporal Le Blanc who'd shared the room with Detective Taylor. Le Blanc confirmed that she had stayed behind to finish her notes.

It was interesting how Eve seemed to be in places she shouldn't be. First in Ace's hospital room, then she was in the same room where a man, who was thought to be a vegetable, suddenly woke from a coma. Both of which he was directly connected to and now, the cop showed up at her house. Although, he didn't appear to be invited by the way he had gained entry to the house. Yet, no 911 call had been made because the police hadn't shown up and he knew she wasn't dead because he was picking up movement from two different individuals in her room and they were close, about as close as two people could get.

He lowered the new Refractor scope. A long-range, portable x-ray unit capable of detecting movement through walls and it fit in his hand.

He grinned to himself. Nice toy.

* * * *

Eve was still in the same position on the bed when Alex came out of the bathroom. Grinning, he climbed onto the bed and fell on his back next to her, staring at the ceiling.

After a few minutes he noticed her shiver and, sitting up, pulled back the duvet on her bed. "Get in," he ordered lightly.

She rolled towards him and pushed up onto her knees with the intent of following his order. He stopped her when he saw it. He traced his fingers over the tattoo on the front of her hip. It wasn't big, maybe the size of a two dollar coin. How did he miss this?

Slapping his hand away, Eve reached for the covers. He allowed her to slide into the bed but held the duvet in place when she tried to cover herself. He splayed his hand over her abdomen and touched her painted skin. "What is it?"

She shrugged. "It's just a copy of an old medallion my family owns." She pushed up on her elbows. He didn't miss the uncertainty before she answered him.

Naturally cautious, he studied it closely, knowing Eve wouldn't share the whole truth with him. It was odd looking, like bits of black string woven together forming a complex shape or shapes. There was also strange writing, which formed a circle around it. "What does this writing say?" He traced the words with his finger.

She didn't answer him right away.

"Eve?" he pressed.

"It's my family motto." She was staring at him with a worried expression.

"What does it say?" he asked again.

"It's Scottish Gaelic. It means Commit thy work to God."

Interesting. He glanced at her and back to the tattoo studying the pattern, almost certain there was more to it than just a family heirloom. He bent his head and brushed his lips over it. "It's different. I like it."

"Really? You don't think it's weird?"

"It doesn't matter what I think." He met her eyes. "Tattoos are personal. It only matters that *you* like it." He ran his hand back and forth over her belly. "Do you like it?"

"I need it." She nodded sincerely. "It's very important to me."

Now that was an odd answer. He continued gently touching her body as he studied her expression. He wasn't expecting *need it*. That was a very telling answer. There was something more to this tattoo and he didn't like that she was hiding it from him.

He stroked her belly again, dropped his hand lower, and stopped when he felt a long thin scar resting just above her pelvic bone. He ran his finger along its uneven path. "This was done in a hurry. Noelle?"

"Yes." — she paused, then explained — "I didn't take my mom's death too well and fainted." Her admission caught him off guard, but she was being honest with him, he could tell and he liked that. He pressed his mouth to her skin, realising that Eve had more secrets than he did. He also realised that he wanted to know each one of them.

Eve felt the muscles in her stomach clench when Alex kissed her scar. His mouth lingered against her for a second or two — it was incredibly sensual. Almost as erotic as when she felt his warm breath tickle her stomach. He broke the contact and moved up the bed next to her pulling the covers over both of them. Placing his hand on her hip he rolled her onto her side so she was facing him. He studied her for a long time, a hard, brooding look appearing every so often. That was not a look she wanted to see after they had just made love. So she closed her eyes against his stare and relaxed against the pillow.

"Eve?" he began quietly.

Keeping her eyes closed she answered with a simple, "Mmm."

"Noelle's father isn't in the picture at all is he?"

Okay, she would open her eyes for that question. "No, he isn't. Why?"

"I don't think the father of Jillian's baby is in the picture either." He pulled her close.

His statement confused her. "Okay. What does it matter?"

"I don't think Jillian has anyone to help her with her baby. And even if she did, I couldn't take them to her or her to them, because Miles is hunting her. I can't even risk taking her to the hospital if she delivers early."

"What are you going to do? You must have medical training."

"Not like you." He lowered his head, his gaze burning into hers.

Oh no! She knew what he wanted. When she shook her head, Alex slowly nodded his. "I need your help, Evening."

She groaned as she rolled onto her back. *No!* This was none of her business, she couldn't help. It was too dangerous. This could affect Noelle, *her* baby. Her train of thought stopped.

Baby.

Damn it! "How far along is she?" She left her hand on her forehead as she waited for his answer.

"Close to seven months now, would be my guess. She looks pretty big though."

She turned back to face him. "Are you sure?"

Alex shrugged. "That's what she told me. She's petite, about five foot nothing, with blonde hair and brown eyes..." he trailed off with a puzzled scowl on his face.

"What's the matter?"

He shook his head then flung the covers off and searched the floor until he found his jeans. With two wallets in hand, he got back in bed, throwing the covers back over them. Sitting up, he began pulling the contents from one of the black leather wallets.

"Alex?"

He ignored her, flinging money and credit cards on her bed. She picked up one credit card. "Oh, platinum!" Alex glanced up at her, she nodded her head. "Nice!"

He chuckled, threw the wallet aside and continued searching through the mess on the bed. Eve picked up the second black wallet and flipped it open. A police picture ID card with Cade's face was on one side and a silver badge was on the other. She looked at the photo. It was Cade as she had seen him in the hospital. With brown eyes and sandy blond hair. He had an easy-going look about him, a friendly smile, nice eyes, he was relaxed. She turned to Alex. Same face, same hair, same body. He turned to look at her. But that was where the similarities ended. He narrowed his blue eyes. She doubted if Alex was ever relaxed.

She handed him the badge. "What are you looking for?"

"The one thing I can't find." He reached for the cards and began sliding them back in the wallet.

"And that's...?"

"I have to go," he said suddenly, facing her.

Her heart sank into her stomach almost as fast as he said the words. *Already!* She fought to keep the words inside. She wasn't the type of woman who begged her lover to stay. Besides, she shouldn't really be surprised, Alex flat out said he didn't want to be attracted to her and that he didn't date women with families. Shit, she should be ecstatic, he hadn't killed her and they'd had really hot sex, the hottest.

She inhaled slowly keeping her disappointment to herself, "Okay."

He glared at her, throwing both wallets on the end of the bed. "I can't take you with me."

"Okay." Leaning back she pulled the covers up to her shoulders. Closing her eyes, she automatically lifted her arm above her head and began toying with a strand of her damp hair.

The room was quiet for some time before the bed moved and Alex suddenly pinned her other arm above her head. His heat spread through her while his fingers threaded with hers. "You didn't answer my question." His voice was low.

She blinked up at him. "What question?"

There was a low groan when she licked her suddenly dry lips. His nostrils flared. "I need your help, Evening." He looked at her lips. "Will you help me?" He lowered his mouth, hovering just above hers. His breath warm on her face.

"Why?" she asked, why would he need her help? There was no soul to be called and she had no idea how to fight off a trained killer. The only thing that made sense was her medical background but she hadn't worked as a nurse in a long time.

Not wanting to take any chances, she altered the pitch of her voice lightly—"Why do you need me? What can I do to help besides get in the way?"

He relaxed the full weight of his body onto hers while his face turned dark. "Do not, do that."

His quiet tone startled her enough so that the only thing she could do was stare up at him.

"You don't have to use your voice tricks to get the answers you want." He squeezed her fingers to emphasise his point. "Do you understand me?"

"But you've already lied to me once. I only wanted the truth."

"I was going to give you the truth." His golden brows pushed together, drawing attention to his scar. "I can't promise it will always be that way, but believe me when I say, my intention is only to protect you."

Eve wasn't sure what to believe, but her heart lifted a little in hope when he said that.

"I wasn't trained to deal with pregnancies. It's not something you run across on a battlefield. You've been pregnant and have the basic knowledge to help Jillian if need be. That is why I need your help. Plus—" he paused, but didn't continue.

"Plus what?"

His face went blank when he answered, "I can keep you safe."

Eve couldn't help but gaze around the room. "I'm not safe?"

"You were no longer safe the second Miles saw you in my hospital room." Alex gripped her hands tightly. She wasn't going to like what she was about to hear. "He has already found your house, seen you and Noelle, and watched your daily activities." He threw a leg over hers as she tried to get up. He felt her large breasts graze against him.

"He knows where I live? How do you know that?" Her voice was high.

"Because I saw him watching your house." He saw the panic in her eyes, felt her grip nervously at his hands.

"Noelle," she gasped. "Will he hurt Noelle?"

"No." He gave her a straight-faced lie as he stroked his thumb along the side of her hand. He couldn't stand seeing fear in those lovely eyes—besides, he needed her calm. "He's just curious right now. He wants to know how you know me." The fear was still there. He needed to say something to ease it. "He wouldn't do anything to harm you during the day. Too many people come in and out of here. And I've been here at night, just in case. So, there's no reason to panic."

"That's why you're here? Just in case Miles tried to hurt us?"

This time he told her the truth. "Yes."

She released a breath slowly, the tension along with it. "Thank you." She blinked, adding, "Of course I will help you. I'm a little rusty though, I haven't worked in obstetrical since before I had Noelle."

He gazed into her pretty face, watching as her pupils grew large. "I'm sure you will do fine."

Her hands weren't gripping his any longer, they just sat inside his palms. Lying on his side next to her, Alex felt her full breasts move against his chest when she drew in a shaky breath. The plump skin teased his nipple, causing it to harden. He wanted to kiss her again, wanted to see her shiver. But he needed to head over to Cade's house. "I need to get going. It's better if I go while it's dark."

She ran her tongue along the seam of her mouth. It was as though she knew he couldn't resist her when she did that. "So no one sees you?"

He nodded and tried to block out how the slide of her flesh against his could stir such need deep within him. She paused briefly before moving again, but he didn't like the idea of her not touching him. *Don't.*

"Stop moving," he mumbled, closing his eyes. Her body, the temptation, was becoming too much.

When she became still, his eyes snapped open. "What are you doing?"

"You asked me to stop moving." She stared up at him confused.

"*Don't*. I meant don't stop moving." He covered her mouth with a hard kiss. He didn't wait for her to open her mouth. He did that for her and slid his tongue along the sweet length of hers. She groaned when he covered her and pushed between her legs. Both ripe breasts pushed at his chest when she arched her back, both of them begging to be tasted. He pulled his mouth and hands away from hers and, grasping both, he took his time licking and sucking until they were pink and swollen. She dug her fingers into his shoulder and moaned when he stopped.

Alex flung off the covers as he knelt between her legs and lifted them onto his arms. Leaning above her he captured her mouth in a long probing kiss. He drew in a deep breath and stopped when the smell of her desire filled his nose. His control snapped and he growled in satisfaction when he thrust deep inside her.

Oh God! This is so good. Eve turned her mouth away so she could catch her breath, but every time she tried to, Alex moved, sending a bolt of pleasure through her, causing her body to grip and clench at his...*oh God!*

He reached up and smoothed a thick curl back from her face. His eyes were glowing down at her again and his face was dark. Alex was looking back at her, not Alex inside Cade's body, with Cade's features…but Alex. "You are so fucking wet and hot…so hot. Why can't I get enough of you?"

"I don't know." She cupped his face and traced her thumb along his bottom lip. "Is that so bad?"

He eased out of her and then plunged back in, stealing the air from her lungs. "Yes, it's very bad."

She gasped when he repeated the motion, driving harder into her.

He touched his forehead to hers. "I've lost control with you, I never do that," he informed through clenched teeth, then kissed her hard. He pulled out of her and sat back.

Confused, Eve watched as he reached for the box of condoms and pulled a foil wrapper from the box. He caught her surprised look and raised his eyebrows. "I never lose control." He covered himself quickly and pulled her up so she was facing him.

Clasping her waist, he lifted her above his, now protected shaft and slowly lowered her until he was deep inside her. He grabbed her legs, bent at his sides, and wrapped them around his waist. His hands moved over her, squeezing her behind, forcing her to rock back and forth grinding their bodies together. She held onto his shoulders while he kissed her neck. The pressure from his lips and warmth of his mouth mixed with the rough texture of his stubble caused her to shiver, even though the heat from his body surrounded her. She sucked in a breath when her body tightened in response.

"Lean back," Alex suggested. "Don't worry, I have you." He did have her. In more ways than one.

She did as he asked, rocking her hips.

"Keep moving. Don't stop," he commanded, in a harsh whisper.

She didn't stop, couldn't have stopped even if she'd tried. The pulsing deep within her core was taking over, causing her body to move on its own. Alex tensed at the same moment and pulled her against his chest, wrapping his arms around her. Then the euphoric throbbing was there, shooting its way through her body causing her thighs to tingle and her head to spin. His hand tangled in her hair as he turned her face into the side of his neck muffling her cries. His heavy breathing warmed her shoulder as he groaned out loud. Their hips and bodies moved in rhythm, their orgasms rocking the bed.

Chapter Nineteen

Not that he expected any trouble from the guard at the front door to Cade's building, but Alex clicked off the safety on his gun, out of habit. If there was trouble, he would be prepared, and looking at the young kid behind the counter, he doubted he could pull himself away from his texting long enough to do anything. As it was, he walked through the front lobby without a problem, and only received a nod from the security guard.

Once he reached the fourth floor, he pulled Cade's keys from his pocket and found apartment four-ten. Holding the key ring he systematically began trying each key. He opened the door on the second try and entered the apartment closing and locking the door behind him. He strolled around, taking in Cade and Justine's former life. It was your basic apartment, with a galley kitchen, large dining room and living room combined, a small guest bath and bedroom and a good size master bedroom with its own bathroom. It was nice, low key and low maintenance. It was an apartment that a newly married couple would own before having kids.

Spotting framed photos on a group of shelves, Alex went to investigate hoping to find evidence. A picture with blonde twin girls stared back, they looked to be about ten or so. He picked it up and then picked up the more recent picture sitting next to it with Justine and her twin sister *Jillian*. Their faces were, of course, identical, but their hair was different. Justine's was cut above her shoulders in a straight line, where Jillian's was longer and wavy.

He chuckled, he couldn't help it. "That bitch," he mumbled carefully putting the pictures back.

"Well it's about time you figured it out."

Alex continued to smile as he turned and asked dryly, "Why are you back? Shouldn't you be tormenting a saint or something?"

Justine gave him a sweet smile. "I'm doing that right now, by coming to see you."

Shaking his head, Alex demanded, "So what do you want?"

She ignored his question and walked around the room. "So how's it going with Eve?" She gave him a wink. "She's pretty and a little feisty." She waved her hand. "And that little girl, oh what a cutie."

Why had she been in Eve's house?

She caught his raised eyebrow. "Oh don't worry. They didn't see me. I was just checking up on you, making sure you've got your eye on the ball." She stopped and turned, pointing at him. "The ball is my sister by the way."

Raising his eyebrow a second time, Alex followed her movement as she walked in a circle around the room. "I know you have a lot going on, what with Miles shooting you, and Eve being so stubborn about merging you, and now that you and Eve are..." — she wiggled her eyebrows — "...together. You're now worried that Miles has shown interest in her. But the sooner you get to Jillian, the sooner this will be over. Besides, I don't think she is doing too good." She frowned anxiously at him. "She says she's okay, but I'm not too sure. She needs you and Eve to get up there."

Alex felt the muscles in his back and shoulders grow tight. "This will be over," he repeated. "You're referring to Miles hunting Jillian?"

"Of course! What the hell else would I be talking abo—" She stopped abruptly and glanced up rolling her eyes. "Okay, sorry." She looked back at him and sighed, "I meant what the 'heck' else would I be talking about?" Then, mumbled under her breath, "Geez, it's just a word. But, yes. What did you think I meant?"

The first thing that had come to his mind was that he and Eve would soon be over. He didn't like that idea. It would end eventually and he would be the one to do it, but not yet, he wasn't ready. There was just too much to learn about Eve for it to be over so soon.

Justine floated closer and grinned up at him. "You like her don't you?"

He didn't answer her, just stared as her face went blank. "What?"

Her voice was deep. She rested her hands on her hips still smiling. "You think we haven't been watching you two. We see it, even if you don't." Alex stared into ancient eyes. "If it ends, it will be because of you and you will regret the choice you made."

The old eyes blinked up at him and began to fade.

"Wait," Alex said quickly. They blinked again and Justine's head nodded in jerky movements. "Why do you care?"

The Being using Justine's soul gave him a warm smile. "Because Evening is one of ours." It nodded once again and Justine was suddenly back, blinking and confused.

She threw her head up and yelled, "What the *hell*! I thought we talked about this." Then mumbled, "Saints my ass. They're just a bunch of brats."

He laughed. What else could he do? The situation was spiritual and supernatural, and so fucking weird. If he hadn't been part of it, he would have never believed it. He changed the subject. "This body is bigger than my old one, I need clothes."

Justine sauntered past him. "Come on, I'll set you up real nice."

After a thirty minute debate about what Alex had wanted to wear and what Justine had thought looked good on Cade's body, Alex finally threw a mixture of both styles in the duffel bag Justine had pointed out to him. Lifting the bag Alex asked, "Does Jillian have anything here that she can wear?"

"I was just thinking that." She moved to a lower dresser with six drawers and pointed to the bottom drawer. "I have workout clothes in there, they should be loose enough to fit her and I bought her a cute top and jeans, but I didn't get a chance to give them to her." She smiled sadly and shrugged her shoulders. "They're in the guest room on the bed."

Alex nodded, quickly sorted through what he thought might fit Jillian and then grabbed the bag of new maternity clothes Justine had bought.

Turning at the front door, he stopped and asked, "When was the last time you saw Jillian?" He sat the duffel down.

Justine looked at him warily. "Today."

"Do you talk to her?"

Justine slowly raised her eyes to look at the ceiling. He looked up when he saw her do it and wondered what she saw. He lowered his gaze and waited for her to look at him.

She froze, then sighed in defeat. "Yes. I talk to her." She glanced up one more time then back at him. "I'm not supposed to though. They," — she pointed up — "don't like it. They said I'm supposed to let things happen naturally." He could see the distress clouding her face, the beginning of tears in her eyes. "How can I do that? How can I just let my sister die?" Then, out of nowhere, Cade appeared and walked across the room. He stopped behind Justine and wrapped his arms around her, protectively. "What's wrong?"

She shook her head. "I'm okay, just worried about Jillian."

Cade kissed her head and whispered in her ear, she sniffed nodding her head.

Glancing up Cade asked, "How's the new equipment?"

Alex shrugged. "Little big at first but I filled it quickly enough."

"Good." Cade's face turned serious. "You are going to help Jillian, aren't you?"

Alex immediately caught on to what Cade was doing. "Yes."

"And you will do your best to protect her and her baby, right?" Cade asked still holding Justine.

Alex focused on Justine and answered without hesitation, "Yes."

Cade bent his head down and said gently, "Will you please stop this now? Let Alex do what he was trained to do. He will stop Miles. You have to have faith."

"Oh Geez!" Justine rolled her eyes. "You sound like those guys."

Cade shrugged. "Those guys are pretty convincing when you sit down long enough to listen to them."

"That's the problem." Justine turned throwing her arms in the air. "I just can't sit and wait. I don't have your patience I want my sister safe now."

Cade glared down at his wife. The two stared at each other in silence, then Justine huffed and rolled her eyes again. Watching the couple, Alex got the feeling that they were having an argument he couldn't hear. Finally, Justine sighed and said, "All right." She turned back to Alex and just stared. Cade glared down at the back of his wife's head, crossing his arms.

"Fine," she snapped over her shoulder. "I'll stop bothering you," — she paused — "for now." Then threatened, "But you better help her, or I'll come back and annoy you for the rest of your life."

Alex raised an eyebrow, the same eyebrow at the same moment Cade did. *Whoa!* It was like looking in the mirror. He shook his head. "Tell Jillian to hang on, we'll be there in three days. I need to get a few things together." He didn't mention the things he needed were to do with Miles, and Jillian, and them being in the same area. Justine would flip out and Cade...being a cop would probably insist on helping. *Help.* He didn't need help, what he needed was a cop. He locked his glare on Cade. "You trust your partner?"

"Trevor?" Cade gave him a confused look. "Of course. Why?"

Alex swung the duffel onto his shoulder. "Because I'm having trust issues right now."

Cade didn't ask any other questions. "Trevor's a good guy. If you need him, he will back you up, guaranteed."

Alex studied him. "I hope you're right." *Because if the cop fails me, there will be hell to pay.*

He checked his watch and swore, he had already been gone longer than he wanted, Miles would notice soon. "Gotta go. I have to get back to…" He stopped, when knowing smiles appeared on both Justine and Cade's faces.

Justine wiggled her brows. "Go on, say it." She smirked at him. "You can't hide it from us," she teased. "Because we already know. Ha!"

Cade smiled at him sympathetically while he clamped a hand over his wife's mouth. She wiggled against him but he held firm. "Pay attention," Cade joked. "You may need to do this to yours one day."

Alex laughed out loud as he left the apartment.

* * * *

The last thing Eve remembered was that Alex had kissed her gently on the mouth and had told her that he would be back soon. She hadn't asked where he was going or why, she had been too tired and pleasantly satisfied to even think about such things. That, of course, had changed when she'd awoken and realised he wasn't there. Now she could honestly say — to herself only — that she was worried about him. Then, she would remember his training and she would begin to relax, only for it to start all over again. By the time she got out of bed, dressed and got downstairs she was running late. Noelle came into the kitchen, clearly unaware of the night's events and Eve's confused state.

"Good morn'in, Mum."

"Good morning. How'd you sleep?"

Noelle shrugged. "Good." She reached for the fridge door when the doorbell rang. They both looked at one another. Then back to the door. "Who's that?" Noelle asked.

"I'm not sure." Eve looked to her watch. "Too early for patients."

Noelle shrugged. "Can I get it?"

"No!" Eve caught herself a little too late. "I mean, you decide what you want me to make you and I'll go see who it is." Noelle turned, unaffected by her sudden outburst. Moving towards the front door, Eve felt her eyes grow wide and mouth become dry. A large shadow moved on the other side of the glass pane. Was it Miles? Was he here to kill her and Noelle? Alex said he wouldn't, not during the day, but he had described Miles as desperate and desperate people did unpredictable things.

As she reached the door the large shadow turned, she sighed as she opened the door.

"What's wrong?" Alex entered and quickly closed the door.

She shook her head. "I thought maybe it was Miles." Her face flushed at her admission.

"He left a while ago. He likes to take his kids to school when he's in the area." He held up a large shopping bag. "I thought you might have slept in, so I brought breakfast."

"Oh." Eve blinked. "I wasn't expecting…"

"You're welcome," Alex teased.

"Thank you." He held out the bag, her hand shook as she reached for it.

"Hey," Alex stilled her and pulled her to him by her shaky hand, his heat easing the fear. "Take it easy.

He's gone. And we won't be here tonight." He lowered his voice, "Now introduce me to your daughter."

Breakfast was delicious, and there was lots of it. Fresh bagels with cream cheese, sliced fruit with yogurt, and very tasty latte's. Heavenly after a long night of…

"What time is your bus?" Alex asked Noelle, interrupting her daydream. Eve glanced at her watch. "Oh, you've got five minutes, let's get moving. I'll meet you out on the front porch."

Eve excused herself and quickly ran upstairs. She had been a little embarrassed when Noelle caught her standing in Alex's arms. The look on Noelle's face was a mixture of recognition and confusion but, when she stepped forward and stared at Alex, or rather Cade, as he introduced himself, she blinked wide eyed and gave him a big smile. It was great that Noelle seemed to like Alex. It surprised her a little too. Noelle wasn't the type of kid that just talked to anybody, but she had no problem with Alex.

Then again, Alex was easy to talk to. He had to be, a requirement of his job she supposed. He could probably strike up a conversation with anyone, and yet it seemed personal when he spoke with Noelle. She enjoyed listening to him ask Noelle questions about school and what subjects she liked best. There were many different sides to Alex but she would never have guessed that he was good with kids. She was strangely moved by it.

Stopping behind Alex and Noelle, she watched the two standing together on the porch. Noelle needed a man like Alex in her life. Not the killer, but the man that showed an interest in her, who would talk to her, who wouldn't pretend she didn't exist.

"I'm glad you came back, Alex." Eve's mouth dropped open as Noelle smiled up at him.

Alex looked down, returning the smile. "Me too."

"Why doesn't mom want me to know it's really you?"

"Because she worries about you and she knows I'm not an entirely good guy."

Noelle wrinkled up her face and Eve knew she was confused. "But you're going to stop that guy from hurting us, right?"

"Did you hear me and Eve talking?"

Noelle leant back, shaking her head.

At once Alex squatted down, so he was eye level with her. "It's okay," he soothed. "Tell me, did you see him?" he asked seriously.

Noelle nodded with wide eyes. "Not last night but the night before. He looked in my window."

Eve gasped and went to them. Her body was shaking so badly, as she knelt down next to Alex the she almost fell into him. He wrapped an arm around her waist and held her still. "Honey, why didn't you come and get me?"

Noelle's eyes shifted back and forth between her and Alex. "I don't know." She shrugged. "Maybe I thought it was a dream. But I wasn't scared or anything. I knew Al…I mean Cade was close."

Eve rubbed at her forehead. *Please don't let her have it, please say it stops with me.* She pleaded in her head. "Honey, you saw Alex before today didn't you?"

Noelle's eyes began to fill with tears as she nervously played with her necklace. She shifted her eyes, looking to Alex for help.

"Easy, it's okay. Answer your mum, she deserves the truth," Alex suggested.

"Yes." Noelle wiped the tears with the back of her hands.

"Oh, honey." Eve reached out and pulled Noelle to her. "Of course it's okay. Why didn't you tell me?"

"I thought you might get mad. Gran says you don't like seeing medians, that they scare you."

Eve pushed Noelle back. "Does Gran know you see medians?"

"Yes."

"That old coot." Eve shook her head. Noelle giggled.

"That's what she calls you."

"Well, not quite." Eve rolled her eyes and grabbed Noelle's hands to stop her from tugging on the necklace. "I never want you to hide something that important from me again. Okay?"

"Okay, Mom."

"Good, now it's time to go." She gripped the round charm hanging at the bottom of Noelle's necklace and dropped it inside her shirt. "Get your bag. It's in the front hall."

With Alex's hand on her elbow, Eve stood.

"You're pissed?" he ventured.

Eve really didn't know what she was feeling, she hated the idea of Noelle having this curse, having to go through the rest of her life seeing medians and there was the added kicker that she might be able to see the dead too. What bothered her was the fact that Alex had known that Noelle could see him but he hadn't said anything to her, her own mother. It also bothered her that she had been excluded from their secret. That hurt more.

"You should have told me." The brown of Cade's eyes began to flicker and change to blue. His hair was becoming darker too.

Alex was plainly visible when he finally answered her, "I promised I wouldn't. She was very worried you would be upset with her."

"Of course not. I don't want her to have this, but I would never get upset at her because she did. It's not her fault." She stopped and blinked, surprised. "I can't believe you kept a promise to an eight year old."

Scowling he informed her, "A promise is a promise. Age has nothing to do with it."

"Ready, Mom." Noelle hopped past her and down the porch stairs.

Alex joined Eve and Noelle as they walked to the bus stop. He waited next to Eve as Noelle joined her friends on the bus. She sat at the window closest to them and waved as the bus pulled away. The strangest thing happened then, Alex found himself waving back. He suddenly dropped his arm. This was beginning to feel very domesticated. The family breakfast, walking the kid to the bus, waving goodbye, walking with the wif... He stopped himself from thinking about it. It would not happen. He was not domesticated, not any more, that'd ended the day his parents were killed.

Eve looked up at him. "Alex, what's wrong?"

"Nothing, why?" he snapped. She moved around him, walking back towards the house.

Sighing, he caught up to her and grabbed her hand. The second he touched her she tried to pull away but he held tight. "I didn't mean to snap at you." He waited, wondering if he should tell her what he was thinking about, then decided against it. "We need to get moving. We've only got a few more hours before Miles is back."

"Where are we moving to?" She tried to pull her hand away, again.

"I'm not letting go, so stop it." He kept walking as he spoke. "We're going to my apartment. I need to get a few things."

"You're taking me and Noelle to stay at your apartment?"

"No. You are coming with me. Noelle is going to go to your Grandmother's."

She stopped and whispered, "No." She shook her head, concern on her face. "Noelle has never been away from me, not even for one night. I don't think—"

"She'll be fine. It's only for three or four nights."

"*She* will be fine." She began walking after he gently tugged on her hand. "It's not *her* I'm worried about."

They reached the house and Alex pulled her up the porch steps and through the door. Closing it behind her, he asked, "Why so scared? You won't be alone, I'll be with you."

"It's not that." She moved into her office and stopped in front of the old picture with the tartan border. "Noelle is all I have, besides Gran. I can't protect her if I'm not with her."

Alex stood beside her as she stared at the photo. "Noelle will be safe. Do you want to know why?"

"Yes."

"One, I'm sending her to a place that Miles doesn't know about yet. Two, when he does find out about it, he won't bother wasting time by going out there. Three, I'll make sure both Noelle and your Gran are protected. Does that satisfy you?"

She shrugged. "What other choices do I have?"

"None," he informed. "I will not risk taking Noelle with us, just so you feel better."

Eve pulled her lips into a straight line and turned from him. "Fine. How long will I be gone for? I need to rebook my appointments and pack some clothes."

Chapter Twenty

"So, you've found yourself a new body?" Gran had blurted out the question the second she'd opened the door. Eve had known Gran would notice. She'd known right away that Alex was the soul resting inside Cade's body. But did she have to be so snippy about it?

"Gran," she sighed, marching past the older women and into the house.

"There's my wee girl. Come give your Gran a kiss." Eve turned back in time to see Noelle fly into Gran's open arms.

"Come in, come in." Eve watched as she ushered in Noelle, then glared up at Alex with narrowed eyes. "You too." And walked inside turning her glare on Eve when she passed. "You should know better."

Eve shrugged at Alex as he closed the door and was about to apologise, but there seemed to be no need. Alex was chuckling, clearly enjoying Gran's rude behaviour.

Eve walked into the main sitting area that normally felt like a nice sized room but suddenly decreased in size when Alex entered behind her. He sat next to her on the old pink Victorian chaise longue and watched nervously as he scanned the room.

"Mom says I get to stay here for a few days," Noelle said excitedly.

"Yes. Your mum told me when she called at the last minute." Gran's sarcasm was lost on Noelle but not Eve. She shook her head. Alex grinned. "Come with me and we'll have tea and cookies before your mum and Alex have to leave."

Noelle skipped ahead into the kitchen but Gran looked back and pointed at Alex. "That blond hair and those eyes don't fool me. I can see through that mask you're wearing." Alex chuckled again as Gran left the room to find Noelle.

He examined the room again. He knew something was different about Gran's house, how could he not tell. Coming into this room was like travelling back to the 1880's. Eve's heart started to race but froze in mid beat when he finally commented. "Your Grandmother has a lot of antiques. Why do I have the feeling these are all originals?"

Eve looked around the room, anywhere but at him. "I'm not sure what you mean."

"Let me put it this way." He leaned into her side, his arm resting behind her. His breath was warm against her ear. "Is your Grandmother the origin—?"

"Tea's ready," Noelle called from the kitchen.

Holy cow that was close! Smiling at Noelle as she came back in the room, Eve could feel Alex grip the back of her neck. Not tight, just enough pressure to let her know that their conversation wasn't over.

Damn it! Why does he have to be so persistent? His grip changed and he ran his fingers lightly along the base of her neck. The tender touch didn't fool her—he wouldn't just let it go. He was going to find out eventually.

Noelle placed a plate of cookies in the centre of the table. Alex stood when Gran entered carrying a tray — he took it from her and gently positioned it next to the cookies.

"Well, at least you have proper manners," Gran said approvingly. Sitting back down, Eve saw that he was studying the cups and saucers, a white china teapot with delicate pink flowers and matching cream and sugar bowls. And to top it all off he picked up a silver spoon and twirled it in his fingers.

Alex raised a dark blond brow, giving her a sideways glance. "You know we should probably get going," Eve blurted out.

"No." Alex clamped his hand around her arm and pulled her back down. "We have time for tea."

"Good." Gran sat across from them in one of two identical Victorian parlour chairs. The material on both was in great shape, considering Gran had bought them brand new. Sitting forward, Gran began pouring the tea. The movement made her Sinclair medallion swing foreword. Eve felt her eyes grow wide when the sun caught the pure silver and brought it to life.

Please don't let him notice. She silently prayed.

"That's an interesting charm on your necklace, Dawn," Alex commented as Gran handed him a cup and saucer. Eve shifted her gaze to Gran. *Oh no!*

"Thank you. It's been in my family a long time." Gran passed her a cup and gave her a confused look. She must have seen how panicked she was. She took a slow breath and tried to calm down.

"I have one just like it," Noelle said proudly, showing Alex. He held it in his fingers and lightly stroked the handcrafted silver medallion. "It used to be Mummy's, but she gave it to me to wear. I have to wear it every day."

Eve groaned inward.

Alex smiled at Noelle. "Is it for luck?"

Noelle gave him an honest answer, "It protects me."

Gran looked at Eve, asking without words if Alex knew about the Sinclair secret. She shook her head, hoping Alex wouldn't notice.

Thankfully, Gran stepped in, offering Alex a cookie and changing the subject. "So how long will I have Noelle here for?"

Alex sat back with his very girlie cup and saucer and eyed both women suspiciously. He might not know what her family's secret was right now, but she had a feeling he would know shortly.

* * * *

Sitting four cars back Miles watched as the cop, Cade Taylor and Eve Sinclair weaved their way through the city. Keeping his distance wasn't a difficult task although he was certain Taylor knew he was there. He dropped back another two car lengths and watched as they took another right. He followed them for another ten minutes until they entered an area he was quite familiar with.

They turned into the underground parking garage of The Platinum Galley—a modern glass and silver building on the expensive side of the city, where playboy hockey players and mistresses of the well-to-do lived. Every apartment claimed to have the same luxuries as a penthouse and were said to be twice the size. It was for the very stylish, and the very elite.

There was only one person that lived in this building that wasn't a millionaire and he'd blended in perfectly with the rich, which had most likely been due to his upbringing. You learnt to work the rich when you had wealthy parents. So he'd never had to fool the other tenants into believing he was one of them, because really he was one of them.

Pulling a U-turn, Miles parked on the main road in front of the building. He had a clear view of the lobby and waited to see if Taylor and Eve would come and ask for help. They would have to. There was no other way to get up to the apartments unless you had a pass code for the elevators.

Waiting, he looked at the giant building. He had always been jealous that this identity had been assigned to Ace. He'd wanted to live the good life, even if it had been for appearances. But he would never have been able to pull it off. The rich always seemed to know he wasn't one of them.

Five minutes had passed since they'd driven into the underground parking lot and he still hadn't seen them in the lobby. How in the hell did this cop get a pass code? He mumbled to himself as he switched off his engine. "And what do you want in Ace's apartment?"

Eve didn't get a chance to get a good look at the building, but it seemed very upscale. Her suspicions were confirmed when they entered the garage. There were high end cars in every stall. BMWs, Mercedes, Porsche, a few old muscle cars in pristine condition and a couple of new sports cars as well. If the cars were any indication about the people that lived in Alex's building, he had some very wealthy neighbours. He pulled into a numbered stall, shut off the engine, and got out. Eve followed, not knowing what else to do. He hadn't talked to her much on the way here. He was stewing over something, she could tell by the annoyed look he kept giving her. She hoped it wasn't about the medallions. Yet what else could it be? He'd recognised Gran's medallion, then studied the one she had given to Noelle, running his finger over it like he had on the tattoo version on her hip. Now he was probably trying to figure out what was special about them.

She opened the back door and reached for her bag.

"Leave it, we're not staying."

"Oh. Okay." She shut the door. "Should I stay here then?" she asked with her hand on the car.

"No." He shook his head. "I want you with me, I'll need your help."

She nodded and joined him at the end of the car. He turned from her and began walking towards a set of elevators. She saw him punch a code into a pin pad and the doors slid open.

Holding the door, he waited for her to enter and stepped in behind her. He hit the button for the fourteenth floor and leant back against the mirrored wall. Eve moved to the other side and tucked herself into the corner. She felt him staring at her, but couldn't face him and focused on the floor numbers. There was a strange vibe between them right now and it unnerved her. Was it going to be this way until he asked her about the medallions or was he waiting for her to tell him? The idea of both made her nervous.

The doors slid open on the fourteenth floor and she followed him down the hall where they passed only one other apartment, before rounding a corner where a single door stood. Eve looked back down the hall, judging the distance between the doors. *Wow!* These apartments were huge.

As she turned back to Alex she noticed the fire exit was opposite his door. "That's handy," she commented.

Alex looked over his shoulder and then at the fire exit where Eve was pointing. "That was on purpose."

Of course, someone like Alex would need multiple exits.

After entering a code into a second number pad, the door to the apartment opened. Alex stood to the side waiting for her to enter. Her jaw dropped open when she walked in. A wall of windows, floor to ceiling, covered the entire outside wall of his apartment.

She slipped out of her shoes and asked, "May I...?"

"Go ahead."

She walked over to the windows and blinked, surprised. "What a beautiful view." She could see the canal and the paths that ran beside it, the fall colours spreading through the trees. The low lying mountains and ski hills were visible in the distance. "I would love to see this every day."

"It's okay." He stood beside her, inspecting the view. "The novelty wears off after a while and you begin to take it for granted."

"I wouldn't. My view is old Mr Moyer's house. He sometimes comes out only wearing his boxers." She looked up at him. "He's seventy-five. It's not a nice view."

Alex shook his head fighting to hide his smile. He was trying to stay pissed at her. She was hiding something important from him, something that had to do with the tattoo on her hip. But it was nearly impossible to remain angry when she looked at him or talked to him... Talk. He narrowed his eyes, scanning her face. Was she trying to use her voice to ease the tension between them? He took a breath. No. He didn't feel that seductive pull which normally accompanied her words. There were no tricks this time. It was just Eve.

She moved away from the windows and walked around, inspecting the apartment. "This is really nice. Very sleek and modern. Why all the grey?"

"It came this way."

"You bought it like this?"

"No." He followed her through the long galley kitchen — watching as she ran her fingers along the polished cement counters. "It was issued to me."

She glanced back over her shoulder as she found the hall to the bathroom and bedroom. She stopped and turned to face an oversized mirror that hung on the wall opposite the bedroom door studying it. "Issued? What does that mean?"

"When you join the military you're issued kit," he explained, watching her. She knew there was something odd about the mirror. Would she guess what it was? He watched her closely. "Boots, clothes, guns. Once my service is over, this apartment will be re-issued to another serving member."

Shaking her head, she turned to the bathroom and peeked inside mumbling, "Guess I should have taken the recruiting guy that came to my school more seriously."

He followed her to the bedroom watching the sway of her hips and stopped behind her in the doorway.

"Wow! This is quite the boring room."

"It's used for sleeping. I don't want it exciting."

She walked over to the long black dresser and picked up a business card with a pair of lips created out of bright red lipstick smeared on it. She held it up and waved it at him. "Not only sleeping I see." She flicked the card with her fingers. "One of many conquests I assume." Then dropped the card back on the dresser.

"Not so many."

He grinned when he heard her snort, "I doubt that."

She sighed and went to move past him. He shifted his body blocking her escape. "Well then you would be wrong. The women I date want exactly what I want...sex. Nothing more, nothing less." He kept pace with her when she backed away.

"I've made certain of it or I wouldn't have been with them. I can't be with a woman that has a family or wants a family, so that limits the playing field."

By the time Eve was done backing up, he had followed her clear across the room and pinned her against the window. He placed a hand on either side of her head. "I have a family," she pointed out.

"Yes." He stared at her lush mouth. "I've met them."

"Why did we have sex, if you don't want to be near women that have or want families?" She tried move under his arm, but he caught her by the waist and held her against the window.

"I don't know." He glared down at her, trying to figure out that very reason. "You're different."

She scowled up at him. "Different how?"

He scanned her face, touched her bottom lip with the pad of his thumb, enjoying that familiar tingle. "I don't know," he sighed. "It's hard to describe this feeling I have." He focused on her hazel eyes, loving the green slivers in them. "It's almost as if I'm drawn to you. As if you have some power over me."

She shook her head, eyes wide. "I haven't done anything to draw you to me. Not my voice, nothing. I didn't do anything, and I didn't ask for this, so just leave me alone if you want."

"That's the problem." He lowered his face, his nose an inch away from hers. "I just can't leave you alone. I can do it with any other woman. But not you." His words turned hard. "I hate that you have lied to me and I hate that you are hiding something from me. Normally, I would just leave, but I can't. I want you, but I don't want to want you."

Tears shimmered to the surface of her eyes. An earthy mix of hurt and anger. "Yah." She inhaled a choppy breath. "You've mentioned that." She pushed hard at his shoulders, forcing him to back up, then marched out of the room. He stared out the window until he heard the bathroom door shut. "Fuck," he swore under his breath.

They needed to get moving. Staying in the apartment Miles knew about was not the best scenario and, if his gut feeling was right, Miles was out there right now, watching the building. He needed to get his bug-out pack and get Eve the hell away from here.

He stopped outside the bathroom door, heard splashes of water and the faint sound of a sniff. He sighed again. He hadn't meant to say those things to her, hadn't meant to hurt her. She stirred things around in him, made him want things he would never allow himself to have. Made him crave the things he'd lost.

Another sniff. His chest constricted.

"Fuck," he swore again and opened the door.

Eve's red eyes grew angry. "Go away," she said, slapping at his hands. Nothing was going to deter him, he'd caused this hurt and he was responsible for healing it.

Pulling her into his arms, he pressed his lips to her ear and gave her the same answer he had every other time she had given him that command, "No." He tightened his hold, moulding her body to his. "I don't understand what is happening to me or why I lose focus and all I can think about is you." He cupped the side of her face as he looked into her watery eyes. "I'm trying to do the right thing. Jillian is out there waiting for me to save her and all I can think about is how good it feels when you wrap yourself around me. How sweet your mouth tastes." He sighed, lowering his head. "How much I want to be in you right now." He pressed his mouth to hers, gently at first, to heal the pain he'd caused. When she exhaled and hooked her hands around his neck, he kissed her with the full force of his need.

With their mouths fastened together, Alex lifted her off the floor, her legs dangling as he carried her into his bedroom. Once they reached the side of the bed they began pulling at each other's clothes. Eve tugged on his shirt and, with his help, pulled it over his head. Eve lost her sweater and pants seconds later, then he forced her back on the bed. Standing between her bent legs he unbuckled his belt, then jeans, stopping when he saw her shift her hips and run her hands over her thighs. A low groan escaped his throat as he covered her body.

Eve moaned when Alex drove his tongue deep, sliding over hers in heart-stopping slow strokes. His touch caused her belly to tighten and her insides to ache. Never had kissing got her this hot. This only happened with Alex, his lips and mouth alone accomplished the task.

She broke away from his mouth and licked the outer edge of his ear, followed by sucking his earlobe between her teeth. He moaned into the side of her neck, thrusting against her wet folds. Next, she kissed his neck, breathing in his potent scent of sweat and desire. Wow, he smelt so good. She nipped at his shoulder, tasted his skin. He groaned and began tugging at her damp panties. She chuckled when he tried to get them down her legs without breaking contact with her body.

He pushed up onto his arms and glared down at her. "It's not funny," he growled. "I need you Eve."

Running her hands down the sides of his neck, she stroked the solid muscles of his shoulders and pushed. He didn't move. Clinging to his neck she pulled herself up and kissed him hard, then broke the contact and very carefully, added a soothing lilt to her words, so that he would do as she asked but not notice her influence. "Please stand up," she asked, her lips stroking his.

His exhale was full of frustration but he complied with her request.

Once he was standing in front of her, she knelt on the bed, touched his chest, stroked the tense muscles. She ran her fingers over the small bullet holes that now appeared on Cade's body. Alex's soul was so strong that he had imprinted himself onto the body he now resided in, every important feature that was Alex was now also part of Cade's body. A hand clamped down over hers the instant she touched the scar. She met Alex's intense stare. Her heart raced as his dark slashing brows gave him a menacing appearance. He shook his head in warning. It was then that Eve realised his wounds were still fresh and tender and very much a part of him, regardless of them now belonging to a different body.

The need to heal his body as well as his soul rose quickly. But how? She would normally talk to him, help heal him from the soul out, except she would need to put a great amount of force behind her words in order to help him, a slight push wouldn't do it, he was too aware of her abilities. Plus, he had already warned her not to use them on him. She looked up at him, then his bare chest. Before the idea came into full view, she had placed her lips over the scars and lightly kissed them, letting her mouth linger on his skin. Pulling away, she looked up at him feeling a little embarrassed. She had no time to dwell on it because he cupped the side of her face, and with a dazed expression, gently pulled her back to his chest. Eve closed her eyes. She kissed his chest again, ran her tongue over the small scars tasting his skin. As she continued to press her lips to his skin she skimmed her hands over his hard chest muscles and sculpted shoulders, down his arms, over his belly and every place she touched she could feel the muscle beneath his skin tighten.

Kissing her way to his stomach, she stopped and slid his zipper down. She locked her eyes on his as she lowered his jeans and boxers over his hips and thighs. She couldn't look away from him as she clasped the hard length of him in her hand. The look he was giving her was mesmerising, even a little dark, but what kept her entranced was the tenderness she saw.

Alex felt his legs shake when Eve closed her mouth around his cock. The heat from her mouth had him melting, but that was minor in comparison to when she moved her warm tongue over the tip, sending excruciating pleasure though his groin and down his legs. He reached out. Touching her face, he felt his fingertips tingle. He brushed his hand over her soft curls.

Once again, the muscles in his chest tightened and his stomach felt heavy. It was the same feeling he'd had when she kissed the scars on his chest. He thought it was a one-time thing. Yet here it was again, making his body and soul crave her.

What the hell was she doing to him? How...why was he allowing this to happen? He had to stop. This wasn't fair to her, giving hope where there wasn't any. It wasn't fair for him either. What if something happened to her? He honestly didn't know how he would handle losing another person he cared for. Eve's mouth pulled hard, the suction driving away all thought.

Tangling his fingers in her hair he allowed another few seconds then pulled at her. Her eyes were heavy with lust when he picked her up and stood her on the bed in front of him. He pulled her mouth down to his. He kissed her hard, he knew, but couldn't help it, she was just...she made him feel...he ran his thumbs over her smooth cheeks. She made him *feel*.

Her breasts brushed his chest, teasing him. He unclipped her bra and bent, capturing a rosy tip in his mouth, sucking it to a swollen peak. She moaned when he repeated the torment and wrapped her arms around his head, forcing more of her into his mouth. Her hips rocked against him. His cock swelled with her desire. He loved how uninhibited she was, if she liked something he was doing to her, she told him, not with words but with her body.

Tugging on the sides of the lacy material he pulled her moist panties down her legs. She stepped out of them and he tossed them away. Lifting her against him, he forced her to wrap her legs around his waist and lowered her onto the bed. Once again, he was face to face with her beautiful breasts. He cupped and squeezed, licked and nibbled until she was pulling at his shoulders. Then, holding her hands at her sides he moved down her body, kissing every inch of her smooth skin. He circled her tattoo with his tongue and grinned when her body tensed. She tried desperately to tug her hands away but he laced their fingers tightly together, stroking his thumbs over the backs of her hands until she stopped fighting him. He dipped lower and kissed her inner thigh, watching as goose bumps appeared on her skin after the second kiss.

Taking a deep breath, he drew her sweet scent, felt his cock throb, his muscles stiffen. Her hips rolled in anticipation when he blew warm air over her moist folds. Watching her hips move enticingly became too much. He pressed his mouth to her glistening lips and groaned when he tasted her.

Many times, Alex brought her to the height of a climax only to take it away and begin again. And every time Eve sucked in a breath and shivered. He sucked on her clit and moaned, the vibration had her hips squirming against his face. "Alex," she panted. "I can't...it's too much." She gripped his hands and tried to pull him up. He was torturing her with his mouth. She pleaded, begged for him to finish her. "Alex please." Her breath caught when he slipped two fingers deep and quickly made her come. It was like nothing she had ever felt. The sensation was so intense, she cried out, her hips bucking of their own accord.

Eve ran her hand over her face. She was shaking. Alex had tormented her for the longest time. Yet each time he did, the sensation grew to the point, that when she finally came, it almost shattered her into tiny pieces.

She was vaguely aware of the rustling of clothes, then heard the tearing of a wrapper. Alex joined her back on the bed and nudged her legs apart. She opened them for him without hesitation. He braced his arms on either side of her head, looking down at her with a satisfied grin.

"What?" A blush flushed her cheeks.

He lowered his head, his mouth hovering above hers. "You taste good."

"I do?" She sighed, feeling his heat seep into her skin.

"Mmm. Like sex and honey, but better." He kissed her. Long and slow until her body was aching for more. "How about a ride?" he asked, nibbling on her lip while she tried to catch her breath. "Ride?"

The only warning he gave was a deep chuckle before he rolled onto his back. Seated now on top of him Eve pouted down at him, doing her best to play innocent. "I'm not sure what to do."

Alex raised a dark eyebrow. He gripped her hips in his big hands, raising her just above him.

She slowly lowered herself over him stopping just before he entered her, then pulling away. "Oops. I missed," she teased. He grabbed her hips again forcing her down onto him but she held firm. "Let me try again." This time she took a little more of him in and pulled away. "This is harder than it looks." She gave him a wicked smile.

She knew she had pushed him too far when his nostrils flared and his hands gripped her hips painfully. He thrust deep inside her. The sensation was so overpowering her head rolled back at his delicious invasion and she groaned in ecstasy. He tugged her down and nipped at her ear. "Don't tease me Eve, fuck me."

Her heart jumped at the passion in his voice and her body trembled. Without any hesitation she did as he asked, moving hard and fast, bracing herself against his chest and shoulders. He slid his hand into her hair and pulling her face to his, he kissed her hard, his lips bruising hers.

Panting, she had to pull away, she couldn't breathe. She sat back and closed her eyes, rocking her hips and covering his hands with her own when he touched her breasts. The steady movement of their bodies grinding together was all-consuming. His hands on her, stroking and cupping, their bodies joined as one. His lips pressed firmly against her. She never wanted it to end.

She locked eyes with him, his look dark and full of need. He tugged her forwards brushing his lips tenderly against hers. At that moment, little wings brushed the inside of her stomach.

"Now," he growled out. "Give it to me now." He clamped down on her hips and forced her to move fast. When her body began to throb, Alex was there, rolling her onto her back, forcing her thighs apart, driving into her harder and harder.

"That's it," he groaned with satisfaction. "I love how tight you are."

She cried out this time as he continued to plunge into her, pushing her body far beyond it's normal limits and she loved it, she wanted more. She wanted him to move faster, harder. She raised her hips meeting his every time he drove into her, wanting, no…needing him deeper. When she didn't think she could stand another minute of his passionate onslaught, Alex's sweat covered body stiffened as he covered her mouth in one more heart-stopping kiss before he called out her name, his entire body shaking.

Chapter Twenty-One

"Bored yet?"

Jillian lowered the book to her chest and glared up at her sister. "I'm reading a book on the evolution of weapons during warfare... Yes I'm bored!"

Justine laughed, perching herself on the end of the long couch as she gazed at her sister. "But you're lounging and taking it easy. Something the doc said to do a while ago if I'm correct."

"It's hard for me to sit still. You know that, we're the same." Pressing her hand to her head she asked, "Is it still like that...?"

Justine waved her hand. "Of course. Except I'm not just driving Cade or mum and dad crazy, I've upped my game to angels."

Jillian felt her mouth drop open. "Are you serious? Angels?"

Justine narrowed her eyes. "Or they could be Saints. They certainly have the patience for it. Well they do with me anyways. Not that I'm giving them much choice in the matter."

Jillian shook her head, giggling. That was Justine, always pushing the boundaries or in this case patience and smiling while she did it. She was blessed with an outgoing personality, with a hint of troublemaker thrown in for good measure. She loved that about Justine. If it hadn't been for her sister, she would never have experienced half the things she had done in her thirty years—trips out west backpacking through the Rockies, white-water rafting, skydiving and getting matching tattoos.

Tears unexpectedly filled her eyes. It was all over now. No more midnight phone calls, no more sappy movie nights, no one to share her fears with over the baby, no crazy aunt for her baby to get to know and love.

"Jill?" Justine appeared next to her, sitting cross-legged on the floor. "Why so sad Jilly?"

"Because, I have no one to have sappy movie nights with any more or talk to about all the weird things this baby is doing to my boobs and the rest of me. You're dead…" She covered her face as she began to cry.

"Don't do that, Jilly," Justine soothed. "You'll find someone else to have sappy movie nights with."

"Who?" she sniffed wiping her eyes. "Cade? He isn't going to want to do that."

Justine gave her sad smile, not agreeing or disagreeing with her, leading her to believe she was right. Would Cade even want to be around her when he woke up?

"Have you seen Cade? How is he?"

Justine just gave her another smile, which confused her. "Don't worry about Cade, you just worry about yourself. Okay?" Jillian nodded.

"Good. Now can I make a suggestion?" Justine began. "Enjoy the large knockers, who knows how long they will last."

Jillian burst out laughing and swiped at her eyes again. "What's going on with Alex? Has that Eve chick got him in his body yet?"

"Ah!" Justine paused then nodded. "He's in a body."

Jillian pushed up and sat back against the couch, nervous excitement making her smile. "Great, so he's on his way."

"Not yet, he said he needed to get a few things together. He said they'd be here in three days."

Dropping her head back, she sighed, "Three more days of reading tactical books, geez at this rate I'll be qualified to join the army soon." She lifted her head. "*They'd* be here in three days? Who's coming with him?"

Justine gave her a wicked grin. "Eve's coming with him."

"Oh!"

"Oh is right. Those two are finally getting along...really well."

"Oh yah?" Jillian rolled onto her side pushing herself up, then propped her feet on the coffee table.

"Yah! You should see those two, very hot!"

"You watched them?" Jillian giggled. "You perv."

"Not all of it," Justine admitted sheepishly. "But let me tell you, there is more than hot sex between those two, much more."

* * * *

Alex watched Eve as they dressed in silence. Her mouth was dark pink and swollen and so was the rest of her. Had he been that rough with her? He couldn't

231

remember. The only thing he remembered was how she'd touched him, how her mouth and body had tasted, how her tight, hot body had gripped him. She pulled her sweater over her head and walked out of the room towards the bathroom. He grabbed her before he knew why.

"Evening?" He turned her, searching her face. He framed her cheek when she flushed in response. "Thank you. I feel…" He shook his head not knowing how to describe what he felt. It was as though he had been fighting to breathe but didn't know until he took his first real breath. He looked at her realising that, whether he wanted it or not, Eve was healing him like she had the other soldiers. He sighed, "I feel."

With the green flecks in her eyes twinkling, she gave him a tender smile. "You're welcome."

He pulled her into his arms, her head resting against his chest. "I got a little forceful when you teased me. I hope it didn't scare you."

She giggled but gave no response. "Eve?" He forced her away from him, annoyed, but he lost a little steam when a curl fell in her face. She was still giggling. "What does that mean? Did I…hurt you?" It was never a question he had asked any woman before, there had never been a need before. He hated that there was a need to ask it now.

"No." She touched the side of his face. "You didn't hurt me, not at all. I was just giggling because, I really liked it," she admitted then shrugged, "Guess that makes me a slut."

He laughed, relieved by her admission. Her words and actions had eased his pain and fears and she made him feel…again.

"Are you done getting dressed? We should get moving." Alex asked, stepping away and taking his heat with him. Why did she always seem to notice his heat?

She needed to use the bathroom and agreed to meet him in the kitchen when she was done. When she entered the kitchen a few minutes later, she found a green duffel bag on the floor, but no Alex.

She was about to call out when his hand went over her mouth. He pressed his lips against her ear. "Shhh. We have a visitor." He pointed to the front door, shoving her purse and shoes into her hands. He reached down, grabbed the duffel, and clasped her arm, pulling her behind him. Stopping in front of the oversize mirror next to the bathroom, Alex traced his fingers behind the frame and stopped, a muted click filled the area surrounding them. The word PASSCODE appeared in a red glow on the mirror. He leant forward and spoke in a low voice. "Delta-Charlie-eight-seven-three-nine-one." There was another click and the mirror swung away from the wall.

"Holy cow!" she whispered, then covered her mouth with her hand. He grinned at her as he helped her step through the wall and into the narrow opening. She pinned herself against the wall when he closed the door and waited silently in the dark. She heard a snap and Alex shaking something—a green fluorescent glow lit the way. "Hand," he ordered. She held out her hand and he clasped it in his, tugging her down the black passage.

They hadn't walked twenty steps when Alex stopped at a dead end. He pushed against the wall blocking them and it swung open into a room about the size of Alex's bedroom, minus the windows and bed and any other furniture except a steel work bench. The walls were covered with steel cupboards and each one had a lock, as did the matching cupboards that sat on the floor. He dropped her hand and flipped on the light as he moved into the room.

Throwing the duffel onto the bench, he quickly moved to a keyboard and flat screen. He punched at the keys and four pictures appeared on the screen – two of the hallway outside of Alex's apartment, and two inside the apartment.

Eve joined him and watched the screen. A man moved quickly past the hidden cameras. She didn't see him again. But knew he was close because a warning flashed onto the screen. The word MOVEMENT, flashed repeatedly at the bottom of screen.

"Is it Miles?" she whispered her question.

He nodded, staring at the screen. "You can talk normally in here."

"How did he know where to find us?" She turned and watched as he moved away and opened the cupboard closest to them. She found herself moving to the other side of the room when she saw the knives lined up on the wall next to a variety of small hand guns. Her heart began pounding in fear as he reached for a pair of short handled silver knives.

"I saw him following us, plus there is probably a tracking device in your…" He turned to face her but stopped when she wasn't there. He slowly scanned the room until he locked Cade's eyes on her. "Eve?" When he moved towards her still holding the knives, she stumbled back, bumping into the wall.

How could she have forgotten that this man was a killer? He killed dangerous people to protect society, sure, but he was still a killer. He stopped and studied her briefly before placing both knives on the bench behind him. He sighed and leant back.

Eve peeked at his face and saw his eyes were blue and the scar was running through his left brow. "I shouldn't know about this place, should I?"

He simply shook his head.

She began to panic. "I shouldn't be in here." She leaned towards the door. "I'll wait in the hall."

"No you won't. It's not safe for you in there, it's not soundproof." Her pulse pounded in her neck as he crossed the room. Her breath was coming in short choppy bursts.

He stopped in front of her and glared down, his blue eyes glowing. "Stop it right now!" he commanded. "If I'd wanted to kill you, you would already be dead and this—" he waved his finger between the two of them, "—wouldn't be happening." He sighed, running a hand through his darker hair. "I don't understand where this is coming from. We just had sex, I assumed we were good."

"We…I…those." She pointed over his shoulder to the weapons in the cupboard. He quickly grabbed her hand and pulled her forwards. "Calm down." He fixed his eyes on hers and encouraged patiently, "Try again."

"We are good." She swallowed and looked over his shoulder. "It's just that seeing all those guns, scares the shit out of me. They reminded me what it is you do and that scares me too."

"Evening." He tugged her closer, fixed his intense eyes on her. "Do you really believe that would I hurt you because you know about my weapons vault?" There was a look of insult on his face.

She pressed her lips together and shrugged, not sure what she felt.

Alex turned away from her and grabbed the knives, flipping them closed as he watched the screen. He reached up and pulled a sliver gun and corresponding clip from the cupboard. He checked the gun and loaded the clip before sliding it into the back of his jeans.

He was quiet as he worked, moving with precision as he filled his duffel with a variety of smaller weapons, the corresponding bullets, and a stack of small disks — leaving five on the bench next to him. He opened another cupboard that housed a safe and opened that too, pulling money, along with an assortment of ID's. Eve stood watching his back and, after debating with herself, she said, "I won't tell anyone."

"I know," he answered, sliding a black rifle into a basic canvas case. "You can keep secrets better than anyone I know. It annoys the hell out of me. Then again, if I had your ability, I would keep it to myself too."

He was so damn reasonable about it, it made her feel all that more guilty about being scared of him. "Thank you for understanding."

"What's to understand? Just because I know where you're coming from doesn't mean I like you keeping secrets from me." He assessed her over his shoulder. "You will tell me eventually, but now isn't the time — we have to go." He tapped the lower right side screen. "Miles has found the entrance to the vault. It won't take him long to get in."

Eve moved next to him to watch the screen, he could smell her light scent. "How do we get out?"

"I have an exit into the hall from this room." He pointed to a tall storage cabinet. "Behind it."

He scanned her face. Damn she stirred him up. He understood that his life was scary and he had scared her in the past, but with the recent time spent together he'd thought she had got past it. Realising now that she hadn't, he wanted to do whatever it took to help her come to terms with it. Though why he needed to do that, he had no idea.

He took her purse from her and ordered, "Put your shoes on." As she did so, he went through her purse until he found her wallet.

"What are you doing?" She stood next to him watching as he opened and pulled all her cards from her wallet.

"I've let Miles follow us this far." He studied the black strip on the back of a card. "I don't want him following us to my apartment." Nothing, then he picked up the next one.

"But, we're at your apartment."

He grinned, picking up the next card. "We're at the one he knows about." Nothing still. He went through every piece of plastic in her wallet and held up the last one, a credit card. "Here it is."

"What?" Eve leaned in closer and gasped when he peeled off a clear strip of tape with a black line running through it from the back of her card. "What is it?" she asked.

He held it up. "This is a shadow strip. It sticks to the magnetic strip on your credit card. It's easy to use and very hard to see if you're not looking for it. We can follow you via GPS with this and it will inform us of any purchases you make."

"What like gas or something?"

"Yes, but in most of my cases it's usually guns and ammo, sometimes large plastic bags or dissolving chemicals and medical supplies."

"For serial killers?" she whispered.

"Sometimes, but in your case Miles is using it to follow you and if, by some chance, he loses you, any purchases you make will send him your location immediately."

"This is really high-tech. I had no idea there were such things available."

"It's not available commercially." He began putting her cards back into her wallet.

He picked up a school picture of Noelle that had slipped from her wallet. "She looks like you, especially the eyes and hair," he commented, handing her the picture. "The rest must be her father."

"Yah," she said lovingly, and for some reason that pissed him off.

Eve tossed the rest of her belongings into her purse and threw it over her shoulder grabbing Noelle's picture in her hand. "I'm ready whenever you are."

Moving to the passage between the vault and the main apartment, he grabbed two micro mines, opened the door and threw one down the dark hall. The tiny red light flashed indicating where it had landed. Satisfied he tossed the second just inside the door and closed it behind him.

"What were those?" Eve asked, standing next to the storage cabinet.

"Micro mines." He grabbed the remaining three and placed them around the room.

"As in bombs?" she asked slowly.

"As in micro bombs. They're small,"—he held one up—"Light weight, easily concealed but they make a hell of a mess." He opened the DVD drive of his computer and placed the last bomb on the tray, then watched as it slid back into the hard drive. "When they go off, nothing in this room or the apartment will be identifiable."

"You're going to blow up your apartment?" Her eyes were huge.

He laughed. "I don't want to. It will attract more attention than I want, but I can't risk Miles getting in here and seeing my hard drive."

"Why?"

"Because," —he hit a button on the keyboard and his bedroom appeared—"there is footage on there of you and I..." he felt his chest squeeze, then sucked it up and said it, "...making love. Nobody gets to see that except us, and I don't have time to make a copy." He gave her a teasing wink when her face flushed.

"Oh! Good thinking." She took a deep breath. "What's going to happen when we leave?"

Alex shouldered the duffel and rifle case. "When I tell you it's safe, we are going to go through this door, out into the hall where we will turn left and head to the elevator. The mines will go off in the hall that lead in here, first." He pointed to the hall that connected his apartment to his weapons vault. "Then the ones I hid around the apartment and then finally the weapons room."

She interrupted him, "You hid some around your apartment?"

He nodded. "When you were in the bathroom."

"You knew he would come, didn't you?"

"Yes." His frankness sent shivers down her arms and legs.

"Easy. By the time they go off we'll be in the fire escape on the far side of the building."

"What will happen to the building? I have this picture of a massive explosion in my head."

"No, nothing like that. This apartment was set up with a backup sprinkler system and is re-enforced, besides the mines aren't that strong, they can't blast through the extra concrete that surrounds this apartment."

Eve jumped when a loud, thundering blast sent a small dust cloud under the door leading to the passageway.

Calmly Alex grabbed her arm — "It's time to go." — and dragged her behind the tall cabinet and into a small black room. He closed the door behind them just as the second blast went off. The walls and floor shook for a long time until Alex slid his arm around her waist, "Relax, we're okay. Stop shaking."

"Oh-kay."

He pressed his mouth to her head. "Eve, slow breaths. I don't want you passing out on me."

She made an attempt to do as he asked, but found shaking much easier.

Standing in the dark, Alex shoved her behind his back. "Do exactly what I tell you, no questions. Understand?" The words, said between clenched teeth, were not meant to be questioned.

She touched his back so she knew she wasn't alone. "Y-yes." She couldn't see his face but guessed it was set as hard as his words.

The muscles in his back and shoulders flexed once. "Let's go," — was the only warning he gave before the door flew open. He focused on the hall leading towards the apartment and began pulling her out when the first bullet flew past.

With the silver gun already in hand, Alex shoved her across the hall away from him and ordered, "Fire exit, move." She saw him firing back before turning.

Moving back along the hall towards Alex's apartment with her ears ringing and her heart pounding, Eve tried not to look back but desperately wanted to know if Alex was all right. She heard more gunfire and flinched, ducking her head low when she thought she felt the air around her head stir. She made it to within a few feet of the fire exit, when she felt a sharp sting to her thigh.

She tripped and stumbled to the floor, Noelle's picture flying out of her hand. She panicked when she saw Noelle's face smiling back at her, and for some reason which made no sense, she knew she needed to have that picture with her. She crawled, reaching the picture and grabbed hold before standing up. As she stood she saw that she was right at the opening to the small hall leading to Alex's apartment, with the fire escape behind her.

Hearing Alex's voice, she turned and saw him running towards her. That was when she remembered that Alex said the mines in his apartment would go off after the passageway. She turned as fast as she could and reached for the exit but it was too late. Everything went black.

Chapter Twenty-Two

All Alex saw was Eve get picked up and slammed into the door of the fire escape. Her shoulder and the side of her body taking the full force of the blow. Miles fired another couple of rounds as smoked filled the hall. Alex swung around, dropped to his knees and fired back grazing his shoulder. He stared at his partner. "That's one," he called out, "I owe you two more." Miles clamped his hand over the wound, giving him a hard look. Shock drained the colour from his face and he staggered back just as the mines went off in the weapons room.

Mine number one in the vault exploded through the door and out into the hall, knocking him against the wall. He picked himself up and dived for cover before the second and third mines went off.

Alex didn't have time to enjoy the look of alarm on Miles' face. He quickly turned to Eve and felt his heart seize up on him as he ran to her. She was laying on the floor half in the hall and half on the cold concrete of the fire exit stairs. There was a gash in her thigh that looked like a bullet had taken out a chunk of skin and her nose was bleeding.

With a shaky hand, he knelt down and felt for a pulse, fully expecting her to be dead. The blow she'd received from the mine, forcing her into the solid metal door, would have done serious damage to her. Still, he needed to know for sure and silently prayed to whoever was watching them, that she was alive. He pressed his finger deep into her neck then closed his eyes, waiting.

He exhaled, when he felt the strong beat under his fingers. His tense muscles suddenly relaxed. His hands still shook as he lifted her into his arms and wiped the blood from her nose. He quickly checked her limbs, neck, and chest. Except for the wound on her thigh he couldn't find any major damage, which surprised him.

Coughing, he saw smoke filling the exit. He pushed to his feet, throwing the duffel and rifle over his head and picked her up. Probably not the best thing to do, she could have internal injuries, but there was no time to give her a more thorough exam and there was no way he was leaving her. Miles would be itching to finish them off. Even if he didn't come looking for them and Eve was taken to the hospital she would still be at risk. The Project could access any hospital, and Miles would easily hunt her down.

* * * *

"Eve," Alex's deep voice broke through her sleepy haze. She sighed enjoying the sound of his voice.

"Eve." He gave her a little shake. "Can you hear me? Wake up." She came to, a little more when she heard the concerned edge to his voice.

"Yes." She swallowed, her throat was dry. "What's wrong?"

"You were hurt." She could hear his frustration. "Can you open your eyes and look at me?"

She did as he asked and saw a worried scowl on Cade's tanned face.

"Good. Now I'm going to give you a thorough once-over to see where the damage is."

"Okay." She remained still as Alex checked her arms and legs, then he moved to her chest, neck and head where he paid close attention and watched her face for any signs of distress. Despite the sting in her leg and some sore muscles, she felt pretty good for being thrown against a door by a bomb-blast.

He ran his hand down her sides, feeling each rib. "Anything sore?"

She bit the inside her lip and stopped herself from giggling when he touched a ticklish spot on her side. He looked very worried and very confused. He narrowed his gaze on her as he checked the shoulder that hit the steel door.

"Nothing?"

She should try to cover *this* up, somehow. Yet if she lied, saying she was hurt and she wasn't, it may cause him to worry more. But if she didn't say at least something was sore he would question her as to why. "My thigh hurts. I think it got cut somehow?"

He narrowed his eyes, studying her.

"I...my neck and shoulder feel stiff, but I think that's the worst of it right now. I'll probably be really sore tomorrow." she hoped.

He nodded, not saying a word and lifted the covers, exposing her stinging thigh. Pulling a combat medical bag from the floor he unzipped it and pulled the necessary supplies to clean and disinfect the cut on her leg, as well as a sterile needle and thread to suture it back together.

Eve panicked a little when she saw the needle — "It's not that bad is it?" She struggled to sit up.

Alex put his hand on her chest, forcing her down. "It's deep but not bad. A few stitches will help it heal. Now, hold still." He said the words casually like he had done this a hundred times. But it wasn't necessary.

"You know," — she tried to act calm — "It probably looks worse than it is. Just throw a Band-Aid over it. It'll look better tomorrow."

"It will look better tomorrow," he repeated slowly. "You have a gash in your thigh that requires at least ten to twelve stitches and you say it will be fine tomorrow." He narrowed his eyes again. "How do you know that?"

She shook her head, desperately thinking of a way to get out of the corner she'd backed herself into. "I don't know anything. I'm just saying that it's starting to feel better already."

He nodded again, studying her and without a word reached into his bag moving it around but she couldn't see what he was doing. Then he leant forward and grasped both of her hands in one of his. That was when she saw it, a needle attached to a self-injecting syringe. It wasn't big, only about the size of a quarter but she knew what it was used for.

"No!" She fought against him but he was so strong. "Please Alex no! Don't!" It was too late. He pressed it to her neck and she felt the pinch. He pulled it away, tossing the used plastic on the bed and released her hands. Once freed she shot up while she was still able to and slapped him hard across the face. "You're a bastard."

"I know," he confirmed.

Eve fell back against the bed and covered her face, her head becoming foggy. "How long will I be out?" Whatever drug he had given her was fast acting because her arms suddenly felt heavy and she dropped them to her sides. Her body felt heavy too, like a giant lead weight was pinning her to the bed. When he didn't answer, she fought against the drug and turned to look at him. "Why…" Was all she could get out. Her voice cracked and became unsteady.

Alex rested his elbows on his knees, hands gripped together, watching her with a blank expression. Why was he doing this? Tears gathered on her lids. Hadn't she just felt guilty for not trusting him and now that she had tried, he proved he couldn't be trusted. She turned away and tried to focus on the ceiling, but her vision blurred. Finally closing her eyes, she felt Alex stroke her hair away from her face. "I'll be here when you wake up."

* * * *

Standing in the dark, Miles studied Ace lying in the bed. He had been in Ace's room for the past ten minutes deciding whether or not to just kill him and get it over with.

Although at this point, it might just make matters worse. Ever since he'd engaged Taylor this afternoon outside Ace's apartment, his CO had been raining down a shit storm. After he'd had the hole in his shoulder closed he was called into see the Colonel. Things worked out better than he could have planned when he was questioned about the shooting and explosions. He'd simply added to the tale he had already told the CO about the perpetrator shooting

Ace. He'd explained the odd way Eve had become a person of interest and that he'd observed Detective Taylor at Eve's house. All of which was conveniently the truth.

From that point on however, he was just as much in the dark as the CO and the rest of the Project. He had no idea why Taylor and Eve had gone to Ace's building, and he had no idea how they had got into Ace's apartment and weapons vault. He didn't want to guess how Taylor knew about Ace. He wanted the truth, which he would get. Nevertheless, there was one thing that was clear, Taylor was not just your ordinary cop—he was fast, agile and could shoot while under fire. He had the knowledge to get into Ace's apartment, plus his vault, where it was obvious he was familiar with the wide assortment of weapons Ace had on hand.

What confused him about today's event was what he had seen in the hall. He'd seen Ace in that hall, he'd heard Ace in that hall.

'*That's one, I owe you two more.*' Taylor had said that to him, he had been the only one there but he was sure that he had seen Ace. How could Taylor have known about Ace's wounds? How could Taylor have known that *he* had given Ace those wounds?

Slowly walking over to the bed, Miles reached out, touching Ace's arm. It was warm. He looked the same as he had the day before, his black hair was longer than usual and he now had a full beard that the nurses seemed to be taking care of, but which he knew Ace would hate. This wasn't who he'd seen in the hall, he'd seen Ace like he normally was—short hair, clean-shaven.

Miles frowned. Who had he seen?

* * * *

Alex walked into the small house and inspected the room. Like earlier in the afternoon, he felt like he had stepped back through time to when he'd first entered Dawn's house. The light was on in the kitchen and he could hear Eve's grandmother talking to a man. He walked through the living room and stopped just before the kitchen and listened as Dawn spoke.

"Well you can't go in there, my granddaughter is in there."

"I just want to walk around, that's where I go when you're sleeping." The man said. He was wearing an odd-looking farmer's hat and vest with a cotton shirt under it and his pants stopped short before hitting his ankles making them look, at least, two sizes too small for his tall frame.

Dawn clucked her tongue. "I'm not arguing with you about this, Phillip. This is my house and Noelle will stay in that room and *you* will not go near her. Is that clear? Now bugger off!" Her voice was strong and she quickly gained control over the man.

The tall man grumbled as he walked towards him. Alex studied him as he stopped in front of him. "Who are you?" he asked.

Alex could see Dawn through the man as she called, "Out Phillip, now."

He grumbled again as he passed Alex and out through the wall of the house.

Alex raised his eyebrows and turned to face Eve's grandmother. A ghost. Okay. Not what he had been expecting when he decided to come here tonight.

"Well, you might as well come and sit down since you took the trouble to break into my house." She scuffed her slippers as she passed him and entered the sitting room.

He followed her in and sat across from her, resting his forearms on his knees. He noticed how she toyed with the necklace that held the silver charm.

"What exactly is the purpose of the charm?" He watched closely as she smiled down at it.

"The Sinclair medallion has more than one role. It protects and prolongs." She looked up at him with sharp green eyes, too sharp for someone to be living in a retirement village.

He scowled back. "I just saw your granddaughter get slammed through a steel door by a bomb." He waited for the older woman's reaction and was satisfied when her face turned white and her hand flew to her chest. "Is Eve all right?"

"That's why I'm here, she has minor bruising and abrasions, a small bump on her head but that's it. I've seen enough bodies injured by grenades, IED's and such to know she shouldn't be in one piece." He controlled the shudder that tried to run through him. The mere thought of Eve lying there looking dead, scared the shit out of him. It was something he never wanted to see again. "Eve should probably be dead. But she's not. What does that medallion do?"

Dawn sighed and sat back, her hand shook. "Where is she?"

Alex stood and moved to join to her on the small sofa. "She's at my apartment, and she's sleeping," — then thought to add—"She's safe. I wouldn't have left her if she wasn't."

"I believe you." She nodded. "I know you wouldn't hurt someone you care about, and you care about Eve don't you?"

There was no point in denying it, everyone seemed to know. Justine and Cade knew, Dawn knew, the saint or angel or whatever it was knew. Shit even he knew it. The problem was, he didn't want it to happen. They could not be together no matter how much he wanted her, his life was just too dangerous, today's fuck-up proved it.

He shook his head fighting against the truth.

She sighed and gave him a sad smile. "Then you don't deserve to know."

He squeezed his jaw. "Yes, I do deserve to know."

"Why? You just said you don't care for her."

"I didn't say that," he snapped.

"Why are you fighting it?"

He sighed and shook his head again. "I'm not. There just isn't any future for us. My life is too dangerous."

Dawn patted his arm. "Eve will come to accept who you are, and you in turn will bend accordingly."

"I can't change my life for her," he admitted.

"You don't have to change, just adjust," she instructed.

Taking a deep breath, Alex focused on the reason why he had come. "So tell me about the Sinclair Medallion, how does it protect Eve?"

"The same way a bullet proof vest protects police officers or, in your case, soldiers."

"It repels outside attacks to the body? I've worn Kevlar vests; they're hot, heavy and uncomfortable. But all Eve has is a tattoo of that medallion. How can it protect her?"

"Well it all began with William the Conqueror. In 1066—"

"Wait." Alex held up his hand. "I didn't come for a history lesson. I just want to know how Eve is protected."

"If you want the answers then sit still and listen," she commanded. "I'm not telling you this to listen to the sound of my own voice."

Alex took a frustrated breath.

"Good. Now weeks before the invasion of England in 1066, William the Conqueror was having bad luck with the weather and had to wait impatiently to cross the channel. It's said that while he waited for the winds to shift he would set out with his guard and explore the surrounding area. One day while out on a ride he came across an old rundown church in the middle of a large field. With his guards keeping watch, William circled the field and used the time to think about the upcoming invasion. As he wandered around the area, deep in thought, he came upon an old man lying in the field. William approached the man, quickly noticing he was in need of aid. He dismounted and went to assist the man." Dawn shifted in her seat, getting comfortable.

Alex almost groaned out loud. This was going to take a while.

"When he knelt next to the man he saw he was a priest. His name was Father Raphael. The man had hurt his leg carrying firewood. After seeing to the priest's wounded leg, William lifted him onto his horse, picked up the firewood and proceeded to carry it back to the church, while leading his horse with the priest behind him. Once back at the church, William helped the old man get settled in a chair before starting a fire. They spent a good while talking and before he left, William promised that he would send men to make repairs to the Father's small church. Father Raphael was so grateful that he gave William a parting gift and placed two silver coins in his hand.

He told William that it was a gift from God and would protect and prolong the lives of those who owned it."

Alex leant forward onto his knees.

"Thinking the priest was a little off, William refused the coins, saying he didn't require a payment. The priest then suggested that he should take it anyway and pass the gift on to a man worthy of God. William accepted the gift with the intent of following the old priest's request."

"And did he?" Alex asked.

"Yes he did. Shortly after, in fact. But there's more to this part. When William got word that the winds had changed, he rode to the old church that his men had repaired and was going to ask the Father to bless his soldiers. But when he arrived the old man couldn't be found. Instead all that was found was a grave stone with the Father's name and a symbol, the same symbol that was carved into the coins William was given."

Alex raised his eyebrows. "That didn't help me."

"I'm not done. Once William met Harold at Hasting and the battle was over, William walked through his wounded soldiers surveying the damage, until he came upon a woman tending to one of his loyal knights and friend, a man by the name of St. Clare. Watching her work he quickly realised she was a truly gifted healer. Not only did she heal St. Clare's body, but she had lifted his spirit as well. The next day he went back to see his friend St. Clare and, once again, saw the woman treating another knight, except this time St. Clare was standing protectively nearby. St. Clare, you see, had been taken with the woman named Elethea, which means healer. As the days went by he saw the injured men Elethea had tended to and that each one was alive because of her. So impressed by the woman, William gave her to St. Clare thus eventually making her a Baroness. He also gave her the coins the priest had told him to pass on. St. Clare had them fashioned into medallions. Which he and his wife wore until their first child was born." She held up the necklace that carried the medallion. "This is one of the medallions that Father Raphael had first given to William." She toyed with the heirloom. "Noelle wears the other.

"Did you know the name Raphael stands for 'he who heals' or the more popular 'God heals'?"

Alex felt a frown pull at his face. "No. I didn't."

"And so started the Sinclair line and, with it, the ability to heal the body and soul. The medallions prolong our lives by slowing our aging process and protect us from outside forces, so that we may keep healing."

Alex stared at Dawn, startled by the words she had chosen to use, 'heal the body and spirit'. Spirit was another name for the soul. The thing that possessed Justine had also said that Eve was a truly gifted healer. Was it her or was it the medallion? "So, how does Eve have protection? She doesn't wear a medallion, she only has a tattoo."

Dawn wiggled her brows. "Oh she is clever, that one. She figured out that the medallion wasn't what protected us, but the symbol etched into it."

Still resting his elbows on his knees he clasped his hands together. "Does this symbol give her the ability to merge medians?"

"No." Dawn stood. "That was passed down from Elethea. Any Sinclair that is a direct descendent has the ability."

"How did Elethea get the ability to merge?"

"I asked my mother that once." Dawn looked down at Alex in thought. "She didn't know. No one knows."

Alex nodded. "How many Sinclairs have it?"

"There are three of us left."

The back of her slippers scrapped against the floor as she went to the kitchen.

Alex followed and stopped in the doorway as she washed out her cup. "That doesn't make any sense. Sinclair is a popular name, especially in the UK. There has to be more than just you, Eve and Noelle?"

"The Sinclairs were, are a large clan. But," she stressed, "only Elethea's children and grandchildren and great-grandchildren and so on, have the ability and because of our lifespan there really hasn't been that many of us." Dawn changed the subject. "So how about it, should I be excepting to see this Miles in my kitchen next?"

Alex let the matter go. Eve could answer the other questions that he had. "Not tonight. And you should have protection by tomorrow afternoon."

"Well, that's good." She turned from him. "Lock the door on your way out."

He followed her down the hall leading to the bedrooms. "Which room?" Dawn flinched and turned to face him.

"No," She whispered. "You'll wake her."

"Eve will be worried and I can't have her trying to get over here, it's just too risky."

"What exactly is risky about it?" Dawn demanded.

He mimicked her stance, and, keeping his voice low, laid it out for her—"Miles thinks I'm a cop. I'm new. He will research me and will not approach me unless he is positive he can make the kill. Eve is an easier target. He already knows everything he needs to kill her."

"Oh sweet Jesus!" Dawn pressed her fingers into her temples. "What have you got my Eve into?"

"Nothing I can't get her out of. As long as she does what I tell her. So let me see Noelle so I can tell Eve her daughter is safe."

Dawn shook her head and pointed to the door next to him. She rested back against the wall. "I'm timing you."

Alex nodded and quickly slipped into the dark room. The furniture in there was also full of antiques, but as with the rest of the house, everything was decorated tastefully.

He moved to the side of the double bed where Noelle was sleeping and pulled the covers up over her shoulders. She rolled onto her side and smiled sleepily. "Hi Alex."

He squatted down next to the bed. "No reading tonight?"

She smothered a smile and pulled a book out from under the covers. "I had to hide it because Gran checks on me a lot."

He laughed quietly. "Smart lady. It's late now, go back to sleep."

"I will. Where's Mom?" she whispered.

He took the book from her and placed it on the night stand. "Sleeping, like you should be. I just wanted to make sure you and your Gran were okay."

She yawned. "We made cookies."

"Yah, how'd they turn out?" he asked as she closed her eyes.

"They were good, we ate most of them." She was drifting off.

He smiled and whispered, "Goodnight, Noelle." He gently touched her head as he stood. Looking down, he wondered what it would feel like to be the father of a child as cute and smart as Noelle. The memory of the three of them having breakfast earlier replayed in his head. The time had been simple and enjoyable, just like being with family should be. He looked at Noelle, thought about Eve sleeping in his bed. No. It couldn't be. He couldn't risk either one of them.

Squeezing his teeth together, he left the room without a sound and nodded at Dawn who still waited in the hall. "Now, I'll lock it."

"Fine. Goodnight."

"Goodnight, Dawn."

They both turned from the other and headed their separate ways.

Chapter Twenty-Three

Alex hadn't lied to her, he was here when she woke up. But did he have to be glaring at her? After all, he had been the one to give her a shot in the neck and knock her out, not the other way around.

She placed her hand on her head and sat up. "How long was I out?"

"About three hours."

She was surprised by his answer. "Oh."

He lifted a glass off the table next to the bed and handed it to her. "It wasn't my intention to keep you asleep all night, just long enough so I could stitch up your leg and get a few questions answered."

That wasn't fair. She had been ready to curse him up one side and down the other for knocking her out. Now she couldn't because he wanted to help her. Damn.

He placed his hand on her leg, next to the gleaming white dressing. "What do you think I'll find under this dressing?"

She stared at him over the top of the glass and drank about half before finally coming up with an answer. "Stitches."

"Mmm." He took the glass from her and put it down. "Anything else? A wound maybe?"

She opened her mouth but he applied a light pressure to her leg in warning. "The truth please, from your mouth not your grandmother's."

She sucked in her gasp. "You saw Gran? How's…"

He held up his hand. "Noelle is fine and so is Dawn. She was nice enough to answer my questions. But there were others that occurred to me that I didn't want to bother her with."

Answers? To what questions? She suddenly felt sick.

He looked her dead in the eye. "Does your tattoo help protect you?"

She bit the side of her lip. She had been told time and time again not to tell anyone about the medallion or her abilities. People wouldn't understand, her mother had said. She lowered her head, staring at the dark sheet on Alex's bed, feeling horribly guilty. She was about to break a secret she had lived with for many years. "Yes."

With a single finger under her chin, he raised her face to meet his. "Does it help you merge?"

"No, it doesn't." She noticed the scar over his narrowed eyes. He must really be upset with her.

"How old are you, Eve?"

She didn't know what to say, so she lied, "Thirty-five."

He nodded and reached across the bed, bringing her driver's licence and an old photo into view.

"Your driver's licence has a date of birth of July, nineteen-seventy-six. But this picture…" He lifted the photo so she could see the back, with her mom's handwriting on it. He flipped it over and she stared at her mom's beautiful smile. "'Me and Eve. Bristol, 1952.' And by looking at this picture I would say you were at least five or six. So…" He looked her in the eye again. "How old are you Eve?"

She clamped down on her lip again. Yet again, she was going against everything her mother taught her. "Evening," he rumbled her full name in warning.

"I was taught from a very young age not to tell anyone about anything I could do, or of who I am, or where I came from. Mum said people wouldn't understand that they might try to take our gifts for their own gain. This is hard for me, I feel like I'm going behind my mum's back."

Alex leant forward. "I hate to break it to you but the majority of people won't believe you. Besides, who am I going to tell? I'm just a soul that has been merged into a body that doesn't belong to me." His voice dropped low. "Tell me how old you are. Please."

She closed her eyes. "I was born in nineteen-forty six." She peeked up when he didn't say anything. He was simply staring down at her with no expression. She covered her face and rolled back. "Oh shit. I shouldn't have told you. Shit. Shit. I knew this would happen." She swung her legs off the bed and stood. "You're grossed out now aren't you?"

She walked past him towards a window. It was dark out now, and from where she stood, the city was outlined perfectly with little white lights. Where were they?

"What's gross?"

She faced him, crossing her arms. He couldn't be serious? "Us. Cause we…you know…" She stopped, hoping he understood, and she wouldn't have to continue. But he just stared at her like he had no idea what she was referring to. She threw her hands up. "Cause we had sex. And I'm old. And that's gross."

Minutes passed without him saying a word. He just sat there staring at her. Wasn't he going to say anything? Wasn't it bad enough he was making her feel like the freak she was? She snorted. Enough of this, she was out of here. She began searching for her clothes and, when she couldn't find them, she looked for the bag she had packed. She didn't have any luck there either, so she marched over to Alex's tall-boy dresser and pulled open drawers until she found something suitable to wear outside.

Only when she was throwing open his bedroom door did he finally move. She had taken two steps out of his room when he was on her, lifting her by the waist and carrying her back inside the room.

"Let me go, Alex." She fought against him but she doubted he even noticed. He simply kicked the door shut, carried her over to the bed and threw her in the centre of it.

"Where the hell do you think you are going?" His voice was deathly quiet as he stood glaring down at her.

"Away from you." She swung her legs to the side of the bed only to be pulled back into the centre. "Stop it."

"No." He was on the bed in a flash and straddling her. He gently pushed her back when she sat forward. "Why do you want leave?" He kept his hand on her chest.

"Get off." She tried to move but couldn't. "Please," she whimpered. She felt like crying. She wanted to leave, hide her face so he couldn't stare at her like she was a freak. He kept saying that he didn't want to want her, he'd given her reasons, then listed her faults and now he knew her true age and he kept looking at her with either disgust or fascination, she couldn't tell, but she didn't like either one. Tears slowly flooded her eyes and they slipped down the sides of her face when she closed her eyes.

The next thing she knew Alex was off her and she was being pulled to the side of the bed and lifted. When she opened her eyes and faced him, she was on his lap, his arm curled around her back.

"Better?" he asked.

She nodded.

"Why were you leaving?" he asked again, lightly rubbing his thumb against her side.

She sniffed, "Because I feel like a freak."

"You are not a freak," he said each word with more force than she was expecting.

"But you make me feel that way."

"How did I make you feel like a freak?"

"By the way you were looking at me. I know how unusual I am, I don't need to be reminded of it."

"Is that what made you cry?" He made a confused face. "Me looking at you?"

"Yes and everything that you've said to me."

"Which was?"

"How you don't want me, and how I'm not as good as the other women you have been with. That hurt my feelings, more than once."

Alex sighed, "Evening, I never said you weren't as good as the other women I have been with."

She sniffed again, "Yes—"

"No." He cut her off. "I said I like my women tall and blonde. You do remember that you were pointing a rolling pin and knife at me. I wanted to make you angry enough to throw those at me, so I wouldn't have to take them by force. I also said that I was very attracted to you, but didn't want to be, and I told you why."

She shook her head. "All I hear are all the things you don't like about me. None of this is my fault, you came to me, remember? But it's me who you keep insulting. I can handle a lot but with the way you were just looking at me, it became too much."

Alex sighed again and nuzzled the side of her head. "I wasn't expecting you to say nineteen-forty-six. Eve you're sixty-five. But you look like you're thirty. It caught me off guard."

She looked down at her hands. "How old were you expecting?"

"Jesus, I don't know. Maybe mid-forties. It doesn't matter now."

She raised her head. "Why not?"

He stroked the crease between her eyes with the back of his finger. "Because, you told me the truth and we can now focus on helping Jillian."

She blinked. "That's it. You're just going to accept what I just told you? Not get all weird on me?"

"I'm pretty good at accepting the stranger things in life. I hunt very evil people. But with what I've gone through in the past couple of weeks... Yes. I can accept anything at this point. And, no, I don't plan on going all weird on you."

She pulled at his shirt nervously. "So, you aren't grossed out about us..."

"Not at all. In fact I'm thinking I'd like to have a little bit of...us." He gave her a wicked grin. "But I want you to have something to eat and then rest. I don't care what that tattoo can do, it's me who's protecting you. Besides, I need to calm down first."

Her arm had curled around his shoulders and she dragged her fingernails along the base of his neck. "You do, why?"

"'Cause I'm feeling pretty horny and you're a senior citizen. I could break your hip."

After Alex fed them both, he covered her wound in some plastic wrap and ordered her to have a shower. He didn't leave when she asked and stood outside the door until she was done. He knew the wound on her leg would heal, but she had been caught in the middle of a violent clash, he didn't want her alone when the reality of being shot and almost blown up finally hit her.

He had been expecting some type of reaction sooner, maybe some crying or endless nervous chatter but she hadn't even batted an eyelash. The strange thing was, it seemed to bother him more than it bothered her and he asked her why, once she was back lying in his bed. He propped himself up onto his elbow as he waited for her to answer.

"I don't know," she began, looking up at him. "Is that bad do you think?"

"No, I don't think so. It just means you're better at coping than most people." He rolled back onto his pillow. "If it does suddenly hit you, I'm here to help you deal with it."

"You are?" she asked, hesitantly.

Because he had just said he was here for her, he didn't feel it was necessary to answer her question. Instead, he tugged on her hand until she curled into his side. He wrapped his arm around her and she lifted her leg onto his so they fitted together comfortably. He kissed her forehead and let his lips linger on her soft skin, breathing in her clean scent. She was asleep by the time he wished her good night.

Chapter Twenty-Four

Alex shot up in bed when he realised Eve wasn't next to him. He jumped out of bed and checked the bathroom first, then turned and stopped, coming face to face with Justine.

Her hands were held up. "Don't panic, she's downstairs drinking coffee and checking out your house. Which for the record is pretty nice for a single guy. Very homey," she sang, dropping her hands. "I hope you don't plan on blowing up this place too."

Alex felt his heart rate return to normal, then the irritation set in. He placed his hands on his hips. "What's up?"

"Jillian's up. She running out of food but is too scared to go into town."

Alex stared through Justine while he thought. She should have enough food to last at least a month. By his count it had only been about three weeks. Regardless, she was pregnant. She needed to keep her body healthy. If she needed to run the risk and go into town, so be it. By the time the Project traced the car, he and Eve would be up there and his plan would already be in the works.

"Tell her not to worry about it. She needs the food. But she doesn't talk to anybody. In and out, no socialising."

"What about Miles, what if he finds out?"

"It won't matter, by the time he finds her I'll be there."

She eyed him. "You better be."

"How is she otherwise?"

"Bored. But now that she knows you're coming she's calmed down a bit. The time away is probably doing her good, I just wish it hadn't happened like this." She waved her hands down her body.

A thought suddenly occurred to him. "Does she know I'm in Cade's body?"

"No. I didn't know how to tell her." She shook her head. "She was sad enough with losing me."

"You need to tell her."

"Geez, you sound like Cade." She tugged a strand of hair behind her ear.

"What, logical? She needs to know. What happens when she finds out I'm not Cade on the inside. Can't shock trigger early labour?"

Justine threw her hand on her chest. "You're asking me?"

"Yes."

"Well I don't know. Let's go ask your girlfriend."

"No," Alex said quickly. "You'll scare her."

She pulled a face. "Oh yah! Forgot about that."

"You need to tell her."

"I know."

"I'm serious. Tell her." Alex ordered, pointing at her as he left the room and went downstairs to find Eve.

* * * *

Eve wasn't happy when he left her at his apartment for the better part of the day. Ordering her to stay inside and not venture around the area didn't make her pleasant to deal with, but at least she understood the reason why. Did he push her over the edge by locking her inside...definitely. Or at least that was the impression he got when he heard a thump against the back of the door. *Oh well.* She would just have to deal with it, because there was no way he could handle another moment like yesterday when he'd thought she was dead. Special tattoo or not, nothing would happen to her today.

Besides, she couldn't be with him. He needed to talk to the cop. After yesterday's events at his apartment not only would the cops be looking for him but so would Miles. And if he knew Miles, and he did, he would already be searching for Cade.

Jesus, what was Miles doing? He'd never acted this irrationally before. He'd never wanted to kill a witness, never killed an innocent person or a cop. A cop. Christ. The only thing that made any type of sense was that Miles had panicked and thought Justine was Jillian, and had inadvertently killed Cade. Or maybe not. Could he have killed Justine, because she was Jillian's twin? Was Miles desperate enough to kill Justine in the hopes it would draw Jillian out? He didn't know, but there was something more going on here.

He pushed the dark glasses up his nose and adjusted his position against the tree in Ryder's Park. The Project was located in a busy residential neighbourhood. The cover of a computer graphics company fit in well with the surrounding area. The teams were normally free to move in and out with large briefcases or bags without causing suspicion. Normally. However today wasn't normal. By the looks of the people coming and going, it appeared Cade had caused quite the shit storm yesterday by blowing up a member's apartment.

He grinned, sipping his coffee. He had watched Miles enter into the massive three story mansion about forty minutes before. Since then the influx of people had increased. It was nice to know he had made Miles' life a little bit more complicated. That should force him to pick up his pace in order to cover his ass and with a little luck, he'd screw up along the way.

Finishing the remainder of his coffee, he wondered what lies Miles had told the others about him. A better question was, would they believe him? Of course they would, they had no reason not to. Miles was his partner and you always trusted in your partner.

"Jesus, Cade do you have any idea what kind of shit you've caused?"

Alex pushed away from the tree and stood to Cade's full height as the cop approached him. Behind the dark glasses, he quickly scanned Trevor for weapons. He was wearing his jacket open, which displayed his pistol and his badge and he guessed he'd have another gun strapped to his ankle but couldn't be sure because of his baggy jeans.

"Close your jacket. I don't want anyone knowing who we are." He turned and leant back against the tree.

Trevor complied with his order but asked, "Who? What the hell are you doing here? People are looking for you." He raised his red brows and stressed, "Very important people."

"I bet." He glanced over at Cade's partner. There was genuine concern on the guy's face. This cop wasn't only Cade's partner, he was also a friend.

Yah well, he had considered Miles a friend too and look where it had got him. He hoped Cade was right in saying this guy was trustworthy, because he really didn't have the time to kill this guy should he have damaged morals.

Trevor shoved his hands into his pockets and sighed, "What's going on Cade?"

Alex stood up and shook his empty coffee cup. "Let's go grab a coffee and I'll catch you up on what I have so far."

"Coffee?" Trevor scoffed. "You hate coffee."

Alex pulled a tight smile. "My tastes have changed."

It took less than an hour to tell Trevor about Jillian witnessing the murder and re-telling him the rest of the events from a second perspective.

Trevor waited until he was finished before asking any questions.

"Okay." Trevor sat back and crossed his arms high over his chest. "Let me get this straight. Jillian's boss, Brad Rhodes, was murdered and Jillian was witness to it, but was caught by the two guys who committed the murder. One wanted to kill her and the other helped her escape."

Alex nodded as Cade's partner recapped the story.

"You do know the autopsy confirmed Rhodes died of a heart attack?" Trevor supplied. "But that would explain why his office was a mess and why no trace evidence could be found except for Rhodes."

Alex watched some kids run around the open field of the park. "They found nothing?"

"No. It was Jenkins and Wood's case. They thought it might have been a break and enter and that Rhodes surprised them, but when nothing was found to suggest otherwise, they closed it." Trevor ran a hand over his bald head. "I wonder if anyone tried calling her."

"And why hasn't anyone from her office reported her missing?" Alex pointed out.

"Maybe they have. I'll check with missing persons."

Alex nodded. He knew Miles would have called Jillian's work, and given them some bullshit cover story that would have explained her absence.

"Okay," Trevor sighed, resuming the original topic. "The one killer helped Jillian get to a car, where she took off. But she came and saw you first, even though he said not to."

Alex really hated being called the killer, but then again what else should he be called? "She was scared."

"No doubt. Did you get the make of car and plate number?"

"Plates didn't register, I checked local and federal. Nothing."

"Shit. So where did Jillian go?"

"I told her to follow the guy's instructions. From what she told me, he seemed to know what he was doing, so it only made sense."

"And where was that?" Trevor glanced at him.

"Hey." Justine suddenly appeared next to him. "How's it going?"

Alex shook his head, not only to answer the cop's question but to show Justine now was not the time for chit-chat.

"Don't get in a snit. I'm just checking in."

Trevor was clearly annoyed too, but was easier to shut up. "She gave you his description."

Alex nodded.

"And you saw this guy watching the therapist's house?"

He nodded again.

"This therapist broad, where is she now?" Trevor raised his red brows.

"Broad!" Justine chuckled. "I do love Trevor's choice in words."

"Eve," Alex clarified sharply. Justine laughed again. "She's safe. But she's worried about her daughter and grandmother. Can you send a patrol car to keep an eye on them until this gets cleared up?"

Trevor nodded. "Why did you go over to Eve's place to begin with?"

Alex paused, not knowing what to say. "Use me." Justine was now standing in front of them. "Say you had a ghostly apparition of me." She waved her hands in the air. "And I said to go to Eve's house. Oooooh!"

It was all Alex could do to keep from laughing out loud.

"Ha!" Justine put her hands on her hips. "I knew you liked me."

Alex bit his tongue and answered Trevor. "You wouldn't believe me if I told you." He shook his head.

"Try me," Trevor suggested seriously.

Alex stared the cop in the eye. "Justine told me to go." He waited to see what the reaction would be to his answer. When there was none he continued, "She said I would find her killer, watching a woman and her daughter."

"Oh you are good! That was a nice touch." Justine grinned down at him.

There was silence while Alex...and Justine waited to hear Trevor's response. He lifted his sunglasses onto his bald head and nodded. "Okay."

Justine clapped her hands. "You see, Cade told you Trevor was a good guy. Now hurry up and get your ass in gear." And with that said she was gone.

"And this Eve. She was just in the wrong place at the wrong time and now he wants to kill her too?"

Alex exhaled before telling him the truth. "I told you I saw him watching her house when I followed him. I found out she ran into him when she was working on the seventh floor of Memorial Hospital."

"Seventh. My brother was on seven, that's military only."

"Yah. I found that out." Alex rested his elbows on his knees. "She was there to assess a patient and this other guy came in and started asking her questions. He gave her the name Remy Castillo."

"And you think this is the same guy that wants to kill Jillian?"

"The descriptions match."

"I suppose I don't need to ask if you went to check out the parking garage where this shoot-out happened."

Alex raised an eyebrow. He had of course gone back. He'd wanted to see first-hand how Miles had cleaned the area. It had been spotless to the untrained eye, but Alex had known where he had stood and fired his pistol, so he knew where the bullets should have hit the wall behind Miles. And he was right, the holes had been there, just nicely covered up with a filler the same colour as the wall.

"There was nothing there that I could see."

"This patient in the hospital, who is he?" Trevor sat forward on the bench.

"Eve was given the name…" Alex stopped himself. If Trevor checked into the cover name he would find nothing, but if he checked into his real name it would confirm his story. Alex could feel Trevor's eyes on him. Alex fought against his training and gave the cop the truth. "Alex Hunter."

"Do you think this Hunter is the guy that helped Jillian get away?"

"I have no idea. But Eve said he was in a coma, so there is no way of finding out the truth until he wakes up."

"Or if he wakes up. Did Eve say what caused the coma?"

The fight was easier this time as he revealed, "She said he had multiple gunshot wounds."

Trevor rubbed his chin. "Think his partner did that?"

Alex flexed the muscles in his jaw. "It would make sense. This guy wanted to kill Jillian because she can identify him. And then his partner, the one person who should have his back, refused and then helped the witness to get away. He was pissed."

Trevor nodded. "Okay, I need another recap. We have two possible military guys, one of whom is in a coma and could have possibly helped Jillian escape. The other military guy wants to kill Jillian because she witnessed him murdering Rhodes. He is now after Eve because…" He paused and shrugged. "We're not sure why. And he is after you because you blew up his apartment?"

Alex sat up straight. What the hell? How did he know that? "I didn't blow up his apartment."

"We saw footage of you carrying an unidentified woman in a parking garage. After the report of an explosion in the same building."

"It blew up when that guy started shooting at me."

Trevor's red brows shot up. "He shot at you."

"Yes."

He shook his head. "There was no evidence of gunfire. Mind you there was no evidence of anything else either."

Good. Alex exhaled slowly. Both he and Eve couldn't afford to be seen having sex. Jesus, how would it look? A cop, whose wife had been killed less than two weeks before was having sex with another woman. It would raise a lot of questions he didn't have time to answer. And those cameras in the parking garage. He had forgotten about them and the only excuse he could come up with was that he was worried about Eve. He'd thought she was hurt worse than she was. Still, he needed to be more careful.

"How did you find that apartment?"

"Eve got the address from the seventh floor."

They sat in silence for a while, both men deciding what the next course of action should be.

"I don't think it would be good if you came back to the station. I'll fill the boss in, check into Remy Castillo and Alex Hunter, and see what I can find out."

Alex shook his head. "Don't tell anyone else. I think the less people that know the better. I don't think we should trust anyone who is military right now either."

"I agree. But the boss is going to want to know why you didn't come back with me."

Alex stared at the cop. What could he say? That he didn't trust the cops any more than he trusted the members of the Guardian Project? It was ridiculous, he needed to act somewhat like a cop, Cade must have trusted more than just his partner.

"Okay, tell him. But nothing about Eve. I don't want the military knowing her name."

Trevor narrowed his eyes and studied him for a moment before agreeing. "Are you going to Jillian today?"

"No."

"Will you tell me when you do?"

"Yes." *Because I will need your help distracting Miles so I can kill him.*

Chapter Twenty-Five

Alex didn't get back to the apartment until late. He watched the 'shop' a while longer until Miles came out, then followed him over to the apartment he'd blown up. Miles would be going in to do a sweep, making sure nothing was there for the authorities to find and tie the Guardian Project to the apartment. Once Miles had left, Alex followed him home, where he saw his girls playing in the front yard. Alex still couldn't believe that Miles had wanted to kill Jillian. It just didn't make any sense. He was a father, a good father and a good husband. What had made him react the way he had?

Alex left Miles and knew he wouldn't be active until his kids were in bed. So he drove over to see Dawn and Noelle. He received a warm hug from Noelle and the cold shoulder from Dawn. He only stayed long enough to tell Dawn about the police car that would be patrolling the area.

He got a snippy — "About time" — and a container of food shoved at him. After explaining to Noelle that Eve was fine and that he had to go back to her, he accepted another hug and promised to give Eve the picture Noelle had coloured for her.

He probably should have stayed with them, but he didn't want to get too close. He was really beginning to like them. He liked how feisty Dawn was and that Noelle was such a sweetheart. It was going to be hard enough to end things with Eve. If he had these two to deal with as well, it would make things even harder when it came time for him to go.

He stayed in the area watching Dawn's house until he saw Trevor pull up. He got out and went to talk to the cop.

"Why no cruiser?" Alex asked, coming to stand next to Trevor.

The cop shook his head. "There was military at the station when I got back. I didn't feel it was safe to leave this in the hands of a patrol officer, who might let it slip what I asked him to do."

Alex nodded. "You find out anything on Remy Castillo or Alex Hunter?" He asked the question even though he already knew what the answer would be.

"Not a damn thing. I checked federal and even the Defence Department." Trevor held out a phone for him.

"What did they say?" Alex frowned at the phone.

"Nothing. But they were very polite when they hung up on me."

Alex laughed. "What's this?"

"Your phone. You left it at the station the day you and Justine went to lunch and got hit..." He stopped, handing him a piece of paper. "Your number and my number, just in case you forgot."

"Thanks." He slid the phone and paper into his pocket. "I can stay if you want to go home and get a few hours sleep first."

"I got a couple hours before coming here. You go."

Unlocking the door, Alex entered the old converted fire hall. It wasn't a big hall, which didn't bode well for the factories in the area should there be a fire, but it was for that reason he got it so cheap. Besides, it was a classic red brick, two-story firehouse and it was easy to convert into what he needed. A place that no one knew about, not even Miles.

All the lights were off except for a reading lamp above his desk. He closed the door and locked the bolts. Placing Cade's phone and the picture Noelle had made on the counter, he reached for the fridge with the intent of putting the container of food Dawn had given him inside. He paused when he saw a plate of food covered in plastic wrap with a note resting on top of it. *Hungry?* Was all the note said.

He pulled the plate from the fridge and took off the wrap. He found himself smiling like an idiot. It wasn't a gourmet meal, just a simple sandwich with French fries but it looked delicious and after he had finished it, he wondered how something so simple could taste so good. Was it because he was just that hungry or the fact that Eve had taken the time to make it for him?

He sat back in the chair and looked up the stairs to where he knew Eve was sleeping in his bed. A disturbing thought occurred to him. Eve might be in love with him. He already knew she was attracted to him. Her eyes gave her away every time they were together. But, she might actually be in love with him.

He stood, taking the plate to the sink and wondered if he even deserved Eve's love. He caught his reflection in the window. Brown eyes, blond hair, tanned skin. Jesus, Cade looked like he belonged on a magazine cover. He placed the plate in the sink and gripped the counter. Was it him Eve was in love with or was it this body? Cade's body? He hadn't considered that she could be attracted to the body and not the soul. Which meant that she was in love with Cade and not him.

With anger and a little jealousy running through his veins, he moved to the stairs, taking them two at a time. He needed to know if that was the case. He needed to know if she loved him or this fucking body. He went to her, tossing his shirt on the floor, quickly removed the rest of his clothing and slid under the sheets behind her as she lay on her side. He slid his hand down her waist and over her hip and was annoyed to find she was sleeping in a T-shirt and panties but realised that taking them off her would give him the time he needed to calm down.

He pulled her shirt up as he kissed the side of her neck. "Eve," he breathed her name. "Eve, wake up."

She allowed him to tug her shirt over her head and he threw it away. She sighed sleepily when he cupped a single round breast. He nipped at her neck and pinched her nipple.

She clamped her hand down over his. "That hurt," she whispered back.

He inhaled a deep breath and kissed the area he had nipped and ran his thumb over her nipple gently. "I just wanted to make sure you didn't miss out on all the fun."

"So you're not worried about breaking my hip tonight?" she teased.

"No." He kissed her shoulder.

"And you're not bothered by what I told you yesterday…about my…" She stopped.

"About your age?" he guessed, sliding his hand down to her panties. He hooked his thumb in the side and inched them down. "Your true age and your family tattoo don't bother me." He pressed his lips next to her ear. "It was your hiding the truth from me that I didn't like." He licked the outside of her ear lightly. "I always want you to tell me the truth." He dipped his tongue inside her ear as he slid his hand between her legs. She inhaled when he rubbed her core.

"Say it Eve, say you won't lie to me." He slipped his other arm underneath her and rolled her so her back was resting on top of his chest.

Her head fell back onto his shoulder. "Say you won't lock me in your house again."

He chuckled as he licked the side of her neck, teased the nipple of her large breast and massaged her moist centre. Her hands clamped down over his, holding them in place. He roughly moved them out of the way. "I will not apologise for keeping you safe. Now tell me you won't lie to me." He desperately needed to hear the truth from her, that way when the time came and he asked if she was attracted to him or Cade's body she would have to tell him the truth.

"I won't lie to you." The words mixed with her choppy breath. Her hands covered his again as he tormented her and she began to make little whimpering sounds.

"Do you want me, Eve?" His voice was raw and his body hurting.

That was the stupidest question she had ever heard. Of course, she wanted him, she always wanted him and why he found the need to ask her, was beyond her comprehension.

He pulled his hand from between her legs and asked the question again, his voice a little harder this time.

She gripped his hand and tried to tug it back in place but he couldn't be moved.

"Answer me." The command was rough.

There it was again, a dark...anger radiating from him. She thought she was dreaming it at first, not being fully awake, but now she realised it was real. Alex was angry, and, although he was no longer a median, he was powerful enough that she was able to feel his ferocity surround them.

She let go of him and answered him clearly and carefully, "Yes. I do want you."

Before she could blink she was on her back and Alex was pulling her underwear down her legs and over her feet. He glared at her and she froze when she saw dark brown eyes. Not blue eyes, brown and no scar above his left eye. She scanned his chest, as he moved on top of her. No bullet wounds either.

No. This wasn't right. She pushed at his shoulders, struggling to keep him away so she could look at him. She ran her eyes over his face searching for any sign that Alex was there. But she couldn't see any. She shook her head confused. "Cade?" His face turned expressionless. She asked again, "Cade is that you?"

No answer, just dark brown eyes staring down at her. She pushed at his shoulders, repulsed by the idea of Cade touching her. "Get off." He tightened his grip.

Panic rose fast when he didn't move. "No." She fought with everything she had. It seemed silly, she knew Alex was using Cade's body but, when they made love, it wasn't Cade touching her it was Alex, it was always Alex.

"Please," she finally sobbed. He released her instantly and sat back. She flung herself off the bed and backed into the corner of the room. She looked to the door. Damn, why hadn't she jumped off the other way? Her eyes darted back to Cade and, breathing heavily demanded, "Where's Alex?"

"I am Alex." He turned to face her but remained sitting on the bed.

She pointed at him. "You are *not* Alex."

He dropped his head into his hands. "It's me, Eve." His voice held something different, was that regret?

"No." She shook her head. "Alex has blue eyes. I always see his blue eyes."

He lifted his head and she was shocked to see blue eyes staring back.

She inched closer so she could see clearer. She blinked and searched for the scar above his eye. It was there too, as were the bullet wounds. Confused she asked, "What's going on? I don't understand."

"I made a mistake," he confessed.

"Mistake? What are you talking about?" She still felt a little panicked and shifted back from the bed.

"I thought that you might be attracted to Cade and not me." He looked her straight in the eye. "So I thought I'd find out for sure."

Eve felt her mouth drop open. She didn't know how to react to that. Should she be angry that he had not only tricked but also scared the shit out of her, or should she be flattered that he was jealous enough to conduct the experiment in the first place? She stood in front of him. He reached out to her, but anger won out and she slapped him hard across the face.

"How dare you scare me like that." She moved to slap him again, but he caught her arm and held her in place.

He moved his mouth to her arm and kissed her wrist. "I shouldn't have done that to you."

"Then why did you?" She tried to keep back the tears but they still found a way to the surface.

He pulled her closer and cupped her hips, leaving his face open for another hit. "Because the sudden idea of you wanting someone else, other than me, didn't sit well."

Eve shook her head. "I don't understand. Did I say something or do something that led you to believe otherwise?"

"No," he breathed out. "It was entirely me. Cade has a nice body, I suddenly got it in my head that you wanted the body and not the soul."

"But I don't know Cade."

"I know." He ran his hands over her thighs and stopped, looking to where the stitches had been in her leg. The cut, of course, had healed and she had taken the stitches out earlier in the day. He ran his fingers over the area.

She touched his cheek drawing his attention back to her. "I don't see him."

"What do you mean?"

She swallowed a sudden lump in her throat and her heart thumped hard. "When we are together talking or when we make love, it's not Cade I see. It's you. I only see you, Alex." The grip on her thighs tightened as he pulled her closer. "I'm not sure why you're so worried. You don't want me, remember?" She didn't know what possessed her to say that but it wasn't well received, or maybe it was, because Eve suddenly found herself lying back on the bed with Alex looming above her. He was angry again, but the strong, dark feeling didn't accompany it. This time it was different.

"I want you." He lowered his lips to hers, brushing them back and forth. "But the things I do are so dangerous, if my job followed me home, it could get you killed." He kissed her when she tried to speak. "Listen to me. The idea of something happening..."

He squeezed his teeth together, his nostrils flared. "I won't go through that again."

"But I…"

He kissed her quiet a second time. She just wanted to tell him she would be there for him whenever he needed her. He didn't have to live with them or spend all their time together like normal couples did. Hell, they were the farthest thing from normal you could get. Why should their relationship be any different? She would be happy with that, but it was either all or nothing for Alex. Which meant, when this was over, there would be nothing.

The fear of never seeing him again had her pulling desperately on his shoulders. She needed to get as much of Alex as she could before their time was over.

Over. She didn't want it to be over. She wanted Alex in her life.

The comforting heat that his soul produced seeped into her skin, but even that couldn't erase her fear. She felt her body shake, she couldn't stop it.

Alex moved between her legs and, resting an elbow on either side of her head, he buried his fingers in her hair. "Okay?"

She jerked her head. "Yes."

"You're lying."

She looked at his chin. "Yes." There was a sickening piece of lead in her stomach that felt like it was going to drop to her feet and take her heart with it. She wanted to tell him how her body wanted his body. That her soul needed his soul, and how her heart ached longingly for his. But she didn't.

"Why?"

"I don't want to talk about it 'cause I'll start thinking about…and I don't want—" She couldn't say it. She hated that she sounded so desperate. She felt…like she had when her mum died. Small and sad and unbelievably heartbroken.

"Okay, okay," he soothed, kissing the side of her mouth. "No talking." He dragged his lips to her neck and kissed her lightly. "I still want you, Eve." He rocked his hips, pressing the tip of his cock against her.

She rested the side of her face against his head, then truthfully confessed, "I want you too." *More than you will ever know.* She kept that thought to herself.

His hand moved between their bodies as his mouth covered hers. His tongue stroked her tongue in the same rhythm as his hands stroked her body. In no time, Alex had made her fear of the future vanish — for now anyway — and made her focus on him and what he was doing to her.

She loved these incredible feelings he ignited when he touched her. The damp yearning that ached between her legs when he caught her nipple between his teeth and flicked it with the tip of his tongue. How her breasts became wonderfully full when he drew the pink pointed tip into his mouth and fed greedily. And the way her muscles clenched when he kissed a warm wet trail down her stomach and into her bellybutton.

He splayed his hands wide over her abdomen inflaming her skin, building the heat inside her core and melting her heart at the same time. Her thighs quivered as he licked the sensitive flesh, trembled as he tortured her with his slow wet kisses, until she couldn't bear any more and arched her back begging for him without words. He gave in to her and closed his mouth over her slick aching centre. Her hips jerked from his deliberately slow licks over and around her clit and she gripped at the sheet in an attempt to keep still, but it didn't work. Again and again he licked her, blood rushed in her ears, her belly tightened and the tops of her legs began to tingle as she finally drew in a shaky breath and exploded in mind-numbing ecstasy.

Eve barely had time to enjoy the moment when Alex was above her. Without any thought, she reached for him as he draped her leg over his shoulder, positioning himself but unexpectedly he paused. The scar on his brow puckered the skin around it when his eyebrows pressed together. Eve felt a sudden panic rise in her chest. She couldn't wait. She wanted him now, who knew how long she would have with him before he left? Reaching up, she cupped his cheek. "Please Alex."

Shaking his head he began pulling away.

"No." She pulled him back.

"Easy," he soothed running his thumb along her bottom lip. "I'm not going anywhere."

He reached across her to the bedside and pulled a condom from the box.

Yet. Eve sighed. *You're not going anywhere yet.*

He moved between her legs and, once again, lifted her leg over his shoulder.

She stroked the side of his face. "Please." God, how pathetic and desperate she sounded, but she couldn't help it. "I need you now."

He lowered his head and stared hard into her eyes. She had no idea what he was looking at, but a warm smile claimed his mouth briefly before he thrust into her, pumping hard. She cried out when he drove hard into her, his thrusts were so deep that pleasure blended with pain and she reached for him needing him close. He lowered her leg and went to her holding her tight, his body still moving fast in hers. Her body was shaky, her arms were shaky, even her voice was shaky. She wrapped her arms around his wide shoulders, stroked the hard, smooth muscles of his back. "A-Alex," she breathed his name against his mouth, not able to continue. He rested his face next to hers. "One more, Eve." His heavy breaths heated her face and mingled with her own. "Give me one more."

He lowered his hand between their damp bodies and rubbed her throbbing clit until she cried out again. He moved faster, increasing the pleasure, the pulsing—a blissful torment that never seemed to end. He rested his head on her shoulder breathing heavily. She nipped at the skin on his neck then sucked it into her mouth, as he drove into her one final time.

Chapter Twenty-Six

Alex gave her a hard kiss before moving off her. She closed her eyes, listening to him move across the room. She heard the shower turn on and, suddenly, he was back, lifting her off the bed. He stepped under the warm spray and lowered her to her feet, then closed the clear glass door. He gently lathered her body, taking his time as he cleansed her. Each touch triggered a wave of need. It burned her from the inside out. It caused a hot craving to pool between her thighs and her nipples to tighten. He lifted her breasts, moulded them with his hands as he soaped them, then pulled on the nipples making them a dark rosy colour. When she was covered in a thick soapy lather he pushed her back under the water until she was rinsed clean. Then he handed her the soap and let his arms fall to his side.

She enjoyed soaping his body, even though she wished it was *his* body she was touching. When she closed her eyes, she could still see him lying in the hospital bed, the hard strength in his arms and shoulders. See the rippled muscles of his stomach and the dark hair covering his chest and face. She opened her eyes as she lathered his back. Cade had a nice body too, but it was not Alex.

She turned him around and began soaping his chest and shoulders. Covered his arms and hands, stroked his palm and pulled gently on each finger. Moved to his hips and knelt down, running her hands down the length of each leg. When she cupped him, she looked up and watched his face. His only indication that he liked what she was doing was the flaring of his nostrils. She stood and nudged him under the water and rubbed at his body to help remove the soap. She moved her hand to his now hard cock and stroked the length of him. God, he smelt so good, clean and manly. She pressed her mouth to his chest, swirled her tongue over his wet skin. Oh man, he tasted good too. She glanced back up to his face, slowly pumping his shaft. His eyes were glowing but the lids hung low as he stared back at her. She licked at her lips, her mouth starting to water at the idea of sucking him into her mouth. He shook his head. She nodded hers. Then dropped to her knees and took him into her mouth.

He tasted good, so good. She couldn't get enough. The need he triggered deep in her soul was heating her body up. She sucked hard, sliding up and down and received a growl for her effort. Then, she was lifted by her arms and Alex was crushing her mouth with his. He clasped her head between his hands and pulled back panting. "You make me...I want to...I don't know how..." He stopped and took a deep breath.

Eve placed her hands on his cheeks and, in an effort to calm him, adjusted her voice, "I know. It's the same for me."

He shook his head, still confused and pulled her forward, crushing her against him. His mouth was hard and demanding. She allowed him to take whatever he needed.

He surprised her when he turned her away from him and placed her hands on the wall. His hands were all over her, cupping and stroking, gliding down her waist to her hips, then behind. Then, slipping his fingers between her legs, he parted her creamy lips. She groaned and rocked her hips back pushing her backside against his thick cock. She felt him drop his head onto her back as he toyed with her entrance. She rocked her hips again, not able to help herself.

"Fuck." He groaned and, grabbing her hips, plunged deep.

She moaned from the sudden heat of his invasion. His hands never ceased their carnal torment, moving over her body greedily, squeezing and caressing, setting her skin on fire. He fondled her breasts, pinched her nipples, kissed her shoulders. His arms wrapped around her and he pulled her back against his chest, his breath hot in her ear as he moved in long, so-slow strokes. He slid his fingers back into her slick folds and moved them in lazy circles. She came almost at once, grinding her hips back against him.

Alex grunted in frustration as he withdrew from her body. He grabbed her shoulders, turned her to face him and forced her hand to his cock. "Finish me, Eve."

She understood immediately and gripped the slick length, pumping him hard and fast. He framed the sides of her head, kissing her. She tightened her grip and ran her finger over the sensitive tip with each hard stroke. He pulled his mouth away, but held her face next to his. She pumped a little harder, squeezed a little tighter as his hips bucked and he groaned into her mouth as he came.

After they cleansed each other again, they fell into bed. Alex pulled Eve next to him and kissed her forehead. "How do you feel old timer?" he teased.

Eve pinched at his arm. "Not funny."

He grinned into the dark. "Sure it is. But seriously, you okay?"

"I feel..." She hugged him and sighed, "Mmmm."

"I know what you mean." He laughed. "I saw Dawn and Noelle again tonight."

"You did?"

He smiled at her surprised tone. "They're both good. There's a very colourful picture downstairs from Noelle."

"Really?" She tried to pull away but he held her in place.

"I'll get it."

He went downstairs, got himself a glass of water, and emptied it before reaching for Cade's phone. He shouldn't have brought it here, there was a tracking system built into this phone, which meant as soon as he called out or answered a call, Miles would have his location. It was a guarantee that Miles knew Trevor would give it to him, just like he knew Trevor had no idea that this particular phone was standard issue for all Project members and that it wasn't Cade's actual phone.

Holding it in his hand, Alex was tempted to turn it on just to see how long it would take to get a call. He had the urge to let Miles come to him, he wanted this over and done with, but Eve was here and this place was a sanctuary, he couldn't risk having it discovered.

He left it turned off, but it would certainly come in handy tomorrow when he turned it back on.

Refilling his glass, he grabbed Noelle's picture and went back to Eve. He handed her the water and she drank half before giving it back. He turned on the bedside lamp and slid under the covers. He watched her, a slight smile pulled at her swollen mouth as she looked at the picture lovingly. His chest became tight as he watched her. She made him feel...loved. And she loved him, he was certain of it now. Her reaction when she had thought he was Cade was the outcome he had prayed for. He hadn't meant to frighten her but he had got what he wanted and more. Much more. She hadn't said she loved him but she certainly didn't like the idea of him saying goodbye. His heart sank at the thought. Knowing what he did, that she loved him, how in the hell was he ever going to let her go?

"What's wrong?"

He focused on her face and faked a smile. "Just trying to figure out what Noelle drew for you here." He looked at the picture. "Are those flying turtles?"

Eve giggled. "I think so."

"Okay. What do you plan on doing with that?"

"I'm going to give it to you." Eve handed him the picture.

"No. Noelle made that for you." He pushed it back at her.

"But your name is on it too." She pointed to the top left corner.

He could just make out the printing in different size letters. *For Mom and Alex LOVE Noelle Sinclair.* He was touched, the unfamiliar feeling crushed down onto his chest. Shit. These women weren't going to make it easy, were they?

"Why did she put her last name?" He asked, accepting the picture.

Eve rolled onto her side and giggled again.

"Because, if you can believe it, there is another Noelle in her class." She pulled the covers around her. "She was so beautiful when she was born and it was Christmas, I wanted to give her a name that was unique." She shrugged. "Guess someone else had the same idea."

Alex carefully put the picture on his bedside and switched off the light. He pulled Eve up against his chest and kissed her neck. She had no idea that she had just described what Alex saw when he looked at her. Beautiful and unique.

* * * *

As Miles closed the door to his youngest daughter's room, the cell in his pocket rang.

He checked the caller ID before answering.

"Sir."

"Detective Taylor's partner has given him the phone. I assume everything else is already in place."

"Roger." Miles confirmed. He had spoken to Mike, made sure he understood that he was to be contacted first before all others.

His CO sighed into the phone, "I don't like you going at this alone. And if I feel the situation is getting out of your control, I'll send in another team to assist. Clear?"

"Roger." Miles squeezed his fist. He had to get this mess sorted out and fast.

"Good." The line went dead.

Miles clenched his jaw as he went back downstairs to his wife, silently cursing Taylor. *Turn on that damn phone.*

* * * *

"Eve," the deep voice called. A hand touched her face and she slapped it away.

"Eve. It's time to get up." The covers flew off her and she suddenly felt cold. There was a slap to her behind.

"Ouch!" She opened her eyes to see Alex walking away. "What time is it?"

"Ten." He kept walking as he called over his shoulder. "Breakfast is almost ready. You have ten minutes."

Because she was starving, she washed her face, dressed, and was downstairs in record time.

"Hungry?" Alex asked, setting a knife and fork in front of her.

"Starved." She took a sip of the coffee he sat in front of her and wrinkled her nose.

"Too strong? Here put milk and sugar in it."

"Wow. This stuff tastes like lead," she teased.

Raising his eyebrows, he pointed to the milk and sugar before turning back to the stove. Eve watched him flip what appeared to be an omelette and put two slices of bread into a toaster, then turn back to her. He didn't say anything, just stared at her, a knowing look on Cade's tanned face. After a while it became too much and her face began to heat up.

"What?" Why was he staring at her like that? What was he thinking? Alex wasn't an easy person to read.

He turned back to the stove when the toast popped up. While he filled two plates Eve sat back holding her lead coffee. She really liked this place. It was cosy and stylish for a single guy. "This place wasn't issued to you was it?"

"No it's mine. No one knows about this place, including Miles."

"It's really nice, not a bad place to be locked in for the day," she reminded him again.

His response was to grin while placing a white plate, filled with omelette, toast and hash browns in front of her.

"Wow, this looks really good."

"It is. Eat up. You'll need it," he said before sipping his coffee.

"How come no one knows about this place?" She tasted the eggs. "Mmm. Delicious."

"I needed a place where I could go that wasn't touched by my job. So I would come here on my time off and fix it up."

"You did all of this?"

"Most of it." He shrugged. "I contracted out when I needed to."

"I like it, much nicer than the other apartment."

"Even though there's no view?" He smirked.

She nodded. "It's not always about the view and that place felt cold. This place is warm and inviting. I really like it."

He pointed to her plate. "Keep eating, I don't know when we will be able to eat again today."

She swallowed hard. "Oh!"

He watched her from across the table. "We're going to Jillian today."

She set her fork down. "Okay. When?"

"As soon as you eat your breakfast." He began eating.

Eve stared down at the nice breakfast Alex had made for her and wanted to throw up. She had known this was coming. She had agreed to help Alex in case Jillian needed it. But it had come so fast and she wasn't ready to leave this little piece of heaven that Alex had brought her to.

"Eat."

She nodded and picked up her fork again but couldn't seem to touch the food. Their time together was coming to an end faster than she thought it would. Soon he would walk away from her and not look back and she would be alone, missing a small piece of her soul.

"Eve, you have to eat."

She looked up, hearing his concerned tone. His brow was wrinkled as he stared at her. Well, at least he was a little concerned for her. Would he be that way once everything was done and Jillian was safe? Would he worry then? She stared back at him. She honestly didn't know.

"I can make you something else."

"No." She shook her head, lowering her eyes to the plate. "This is fine." She jabbed a potato and quickly shovelled it in. It went down better than she thought it would and she ate as much as her turning stomach would allow.

An hour later they were on the road. Alex had loaded her bag of clothes and medical bag into a Jeep she had no memory seeing the day before, while wandering around his firehouse. He had the nerve to laugh when she asked if he had stolen it.

"No. I didn't steal it. That would be too much trouble. I bought this a few years ago." He looked for oncoming traffic as he pulled out onto a main road.

"This is what I take when I go north. I need the suspension for the dirt roads."

"So we're going north?" she asked looking at him. "Into Quebec?"

"Yes." He looked in his rear-view mirror before continuing. "I sent Jillian to my cottage up north. It's very isolated, a good place to lay low."

She turned to watch the other cars. "How long will it take to get there?"

"About five hours. Once we are out of the city it's two lanes straight there. But if we had left earlier we could have missed all the traffic, this will add on that extra time."

She was the reason they'd left late, she was the one who had slept in. "Sorry. I didn't know we were leaving today, or I would have got up sooner."

He shifted gears, picking up with the pace of the traffic. "It's not your fault. I didn't decide until this morning. And you needed to sleep. We had an interesting night last night."

Eve nodded silently, looking out the side window. What the hell was the matter with her? The second he told her they were leaving to go to Jillian, she became distant, almost withdrawn. It wasn't like he'd suddenly surprised her with a road trip up north. This was the goal after all, to help Jillian and her baby. And if he was lucky he'd get a chance to even up the score with Miles too.

He looked at her again. She was sitting straight with her hands jammed tightly in her lap. He reached out before he could stop himself and slid his hand in between hers, weaving their fingers together. She was nervous, that much was clear, about what though? He would never let anything happen to her or Jillian.

"Everything will be okay," he reassured her. When she gave no response, he wiggled the hands gripping his. "Hey"—he hardened his voice to get her attention—"Look at me." When he saw her turn her head, he made himself perfectly clear. "You will be safe. Do you understand me? You concentrate on helping Jillian and I'll take care of everything else. Okay?"

She nodded. "Okay."

"Good." He rubbed his thumb over her fingers. "Now try to relax. We have a long way to go and there aren't many places to stop until we get to Montcalm. This is why I wanted you to eat before we left."

Chapter Twenty-Seven

"They should be here in a few minutes."

Jillian didn't need to turn to find Justine. She appeared in front of her, sitting on the railing to the porch, her back to the front yard.

"I know, I can hear his car." She kicked her feet against the floorboards, setting the rocking chair into motion. "I'm still mad at you."

"I know. I just didn't know how to tell you and you were already upset over me. I didn't want to add to it."

"I know you didn't, but that's not the point. Cade might have been your husband but he was my brother. You should have told me right away."

"You're right, I'm sorry." Justine gave her a wary look. "Are you going to be okay?"

"Stop worrying." She waved her hand. "I'll be fine."

Justine hopped off the railing and sat in the chair next to her. "No back talk, missy. It's my right as the older sister to worry."

Justine snorted. "Four minutes hardly counts."

"Seriously. It might be weird for you to see Cade when you now know he's dead."

She felt her chest squeeze again. She still couldn't believe Cade was gone too. She had come to think of him as a brother, she had really enjoyed his company. He was so nice and sweet and he'd loved her sister. But they were together and, in the end, that was all that mattered. Now she just had to wrap her head around the idea of Alex showing up in Cade's body. "Yah it will! But I'll make sure Alex reminds me who he really is every once in a while." She rubbed the left side of her belly when the baby gave her a good kick.

"I doubt he'll have to do that. Eve calls him Alex." Justine studied her. "You haven't forgotten that Eve and Alex are…"

"Getting down and dirty?" Jillian supplied with a grin. "No, I haven't forgotten."

"That may be weird too. But remember Cade is with me."

Justine gave her a smirk. "Are you worried that I might go don't-yah-be-cheatin'-on my-sista crazy?" She ended with a snap of her fingers.

"Totally." Both sisters laughed out loud.

"I'll be okay." They both watched the Jeep as it pulled into the clearing. It was still a good distance away.

"I should probably get going. Eve is nervous of us ghostly folks." She stood and stopped at the top of the steps with a mischievous smile that Jillian had seen all her life. "But I think I'll just wait here." A familiar silence fell between them. "Are you going to tell him about the baby?"

Justine sighed, patting her stomach a nervous knot forming in her belly. "Not if I don't need to."

"You should, he deserves to know the truth." Justine turned back.

"What if he changes his mind and walks away from us?" Jillian stood next to Justine. She rubbed slow circles on her stomach, trying to sooth the baby who was suddenly kicking up a storm.

"Alex would never do that."

They both watched as the Jeep drove past the front of the house to the shed at the back. Justine turned back. "I'll check on you tonight."

A sudden fear caused the muscles in her throat to ache. "Justine."

"Yes?"

"When this all over, will you keep coming to see me?" The thought of Justine dead and buried was painful enough but to never see her again was worse. If the only way she could be with her sister was like this, then she would take it. The idea of Justine and her mischievous smile, being gone completely from her life, was downright depressing.

"Jilly, I'm not supposed to be here now. So you tell me if I'm going to keep coming to see you."

Jillian sighed inwardly. "Are you going to get in trouble for coming here?"

Justine shrugged. "What's the worst they can do me? I'm already dead. Besides, they said they need my help with others."

"What does that mean?"

"I'm not sure. Something about me having a good rapport with other souls. I don't know, sounds like a load of crap to me. We'll have to see. But no matter what those guys are having me do, I will always come to see you." Tears shimmered in Justine's eyes. "You're my sister. I love you."

* * * *

"Who was that?" Eve asked turning back to the house.

"That's Jillian." Alex geared the Jeep down and came to a stop in front of the shed.

"No. The other woman who was next to her."

What the hell! Alex stilled, giving her a sideways glance. He had to fight to keep from showing his surprise. Eve had seen Justine. He didn't know what to say without scaring her so he raised his eyebrows questioningly.

She made a face and placed her hand on her head. "It must have been all that bouncing down this road. All those pot holes gave me a concussion."

He smiled, hoping his worry didn't show. "I'd sue the owner if I were you."

"I might just do that." She chuckled, opening the door.

He wasn't sure what to do, should he tell her she had just seen a ghost or wait to see if it happened again? He quickly decided on the waiting approach. This could be a one-time thing, and he didn't need her jumpy. If it happened again, he would help her to learn to deal with it. He reached out and caught her by the back of the neck and drew her close. "Are you ready?"

She nodded up at him with big eyes. He gave her a hard kiss that turned soft when she ran her tongue along the seam of his lips, leaving him wanting more.

With her purse hanging over her shoulder and her old medical bag in her hand, Eve walked towards the house with Alex at her side. She was nervous. What would this woman be like? Did she have any idea what Alex had been through for her? Would she suddenly find out there was more between Alex and this Jillian? She closed her eyes when her heart dropped into her stomach. Where had that come from? No. Alex had said he didn't even know this woman; he had no reason to lie to her about it. Her new found jealously was ridiculous.

With his bag slung over his shoulder, Alex pulled her to his side. "Remember," he spoke low. "Jillian might think I'm Cade. If that's the case, let's go with it. I don't want her going into shock."

He suddenly released her and forced her to step away from his side before they walked around to the front of the house.

Jillian was still standing on the front steps, her hands twisting the sweater she was wearing, as they approached her. Eve stopped, keeping her distance, and watched as Alex approached the woman. "Any problems?" he asked lightly.

Jillian shook her head, her eyes blinking rapidly as she scanned his face. "I think something might be up with the water heater and the door to my...I mean, to the room, I'm staying in doesn't always stay closed."

Eve watched Jillian as she spoke to Alex. It was hard to tell if Jillian knew that Alex was using Cade's body. She appeared okay, but seemed startled by Alex's presence too. Alex must have picked up on it too because he continued to keep his voice low, "How about you, anything I need to know?"

She placed a hand on her swollen belly. "I'm...big. But I feel okay."

Alex nodded. Then looking over his shoulder back at her, he motioned with his head for Eve to step closer. She raised her eyebrows, not impressed by the manner in which he asked. Eve forced a smile when she stood next to Alex. "Hi."

"This is my friend Eve. She used to be a nurse and she is a damn good physiotherapist. I brought her in case you need any help with the baby."

Jillian smiled back at Eve. "I know. Thank you for coming. I hope this is over soon so you can get back to your daughter."

Eve straightened. "How do you know about my daughter?"

Jillian's eyes suddenly darted back and forth between her and Alex. She opened her mouth then closed it.

Alex curled his arm around her shoulder and pulled her up next to him, his heat suddenly seeped into her. "Justine?" He asked Jillian.

Jillian looked back to Eve and confirmed her fear.

Justine! The dead sister!

Fear made her back stiffen and her muscles became painfully tight. She looked around the front yard nervously. "How...d-does she know a-about..."

"Shhh." Alex pressed his mouth to her temple. "I'll tell you later."

"No." She pushed away. Her eyes darted back and forth. "Tell me now. H-how does she know about Noelle?" Alex dropped the bags and reached for her. She stepped back. "No."

Alex let his hands fall to his sides. "I can see Justine. She has been letting me know how Jillian has been doing."

Eve felt her eyes grow wide. No, she must have misunderstood. "You mean when you were..." She stopped and stared at Jillian.

"Yes, then." Alex gained her attention, taking a step towards her. "But now too." He quickly reached out and grabbed her by the arms, hauling her up against his body. Her mind began to spin. How was it possible? How could he still see her?

"How can…?" She trembled as his arms tightened around her.

"I don't know. But I can." He answered her question before she had a chance to ask it.

"Was she in the house, Alex?" The idea terrified her. A dead soul in her house, close to her baby.

He rubbed his chin on her head. "No. I told her about Noelle. So you can stop shaking now."

She took a deep breath and relaxed against him. "Good."

"Better?"

"Yes," she exhaled slowly. "Guess I didn't do a good job keeping your secret identity."

"Don't worry, I'll handle it." He pushed her away and walked to the bottom of the steps, closer to Jillian. She wrung her hands, a distraught look on her face.

"I'm sorry. I didn't mean to scare you," she apologised sincerely.

Eve felt her face flush. She didn't know what to say. Her fear of the dead was so overwhelming at times that she seemed to just come apart. She felt bad that she had blown Alex's plan about keeping his true soul from Jillian, but she was glad to know Justine hadn't been near Noelle.

"Can I assume you know who I am?" Alex asked carefully.

"Yes, I know who you are…Alex." Jillian nodded. "Justine told me." She blinked her large brown eyes.

"Good." He reached down to pick up the bags and teased, "I was worried you'd pass out or something."

Jillian placed her hands on her belly and snorted, "Don't let the belly fool you. It'd take a lot more than that to make me pass out."

Eve smiled at her sudden indignant tone.

"Oh shit. You're just like your sister aren't you?"

"I'm nowhere near as bad. But I do have my moments." Jillian stepped to the side as he climbed the front porch.

"Great," he said drily.

Jillian looked up, studying his face intently. "This is really weird though. You in Cade's body. How do you feel in there?"

Shrugging, Alex looked down. "A little taller."

Eve shook her head as she listened to Alex and Jillian joke about bodies and dead women. They had a bond, beside Cade's body and the obvious one of Miles wanting to kill Jillian. The same dead soul appeared to both of them. It was a bond she didn't understand and wanted no part of. Didn't they realise she was dead? Dealing with the dead was never good, bad things always happened.

Both Alex and Jillian turned to her. "Eve?" Alex asked. He studied her for a moment and, as though he knew she was still feeling nervous, his true face emerged along with a sexy grin. Then as quickly as his face appeared, it vanished and returned to the tanned face that was Cade's.

Eve sighed, walking up the steps of the wide front porch. Everything was okay. Alex was still here. For now.

* * * *

After taking Eve's bag up to the spare room, Alex fixed Jillian's door and had a look at the water heater.

Both were an easy fix. He wandered back into the house and found the bottom floor empty. After washing his hands he went upstairs to find Eve. He still felt guilty about lying to her about Justine. But when she turned white and began to shake, he went into protection mode and did the only thing that would get the result he wanted, he lied. It bothered him that he had to do it, but he'd do it again. He'd do anything to protect her, he realised, absolutely anything.

He stopped at the top of the stairs when he heard the two women talking. They were in Jillian's room with the door closed.

"How long were you a nurse?"

"Quite a few years. And don't worry, I did my time in obstetrics and gynaecology." Alex took a deep breath when he heard the velvety lilt to Eve's voice. He loved listening to her voice even though she wasn't talking to him. He propped himself against the wall and listened as Eve asked Jillian a series of questions relating to the baby and her general health. He rested his head back, Eve's soothing voice, compelled him to close his eyes and breathe. He was going to miss her. Miss her smile, miss her cheeky attitude, and miss her body. His chest suddenly became tight when he thought about his life without her in it.

He hung his head and rubbed at his face. Jesus, he was in deep. What the hell was he going to do? He had to go. He couldn't take the chance of her becoming hurt because of his life. But how the fuck was he going to find the strength do that?

He honestly didn't know if he could let her go and was unsure if he should even bother trying. The idea of having her and Noelle in his life was such a huge temptation, even with all their extra abilities and strange family medallions and lifespan... A thought suddenly occurred to him. If he and Eve were to live together or got married, he would grow old, while she and Noelle would barely age. And what would happen when he died? His chest tightened again. Eve would end up being alone. It was something that hadn't occurred to him before, but now that it had, he felt his confusion grow.

He swore to himself, fighting mixed emotions, but remained next to the door. He wanted to listen to Eve's voice, memorise that beautiful lilt, because it might have to last him the rest of his life.

* * * *

"Well. You look pretty good to me, and that baby's heart sure sounds strong." Eve closed her bag and looked seriously at Jillian. "But I would feel a lot better if we could get you to see a doc just to be sure."

Jillian rolled to her side and Eve helped her to sit up. "But you said I look good and the baby's heart is strong."

"True and I don't believe you have anything to be concerned about" — Eve could hear and see Jillian's sudden concern. She adjusted her voice — "But what I just checked is bare minimum pre-natal stuff. It's no substitute for seeing a specialist," Eve counselled, then asked, "Do you have a doc that you have been seeing?"

"No. I couldn't find one." Jillian lowered her head. "I've been going to the clinic around the corner from my apartment."

Eve patted her hand. "That's okay," she reassured. "I know a few good docs. When all of this is over I'll give them a call and see who has room for you," she soothed.

"Thank you." Jillian took a deep breath. "It's nice to have someone to talk to about this stuff."

"You didn't talk to your..." Eve swallowed. "Sister about this, or the baby's father?"

Jillian stiffened. "Justine listens but there is nothing she can do now."

"And the baby's father," Eve pressed. She watched as Jillian stiffened again. Eve fully understood. "He's not in the picture."

"I thought yes, but then..." She lowered her head as tears filled her eyes. "Not anymore."

Eve gently clasped her hand. "Would it make you feel better if I was to tell you, I went through the same as you?"

Jillian's head shot up. "Your daughter's father tried to kill you too?"

Chapter Twenty-Eight

"What?" Eve grabbed hold of Jillian's hand. They both jumped when the door flew open.

"What did you say?" Alex stood in the doorway.

Poor Jillian jumped again when Alex demanded she repeat her last sentence. She was shaking so badly she could barely get the words out.

"Easy. It's okay," Eve soothed, then turned and glared over her shoulder. "Stop it Alex, right now!"

He pinned her to the spot with glowing eyes.

Her anger flared to match his, "Don't look at me like that. I won't have you scaring her."

"Didn't you hear what she just said?" he barked.

"Of course I heard, I'm sitting right next to her." She focused her attention on Jillian and gently rubbed her back and used her strongest pitch to calm her. "It's okay; don't pay any attention to him. He may sound like a rabid dog, but he's no more than a kitten with a hair ball." She got a shaky laugh out of Jillian.

Alex snorted behind her, "Kitten! More like a cougar." Well she had to agree with that, but that didn't mean he needed to know.

She continued talking to Jillian, both her and Alex needed the clarification. She levelled her voice —
"Jillian, is Miles —"

"Rick," Alex corrected.

She looked to Alex. "Who the hell is Rick?"

"Cover name," he explained.

Eve wrapped her arm around Jillian's slumped shoulders. "Is Rick the father of your baby?" Jillian lowered her head to stare at her hands. Eve squeezed her shoulder. "It's okay."

"No it's not." She sniffed. "Look at me. I'm a pregnant mess."

Alex quietly came to stand in front of them and squatted down gripping his hands together. "When?"

Eve glanced up at him, it would seem the shock was under control. She gave him a worried smile. This was some serious stuff, she wasn't only worried about Jillian and the baby, she was worried about Alex too.

He gave her a wink before Jillian finally spoke.

"I met Rick..." She stopped. "That isn't his real name, is it?"

"No."

Jillian took a deep breath. "I met him over seven months ago now. When he came to work for Mr Rhodes. I worked late one night and missed my bus."

"That happened the night we found you."

"Mr Rhodes worked long hours. I missed my bus a lot. But he always covered the cost of the cabs I took home."

"But Rick took you home one night?" Alex guessed.

"Couple of nights." Her shoulders slumped.

"Hey," Alex said. "No judgement here, we're all human."

She lowered her eyes, and then continued with her story. "I told him when I found out. He was quiet at first but seemed to be okay with it and we still...you know." She shrugged. "And then he was gone for a while. When he came back I was just coming into my sixth month and had gotten pretty big." She shook her head wiping at her eyes. "He wanted me to put the baby up for adoption, but I couldn't do that. He didn't like it but he didn't pester me about it or anything and let the matter drop. And then I worked late with Mr Rhodes and saw you and Rick kill him." She sniffed. "That's it."

Alex stood and looked down at Jillian. Jesus, this was the reason Miles wanted to kill her. Not because she had witnessed them take out Rhodes but because she was carrying his child and refused to give it up. Then an opportunity presented itself and he took it. He clenched his fists. *That twisted fuck.*

"Alex?" The worried tone came from Eve.

He forced a smile. There had been too much screwing around. This had to end.

He turned from the women and went downstairs and out the front door. Cade's cell was still in the Jeep. He needed to turn it on. He'd call Trevor first and get him up here, then let Miles call him.

"Alex?" Eve called from behind.

"Go back in the house, Eve." Too late. She was beside him, gripping his hand. He stopped and glared down at her. "What?"

"I just...it got so cold in there. I wanted to know if you were all right."

"Do I look all right to you? My best friend wants to kill that woman because he got her pregnant." He pointed to the house. "He used her and then tried to kill her because she wouldn't do what he wanted." He glared down at her, then straightened. He was doing the very same thing to Eve. He had threatened her, threatened Noelle, forced her to do his bidding and had believed himself to be in the right because he had a noble cause. In fact, he was still using Eve by dragging her here to help him deal with Jillian. He was no better than Miles.

He stepped back from her. It would end here. If he cared for her at all—which right now he wasn't even sure his feelings for her were actually real or just a result of their circumstance—she needed to know it was over. She deserved to have a man that would love her the way she deserved to be loved.

"Go back to the house and stay with Jillian." He stilled her when she opened her mouth. "No. Listen. Remember when I told you we would end?"

Her hazel eyes became huge, she nodded slowly.

"Well that's now. I've already wasted too much time with you trying to get to this point. I hope it was worth it." Then, added to the harsh words. "Your job is to take care of Jillian and stay the hell away from me. Nothing more. Miles will be coming and I don't need you or her getting in my way. Is that clear?" She swallowed but nodded again.

"Good." He turned from her and marched to the Jeep throwing the passenger door open.

"Jesus, you are a real bastard." He looked up to see Justine sitting in the driver's seat.

"It's not a new thing for me." He opened the glove compartment and withdrew Cade's phone.

"She didn't deserve that." Her eyes flared at him. "Alex. Eve loves you. You must know that by now?"

His heart contracted painfully but he fought it. "She shouldn't." He turned the phone on.

"But she does. You were told she must be cherished and instead you crush her. What kind of man are you?"

He managed a flat smile, his guilt tearing him apart. "I'm not a man," he began. Then repeated what Brad Rhodes had said. "I'm a monster."

It took no time to call Trevor and give him detailed directions to his parents' cottage. He was eager to help and agreed to everything Alex suggested, except killing Miles. Alex had expected that. Trevor was a cop after all, he would want to see Miles do time. The only thing that Trevor didn't realise was that Miles would never do any time, shit he wouldn't make it to a police station to be formally charged. The Guardian Project protected their own.

After hanging up, he leaned against the back of his Jeep and looked at the cottage he had grown up in. During his summer vacations he and his mom would spend weeks, sometimes longer, here, his dad driving up on the weekends to join them. He would ride his bike, go into town and play with the local kids, swim in his own personal lake. Life was simple. He wished he had that now. It was incredible how fast a life could turn into a nightmare.

The cell rang.

He raised it to his ear. "Detective Taylor. Remy Castillo. I'm glad you decided to man up and turn on your phone. How's the weather up north?"

Alex laughed, he couldn't help it. Miles was going to die, there was no question about that. It was just too damn bad that there was still the man Alex had called a brother inside there somewhere. "Remy?" Alex stood up and opened the back of the Jeep. "I always hated that name. Makes you sound like an over-paid porn star. I'm sure I mentioned that once or twice." There was silence on the other end. Alex chuckled, pulling his rifle bag and large duffel from the back.

"How about I just call you Rick Burns? Or better yet Miles Harding, which is, after all, your real name?"

Miles gripped the phone as he sped through the city. He cut two cars off before shooting onto the highway. How the hell did this cop know his real name? And why did he repeat the same thing Alex had said to him years ago about his cover name Remy Castillo. Only Alex had teased him about it over the years. It was a private joke between the two of them.

Alex? No, it couldn't be. He reasoned, with the doubt in his head. It couldn't be Alex. He was lying in a coma at Memorial. But with what he'd seen at Alex's apartment and with what the cop had said, his gut was telling him there was something else going on.

"Sounds like you're on your way," Cade said casually. "When should I expect you?"

"Soon." Miles ended the call as he flew down the highway. There was more to this cop, something he had missed, but what? He was too calm, too casual. It was as though Cade knew what he was planning to do.

Alex sighed, sliding the phone into his back pocket. Miles was on his way. He moved quickly. There was a lot of ground to cover and he wasn't sure how long he would have before Miles arrived. The entire property was ten acres, with other wooded properties surrounding it. He need to set up a defensive ring around the house and shed, leaving only one way in, by water.

By the time he was done it was dark. He walked back down the drive to the house and noticed that a light was still on in the living room. As he walked past the house he noticed Eve on the front porch. She didn't look at him or even acknowledge he was there, just sat still and looked out at the water. He stopped and stared at her. He wished things hadn't turned out this way. He never wanted to hurt her and he fully accepted her hate for the things he had done to her. He still intended to protect her though, whether she wanted him to or not, there was never any question about that.

He cleared his throat, getting her attention. When she turned her head, he swore silently. Her eyes were flat and her face void of any emotion. "I need to show you something." He pointed to the shed behind the house.

She got to her feet and followed behind him as he walked behind the house. She was silent, the only thing he heard was the crunch of her feet on the driveway. He pulled open the double doors and moved beside the BMW parked inside, to the back of the shed. When he turned to show Eve the door on the floor, she wasn't there. He looked up and saw her watching him from outside.

"It's here," he said, pointing to the floor. She walked around the car and stopped next to him looking down. He bent down and pushed on a single slat of wood, which popped open exposing a handle. He pulled open a rectangular door leading down a narrow flight of steps.

"This leads to the house." He placed his foot on the first stair which triggered a light, and a faint glow lit up the tunnel. He waited at the bottom for her and when she was next to him he explained, "That way leads to the house." He turned and pointed under the stairs in the opposite direction. "That leads up the hill, away from the house."

Alex focused on her. "When I tell you, you and Jillian will go down to the basement and take this tunnel to here. Grab this flash light." He pointed to the ground and Eve saw a single long handle flash light sitting on the dirt floor. "Then take that tunnel up the hill. You'll come out next to a fir tree. Wait for me there. If I'm not there in twenty minutes make your way down to the main road and into town and call the cops."

Eve blinked up at him astonished these tunnels were even down here. "Did you dig this out?"

"No. I found it after my parents bought the house from an old couple. There used to be a barn above here, the previous owner didn't like walking in the snow to feed his horses and dug it out. That part" — he pointed back to the narrow tunnel under the stairs — "my dad figured it was a natural part of the area, there are caves all around here. I used to play in it all the time when I was young. It can be a little slippery, so watch your step."

She didn't respond to him, she was so surprised that he was concerned for her well-being all of a sudden. Well there was no need, she could take of herself and Jillian. "We'll be fine."

She pointed in the direction of the house. "I'm going to check out the entrance so I know where it is." She took a single step before Alex grabbed her arm.

"No. I'll show you when we're in the house."

"Don't." She pulled her arm away. She didn't want to feel Alex's hands on her — she was still hurting from his words. She knew he could be controlling and aggressive and she knew he had a very dark side to him, but never once had she thought he could be cruel and that was what he had been to her. Cruel. "I'm a waste of time. Remember?" His eyes were glowing by the time she was done.

Turning away, she climbed the steps, not caring how mad he had become. How dare he treat her like that? She hadn't done a single thing to deserve this, yet she was the one who kept catching the full force of his anger. What was wrong with her that drove Alex to reject her so quickly and in such a harsh manner? Her heart dropped. What was wrong with her besides the obvious not aging, having a tattoo that protects her from harm and being able to merge medians? Her heart broke a little more. Maybe what she should be asking is — why didn't he do it sooner?

She waited outside the shed as he closed the double doors and walked around the side. She followed, assuming he wanted her to and took the corner, stepping wide and was jerked back. Alex's arms surrounded her. She fought to get away.

"Hold still," he hissed in her ear, squeezing her tight. "Look down. See the tiny red light?"

She followed his instruction. "I don't see anythi…" She didn't see anything at first. All she could think about was getting away from him, but then she caught sight of it out the corner of her eye. "A micro mine." She stiffened. "Is Miles here?"

"I put that there. They surround the house and shed." He pointed to another, a little further away.

"Why?"

He didn't answer her. "The mines in my apartment were on a timer, these ones are motion sensitive."

"What does that mean?" She looked the other way and saw another tiny red light.

"It means if you go near them, and they detect the movement, they will explode."

"What if something happens and help comes. They will kill innocent people."

"No. It will be over by then." His breath warmed her neck. "They have an auto shut off for four hours. They've been on about an hour, so do not go past the trees on either side of the house or past the shed." He wasn't holding her as tight now. His fingers were gentle as he held her and his mouth kept brushing her ear.

Closing her eyes, she tried to ignore the heat that warmed her. Alex's heat. God, she was hurting and him holding her only made it worse. She pushed away feeling her throat close up and whispered, "Okay."

She walked carefully to the front of the shed and towards the house. She could hear Alex enter the house behind her and close the door. She jumped when he spoke right behind her.

"Come into the basement and I'll show you the door."

She followed him again and he showed her the door to the tunnel. She should have known it wouldn't be an actual door. Alex had an incredible imagination when it came to secret entrances. The entrance to the tunnel was hidden behind a set of shelves that collapsed in on themselves, folding down when they were moved along the wall. She peered down the dimly lit passageway and could see nothing but shadows.

"Are you good?" he asked, standing behind her.

So much for the concern. She nodded at his cold tone and, with her heart sinking into her stomach, she turned. "I'm going to check on Jillian."

Chapter Twenty-Nine

Alex moved quickly through the house, checking the windows, pausing at each one to search the surrounding area. He lowered his rifle and crossed to the stairs, climbing them silently. He stopped at the top when he saw Jillian's door was open and peeked inside, seeing her sleeping on the bed. He scanned the room. No Eve. He entered the room across the hall. It looked out onto the front of the house. He raised his rifle and looked through his scope at the opposite side of the lake.

No movement.

He scanned the lake in a slow sweeping motion and stopped when he saw ripples in the water. He held his breath and focused on the spot. Nothing. He continued searching further along for any type of disturbance in the water. When he found nothing, he exhaled and finished his sweep, then checked the bank and the front yard.

He lowered his rifle and stared out the window. There was a drowsy sigh behind him in the dark. He turned to find Eve sleeping in his mom's old reading chair. He had sat in that chair with his mom for many hours listening to her read. He'd always loved that chair. It was the only piece of furniture he hadn't given away, when he finally came back here. It was faded and worn and was so big it practically swallowed Eve up.

He felt a sense of peace run through him as he watched Eve sleep. Her head was resting back, her hands were jammed between her knees and her legs were tucked up under her. He noticed her lift her shoulders and shiver, pulling at the sweater she wore.

Grabbing a blanket off the bed, he laid it over her gently. A curl of hair fell onto her cheek as she cuddled under the blanket. He brushed it away and touched her smooth skin. His chest became tight as he gazed at her. She probably hated him now, which would cause him a lot of pain and regret over the coming years. That didn't matter. The only thing that mattered was that she was safe. He would suffer through anything to keep her safe. And it didn't matter that she was good for him, or that she made him feel at peace, or that she fit him perfectly. Because he knew now that he loved her. He loved her. Would always love her. *And you protect the ones you love, even if it causes you pain.*

"Thank you," she whispered without opening her eyes.

That was when the first mine went off.

Alex jumped to the window. There was an orange glow next to the lake. Close to the house.

"Shit." He turned back to Eve to get her up but she was already up and moving for the door.

He was right behind her as she entered Jillian's room. "Let's go." He grabbed Jillian's arm and helped Eve lift her off the bed, then grabbed her hand and pulled her behind him towards the stairs. "Eve come stand in front of her. Help her down." Eve did as he ordered without question and stood in front of Jillian taking her hand from him. Another mine went off. This one was on the other side of the house.

He motioned for Eve to stop.

Lifting his rifle, he crept silently down the stairs. He could see the bright flames reflecting off the lake through the front windows. Then movement. Miles. He rushed down the stairs. "Basement now!" he ordered quietly over his shoulder. He reached the centre of the room and fired at the shadow running along the front porch. He chambered another round as Eve took Jillian through the kitchen to the basement door. Only when he heard the door close did he leave the house in search of Miles.

* * * *

Another explosion. Jillian jumped next to her. "Oh, God. Rick is going to blow us up."

"No. Not Rick." Eve yanked hard on the shelves and exhaled when they opened. *Holy crap.* She was shaking, she needed to calm down. She would be no good to either of them if she fell apart. She dragged Jillian inside behind her, closing the door and listening as the shelves slid back into place. She exhaled. Alex really was good at this secret hiding business.

"Alex is trying to blow us up?"

"Shhh! Keep your voice down, I'm not sure if he can hear us in here," Eve whispered back. She held Jillian's hand and moved slowly down the tunnel. Another mine exploded, but this time it was ahead of them. Little bits of dirt fell from the low ceiling. Eve looked up nervously at the dirt, then at an old support beam.

Please don't let them collapse. She prayed silently to herself.

They travelled slowly down the tunnel, getting further away from the house and the light. Eve stopped when she heard gun shots. She desperately wanted to know what was going on up there. Was Alex okay, was he hurt? More gun shots. And then silence.

They reached the steps under the shed and Eve picked up the flash light Alex had shown her earlier and switched it on. The area lit up. Jillian's eyes were wide as she looked up the steps.

"Is that where we're going?"

"No, that leads to the shed. Alex wants us to go that way. It goes up the hill and comes out on the top of the hill. We're supposed to wait for him there."

Jillian grabbed the light and pointed it to the tunnel under the stairs. It didn't look too bad, until a centipede fell from the ceiling. Jillian yelped and bolted, as fast her belly would allow her, for the steps. "I'm not going in there. I'll wait for Alex in the shed."

"No." Eve reached for her shirt and pulled her back down. "You can't…" Footsteps above them.

Looking up, both Eve and Jillian followed the steps as they crossed to the hidden door. Eve snatched the light away from Jillian and pushed her towards the other tunnel. A sudden thump on the floor had them freezing in place. Another. And another. The ripping of wood from the floor. Oh no! He'd found the handle to the door. Eve thrust the flash light at Jillian and forced her down the tunnel. "Keep the light off until it's clear." She pushed Jillian hard towards the dark tunnel. "Go." The door flew open just as Jillian slipped into the inky shadows.

Miles squatted down looking thoughtfully at her. "You are not who I was expecting." He sighed, "I knew he was fucking you but I didn't think he was stupid enough to bring you here." He moved his head slightly, studying her.

Eve leaned away from him.

"No." Miles gave her a low warning, "Come on up, Eve." He motioned with his hand.

Keeping her eyes glued to his gun, she slowly climbed the steps until she was within his grasp, he locked onto her arm and hauled her up the rest of the way, releasing her when she stood next to him. Holding out his hand, he gestured for her to precede him. She looked him over. He was wet. Soaking. "How did you get here?"

He spoke between clenched teeth, "Your boyfriend is a little more skilled than I gave him credit for. He made a nice little defensive perimeter around you. I'll have to remember to ask how he was able to get into Ace's apartment."

Eve wanted to say 'through the front door', but decided to keep her mouth shut. She walked out of the shed and looked around nervously. Alex was out here somewhere. Or was he? Now that she was out here and Jillian wasn't with her, maybe he realised that Jillian was on her way to the top of the hill. He may have gone to meet her at the opening of the tunnel, help her escape. If that was the case, would he come back? She prayed with all her being that he would. But after the way he'd treated her — what he had said — she just didn't know. She couldn't depend on him, she needed to help herself. But she had no weapons, no training, so used the only thing she had at her disposal.

"Who were you expecting?" she lowered her voice, forced a smooth pitch.

Miles pulled her to a stop and scanned the area. He glared down at her. "You know who I was expecting. Why are you playing dumb?"

"I'm not." She shrugged. "I just wanted to see if you could say her name. She is, after all, the mother of your baby." She packed the words with enough force that he began leaning towards her. He blinked, confused, then straightened.

* * * *

That's my girl. Alex thought as he silently watched Eve talk to Miles. She was working her magic on him and he had no idea what she was doing. He was proud of her for risking her talent and life to stall him.

When he first saw Miles dive into the shed he'd stopped firing on the off chance that Eve and Jillian might be in there. Then he'd heard the yelp. So had Miles. His throat almost closed up on him when he saw Eve march out of the shed with Miles right behind her.

Anger and fear rose in his chest. He was unaware he was squeezing his jaws together until he felt the pull in his temples. He took a breath. *Calm down.* Lowering his rifle silently onto the ground, Alex pulled the Sig pistol Trevor had given him from behind his back and stood slowly. He shifted lightly from the shadow of the trees behind Miles and motioned to Eve to bring him closer. She faltered in her conversation when she saw him, but not enough for Miles to notice. Satisfied that she understood he carefully backed into the shadows of the forest.

"Jillian Reid," he said, keeping a close watch on her movements. "The attempt to make me feel some sort of attachment towards her is very noble, but a waste of time."

"I don't understand. Is having your baby that bad? You must like kids. You have two of your own." Eve shifted her weight to the other foot.

He was on her in a flash looming over her, glaring at her with black eyes. "How do you know about my family?" he demanded. He followed her when she staggered back and clasped the tops of her arms in a death grip. His hands dug into her skin and she could feel the muscles begin to throb. "Tell me," he roared and gave her a hard shake.

She tried to breathe, but she was so scared. Where had Alex gone? She blinked.

"Alex told me."

"What?" he snapped.

Okay, she had another chance to calm him. "Alex told me you like to take your kids to school when you are at home." The soothing call of her words, mixed with the truth of her answer, confused him.

"Alex who?" He shook his head.

"Alex Hunter." She pushed the words at him. "You remember Alex don't you? He's your partner and friend. Though I can't say I believe that. You shot him and put him in the hospital. How could you do that? He only wanted to help Jillian."

"Ace is in the hospital. He's in a coma." He frowned, looking down. "How do you know...?" His head snapped up, eyes dark. "That cop, Taylor. He and Alex are close aren't they?"

Eve didn't know how to react to that statement and laughed. "Very close."

Miles pulled his mouth into a tight line. "He's how you know about my girls. Alex told him about my family." He ran a hand though his damp hair. "Jesus. All those years working together and I never thought, never considered that Ace was a traitor."

"He's not," Eve snapped. "You are." She pointed her finger at him, enraged that his man had the nerve to call Alex a traitor. "You're the one who is trying to kill an innocent woman, whose only mistake was to let you touch her." She turned, moving towards the forest, then swung back to face him. "Love and lust must truly make people blind, because if she saw you for what you really are, Jillian would never have let you touch her."

He closed the distance between them. "You have no idea who Alex is. You saw him yourself, he's in the hospital," he replied through gritted teeth.

She laughed again. It sounded high and a bit crazy, even to her. "I know him better than you. He's compassionate and protective. He has a wonderful sense of humour. But he's not perfect. He is impatient and becomes annoyed when he doesn't get what he wants. He hates to be ignored and, regardless what he thinks is best for him, he doesn't like to be alone." She swayed back towards the forest, hoping Alex was close. "He didn't say but I think he was hurt when you shot him. He considered you family and you betrayed him. You're the traitor, not Alex."

Somewhere during her rant she had forgotten to maintain her pitch and she lost the calming effect she'd once had over Miles because his face grew darker by the word. He quickly reached out to strike her but Alex was suddenly there, standing in front of her, pushing her back. He caught Miles' arm and smashed his fist into his face. Miles stumbled back.

Alex pointed to the side away from the men. "Over there, Eve."

She backed away hypnotised by the scene in front of her. She didn't know who of the two men looked scarier. Miles with his black eyes or Alex with Cade's brown eyes. Both men were ready to kill the other but they remained still, as though waiting to see what the other would do.

"Jesus, Miles," Alex sounded calm. "Why are you doing this? Because you made a mistake?"

"That baby is a little more than a mistake. It could ruin my life. I love my wife and my family. I don't expect you to understand." He nodded to Eve, wiping the blood away with the back of his hand. "You started fucking this one only a couple of weeks after your wife was killed."

"You mean Justine. The woman *you* killed," Alex confirmed. "She's a feisty little thing. When I found out that a delivery truck was used I knew right away it was you. A little of the Project's organic acid on the cargo straps, deflate the tires. Of course, at the time I couldn't figure out why you wanted to kill Justine and Cade. But now I know. You were panicking because of our little disagreement and the fact the Jillian got away."

Eve turned to Miles and watched as his confused look deepened. Alex continued, "You made a mistake. You killed the wrong sister."

"I don't know you." Miles' scowl deepened.

"But I know you. Very well in fact. You were the closest thing I had to a brother. I was at your wedding, and each of Amber's and Emma's birthday parties."

Miles shook his head when Alex advanced towards him.

There was an evil smirk on Alex's face. It was clear he enjoyed confusing Miles. "How about I repeat the last thing you said to me. Will that convince you?" Alex asked. "'Maybe I should let you freeze to death, then I wouldn't have to kill you.' Of course you didn't know I was standing across the bed from you."

"Who are you...how do you know what..." Miles stumbled on his words.

Alex took another slow step towards Miles, and Eve watched as Alex became very evident on Cade's face.

Cade's normal brown eyes suddenly became intense and focused, flickering into a glowing bright blue. Black slashing eyebrows with the familiar scar running through his left brow appeared along with his muscled jaw and full lips and his short black hair materialised last.

Miles was ghostly white when he staggered away from Alex and raised his gun. But the movement was too slow and Alex was already on him, knocking the gun to the ground with his forearm. He turned back to Miles and drove his elbow up. He caught him under the chin and knocked his head back. Miles stumbled, but caught himself. Straightening, he flexed his shoulders and met Alex head on as the two men slammed into one another.

Eve trembled as she inched back watching the violence. She couldn't seem to make herself look away. The sounds of fists striking flesh, the cracking of bone, the grunting, and the blood. There was so much blood. Blood on Alex. Blood on Miles. Blood on the ground. She finally squeezed her eyes shut and dropped to her knees, covering her ears. She couldn't take anymore. She couldn't watch Alex get hit and she couldn't watch Alex hit. The anger on his face, in his eyes was terrifying. He was consumed with rage.

This wasn't Alex. The situation was causing this behaviour, she lied. She had to lie. She began talking to herself. Using her voice, she forced a much needed calm on to herself. Chanting an old Gaelic nursery rhyme her mother would sing to her, to help quiet her down when she had nightmares. Over and over in a low voice she repeated the tale until she took a deep breath and felt her heart slow.

When she felt calm enough to look back to the men, she found Alex looming above her, covered in blood. She searched and saw Miles lying face first on the ground just behind Alex.

As Alex bent down, Eve couldn't help but shy away from him, shaking her head fervently. He wasn't fazed and lifted her by the arms until she stood in front of him and pulled her into his chest. His arms curled around her gently, pinning her in place.

"It's over," he soothed.

She turned her head, heard his heart beating strong in his chest. Closing her eyes, Eve gripped at his shirt.

"Eve, honey. It's over. Stop crying." Was she crying? She touched her own damp cheek. She hadn't realised.

Alex raised her head. A worried frown creased his brow. "Okay?"

She nodded then answered him, "No" — disagreeing with herself.

His concern was still evident when he soothed the hair back from her face.

"What were you saying when you fell to the ground? I didn't understand it."

"What?" She blinked.

"You kept repeating something, but I didn't understand the language. Was it meant to calm me?"

Shaking her head, Eve admitted sadly, "No. I did that for myself. I couldn't handle watching you two…it was so violent."

He pulled her back into his body, into his warmth. "Well, it worked on both of us. Thank you."

Eve pulled back and tried to look at Miles lying on the ground. Alex shifted his weight and blocked her view. "Is he dead?" Her throat closed as she waited for him to answer.

"No. I tried but I couldn't do it," he sighed. "I thought about his family and stopped. His girls would be without a father. I couldn't do that. Trevor will be more than happy to take him to the cops."

Eve hugged him tight. Thank God! She knew it went against his instinct but his restraint proved that he was a good man. Even if he didn't think he was. "I'm proud of you." She wasn't embarrassed to admit what she felt because it was the truth.

"You are?"

She leant back, his arms still around her. "Yes. You could have killed him but you didn't."

"But, according to you I should be annoyed because I'm not getting what I want, or maybe I was just too impatient to kill him." There was a glint in his eye as he offhandedly told her he had heard her rant.

"That would make sense."

He chuckled as he kissed her. His lips were warm and tender and very loving. Oh how she loved him.

"Where did you leave Jillian?"

"She's in the tunnel. I sent her up the hill like you told me to."

"Good. I'll stay here and you go…" He turned into her without warning, wrapping himself protectively around her, just before she heard a harsh whisper of air followed by a crack. Alex's body jerked forward and a hot pressure exploded in her upper chest by her shoulder.

Alex fixed his beautiful eyes on her and whispered, "I'm sorry Eve." He leaned into her, suddenly grabbing and holding onto her tightly. She tried, but she just couldn't hold his weight and fell to the ground, his weight knocking the wind from her.

Cade's larger body covered hers. "Close your eyes honey, don't move," Alex breathed lightly.

Eve heard huffing and scraping. She closed her eyes, knowing Miles was standing above them.

"Two for the price of one," she heard him spit. "I should have just done this from the beginning. Would have saved me a lot of time."

Eve could hear Miles move towards the shed. He was going after Jillian. Oh God! Were they all going to die, was this all for nothing? When she didn't hear any movement she slowly opened her eyes and searched what areas she could from under Alex. When she didn't see anything she tried to wake him.

"Alex," She breathed out. Air was caught in her lungs, the pain in her chest and shoulder were incredible but Alex's weight made it worse.

"Alex get off me." She struggled beneath him, but nothing. She froze. "Alex." Fear was building. "Alex," she whimpered his name. "Please wake up."

Chapter Thirty

Knowing the tunnel would be black, Miles grabbed a glow stick out of a small camouflaged rucksack stowed in the back of the BMW and took the steps leading down to the tunnel, two at a time. He didn't know how long the tunnel was so he had no idea how far ahead Jillian had got. Moving swiftly, he gripped his gun in one hand and held the white glow stick out in front of him.

He looked back over his shoulder, expecting to see the cop behind him. Christ, he was jumpy. He wiped sweat mixed with blood from his face with the back of his hand.

He was still having a hard time trying to figure out what he had just seen. He could have sworn he just got his ass handed to him by Ace. But it wasn't Ace, it was the cop—but he'd definitely seen Ace- his face appeared on the cop - it was Ace, the dark hair, the colouring of his skin, right down to the scar that ran through his left eyebrow.

Ace. Fuck. He really wished it hadn't come down to this. Once he killed Jillian and buried the bodies, he would have to go back to Memorial and kill Ace. He had hoped things wouldn't turn out this way, Ace had been his partner, his best friend he never wanted any of this. He shook his head and looked behind him again. He didn't actually believe what the cop had said, that bleeding heart crap about them being brothers? Taylor didn't know Ace, who was that guy trying to fool? Eve? Was he trying to impress her?

He snorted. It wouldn't make a difference now, he thought, focusing on the darkness in front of him. They were both... He stopped when he saw the cop standing no more than five feet in front of him.

Detective Cade Taylor stood in the middle of the tunnel, blocking his path. His hands rested on his hips, legs braced apart.

"What the hell?" Miles quickly raised the gun and fired one shot. Heart. There was no way he'd get back up after that.

The cop looked down at his chest then back to Miles and laughed out loud. Then, Taylor charged him out of nowhere. Miles fixed his stance and tightened his body ready to take the blow but nothing came. Just a cold gush of air. He swung the glow stick back and forth lighting the area in front and behind — nothing. "Where the fuck did you go?"

A deep laugh echoed through the tunnel.

* * * *

Eve jumped when she heard the muffled gunshot. With fear taking over, she finally managed to get out from under Alex. His head was turned to the side and there was blood everywhere. Pooling under him, soaking into his shirt. She moved to lift up his shirt but stopped short when pain torn at her shoulder.

There was a hole in the fleshy part of her shoulder. It throbbed when she moved it but it would heal. Of course it would heal, she was a Sinclair. She thought dully as she looked at Alex. Her hand shook as she raised his shirt. There was a hole in the lower part of his back. She put pressure on it and tried to roll him over to look at his front. She knew the bullet went through she just didn't know where.

She pulled off her sweater, crying out as she slipped her sore arm free. She jammed it against the hole in his back and after gripping his shirt and giving him a good tug she was able to roll him over, his weight providing the pressure needed to help slow the bleeding. It wasn't hard to find the exit hole in the upper part of his chest, a thick steady flow of blood was pouring from it. She clamped both hands over it and pressed hard.

* * * *

Miles stopped and held his breath, listening. There was a soft whimpering up ahead. He had heard that muted cry before…Jillian. He charged forward holding the light in front of him. He stumbled on a slick rock but caught himself and carried on until he saw a small form curled up against the side of the tunnel.

He inhaled the damp air. Finally. His life could get back to normal and Nicole and the girls would never find out about this.

"Stand up, Jillian," he ordered raising his gun. He wouldn't shoot her in the back. She deserved more than that cop did. She was carrying his baby, after all. When she didn't comply he ordered her again. She finally struggled to her feet and cried louder. He was beginning to lose what patience he had left. "Shut up. Jesus, you brought this on yourself. I told you to put it up for adoption and you wouldn't. I can't risk you coming by the house. My family means too much to me to let you ruin it."

Her crying became louder and almost piercing, as it echoed in the tunnel. Miles yelled over top of her, "Shut the fuck up and turn around."

She suddenly became quiet and slowly faced him.

Blood — everywhere — coming from her one remaining eye and mouth. There was a long gash running though the centre of her face, so deep he could see the bone. Another gash ran parallel to the first extending up into her blonde hair — blood and bits of grey matter clumped the once satiny strands together. Miles reeled back and exhaled. The area around him suddenly grew cold, very cold.

"This is what you did to me." Her jaw moved. Miles stared at her in horror as it swung almost completely detached from her face. Bubbles of blood escaped from the holes in her chest where her ribs had broken through the skin.

Her hands, held over her belly were also covered in blood and two fingers were bent grotesquely back and he followed her gaze as she looked down. Her hands pulled away and he saw nothing. He looked back up to her face and it was...beautiful. Like the first time he'd seen her. No missing eye, no deep cuts, no blood, nothing but perfection. She stepped towards him, an evil grin on her face. Another step and her face darkened. Another step and her eyes were black. One more step and she lunged at him, an inhuman scream coming from her smiling mouth.

* * * *

Eve whirled to look over at the shed when she heard more gun shots. She couldn't worry about that right now. The blood coming from the hole in Alex's chest wouldn't stop. It seeped through her fingers and over the backs of her hands. "No!" she whispered.

She glanced at Alex's face and was startled to see him staring back. The blue was flickering in Cade's brown eyes when normally it was strong and bright. Her stomach clenched, the reality hitting her. She was going to lose him.

"You have to leave, Eve." He spoke so low she could barely hear him.

Bending closer to his head, she brushed her hand through his short hair. "Shhh. I can help you."

"You have to leave here Eve. Before Miles comes back."

"I don't want to go. I don't want to leave you." Her face cracked and the tears fell.

But he kept talking as though he hadn't heard her. "Swim across the lake to the opening on the other side. Go into town and call the police. Don't go looking for Jillian." The blue was almost completely gone from Cade's eyes.

What would happen when it was all gone? For the first time since he'd begun haunting her Eve demanded the opposite of Alex. "I don't want you to go away." She brushed her hand through his hair again, watching the last of the blue flicker away. "Please don't go away."

* * * *

Miles' heart pounded in his chest. This couldn't be happening. What had he just seen? Jillian's twin? But she was dead. Killed by the truck he had rigged. And the cop, who should have been killed at the same time, but had survived. *And Ace*. He had seen Alex's face replace the cop's face. He stopped and looked around, leaning against the side of the tunnel. He needed to catch his breath. What the hell was the matter with him? He was never this jumpy and he had seen and done things in his life that would make most people cringe. But with what had just happened...he looked back down the tunnel, or maybe it hadn't happened.

He rubbed a shaky hand over his face and forced himself to carry on. This had to get done, Jillian had to die. He wouldn't take any chances.

He held the glow stick out in front of him and saw movement up ahead. His heart actually thumped against his chest. He thought it might be another...he scowled. What? Ghost? He didn't believe in ghosts. When you're dead, you're dead. That was it. Sweat slid down the side of his face. Still. It could be one of them waiting for him.

He raised the gun, just in case, and squinted. The small figure moved against the tunnel, using the wall for support. She turned back when he kicked a stone and it bounced off the side of the tunnel.

The light from the glow stick lit up Jillian's face. She gasped and moved as fast as her body would allow, tripping as she did.

Miles snarled and pressed forward, stumbling. He lowered the glow stick and lit up the ground. Mud, leaves, sticks and moss covered rocks stretched out before him. There was no safe path, so he shifted his weight carefully, stepping from stone to stone.

He was closing the distance until Jillian began to climb up. He saw her clawing at the dirt, pulling herself up. Shit. The opening to the tunnel. He moved quickly, dancing lightly over the slick stones until he reached the bottom of the incline. Jillian peered over her shoulder and sobbed when she saw how close he was.

Almost there.

Miles jumped, landing right behind her. He reached for her foot, but slid backwards, thanks to the mud and moss covering the entrance. He dug his hand into the dirt and pulled himself up, closing the gap. She cried out when she saw him lunge and pulled her leg away at the last moment.

Watching her reach the crest, he swore and leapt up the embankment one last time. This time he locked onto her ankle. She struggled to keep her balance as he pushed up onto his knees. He raised his gun and took aim. He had had enough fucking around and only wanted to do this once.

As he lined her up in his sight she was suddenly plucked from his grasp and pulled behind a man pointing a gun at him.

Miles cried out enraged.

"You have the right to remain silent," the man began.

"Christ, not another cop." He shifted his aim to the cop with the goatee.

The man nodded as he forced Jillian's small frame behind his back.

Miles curled his lips up into a smirk and huffed, "That won't save her." He couldn't believe this man had it in his head that he was going to arrest *him*. He really had no idea who he was dealing with.

The cop studied him for a second. "You're not coming quietly are you?"

Miles chuckled, tightening his finger on the trigger.

Miles blinked once before the bullet tore through the centre of his forehead.

Chapter Thirty-One

Eve straightened when she heard Jillian cry out, followed by a shot. *Oh God!* She had to go. Miles might come back. She stared down at Cade's body. Alex was no longer here. Her heart ached at the thought. Alex wasn't here. She inhaled the cold night air.

She hated the feeling that was surrounding her — it was so strong, so painful it crushed her from the inside. She sniffed. But it had happened. She had been touching Cade's body when she felt Alex go. One second Cade's body was giving off Alex's heat and the next second, nothing. She sucked in a choppy breath and felt the tears continue to fall. He wasn't here anymore. Her lips twitched as she tried not to cry, but she couldn't help it, her heart was just ripped in half. She covered her face and cried, heartbroken, into her hands.

After a few minutes, she finally pushed to her feet. She had to think about Noelle. She had to get home and get Noelle and Gran away in case Miles came looking for them.

Turning towards the lake, she did what Alex told her to do. She walked into the water. The tears sliding down her face as the cold water surrounded her. Her shoulder throbbed but the cold water helped numb the pain. Why couldn't it do that with her heart? She made it over to the opposite side of the lake and crept by a dark four door sedan which, she assumed belonged to Miles and out onto the main road.

Numb and cold, she started towards town. She hadn't walked very far when a car came down the road from the direction of the lake. It was travelling at such a high rate of speed she only just moved out of the way before it reached her. She jumped into the trees on the side of the road when it came to a stop. She hid behind a large evergreen and held her breath.

Was it Miles? Did he see her?

She heard voices and a man ask, "Are you sure that was her?"

"Yes that was Eve."

Jillian? Was that Jillian? No her mind was playing tricks on her.

"Eve Sinclair," the man called out. "I'm Detective Trevor Daniels. I have Jillian Reid with me."

Eve had almost fallen to her knees when he'd called out to her. She vaguely remembered Alex saying something about Trevor wanting to arrest Miles. Chilled, she moved out from behind the tree and stumbled to the road where a bald man with a red goatee stood next to Jillian.

He helped her up the small gulley next to the road, where Jillian rushed to her side. "Eve. Are you okay? How did you get here?"

She suddenly felt very cold and shivered. "I swam across the lake like Al...Cade told me too." She lowered her head, feeling her heart break into tiny pieces.

"Where is Cade? I heard so many shots I..." Trevor frowned at Eve. She couldn't hide the fact that she had been crying, she didn't want to. The man she loved had just been killed, her heart was in two pieces and she didn't know if it would ever heal.

She shook her head and whispered, "Miles shot him."

Trevor handed her the blanket he pulled from the car. "That doesn't mean he's dead. Maybe just passed out."

Eve shook her head again and explained, "The bullet entered in his lower back and came out his upper chest and then hit me here." She pointed to the hole in her shirt. She then drew the line the bullet had followed across her own chest. "I can't even begin to imagine how much damage it did." If she thought about it logically, Alex shouldn't have been able to speak to her at all. That'd proved how strong Alex had really been, telling her what to do while suffering a great deal of pain. She exhaled a choppy breath as new tears gathered. Pain. She closed her eyes and prayed. Please God don't let him be in anymore pain. Let him have peace.

She swayed and let Trevor lead her to his car. She leaned against the side as he checked her shoulder and commented that it didn't look too bad.

"What about Miles?" she asked quietly. "I heard you scream. I thought you were..." She didn't want to say the word, there had been too much death tonight, and she was afraid that if she uttered the word it might trigger another disastrous event.

Jillian shook her head, her lips suddenly trembling. "It's okay." Trevor moved to her side and wrapped his arms around her. Eve's smile at the tender show of affection didn't last long.

Jillian leaned into Trevor as he spoke over top of her head. "Miles was trying to kill her. I did what I had to do."

Eve nodded, understanding perfectly. Miles was dead. Jillian and her baby were safe, she was safe, and Noelle and Gran were safe. Looked like everyone was safe.

She stared off into the trees on the side of the road. Did Alex even know? She shifted her eyes around the area. Could he be here watching? She would never know she couldn't see the dead. She chuckled to herself. How crazy was this? For years she had been terrified at the thought of seeing the dead and now, with the idea that Alex might be close, she wanted more than anything to have that ability. Just so she could see him, even if it was only for a minute.

"I have to call this in," Trevor interrupted her wishful thinking. "Will you be okay here with Jillian?"

Eve struggled, opening the blanket hanging around her shoulders for Jillian. Trevor helped her rest against the car and pulled the blanket around both women. "Call out if you need me." He didn't leave until Jillian promised.

Standing next to her, Jillian hugged her close.

She smiled, but doubted it looked genuine. "I'm so sorry, Eve." Jillian gave her a knowing look, and lowered her voice, "About Alex."

Eve nodded. What else could she do?

* * * *

When Alex opened his eyes he could hear whispering in his head, telling him what he needed to do. But it was hard to understand, the deep voice wasn't clear. He rubbed his face and looked around. He was standing at the end of his bed in Memorial. His body was still in the same room, with the same blanket covering him. His beard and hair had grown longer, but the holes in his chest were healed. He looked around again and swore.

He was back. He was a median again and Eve was stuck out there, hurt with Miles hunting her. Or worse, she was dead.

Leaning forward, he gripped the metal rail at the end of his bed, squeezing so tight his hands went white. "No." He wouldn't believe that, she had to be alive. She was strong, a fighter, plus she had the Sinclair tattoo. She had to be alive, she had to be safe. But what if she wasn't? What if Miles was hunting her, what if he had her?

A low growl vibrated through his body and the room began to shake. He couldn't save her. He wasn't able to save her because he was stuck in this fucking place. The idea had him moving his head back and forth in denial as the force of the vibration grew.

He remembered hearing Miles running towards the shed, had heard the gun shots. Eve. The idea of her lying dead in the forest by his parents' cottage flashed before his eyes. "*No!*" he roared lifting the bed and slamming it back down, the force rocking his body in the bed.

"Easy, big guy. No need to trash the place."

He whipped around and saw Justine emerging from the corner. He stalked over to her, blinding fury coursing through him and for the first time since she first appeared to him, the grin disappeared from her face. She backed away raising her hands. "Hey, calm down."

"Where is Eve?" he roared. "I need to know, now!" He clamped his hands into fists, frustrated by his sudden lack of control.

Justine lowered her hands but still kept her distance. "She's fine. She spent four days here and was released a couple of days ago when she healed faster than expected." She wiggled her eyebrows. "No surprise there."

"Four days?" Alex snapped. "How many days have I been gone?"

Justine smiled sympathetically. "It's been a week.

A week!

"Miles?"

"Oh! He's dead." Justine grinned. Then, looking up, she rolled her eyes.

Alex looked up too, now used to the interruptions from above. "What are they saying?"

"That I'm not supposed to be so happy that Miles is dead," she huffed. "They consider him a wounded soul and will heal him before he goes back out there." She dropped her voice and leaned into him. "I don't care. I'm still happy Trevor shot that prick."

Alex straightened. "Trevor?"

"Yup. Cade told you he was a good guy. You should have had more faith in people," she teased.

Relieved, he took a breath. Okay, Eve was alive, Miles was dead, and Trevor had shot Miles. "Where is Jillian?"

Justine's smile turned warm. "She's here. Down in maternity. The doc's are nervous about letting her go because of everything that has happened. But Trevor has been great, taking care of mine and Cade's funerals and coming to visit her every day. I think there might be something there," she sighed. "God I hope so. I hate to think of Jillian being alone."

Now that Jillian and her baby were safe, his job was done. He could move on! *Fan-fucking-tastic!* He thought sarcastically. Except, he could not just move on. He couldn't go anywhere, he was still stuck being a median. What the hell was he going to do? He couldn't do this anymore, he wanted a body. He wanted his body. "Now what?" He opened his arms. "I find Eve and have her merge me? I don't know if I can put her through that again."

"Put her through what?" Justine snapped. "You dumped Eve, remember? Wanted her out of your life."

He stared at her. Felt the guilt turn his stomach. Eve's face filled the light and dark places in his mind. Her love filled his heart and her soul had healed his without him even realising she was doing it. He could breathe because of her. How could he want someone as precious as Eve to walk out his life? He knew now that he couldn't live peacefully without her.

But even that wasn't a possibility right now because he was a fucking median again.

"I remember. I was…"

"What?" Justine snapped. "You don't deserve her if you plan on treating her that way."

"I only…"

She cut him off. "Let her go and find someone who will treat her right. It may take time but she will get over you."

Her words hit him hard and he rebelled at the idea of another man loving Eve. "No." He gritted his teeth. "I can't let her go." He lowered his voice and admitted, "I know I don't deserve her but I can't live without her. And this feeling I have for her, it's only growing stronger. It's been this way since you first sent me to her. I don't understand it, but I know with my entire soul that I cannot live without her. I can't let her go not when I know she loves me."

"And you're so sure Evening loves you?" Dawn asked as she stood in the doorway of his room.

He nodded, unfazed by her sudden appearance. "Yes."

"I knew she did." Justine drew his attention, giving him a stunning smile. Pointing her thumb towards Eve's grandmother, Justine said, "But the old bird needed to hear it from you."

Dawn entered the room and closed the door behind her. "Watch it young lady," Dawn snapped.

Justine gave Dawn the worst salute Alex had ever seen. "Yes, ma'am."

Confused, Alex asked Dawn, "How did you get past the guards?"

Dawn tossed her large bag onto the bed next to his legs. "A grandmother is allowed to visit her only grandson."

Alex shook his head. *Incredible.*

"Alex," Justine began. Her voice had dropped in tone and her normally mischievous eyes held a serious glint in them. "I would like to ask you one more question, before we can begin."

Alex narrowed his eyes. "Begin what?"

"Do you love Evening? Enough to spend the remainder of your life with her?"

The question was ridiculous, but his answer was instantaneous. "Yes."

"Evening will outlive you. You will grow old, but Evening's aging will be slowed by her…" The Being in Justine laughed. "By her family's *tattoo*." Old and wise eyes studied him. "Would knowing this change your feelings towards her?"

"In the beginning when I first found out, but not now. The only thing that bothers me about all of this is what will happen to Eve and Noelle when I'm dead and buried." Alex sighed, "I don't like that they will be alone. I'll have to figure something out for them."

Apparently, the question was answered to the Being's satisfaction because he received a slow but genuine smile.

Gracefully crossing to Dawn, the Being controlling Justine nodded to the older woman. "Nice to see you again, Dawn. Did you bring the address?"

Dawn smiled back like they were old friends. "I did." Both Dawn and Justine looked over at him. Dawn winked knowingly.

"This has turned out better than I could have hoped for." Justine placed her hands on her hips and stood, looking very masculine. "He will be good for her don't you think?"

Dawn agreed then added, "And she for him."

"Very true." There was another approving nod before a serious expression crossed Justine's pretty face. "I certainly hope you understand how precious the gift is I'm giving you? I would hate to regret my decision."

"I understand and there will be no cause for regret," Alex said with conviction.

The Being glided the short distance between them and glared at him. "Good. I would hate to come back and deliver my own personal form of justice."

With that said, the Being moved back and stopped. Justine blinked several times before looking back to Dawn. "I really hate that. Everything better be cool?"

Dawn laughed. "Everything is cool. Now stop complaining, you agreed to it."

"I know." Justine rubbed her shoulders and wiggled her arms. "I don't like when my soul is used like a sweater."

Sighing, Alex joined the women. "Who was that who just threatened me?"

Dawn answered the question, "That was Raphael."

Alex raised his eyebrows, surprised by the answer. He narrowed his eyes and clarified. "As in...?" He couldn't finish, it seemed so unearthly.

"Yup! That's him." Justine grinned.

"Okay." Dawn sighed, pulling a large leather bound book from her bag. "Let's get moving before the nurses do their rounds."

Alex stared down at the book. It was Eve's book with the poem to merge him back with his body. "So that's why you're here." He shook his head. "Eve said you were too old to merge."

"She lied. But she only did it to protect me, so don't go getting all mad at her."

Of course, she was only protecting Dawn. He understood that now about Eve. She protected the ones she loved.

"Oh!" Dawn called pulling a chair next to his bed. "Before I forget..." She stepped next to him and pulled a card from her pocket. "You're supposed to memorise this address." She held it up for him. He read the address and knew exactly where the building was located.

"What is this place?"

Dawn turned the card over. "Ask for Ralph, he already knows why you're coming."

Alex grinned like a fool. He laughed reading the name on the card. "A Little Piece of Heaven Tattoo Parlour."

Chapter Thirty-Two

A month had passed since the shooting and Christmas was fast approaching—so was Noelle's birthday. Eve sipped her tea as she huddled under the heavy blanket she'd brought out to the front porch with her. She needed to be out here, the house had felt stuffy since she got back from her brief stay in the hospital.

She wasn't a fool. She knew it was more than the house feeling oppressive. She just didn't want to be in there. There were still too many memories of Alex. Alex in her office, Alex in the studio, Alex closing the fridge in her kitchen. She even hated going into her own room because the memory of Alex making love to her was still so fresh, even after four weeks. Her chest would begin to ache and then it became hard to breathe—that was when she came out here. The very same thing had happened after her mum had died, so the routine was easy to slip back into.

She pushed her foot off the floor boards, setting the swing into motion. Resting her head back she sighed and closed her eyes. Maybe the rocking would calm her enough to want to go up to bed.

"It's getting cold, why are you still out here?"

Eve's snapped her eyes open when she heard the voice. Quickly turning her head, she sucked in the cold night air. Tears came to her eyes and goose bumps formed on her skin.

Alex. Her throat closed up on her.

"Oh my God," she exhaled the words. She turned away, out into the dark, her body remaining perfectly still. What should she do? She couldn't be scared, it was Alex. But was it? The dead were different, or so Gran said.

She pulled in a choppy breath when she realised she had been holding her breath.

"Evening, I need your help." Was he closer? He sounded closer. The swing stopped and she hadn't been the one to stop it.

When Alex had first died and she had been lying in the hospital, she'd prayed every night that he would come to her, so she could see him again. She knew what that meant. It not only left her open to seeing Alex but others who were dead as well. And at that time she hadn't cared, she'd only wanted to see Alex. Then she went home to Noelle and she'd realised what she'd been praying for might not be Alex. It hurt, the idea of not seeing him ever again. She loved him, she still did. But she could do nothing for him now. He needed to move on.

"I c-can't do anything for y-you now. It's t-too late." She shivered under the blanket.

"Calm down. It's not what you think."

Still focusing into the dark, Eve tried again. "It's too late, Alex," she whispered because her throat was closing up again. "I really can't help you now."

"Eve, honey," he pleaded. "Look at me."

When she didn't, he asked again. "Please Evening, look at me."

She didn't want to, she wanted him to go away so she could cry and start grieving for him again. But despite what she wanted, she looked at him anyway.

Alex was staring at her. Not Alex in Cade's body or Alex before she had merged him, but Alex. He was sitting on the bench, only an arm's reach away from her. His black hair was short and neat, the beard she had seen on him in the hospital was gone. But the scar running through his left eyebrow was there and so were his blue eyes. She blinked and looked at the rest of him. He was wearing a black wool coat that hung open with a pair of jeans, buttoned shirt and a pair of black casual shoes. It was a completely different outfit. Not the covert pants and shirt he had been wearing when she first saw him.

She gawked at him as he held a soccer ball, wearing regular clothes, she couldn't help it. He was so handsome and normal, how would she ever block him out now?

Leaning over, he placed the soccer ball—which was still wrapped in cardboard packaging—on the floor next to his feet. "You think I'm dead, don't you?"

Soccer ball?

She held the cup tightly in her hands. "Yes."

He sighed and reached for her. She jerked back moving her head back and forth and pulled her legs up close to her chest.

"Eve," he commanded her attention. "I know how scared you are of the dead. And, even if I was dead, which I'm not," he pointed out. "I would never come here knowing I would scare you."

She wanted to believe him, she really did. She just couldn't. He sighed again and reached out for her. She clamped her eyes shut, squeezing into the arm of the bench, waiting.

The cup in her hand was taken and the blanket was tugged away before a warm hand locked around her wrist. It didn't pull at her like she was expecting it to do. It simply held her in place. Eve opened her eyes and stared at Alex's hand when she felt a warm soothing heat seep into her skin. At that moment he moved his thumb and lightly stroked the sensitive skin on her wrist.

He began to tug lightly on her wrist but she snatched her hand back. This wasn't real. It couldn't be.

"I-I felt you die. This c-can't be."

"It's me Eve. I'm not dead. I'm alive." She looked to his face—saw his intense blue stare. But she just couldn't believe...

He tore off his jacket and ripped open his shirt, buttons flying everywhere. Suddenly, he was sitting next to her with a bare chest. He grabbed her hand and dragged her across the bench. He placed her hand on his chest over the small round scar by his heart and covered her hand with his. "Close your eyes and feel my heart beating." She froze, not knowing what to do. "Do it," he ordered.

Flinching, she followed his command. She felt the heat first, then the scar the bullet caused and the crisp hair on his chest, and finally a...heartbeat. And another one, and another. She squeezed her eyes shut and felt the tears roll down her face.

Alex pulled her closer. "You can feel it, can't you?"

Opening her eyes, she focused on his bare chest and placed her other hand on it. "Yes."

"I'm *not* dead."

She ran her hand up his chest to his neck, his face. Touched his cheek. She felt her face crumble just before he hauled her up against him. She curled up on his lap, buried her face in his neck and let the tears fall. He held her tight, probably tighter than she was holding him.

When she was finally calm enough, Alex sat back and set the swing into motion, gently rocking them. Eve rested her head on his shoulder and shivered. Instantly, they were both covered by her blanket.

They sat for some time together, doing nothing but holding each other. "Better?"

"Yes," she whispered. "I've missed you."

His arms tightened around her. "I've missed you too."

She gripped his shirt. "I don't understand. I felt you die."

He kissed her forehead. "Can I answer that question after I make love to you?"

She laughed lightly.

God he had missed that sound. That light, musical laugh. It warmed his heart and calmed his soul.

"Okay."

Lifting her off his lap, he clasped her hand, quickly bent and picked up the new soccer ball.

"What's with the ball?"

He shrugged as he pulled her in the house. "I picked it for Noelle."

"To play soccer in the park…" Alex had just turned from locking the door when Eve stopped in mid-sentence. He sighed. Eve was staring in shock as Justine sat on the steps blocking them from going upstairs.

Curling his arm around Eve's waist, he pulled her stiff body close. "Easy. Justine is harmless. Although, quite annoying at times."

There was a snort from the stairs, "Well, that was uncalled for."

Alex shook his head. "What's going on Justine?" he asked dryly. He wasn't in the mood to chat.

There was only one thing he was in the mood for and the only female he required was Eve. It had been weeks since he had held and kissed Eve, the time away from her had seemed like torture, as he'd spent time doing what he needed to do in order to get back to her. There wasn't one minute of every day that he hadn't thought about her, and now that they were finally together he wanted nothing more than to explore her body with his own hands and mouth. Hold her and talk to her, tell her how much he loved her. But that wasn't going to happen while Justine was here.

Eve shivered.

"Eve, honey." He pressed his lips to her head. "If you are beginning to see the dead then we will deal with it together. I'm here, Eve, and I will never let anything hurt you, dead or otherwise."

Eve exhaled a shaky breath. "Okay."

"And I would never hurt you," Justine added sincerely. "I just wanted to catch you before you became indisposed for the night." Justine gave them a knowing wink.

"What for?"

"To say thank you." The smile she gave him was genuine. "You got shot and lost your best friend to save my sister." She looked to Eve next. "I'm sorry you were hurt and that you were away from your daughter, but you helped Jillian too. She says you visit her every day."

Eve took a deep calming breath. "I like Jillian, we've become friends."

Alex kissed her head again. He knew she was still scared but she was making an effort and he was proud of her for that.

"See." Justine stood and walked down the few steps to stand in front of them. "The only way I can repay you is by saying thank you. So thank you."

Alex nodded as Eve replied, "You're welcome."

Justine blinked up at them, sadness clinging to her smile. "That's it. I'm outta here." She turned, walking down the hall to the kitchen.

"Justine," Alex called out.

"Yes."

"We'll keep an eye on Jillian."

"She'll be okay," Eve added.

Her smile widened as tears flooded her large brown eyes. "Thank you." She turned again and faded from sight.

* * * *

Alex ushered Eve up stairs and into her bedroom. He closed the door as he watched her walk to the side of the bed and sit down.

They stared at each other until a scowl wrinkled Eve's brow. "I'm so happy you are all right, Alex. You, your body...look so good, so healthy. But, I'm confused as to why you're here. You said we were over."

He shrugged, crossing to her. "I changed my mind."

"That's *it*, you changed your mind. You're a jerk." She slapped his hand away when he tried to touch her face.

"Don't like that answer eh?" He knelt in front of her, nudging her legs apart. He ran his hands up her flannel covered legs, stopping on her hips.

"No."

"Okay. How about this. I love you."

The scowl dropped from her face and her eyes became huge. "What?"

Cupping her behind, he jerked her forwards. "I love you, Evening."

"You do?" She placed her hands on his shoulders.

"Yes, very much." He kissed her lightly then, let her get use to the feel of his lips, the taste of his mouth. Then, slowly he slipped his tongue inside, to her warmth and savoured the sweetness that was Eve.

She pulled away, licking her lips. "You said you didn't want me."

"Eve, I've come here almost every night for the past three weeks making sure you and Noelle were safe. If I didn't want you would I do that?"

"But I didn't know you were doing that." The concerned look in her eyes had him kissing the top of her cheeks. "Why did you suddenly push me away when we were at the lake house?"

His mouth compressed into a hard line. He was ashamed to admit the truth but he refused to lie to her. "Miles had used Jillian and when she told him she wouldn't put the baby up for adoption he got mad and decided killing her would be easier. Eve," —he locked eyes with her—"I used you to get what I wanted. I scared you, threatened you and Noelle, but that wasn't enough for me. I then dragged you into the middle of a war and ordered you to take care of a pregnant woman and then I get you shot in the process. I'm no better than Miles, in fact I'm probably worse. I pushed you away because you deserve to have a man that will treat you better than the way I treated you." He closed his eyes and took a deep breath. "Then I was back in the hospital, stuck in the same position, and all I could think about was getting back to you and when I couldn't, I went crazy."

"When did you realise that you loved me?"

"When I saw you smiling at Noelle's picture of flying turtles. I knew I cared for you before then, but it was at that moment when it hit me. I guess I was fighting it harder than I thought."

"Why did you fight it?" she asked carefully.

"The last people that I truly loved were my parents. What I feel for you is different and strong, it goes far beyond anything I've ever felt before and it happened fast—I wasn't prepared for it. You and Noelle and Dawn are a family and I haven't belonged to a family in a long time. With my life and the things I do, I'm the last person that deserves to be part of a family." He was babbling like a fool. "But I'll be damned if I'm walking away from you."

She looked angrily at him. "First off, you are nothing like Miles. You would never hurt me or Noelle. And I was only scared of you because I thought you were dead. Second, by the time you made love to me, you were already becoming part of my family." She poked him in the chest. "I don't just sleep around, buddy. Third, I don't want any other man, I want you."

He smiled at her insistent tone. But he still hadn't got what he was after. "And?"

"And what?" she asked confused.

"I need more than you want me. I want to hear you say it."

"Say what?" The smile was full of mischief. "I'm not sure I know what you're talking about?"

He wasn't in the mood to be teased but he liked that she wasn't scared to do it. He sealed their bodies tight, growling her full name.

She laughed, wrapping her arms around his neck. "I love you too, Alex and I want you to be a part of my family for as long as you like."

What? He pulled back. "For as long as I like?"

"Yes. For as long as you like." She stared at him with wide innocent eyes.

"You think I'm going to up and leave one day?"

"I hope not, but I will understand if you do. I'm not exactly normal and your work is very different. I'll stay..." She waved her hand down her body. "And you will...change."

He huffed, "You don't get it." He lifted her back onto the bed and stood looking down at her as he took off his jacket and shirt. He bent his arm and rolled his shoulder forward.

Her breath caught when she saw his new tattoo.

"I'm not going anywhere, Eve." A sweet smile pulled at her lips. "You're stuck with me for the remainder of our lives, however long that may be."

"How did you..." She gingerly traced the Sinclair medallion on his shoulder. "I only thought..."

"Does it matter how I got it or who gave it to me?" he asked.

Eve looked up at him, her fingers still tracing the symbol. "No, it doesn't matter."

He dropped to his knees again and tugged her back against his chest. He fastened his mouth over hers in a heated kiss. She tasted so good. Her mouth sweeter than before, the touch of her tongue more alluring. When he finally pulled away they were both panting.

She opened the bedside drawer and pulled out the box of condoms. She gazed over at him, the top of her cheeks pink. "I assume we're going to need these?"

Chuckling he took the box from her. "For the next little while anyways."

Her brows pushed together. "What do you...?"

"I love you, Eve." He cupped her face. "I want to have a family with you. I want to have family dinners and walk Noelle with you to the bus." He dropped his voice low and kissed the side of her mouth. "I want Noelle to have a brother or a sister. But not yet, I'm content to be with you two for now and you need time to get used to me."

He stroked her face when tears clouded her eyes. "You okay? Was that too much to dump on you at once?" His heart paused while he waited for her answer. If Eve didn't want another baby...that was okay too. He still had her and Noelle and if that was all he ever had, it would be enough because he'd never expected to have a family to begin with.

"No not too much. I love the idea of having a family with you."

"But."

"Are you sure? I mean, look what I'm bringing to the table. Are you sure you want your kids to have what Noelle and I have, because it will happen. What we have doesn't skip a generation."

"I'm sure. And when our children begin seeing medians and, or the dead we will teach them how to deal with it." He wiped away the tear sliding down her cheek. "You're killing me with these tears. This isn't what I pictured when I was driving here tonight."

"What were you picturing then?" She stroked his chest.

"Me, throwing you on the bed and fucking your brains out while I told you how much I love you."

Her eyes were twinkling by the time he was done. She nodded fervently. "That sounds good to me. Let's do that. But" — she pushed him back — "No bed."

Alex groaned as they fell back to the floor. She sealed her body against his and covered his mouth with her sweet lips. He was aching when he finally pulled away. He removed her clothes in record time and stared down at her exposed body. It was flushed and swollen and ready for him. Eve didn't hide or hold anything back, touching and kissing with as much passion as he did.

"Alex?" She ran her hand down his chest.

He pulled her hand away and kissed her wrist before pinning it to the floor.

"Soon," he promised. There was one thing he needed to do first before he came to her. He bent his head and kissed her breast, circled her nipple with his tongue in a long slow stroke. Once he'd finished tasting her entire breast he proceeded to the other, squeezing them both gently during the process. He took his time, covering every sensitive piece of skin then moved to her stomach and legs, to her arms, back and behind. When he was satisfied that he had covered every inch of her with his hands and mouth he dipped lower to the sweet folds between her thighs. He made love to her with his mouth, drove his tongue deep, got lost in the honeyed essence of her all the while loving the way she ran her fingers into his hair, the heat of her body, the way she loved him back.

"Alex," she cried out his name shivering. "Is it time yet?" Her hips rolled seductively.

"Yes." He kissed her now dripping lips one more time and rose to his knees undoing his pants. He looked over her body as he covered his shaft with a condom, searching for any spot he might have missed. A possessive grin, curled his mouth. Cade's touch was erased and replaced with his own. Eve had given him her soul when she'd said she loved him, but it still wasn't enough. He wanted her body for his own too and the thought of another man's hands on her drove him crazy. It didn't matter that he was the soul on the inside, it was Cade's body he had used to touch Eve with and that was something he couldn't let go of.

Lifting her hips he drove forward, her body welcoming him eagerly pulling him deeper than before. He covered her mouth as she cried out and moved quickly, reducing Cade's touch to a distant memory, moaning in pleasure at how incredibly tight she was. Something was different. Mind-numbingly fantastic but different. Eve tasted sweeter, her skin was softer, her body tighter. It was like all his senses were heightened, that Cade's body had dulled them somehow. But now that he was back in his own body, everything was crisp and clear.

Eve dug her nails into his shoulders, as desperate as he was. Grinding his body tight against hers, Alex kissed the ultra-sensitive area under her ear. Within seconds her body clamped down on his. He grunted, allowing the pulsing of her body to coax him into coming.

* * * *

Eve rested her hand over Alex's heart as they lay on the floor. She closed her eyes and sighed happily when she felt the strong beats. "How are you alive, Alex?"

"I asked that very question after I was merged back into my body."

She curled her fingers and traced the bullet wound. He was alive, did it matter if he told her? No. But she wanted to know. "And?" she pushed.

"My soul didn't die with the body because it wasn't my actual body. Apparently the soul only dies when the body it belongs to dies. Looks like your theory was right about there being a psychic connection between body and soul."

She placed her hand back on his chest and splayed her fingers wide. His chest was hard, the firm muscles beneath her hand was warm and comforting.

"How did you find that out?" She ran her fingers through the hair on his chest, loving the way it tickled her palm.

"Your Gran."

Eve froze and pushed back to look at his face. "What did you say?"

"Dawn merged me." Alex chuckled.

She was so stunned to hear Dawn had helped him that her mouth dropped open.

"Really?"

"Yes she helped me."

Tears pooled in her eyes again. "I think that crazy old bird must like you."

"Of course she does." Then announced, "Though I doubt she will ever admit to it."

Eve laughed. "When did she merge you?" She began stroking his chest again.

"A week after the shooting." His hand covered hers.

"Oh."

Silence. It had been a full month since that night, what had he been doing between then and now?

As though he could read her mind he said, "I had things to take care of before I could come here," he began.

She simply nodded and waited for him to continue.

"When I was given a clean bill of health I was called in to explain what had happened the night Miles shot me."

"What did you tell them?"

"I told them the truth. About how he'd wanted to kill Jillian because she had seen us kill Rhodes. But I also told them what I'd learnt after. How Miles was the father of Jillian's baby. I told them that I believed he'd used the Rhodes kill as an excuse to eliminate her so his family wouldn't find out."

More silence.

"You spoke with the cops and members of my unit didn't you?"

"I'm not sure, I mean I don't think I did. I assumed I was speaking to police officers, though I did find it weird that everyone kept asking me the same questions." She climbed onto the bed. "Which ones belonged to your unit?" She turned to find him standing next to the bed.

Alex gave her a secretive smile as he followed her onto the bed. His now naked body pinning her down. "What did you tell them?"

"What you did. Well, I told them that Cade had asked for my help because he'd believed Miles was responsible for killing his wife." She narrowed her eyes. "Although, one group of officers didn't quite believe what I was saying and pressed me for more information." Her eyes widened. "Those were members of your unit. Weren't they?"

"Could be. What did you say?"

"I told them I was there when Cade woke up in the hospital and that he came looking for me. I also told them that I had gone to see you and the reason why and that was when I met Miles."

Alex nodded. "My CO told me about you being dragged into Miles' line of sight. They were puzzled over why Miles had suddenly targeted you. But decided because Miles had first met you in my hospital room and because he was already acting irrationally, my CO concluded it was most likely, fear over being discovered that he had shot me and was trying to kill Jillian."

"I also told them that Jillian, told me and Cade that Miles was the father of her baby. I felt that they should know — I was hoping it would help close the case faster."

Alex nuzzled her ear then pushed between her legs.

"Did I say the right thing?" She heard the dreamy tone to her voice. "They aren't going to bother Jillian are they?"

He pulled back a hand on either side of her head. "You didn't lie, that was good. They would have known if you had." He tangled his fingers in her hair.

"But I did lie, about Cade."

"No. I was Cade and I did come looking for you. The rest was the truth and even if you think it wasn't you must have been convincing enough for them to leave you alone or they would have kept you in the hospital until they were satisfied."

"They can do that?"

Alex shrugged knowingly.

Eve shook her head. "That is scary to know. What about Jillian?" she asked. "Will they leave her alone?"

He cupped the side of her face, ran his thumb over her lower lip as he answered, "Yes. Though they will check up on her, to make sure she is doing okay."

"Who will do that? They won't scare her will they?"

"I volunteered." Then, shrugging, he admitted, "I want to know she will be okay too and I thought you would want to as well."

"Yes I do. I meant what I said to Justine. I like Jillian very much, we've become close."

"I know."

Eve lowered her eyes and toyed with the hair on his chest. "Besides answering questions, where have you been?"

With a single finger under her chin, he raised her head so she was looking into his face. "I went up north to make sure the clean-up was done accurately. Then I went to check out the damage done to the apartment Cade" — he winked at her — "blew up. And then I was sent into the field with a new partner. They wanted to know if I can work with anyone other than Miles."

"And can you?" She licked her lips, hoping the answer would be no, so they would have to send another set of men out to kill the guilty. "Work with another partner?"

He looked her in the eye. "It will be an adjustment, but I don't see any problems."

She tried to turn away before he saw her disappointment, but it was too late. "Evening. You know what I do and you know why. There are far too many people out there that enjoy hurting the innocent. I won't stop hunting them." He turned her face to his. "But I have asked to do less field work and more research. So I won't be as busy as I was before. But I had to agree to go whenever a team needs extra help."

"So you won't be away from us that much?"

"No. I won't be away that much."

"Okay. I just hate what all that...hunting is doing to you." She touched his cheek.

"Then it's a good thing I'll have you to heal me when I get back."

Eve sighed and wrapped her arms around his neck when he kissed her. The kiss was so gently and loving that Eve felt her heart flip over.

He ended the kiss suddenly. "You still haven't answered my question."

"What question?"

He gave her naughty grin "I need your help."

"With what?" She looked up at him, amazed that he was alive and here with her, loving her.

He brushed her ear with his lip, his warm breath making her shiver. "Finding a church."

About the Author

Nancy's addiction for a good trash novel began in her late-teens when her grandmother gave her a bag of Harlequin Romance books. She was hooked and spent the next few years lurking in the dark corners of used bookstores searching for her next fix. Until, one marriage and two kids later, her own ideas had her jumping up at 3 am (much to her husband's annoyance) and typing them into her laptop. Beside her husband and children, Nancy has three passions, rearranging furniture, buying bed linens and, of course, writing. Nancy lives in Eastern Ontario with her family and two over sized lap dogs.

Nancy Adams loves to hear from readers. You can find her contact information, website details and author profile page at http://www.total-e-bound.com.

Total-E-Bound Publishing

www.total-e-bound.com

Take a look at our exciting range of literagasmic™
erotic romance titles and discover pure quality
at Total-E-Bound.

www.ingramcontent.com/pod-product-compliance
Lightning Source LLC
Chambersburg PA
CBHW030809260626
47169CB00001B/257